Don't Snap
an Elephant to a Tree

Plus Other Important Stuff

Jeanne Robertson

Published in the United States by JSR Inc.

Edited by Peg McCree
Cover design by Tanja Prokop of BookDesignTemplates.com
Layout by Adina Cucicov

ISBN 979-8-9861400-4-9
eISBN 979-8-9861400-5-6

Printed in the United States of America

Dedication

In honor of the legacy of Jeanne Robertson
and her beloved husband Jerry

Table of Contents

Introduction

Jeanne would have been the first to admit that she was a packrat. One of the items she saved was a copy of each magazine to which she submitted an article for publication. Once "Thuh Nashville People" discovered this trove of material, they began to explore the possibility of publishing another collection of Jeanne's stories. The first step was to get permission from her son, Beaver. He was on board immediately.

Once the printed articles from the magazines were scanned, the next step was to acquire the online articles Jeanne had submitted to the *Southeast Gazette* (*SE Gazette*). Marty Heim, publisher of the *SE Gazette,* graciously made the electronic files available to us. Once all the articles were compiled, we had over 180 articles Jeanne had written between 2000 and 2021. Surprisingly, there were only a few duplications. We knew that Jeanne would not want the stories in her previous collection, *Don't Bungee Jump Naked,* to be included, so we removed those from consideration, leaving over 120 stories for this current project.

We made one additional discovery. On Jeanne's computer was a copy of "The Body Suit," later titled "Don't Snap an Elephant to a Tree." At the top of the first page, Jeanne had typed—

Story: Body Suit . . . Lots of body language in this story. I hope it comes across on paper—

Her note suggested that she was preparing the story to be submitted as an article. We also discovered that a version of this story has never appeared in print, although it is one of her most popular YouTube clips, having amassed over 2.8 million views since it was posted six years ago. In honor of this accomplishment, we titled this book *Don't Snap an Elephant to a Tree, Plus Other Important Stuff* and have included the story in the collection.

Since we consider *Don't Snap an Elephant to a Tree, Plus Other Important Stuff,* to be a companion to *Don't Bungee Jump Naked,* the latter was used as a template for this current project. For example, we separated her articles into sections similar to those used in *Don't Bungee Jump Naked.* The stories are presented chronologically within each section, and each article is identified with the publication date and the title of the publication in which it was published.

Because these articles were intended for a monthly publication, Jeanne often added a comment to introduce each story. Toni Meredith, Jeanne's long-time Executive Assistant, told us that she and Jeanne often checked to see if there might be a special event or day that month that would inspire Jeanne's writings. Toni stated, "In true Jeanne fashion, she always came up with the perfect idea and would soon send her the article to proofread so they could get it to the publication before the deadline." These introductory comments have been retained.

All the articles in this collection were written for one of four publications: *City-County Magazine: Alamance County's Only Magazine; Alamance County Magazine: Celebrating the Character of Our County;* and *Southeast Lifestyle* that became *Southeast Gazette.* Jeanne knew the region well. It included Burlington, where Jeanne and her family resided for many years; Graham, where Jeanne grew up and lived until she left to attend Auburn University; and Elon, the home of Elon University. Her love for this region and the people is evident in her writing. We hope you will also gain an appreciation for Jeanne's southern roots.

Finally, the editor has retained Jeanne's unique writing style and spelling and has kept revisions of the original articles to a minimum. Any errors in spelling or punctuation are the fault of the editor alone.

Plus, More Important Stuff

This project would not have been possible without the assistance of Marty Heim, publisher of the *SE gazette* and the long-time host of Jeanne's website. In addition to providing us with the articles published in the *SE Gazette*, she briefly explained how and when she met Jeanne:

In the Spring of 2000, I attended an awards luncheon that was life-changing.

As I was waiting for the ballroom doors to open, this very tall woman walked past me. I thought I was thinking, but I must have said it out loud, "Gosh, you're tall."

Her head swung around; she looked down at me and said, "Yes, 6'2." I'm Jeanne Robertson, the speaker today, and your name is and what do you do?"

Eight months later, I found myself standing in her home office. Her legacy accomplishments covered the walls, and I could not wait to share her with the world on the www [World Wide Web].

Jeanne liked things done in steps; her website was getting popular. Not long after, we added her first YouTube clip, after which we started product sales and Facebook. I asked her to provide short stories for a newspaper I was starting. She was so thrilled.

When we spoke for the last time, we shared a good laugh together. We talked about life things and being humble. In closing, she said she was late getting me the column for the paper. I told her we would reprint the one we had started with about her mother.

A few days later, Jeanne had passed on. My memories with this great woman can go on forever, and they will. I think a reader said it best: "The world lost a true ambassador of joy." Enjoy this book. Her articles were her pride and joy.

This project would also not have been possible without assistance from Toni, who offered the following addendum to Marty's reflections—

Marty failed to mention that this luncheon was honoring businesswomen in the area—and that she, Marty, was awarded Women of the Year. When each woman was introduced, a picture of them was put on a large screen, telling a little about them and their business. When Marty's slide went up, she was upside down—not the entire slide—just Marty. It was very intentional—and it certainly caught our eye. Jeanne turned to me and said, I think we should work with that person. I can tell she definitely has a sense of humor! And, as they say, the rest is history . . .

Biography

Jeanne Robertson, one of America's most loved and respected speakers and humorist, has amassed over 142 million views on YouTube and thousands of followers on Facebook. She is the author of 4 books and 9 CDs/DVDs that are filled with hilarious stories, including "Don't Send a Man to the Grocery Store," "Don't Bungee Jump Naked," and "Don't Snap an Elephant to a Tree." She also wrote a regular column for one of several local magazines for over twenty years. During the pandemic, her "Live From the Back Porch" Facebook shows were frequently in the top 10 for worldwide viewership, according to *Pollstar Magazine*.

Originally from Graham, NC, Jeanne lived in Burlington, NC, for many years. In 1963, she won the Miss North Carolina Pageant and participated in the Miss America Pageant, where she was voted "Miss Congeniality." She was proud of the fact that she was the tallest woman to ever compete in the Miss America Pageant. After graduating from Auburn University in 1967, she taught physical education, coached basketball, and was a part-time professional speaker until 1976, when she began speaking full-time.

As a professional speaker with over 50 years of experience, Jeanne helped thousands of people add humor to their lives. She won numerous awards, including every award and honor bestowed by the National Speakers Association (Certified Speaking Professional award, Council of Peers Award for Excellence, Master of Influence Award,

Philanthropist of the Year Award, and the Cavett Award). She also received the Toastmasters Golden Gavel and was named the Alamance County Boy Scouts MAN of the Year in 2010. Jeanne proudly asserts that speaking two languages—English and Southern—helped her achieve these honors.

In 2010, she teamed up with Al McCree Entertainment and "Thuh Nashville People." Together, they took her humorist performances from the convention halls to theatres where she introduced her audiences to her cast of beloved characters, including her husband Jerry, a.k.a. "Left-Brain;" son Beaver; her long-time Executive Assistant Toni, a.k.a. "The Queen of the Tickets;" her "Bestest Friend" Norma Rose; and Jane Tucker "from NYC."

In addition to her successful professional career, Jeanne was married to Jerry (Left-Brain) for 47 years. She and Jerry were avid fans of Elon University and supported the university with numerous monetary gifts and their time. Her beloved Jerry passed away on June 7, 2021.

On August 21, 2021, the world got less funny when Jeanne passed away peacefully at her home after a short illness.

Jeanne's friends, family, and fans continue to remember her stories, ensuring that her legacy lives on as we all follow the advice that she consistently gave: to keep laughing and look for the humor in any situation.

Cast of Characters

If you are familiar with Jeanne's stories, you are already acquainted with her characters. However, if you are a new fan, the following descriptions will save you time trying to figure out the cast of characters.

Jerry Robertson: Jerry was what many people called Jeanne's husband because Jerry was his name. She called him LB or, more often, Left Brain. He was a willing source of much of her material and was the greatest sport in the world. He was famous for quietly saying to Jeanne, "I may have just done something you can tell about in a story, but I'm not sure."

Toni: She began running Jeanne's office in 1979, and she is still in charge of handling requests for Jeanne's books, CDs, and DVDs. Jeanne's fans know Toni as the "Queen of Tickets," but Jeanne often referred to her as the "Queen of Everything." As Jeanne stated in an early book, "My career has been a great ride, but it wouldn't have been as much fun without Toni." In addition to working together all those years, they were both proud Auburn fans. "War Eagle!"

Norma Rose: Jeanne's "Bestest" Friend. (Jeanne always added, "We always give our little girls in the South two names, in case they want to be in a pageant.") According to Jeanne, you can have only one "Bestest."

Jeanne met hers when their sons played high school sports together. Norma Rose has more of a Southern accent than Jeanne, and people often thought they were sisters because they sounded so much alike.

Jane Tucker: From New York City! Jane was the fashion expert who came to North Carolina in 1998 to "Tuckerize" Jeanne by improving her wardrobe. Jane became a regular visitor and friend. When Jane showed up in Burlington, Jerry knew it was going to cost him money.

Beaver: Only child. According to Jeanne, he always had her in the palm of his hand. He was also the source of many stories. (Some she couldn't or wouldn't tell.) Jeanne considered him the quickest and funniest person she had ever known, but he could also be irreverent and push his mother's buttons. He remains Jeanne's biggest fan and a fierce trustee of her legacy.

"Thuh Nashville People": The label Jeanne gave to Al and Peg McCree and the other members of the Al McCree Entertainment team. Al was responsible for bringing Jeanne to theater audiences. With the approval of Beaver and assistance from Toni, "Thuh Nashville People" continue to work to preserve and expand Jeanne's legacy.

The National Speakers Association (NSA): Jeanne joined this organization in 1978 and remained active throughout her life. She served as National President and received every award given by the Association. Her last speech was delivered at their National Convention in 2021.

The Andy Griffith Show: Jeanne considered *The Andy Griffith Show* to be the greatest program ever to appear on television. It ran from 1960 to1968 but is still seen regularly on numerousof TV channels and streaming on the internet. If you read Jeanne's book *Mayberry Humor Across America*, you know she was an expert on the show. She often remarked on the similarities between the events and characters presented in the television series and the people and events she experienced as she traveled across the US. Some of the characters from the show you may encounter in the following pages include Andy Taylor, the sheriff in the fictitious town of Mayberry; Opie Taylor, Andy's son; Aunt Bea, Andy's aunt and housekeeper; Ernest T. Bass, a wily mountain man; Barney Fife, the Deputy Sheriff; Helen Crump, Andy's girlfriend, a school teacher; Floyd Lawson, aka Floyd the Barber; and Ben Weaver, a miserly old landlord and the owner of the local department store.

Strangers: In *Don't Bungee Jump Naked*, Jeanne included a short paragraph on the strangers she encountered in her travels and at her theater shows and pageants. She wrote, "Wish I knew all their names so I could say a more personal thank you. They have given me countless hours of laughter and story ideas simply by something they have said or done." Many of these strangers also found their way into Jeanne's articles. We are sure she would offer her thanks to these folks as well.

Family and Friends

Don't Shrink the Turkey

November 2000, *City-County Magazine*

It's stuffing season, the time of year for all the good cooks to come to the aid of their families and load the tables with home-cooked meals. The rest of us have to wing it.

I inherited my inability to cook, quite honestly. My Grandma Freddie hated the kitchen, although she did love to entertain. Even though she was extremely tight with her money, she believed that as matriarch of the clan, she should host the large family holiday dinners. One of them stands out.

Everyone was gathered at Grandma Freddie's home for the traditional turkey feast. Her contribution to the meal was the bird. While she and most of the family socialized in the living room, my Uncle and Aunt sneaked into the house through the kitchen door. They had a small Cornish hen that they had browned and cooked, just as one would cook a turkey. It looked for all the world just like a miniature gobbler.

They opened the oven door and carefully lifted out the twenty-five-pound turkey Grandma Freddie had cooked for dinner. They substituted the Cornish hen and hid the real thing outside.

After a while, Grandma Freddie went to the kitchen to check on the turkey that she was to feed to 28 hungry people. Family members, who were all in on the joke, casually followed her to the stove or hung around outside the kitchen to hear the reaction.

She opened the oven door and peered in. "Good Lord!" she screamed and slammed the hot pad down on the counter. "That's what I get for buying a cheap turkey. It shrunk!"

Gotcha' Last

January 2000, *City-County Magazine*

When our son Beaver was younger, I often played that old "gotcha last" bit on him. I would trick him, grin, and proclaim, "Gotcha last!" It frustrated him as a child, but that was years earlier and long forgotten by me. Children never forget.

Beaver dated an interesting assortment of young women ranging from "girls a mother would like" to "she brings tequila with her." Then, to our delight, he settled down and married our friend's daughter. The parents were thrilled!

There was discussion of having a short, sweet wedding, but it didn't work that way. Not at all. It wound up being a small town, southern "happening" with parties, luncheons, and dinners for days before the event and relatives everywhere inhaling food. Beaver fell right in line as a typical groom and had little to do with the overall planning, but he was granted one request. He wanted a band to play at the after-rehearsal party that often played at The Lighthouse Tavern in Elon College, where he had his own personal booth.[1] They were called "Big Bump and the

---

1 In 2000, the Board of Trustees voted to change the name from Elon College to Elon University.

Stun Guns." Big Bump could play the electric guitar with his teeth from the parking lot while the dancers remained inside. What a talent!

The day finally rolled around, and everyone crammed into the Front Street United Methodist Church for the thirteen-minute ceremony. The couple was pronounced husband and wife and proceeded up the aisle as their high school buddy blared forth on his trumpet. I choked back a tear because I didn't want to walk out crying and have people mumble, "I bet she wishes she hadn't traveled so much when he was growing up."

The twelve bridesmaids and groomsmen walked out by twos. Why twelve? I had asked the same thing. The bride had explained innocently, "The church won't let you have fourteen." I love her!

My husband, the best man, escorted the maid of honor up the aisle. Everything was progressing in the strictest Methodist tradition, just the way we like things. I had been repeatedly reminded that it was not a time to be funny. What did people think I would do? Stand up at my son's wedding and start dropping one-liners?

The bride's mother was escorted out, and husband Gene, in his role as father of the bride, trailed along behind. Before she left, the bride's mother smiled at me. We had done it! Looking back on it, I am surprised we didn't exchange high-fives at the front of the church before she was escorted up the aisle. Now I waited for my turn to leave . . . and waited . . .

When the trumpeter started through the hyperboles the second time, beads of perspiration popped out on my forehead. I glanced backward at my two sisters, who shrugged. Hey, it wasn't their wedding.

More seconds ticked by, and my mind was racing. Where was Michael Pittard, Beaver's friend who was to escort me? Hmm, in the tenth grade, he was the one who . . . . Nah, he has forgotten I told his mother about that. He'll be here. This is a religious ceremony. All these people, months of planning, and the groom's mother—certainly a prime player even dressed in pale—is waiting.

Come on, Michael. Come onnnn.

A murmur started faintly through the congregation and grew louder. Then, commotion! What in the world? Suddenly, there was a huge tuxedo standing next to my pew. I looked up in relief, expecting the usher. Instead, there was a big ol' 6' 8" grinning groom looking down at his mama.

A mass of emotion ran through my heart. A great deal of strict, southern Methodist tradition had been tossed aside by my son and his bride. We don't often step out of the lines at our church, and I was so startled that the guests laughed.

By the time I was able to get to my feet—fighting back the onslaught of tears—and take my "little boy" by the arm, the congregation broke into applause. Mother and son walked proudly up the long aisle toward the bride, waiting at the rear of the church with outstretched arms. Her parents were standing beside her, laughing. All of them had set me up!

Five feet from the door, Beaver looked down at me and said, "O.K., once and for all. Gotcha last!"

A Tall Trick or Treat Tale

October 2001, *City-County Magazine*
October 2009, *Southeast Lifestyle*
October 2018, *SE Gazette*

I once read a letter to an advice columnist from the mother of a tall girl. She explained that at Halloween, her daughter had gone trick-or-treating with friends. At one house, a woman judged the youngster by her height and proceeded to inform her that she was too old to trick or treat. The daughter was embarrassed in front of her peers and returned home in tears. The mother's letter went on to discuss the woman's rudeness and how her daughter had been mistreated.

Granted, the woman at the door had been insensitive, but maybe it was the mother of the tall daughter who reacted poorly. It's too bad she didn't have what my mother had—ingenuity. She could have used a dose of it. A similar situation illustrates my point.

When my classmates and I were seventh graders, our parents decided that we could go trick or treating one last year. Then, on Halloween night, some of my friends said they didn't want me to go with them. I was already 6'2" at thirteen. They thought I was "too big" and stated specifically, "People will think we've got a grownup along. We won't get as much candy." (Wasn't seventh-grade fun?)

I was crushed and went home to tell my mother what happened. Mama listened intently and could have said, "Well, you didn't want to go with them anyway. Stay home, and we'll pop popcorn." But she didn't. She was determined to influence me to see the humor in the situation.

When I finished relating what had happened, Mother rose to her full 5'5" height, looked up, and proclaimed, "You can go trick or treating, Jeanne. We just have to get you the right costume."

The costume turned out to be two sheets. Mother tied one around my waist, and jumping as high as she could, she threw the other one over my head. "Now, crouch down low," she instructed, "and hurry and catch up with everybody."

It was wonderful! I bent my knees, which took me down to half my size, and waddled along with the crowd. My friends thought it was hilarious. I did, too. At each house, I practically pushed my buddies out of the way, rang the doorbell, and thrust my sack forward. "Trick or treat" . . . and brought the candy in. My sack was filling up, and I was having a ball. Unfortunately, I was having so much fun that I began to forget to crouch down.

At one house, I ran ahead of the pack and rang the doorbell. A woman answered, and I stood a full six feet, two inches tall, under those sheets. I stuck my bag out. "Trick or treat."

The woman took a big step back and grinned as she looked at the mass of sheets in front of her. Then she turned and screamed, "John! Come out here and see these two children, one on top of the other under these sheets!"

It's not easy to walk up a sidewalk trying to wobble under sheets as though you were two people. My friends were howling, having arrived just in time to hear the woman's remark. They fell on the grass laughing. I ran toward home, glad that the sheets covered tears trickling down my face.

When I told Mother the story, she was faced with an interesting choice. After all, she had used her ingenuity to influence me once, and it had apparently backfired. As a parent now, I also realize how her emotions were probably churning. No mother enjoys her child feeling ridiculed, however slightly. Surely, now she would say, "You don't need those people. You've got cousins in Alabama. Let's go to the movies." Right? Not a chance. Mama knew that sometimes it takes more than one try. She put her thinking into high gear. In a few seconds, her eyes widened, and she jumped up and ran to the kitchen. I heard her rummaging around as she shouted, "We've been missing the boat!" In a few moments, she emerged carrying . . . a second sack. "From now on," she announced, "you go as two people!"

I caught up with my friends, clutching two sacks under the sheets and standing proudly at six foot two. At each house, I stuck out one sack with my right hand up near my head and, in a high voice, said, "Trick or treat." And with my left hand, I stuck out the second sack near my waist and boomed in a deep voice, "TRICK OR TREAT!"

Guess who went trick or treating every Halloween until she was twenty-three years old?

The Truth Hurts

May 2002, *City-County Magazine*

At one point in my career, I competed in the *Great Atlanta Laff Off* for Showtime Cablevision. Five of us were featured in the televised competition that was held before a live audience of 1,300 people. My family and a few close friends gathered in Atlanta to cheer me on. When I had finished my allotted 15 minutes, they quickly gathered around me to tell me that they were SURE I would win. Of course, they told me that before I even walked on the stage.

I finished fourth out of five. As loyal friends and family have a tendency to do, they again gathered around after the announcements to tell me that I "should have won."

Our son was more honest. We noticed son Beaver was not anywhere to be seen at the conclusion of the taping, and it turned out he was so upset when I came in fourth that he walked back to the hotel. When we returned to the room, he opened the door and, with tears in his eyes, shouted, "Mom, you were robbed! You should have come in second!"

Bestest Friend's Ring Guards

December 2004, *Alamance Magazine*

"Good, better, best. Never let it rest," etc.[2] We know that from Junior High English. But in the South, "best" loses its lofty position because women have a tendency to refer to anyone they see once a week in the Harris Teeter grocery store as their "best friend." Then there are hordes of "really best friends" and "very best friends." Therefore, my really best friend and I decided years ago that we would throw grammarians into a tizzy and call ourselves "bestest friends." You can have only one—I repeat, only one bestest friend, and sometimes you have to cut them a little slack.

"Have you ever thought about getting a bigger diamond ring?" The question came out of the blue one fall afternoon from my bestest friend Norma Rose White, who is always concerned about how I look when I give speeches.

"What's wrong with my wedding rings?"

"Well, nothing. Nothing really," she drawled and glanced away.

Uh-oh.

"You know I wouldn't bring it up if you weren't my bestest friend."

2 Good, better, best. Never let it rest till your good is better and your better is good.—attributed to St. Jerome.

Look out, Nellie.

She shifted around in her chair a little before zeroing in. "Jeanne, you know you have a large body."

"I know that, Norma Rose. I'm sitting right here in it."

"Well, your wedding rings look small on your large body. Sometimes, when you're on stage, the audience can't even see your small rings. You ought to hint to Jerry that you want a bigger ring for Christmas."

I looked down at the rings Jerry had saved to buy years ago when he worked at the YMCA. They looked all right to me. Granted, you might not see them from a back row, but if you come to my speeches to see my rings, get there early and sit in the front. My bestest friend Norma Rose had never mentioned my small rings before. Why now?

Norma Rose swallowed hard and kept going. "I wouldn't hurt your feelings for anything."

Okay.

"Lately, your rings just look smaller for some reason. Maybe because they're next to your arthritic knuckle."

As I said, she's my bestest friend, and you have just one. But I didn't want another ring, and I told her so. No problem.

A month later, Norma Rose came hustling through the front door. "I've thought of a solution for the ring situation."

Now, there was a "ring situation?"

She plopped two gold circles on the table as though she had discovered the solution to cellulite. "Ring guards! Put them on either side of the rings Jerry gave you, and the overall effect will be that you've got on a bigger ring. I've had these for years, but I'll sell them to you for fifty dollars."

Right there is where I messed up. Fifty dollars seemed fair for old, used ring guards, but I didn't particularly like them. She had evidently worn them, though, and I didn't want to hurt her feelings because, after all, she's my bestest friend. First, I lied. "Oh, they're *wonderful*. I love them. And look, I can get them over my arthritic knuckle." Then, my exit. "But I've always thought that Jerry should give me personal items such as rings. I wouldn't want to buy them for myself."

"No problem," she said and put the ring guards back in her purse.

On Christmas morning . . . (Do I really need to go on?) . . . Jerry pulled a small box from under the tree. "Norma Rose said you really liked these ring guards but wanted me to give them to you. They're not new, honey, but I got a good deal. She sold them to me for seventy-five dollars."

I let my bestest friend call me. "Merry Christmas! Did you get the ring guards?" she asked.

"Yes."

"Were you surprised?"

"Yes."

Bestest friends sense things. "What's wrong?"

"Norma Rose, are these the same ring guards you offered to sell me two months ago for fifty dollars?"

"Yes."

"Did you sell them to Jerry for seventy-five?"

She paused before she defended herself. "Yes. But I remind you, Jerry is not my bestest friend."

Trying to Get to the Library

September 2011, *Southeast Lifestyle*

September is here, which means that Fall is on the scene. Young men and women are pouring into the numerous institutions of higher learning we have in the Piedmont, North Carolina Triad, and we're glad they're here. They bring with them youth, ideas, enthusiasm, leadership, etc., and they also bring with them an assortment of modes of transportation. If it has wheels and will get a student from place to place, it's being parked on a campus near you. I suggest we keep our eyes peeled for these future leaders and remember that we were all young once. In other words, cut 'em some slack.

Our son, Beaver, graduated from Elon University by the grace of God. He loved Elon. He thought he'd died and gone to heaven. Even though we live in the vicinity of the University, we never saw him unless he needed something. And "needed something" he did when he frantically called home late one afternoon.

"Mom, MOM! I was trying to get to the library, and I've had a wreck! I'm okay, but the car's torn up."

In hindsight, this was a funny comment by itself. Beaver drove, as we say in the South, "a piece of a car." It was a moving wreck that gulped gas but could still roll. He inherited it when an older family member passed away. The thing was big and heavy, but we considered it to be safe. Generally, though, it was safer when Beaver wasn't in it.

"Calm down, Beaver. Was anyone hurt?"

"No. There were two guys in the front seat of the other car, but I hit their side door at the back seat. They were jolted, but they weren't hurt. I can't believe this has happened. I just can't believe this! Mom, I was trying to get to the library. To the library, for Pete's sake."

Because I had no medal to hang around his neck for trying to get to the library, I ignored all that. Quite honestly, the mother in me was suspicious that he was headed anywhere near the library.

"Okay," I replied. "At least no one is hurt. Exactly what happened?"

He was talking so fast that his sentences were running together, but essentially, he said, "Mom, I was leaving basketball practice, and I was backing out of a parking place in the parking lot right next to Alumni Gym. I didn't see anyone coming—I swear I looked—I always look—you know I always look—but like I said, I was in a hurry trying to get to the library, and I put it in reverse. My foot must have slipped off the brake onto the accelerator, but whatever happened, I didn't see anybody behind me. I guess I backed out too fast, and wham, I backed right into a car that was cruising by. I just can't believe it. Both cars are messed up."

"Beaver, please calm down. We'll be right over there, but the first thing you have to do is call Campus Security."

Bless his heart. Bless his heart right there in his 6'8" body. It took a few seconds, but he finally calmed down and responded dejectedly, "They're already here. Campus Security is who I hit."

The people at Campus Security later said it was the easiest report they ever filed. They didn't need to interview a single witness.

And just to be a good mother, I ignored the fact that the closest parking lot to Elon's Alumni Gym is also the closest to the library. If he had truly been going to the library, he would have already arrived.

Welcome students. Y'all drive carefully now, ya hear? And the rest of us? Be on the lookout and cut 'em some slack.

"Wrong Way" Grandma Freddie

January 2012, *Southeast Lifestyle*

Before my Grandma Freddie passed away and way beyond when she probably should not have still been operating a moving vehicle, she drove the wrong way down a one-way street in Auburn, Alabama. In fairness to her, Tichenor Avenue had been a two-way street for years, and she missed the notification that it had changed.

As she drove along, she noticed people waving, shouting at her, and blowing their horns, but because she knew everyone in Auburn or thought she did, she smiled, nodded, and waved in return. This continued until an Auburn student ran into the street to flag her down. At home that afternoon, she started thinking about it, got back in the car, and drove to the Police Department to turn herself in.

At the family drugstore later, she told her son what happened. Standing proudly with her good name restored, she recounted the story, but a hint of agitation also surfaced. "I told the first policeman what I had done. That was hard enough. But he started laughing and called in some other policemen and the clerical help, and I had to tell the whole thing over again. In a few minutes, the Chief of Police came in, heard what happened, and solved the problem. He said, 'Don't worry, Miss Freddie. It doesn't count if we don't see you.'"

So go ahead, everyone. Make New Year's Resolutions. List 'em. Post 'em. Tell your friends about your good intentions. But the good news is that you can take consolation in the police chief's words. When you break those resolutions, it doesn't count if no one sees you.

Andrea's Favorite Restaurant

March 2012, *Southeast Lifestyle*

When my sister Andrea lived in Atlanta, her favorite restaurant was Houston's. She loved it so much that not only did she insist her out-of-town visitors dine there, but she also pressured us to select her favorites on the menu. We usually ordered what she suggested. I guess it's "Southern politeness." It made her happy, and most of our friends and family will eat anything. Why not take her suggestions?

According to Andrea, Houston's had "the best margaritas in the world." We had to have a certain salad with a "hot bacon dressing you'll never taste anywhere else." Houston's heaped-high-baked potato was a must! "See if you can guess everything they put on it," she always said with pride to first-timers she took there. And, of course, the greatest dessert we would ever eat was the "such-and-such."

Andrea left Atlanta for law school and ended up practicing law in Portland, Oregon. One cousin who went "out there" to visit reported upon return that "Andrea's into that healthy West Coast lifestyle where they mostly eat bean sprouts. I couldn't wait to get to the airport to get some food." Deputy Sheriff Barney Fife might have said that Andrea had started watching the "ol' carbs and glucose." More accurately, she went on a fat-free diet.

On a return trip to Atlanta to visit our niece Elizabeth, Andrea just couldn't wait to return to Houston's. The first night she was in town, Elizabeth gathered up several of her girlfriends, and away they went. All the way there, Andrea told them how great the food was going to be and how much she missed eating there. And she assured them that they were in for a treat.

As soon as the group was seated, Andrea announced that she no longer drank margaritas and, instead, ordered lemonade. Everyone shrugged and ordered their margaritas. Great! Andrea could be the designated driver.

When the time came to order the real food, and at Andrea's urging, everyone ordered the famous Houston's heaped-high baked potato. But when it was her turn to order, Andrea also wanted the baked potato but said she'd like it plain. Plain? The waitress arched her eyebrows upward because she had heard Andrea telling the others to get the potato "all the way." The group exchanged quick glances. But they didn't say anything. More "Southern politeness," I guess. They reacted the same way when Andrea ordered her favorite salad—the one they had all just ordered at her recommendation.

Their mouths dropped open when she asked the waitress what exactly was in the salad. Seconds later, a couple of the "girls" nudged Elizabeth under the table when Andrea told the waitress, "Hold the ham and steak strips; no chicken chunks either. Oh, and is the cheese low-fat? It's not? OK, leave the cheese off too."

Elizabeth swears that by the time Andrea finished changing the salad, all they put in front of her was a bed of lettuce, a few carrots, and the restaurant's hot bacon dressing on the side. Andrea pushed the latter out of the way and brought out a bottle of fat-free dressing from her purse. By that point, everyone else in the group was fighting to keep from laughing out loud. But they didn't know Andrea very well so, being polite, no one said anything.

Elizabeth watched all this, quite perplexed but thinking her aunt was perhaps saving room for several desserts. No. When that time came, Andrea was full. No dessert for her except for the one spoonful she ate from someone else's plate just to see if it was as good as she remembered. (I suppose you can only watch the "ol' carbs and glucose" for so long.) The group of friends said later they thought Andrea must be on some sort of strict medical diet. They hadn't mentioned what she ordered because she offered no explanation. It just wouldn't be polite. But eye contact told them they were all thinking the same thing, "What in the world?" All of them, including Elizabeth, were struggling to hold back laughter the entire meal. To their credit, they were able to do so until they piled back in the car and headed down the freeway.

That's when Andrea sighed and announced casually, "Well, I'm glad we went, but I don't think Houston's is as good as it used to be."

"Politeness" flew right out the window. Elizabeth almost drove off Interstate 85, and the girlfriends bent over double laughing. Especially when a bewildered Andrea asked, "What's so funny?"

Don't Tell Me Who Won

June 2014, *Southeast Lifestyle*

The eyes of the golfing world will be on North Carolina this month. That's because Pinehurst has the honor of hosting both the 2014 U.S. Open (for the men) and the U.S. Women's Open Championships. It will mark the first time in history that both golf tournaments will be played in the same year, on the same course. When complete, Pinehurst No. 2—and thus NC—will become the only golf course and or state to have hosted all five USGA Championships. Sir Walter Raleigh could have never "thunk" it would happen.[3]

But wait! There's more!

August 11-17, the eyes of the golf world will turn toward us again for the 75th Wyndham PGA Championship at Sedgefield Country Club in Greensboro. People in my age bracket will remember it as the GGO—the Greater Greensboro Open. As a child, I still remember the night my Daddy came home after spending the day watching Slammin' Sammy Snead capture one of his eight GGO titles. Good days.

Whether or not we have a smidgen of interest in golf, we can't help but "bust a gut" with pride about what's happening in NC this summer.

3 "In 1587, Sir Walter Raleigh explored North America from North Carolina to Florida." History.com

Many North Carolinians will be in the gallery as spectators for a round or two as the pros tee off. Others will follow the tournament live on TV. Still others will record the action to be watched later in the privacy of their homes. This last group—the group that records golf matches to watch later—may need a little help from the rest of us this summer.

My sister Andrea and her husband Bob lived in Portland, Oregon. She was a lawyer; he was a judge, and they loved following the game of golf. When they couldn't be home during a big tournament that was televised, they fell into that group that recorded the match and later watched the entire event from tee-off to last putt. Naturally, they didn't want to know the outcome in advance. They enjoyed seeing it unfold, especially the last round. This often presented a problem.

The scenario is familiar. One person records a movie or sporting event to watch later, and another person calls or sees them and tells them the outcome before the "recorders" have had a chance to enjoy the replay. (So much for suspense.) In this case, Bob's mother, Phoebe, well into her eighties, was often the guilty culprit.

"What are you doing?" Phoebe would ask when Andrea or Bob picked up the phone.

"Watching the golf match we recorded."

To which Phoebe would reply, "Oh, so-and-so came from behind on the seventeenth and won. It was a thrilling finish."

!!"!?##!

This happened so often with Phoebe and others that when Andrea and Bob were engrossed in a match, they started answering the phone with a somewhat blunt threat disguised as a plea. "Whoever you are, if you know who won the golf tournament this afternoon, please don't say the name. We are watching the replay now." The tone was serious. They meant it.

This was similar to what Andrea said when the phone rang as she and Bob watched the final round of one big PGA tournament in partic-ular. Golf fans in the Portland area had been following the tournament all week because an outstanding local golfer, Peter Jacobsen, had been doing extremely well. He was among the leaders when the final round began. Andrea and Bob were especially interested because he had grown up in Portland and played out of their club. Unfortunately, they had to attend another event that afternoon but hurried home as soon as it ended. They had just settled down in front of their TV to watch their recorded replay when the phone rang. Andrea picked up the receiver and quickly announced emphatically, "Whoever this is, do not tell me the winner of the golf tournament."

There was one of those long pregnant pauses we hear so much about, and then Bob's mother Phoebe, evidently slightly offended to have been talked to in that manner, announced, "Well, I am certainly not going to tell you who won."

"Thank you, Phoebe. We're watching now," Andrea said, her eyes staring at the screen.

That's when Phoebe said in her defense, right before she hung up the phone, "All I'll say is . . . Portland is very proud!"

Regardless of each of our interest in the sport, when it comes to golf this summer, all of us in the state can stand a little taller and say . . ." North Carolina is very proud."

Don't Confront the Governor

November 2014, *Southeast Lifestyle*

Just a few more days, and it will be over—for a while. I'm referring to the incessant, nerve-wracking, political ROBO calls about the upcoming election.

Perhaps it's a good time for me to remind everyone that without politics and politicians, we wouldn't have some of our best humorous stories.

Thanks to my Aunt Lettie, our family has a good one.

My great-grandmother, Cora McAdory, was president of the Alabama Women's Christian Temperance Union. The WCTU was organized by women who were concerned about the destructive power of alcohol and the problems it was causing their families and society. They met in churches to pray and then marched to saloons with picket signs.

We don't think our great-grandmother ever marched, but she must have been adamantly opposed to alcohol to have been elected WCTU State President. During her tenure, Big Jim Folsom was elected Governor of the state for his first term. At 6'8 ", size 15 1/2 shoe, size 18 collar, and 270+ pounds, one can understand the nickname. (The widower was also called "Kissing Jim" Folsom, but that's another story.)

Big Jim was something of a character. He eventually served two terms as Governor and probably would have been elected again if he hadn't gone on live television to debate his opponent while under the influence of alcohol and, some say, without shoes. I say, cut him some slack. Maybe he could only find size 14s, and his feet hurt. That said, if you're slurring your words, can't remember your children's names, and do an extended imitation of a cuckoo clock on statewide TV during a political debate, it can't help a politician. As we say in the South, "Bless his heart."

The WCTU was adamantly opposed to Big Jim's drinking and use of profanity, so they implored their president, my great-grandmother, to lead a group of women from Auburn to Montgomery and make sure the Governor heard—in no uncertain terms—exactly how they felt. In planning their meeting, the women decided to also talk to him about the many rumors of his womanizing.

"Mamahdee," as I called her, drove to the state capitol with my Aunt Lettie and several other ladies for the appointed rendezvous. Apparently, they continued to coach their top officer the entire trip. "Now, remember, Cora, talk to him about all three areas of concern—drinking, cursing, and womanizing."

"I certainly intend to do just that," Cora said. "Drinking, cursing, and womanizing. He'll think twice about continuing those habits after I've talked to him."

"Do you know what you're going to say?" one of the ladies asked.

"Absolutely. When we leave, he'll remember whom we represent and why we came."

Aunt Lettie even assured Mamahdee that, "We'll be in the room, right behind you if you need us, but it sounds as though you have it well planned. We probably won't need to say a word." That was just fine with Cora.

My reliable source was Aunt Lettie, of course, who told the story until the day she died. An hour later, the determined ladies were escorted into the Governor's office in Montgomery. Big Jim stood immediately when they came into the room. Then he quickly came from behind his desk and approached each lady one at a time, shaking her hand, looking down in her eyes, and smiling. "Thank you so much for coming today," he proclaimed, "I've been waiting for your group because I knew you would brighten up this place." A couple of the ladies almost smiled back but got stern looks from the others. No one said a word while they waited for their president to take over.

Before Mamahdee could speak, however, Big Jim offered them lemonade. He had glasses and a big pitcher of it on a beautiful tray on his desk. Later, the women said they felt it would be poor manners to turn down the offer. He already had a glass. (I think they got lucky it was lemonade.) They told him the tray was beautiful, as were the pitcher and glasses. They all agreed later that the lemonade was quite good and the tray was absolutely gorgeous.

With the lemonade served, the Governor returned to his big chair behind the desk. "What can I do for you charming ladies today?" Mamahdee sat up a little straighter and assumed a serious look. As planned, none of the other ladies said a word. Except for the comments on the pitcher, glasses, and tray, one would have thought they weren't in the room.

Finally, in the most stern voice she could muster, my great-grandmother began. "Governor Folsom, I am Cora McAdory, President of the Alabama Women's Christian Temperance Union," she announced firmly and with authority.

"What a fine organization," Big Jim quickly inserted. "May I thank you on behalf of the state of Alabama for your good work?" Silence from the group. After a few awkward seconds of quiet, Mamahdee forged ahead and launched into her memorized opening statement.

"Well, um, yes. Thank you, Governor Folsom. Our members, as well as I, are quite concerned about the rumors of your drinking, womanizing, and use of bad language."

BAM! Governor Folsom slammed his hand down on his desk, startling the women and almost turning over the lemonade. "Mrs. McAdory, I'd like to know the name of the su!mpb@#h who told you that d*@# lie!"

Before Madam President could recover, the Governor strode from behind his desk, came over to where she was seated, put one arm tenderly around her shoulders, and looked down into Mamahdee's eyes as he said in a hushed tone, "Can't you tell by looking at me that I'm not the type of man who would do such things?"

Madam President gazed upward and smiled demurely. "Why, yes, I can." And that is precisely what she reported at the next state meeting of the Alabama Women's Christian Temperance Union. And none of the others said a word.

FABulous NYC Buttons

November 2015, *Southeast Lifestyle*

It's beautiful, colorful November but winter's "a'coming." If you still need to attack the task for this year, it's time to pull out your bulky winter clothes and see what can be salvaged for the coming months.

Some of you who have heard me speak know about my friend Jane Tucker from NYC! I've even written about her a couple of times. She often comes to North Carolina to go through my closet and "Tuckerize" me. Jane is in the fashion industry and has a 6'4" daughter, so she knows who will help me get clothes that fit. She's determined to keep me at least pointed toward stylish. It's a tough job because at age 72 (Gasp! No way!), I still prefer jeans and a T-shirt. Several years ago, she sent me a Pashmina from NYC to fling around my shoulders. When I told my husband, Left Brain, that Jane Tucker was sending me a black Pashmina, his reply was memorable, "We don't need another dog."

Well, Jane's been back. While rummaging around in my closet, she came upon my black St. John knit suit again.[4] It had found its way to the front of the clothes after residing in the back for several years. This suit has a history. I bought it in 1996, and through the years, Jane and I

---

4 St. John Knits is a luxury American fashion brand specializing in women's knitwear founded in 1962.

have altered or changed it at least eight times. The shoulder pads have been put in and removed. The whole suit was taken up one "thin year" and then let back out after the Thanksgiving and Christmas holidays. (A timely subliminal message.) The skirt has been shortened twice and then lengthened back to where it started by adding a piece at the waist. But I'm still wearing it after all these years because I want my money's worth out of it. It was the most expensive suit I had bought until I met Jane Tucker. I told Left Brain I found it on a rack at Big Lots.[5]

We hadn't changed the suit in the past several years, but on this particular trip, Jane took one look and said, "This needs updating." I honestly didn't think the poor thing could have anything else done to it. It seemed to me that, at that point, it ought to be put out to pasture in the back of the closet with an old watch around the sleeve in honor of its years of service.

Jane saw it differently. She thought the shiny gold and black St. John buttons should be swapped for all-black buttons. She said the current buttons shouted, "St. John! St. John!"

I had never heard the buttons say or shout anything, but changing them sounded good to me.

"Okay, Jane. Let me write 'Get black buttons' on my to-do list." Her response was quick. "No, no, no. I'll send the perfect buttons from New York, so they'll be right."

Sometimes, Jane's NY approach can be bothersome to a Southerner. I chose my words carefully. "Jane, I don't know how to break it to you because I'm aware that people in New York City think they have the best of everything, and we don't have squat down here but trust me. We've got black buttons right here in North Carolina. I'll get the buttons."

She was adamant. "No, Jeanne, I know exactly what this suit needs. I'll send them from New York. They'll be fab'ulous." Left Brain says when Jane adds the word "fab'ulous" to anything, the price goes up.

---

5 Big Lots is an American discount retail chain.

This time, he later said, "You should have told her you'll go back to Big Lots, where you bought the suit and find some buttons." I love him, but we don't call him "Left Brain" without reason. If y'all see St. John suits hanging in Big Lots, call me first.

I also told my "bestest" friend Norma Rose about the buttons. Her reaction was the same as mine. "We've got buttons in North Carolina." But when I explained these would be special, fab'ulous New York City buttons, she said, "Call me when they come in. I want to see if these New York City buttons can be worth what I'm betting you paid for them."

Soon, a small box arrived from Jane. I called Norma Rose without opening it. It was as though two spies were whispering into phones. Pick up. "Hello." "The buttons are here."

"Don't open them until I get there. I'm on the way." Click.

We opened the package at the kitchen table, and the buttons took our breath away—Jane's good. The buttons were perfect for the suit. We sat speechless and in awe. Finally, Norma Rose whispered, sounding as though she were from NY, "They're fab'ulous."

I nodded because she was right, but I was thinking, "You grew up in Reidsville. You don't talk like that." She also asked what was next, and I told her that I was going to change the buttons that afternoon. She was aghast.

"You don't sew a lick, Jeanne. You can't put buttons on anything, much less a knit suit. You'll ruin it after all these years. If you clip one little piece of knit, the way you move around on stage, that suit will unravel on you in the middle of a show. I sew. I'll put them on."

"No, Norma Rose, I don't sew, but I can certainly put buttons on a suit." (That's what I said, but I was thinking, please offer one more time. She did.) In minutes she left with my expensive black St. John suit and the fab'ulous New York City buttons.

A short time later, she came back with the updated suit on a hanger. "Ta-da!" It was amazing. The NYC new buttons truly did update the look. We both oohed and ahhed over the suit for a few minutes and then I asked, "Where are the St. John buttons?"

She swallowed and stood there a few seconds before saying, "It's best if I keep the gold and black St. John buttons at my house, Jeanne. I've been watching Jane Tucker for some time now. She'll be back in two years telling you it's time to put the St. John buttons back on the black suit. No offense, but you'll never find them in your cluttered house. Sometimes, you can't even find Left Brain. I'm doing what's best for you. I'll have the St. John buttons in a special place. When you need them, just ask for them."

Again, I chose my words carefully. What I wanted to say had to be said delicately. "Well, exactly where in your house will the buttons be, Norma Rose? If something should happen to you—God forbid, of course—I don't want to have to say to your daughter-in-law, 'When you're cleaning out things, Amy, if you come across some St. John buttons, they're mine.' It would be awkward with you dead and all. If I know where you've put them, I can go there and get them when Amy goes into another room. Exactly where will the buttons be?"

Norma Rose swallowed again and shifted her weight nervously before finally making eye contact and answering, "Okay. Okay. They'll be in my closet. I'm keeping the St. John buttons on a black suit I got at TJ Maxx."

It's November. Get your winter clothes in order—especially the buttons.

Grandma Freddie's Trip to the Holy Land

March 2016, *Southeast Lifestyle*

I grew up on Main Street in the wonderful town of Graham, NC. We rented the house, but Daddy put up a basketball goal in my backyard. Young people today don't always realize that every house didn't have a basketball goal back then. Instead, there was usually a neighborhood goal where everyone played, and during my childhood, it was outside my backdoor. Mostly, boys played there, but if I came outside, they put me in the next game fast. That could have been because I was 6'2" tall in the seventh grade. More than likely, though, they let me play because of something I heard one of the regulars tell a boy from another neighborhood. He had asked, "Why is she playing?" The regular said, "She owns the goal."

I was reminded of this incident several years ago when I was asked to speak at the 100th-year celebration of women at Auburn University, my alma mater. (No, I was not in the first graduating class.) The ballroom was filled with women, many of them older and from the town of Auburn, where most of my family lives. When my speech was over, three of these Auburn matriarchs said the same thing to me, but independent of each other. "Jeanne, you got your speaking ability from your Grandmother Freddie."

Because I'm a professional speaker, that intrigued me. I thought I knew my Grandma Freddie well. I had often been told by those who knew us both that I inherited her sense of "showmanship," which is the polite, southern way of saying, "You both like to be the center of attention." But I had never heard that I had inherited her speaking ability.

That afternoon, I asked my Aunt Carolyn about it. Aunt Carolyn said, "Oh, darling, your Grandma Freddie was an excellent speaker. Not anything like you—she didn't have a professional brochure—but she counted on that 'word-of-mouth' you always talk about. And Jeanne, I've heard you say a thousand times that you have a speaking career because 'From time to time, every group needs a little program.' Grandma Freddie knew that too and would put together a little program, giving it all around Auburn at churches and civic clubs and even around the state. When it ran its course, she put together another program and started over. I'm surprised you didn't know this."

I was surprised, too.

Aunt Carolyn continued. "I think Grandma Freddie's best program was her last program. It was on her trip to the Holy Land. The reason that program was better than the others was that she had a box of slides of the region. She had even gone over to the University and borrowed a pointer from a history professor. She would show a slide, tell a story about something in that location, and point out the spot with the pointer. It was quite impressive." (I couldn't help but think, what if she had just lived to see PowerPoint.)

"Well," I replied, "I didn't realize it living up in North Carolina. I guess everyone in the family who did know about it was proud of her."

Aunt Carolyn suddenly seemed pensive. "Oh, we were. We were. You could certainly say that everyone in the family was proud of her." Then, cutting her eyes toward mine, she added, "Of course, we would have been so much more proud if she had ever actually been to the Holy Land."

"Aunt Carolyn! Grandma Freddie went all over Auburn and the state of Alabama, giving programs on her trip to the Holy Land, and she had never been to the Holy Land?"

"Never stepped foot there. She went on a trip. I know she went on a trip because I booked the tickets and took her to the airport in Montgomery, but she didn't go to the Holy Land. She went down the Rhine, but she thought it was the Nile. Then, in a gift shop somewhere, she bought a box of slides of the Holy Land and wah'la! Her next program was born. The first time she gave the program, Jeanne, it was for the Auburn Methodist women, and she simply showed the slides and told interesting stories. I know because I ran the slide projector. But somewhere between the Methodists and Catholics, she started slapping that pointer on the screen as she said, 'When I was here . . .'"

"Oh, Aunt Carolyn, I can't believe this."

"Why not? You, Jeanne, of all people, know about stretching a story . . ."

"But Aunt Carolyn, what if people in Auburn had found out?"

"Oh, Jeanne, everybody knew. It didn't matter. And may I remind you—Grandma Freddie owned the slides."

Forget at Your Own Peril

April 2016, *Southeast Lifestyle*

Consider this your friendly reminder—"Administrative Professionals Day" is this month. It is always celebrated on the Wednesday during the last full week in April. If it applies to you, my advice is to remember it. Write it down. Put up sticky notes. Email or text yourself a message. Whatever you do, make it a priority. Forget it at your own peril. That stated, we don't have to limit our "special recognition" for these terrific individuals to only one day of the year. There are plenty of other days that will work.

Toni Meredith has been my Administrative Professional for over 37 years. We were both students at Auburn University "down" in Alabama, and both wound up near Southeast Guilford in Alamance County with our families. I had grown up in Graham, and my husband, Left Brain, in Burlington, so we came home. Toni and her husband Tom moved to Burlington for business so, as Deputy Barney Fife might say, "They were from somewheres else."

To refresh your memory, "Administrative Professionals Day" or "Admin Day" was known for years as "Secretary's Day." In my office, from time to time, Toni has been known as "Queen of Everything," "Queen of the Tickets," and "National Coordinator." (I'll never forget the time she booked me for my first speech in California and pronounced herself "International Coordinator.") But the current, politically correct term is certainly Administrative Assistant or Administrative Professional.

Several years ago, I returned home from a speaking trip in January and, as usual, soon had a meeting with Toni to catch up on what was happening business-wise. I write my material, travel, and do the speeches and shows. Toni handles about everything else, including booking all my engagements. At this particular meeting, she told me a meeting planner had called about booking me the following summer on Saturday night, August 18. It was unusual for her to tell me about every call. Usually, she just reported on what had been booked. That day, she told me the gentleman's name and the name of his organization.

"Did he book it?"

"Well, no. Not yet," Toni explained, avoiding eye contact. "We're holding the date for him, but I needed to talk to you about it first." Again, this was odd. She has full authority to book dates.

I responded, "Is there a problem with travel? I can't get there? Is he deciding among several other speakers and me?"

"No, you can get there from another speech with time to spare," she said, still glancing at her notes rather than at me. "He definitely wants you, and he has the fee. It's just, well, August 18 is the exact date of Tom's and my 50th wedding anniversary. We've been planning a big party. One of those events where we send out 'Hold the Date' cards to let old friends from around the country have time to plan if they want to come. And, naturally, there'll be a long list of local friends. It's going to be a big deal, Jeanne, and I wish you could be there."

Priorities. I sized up the situation immediately and, without blinking an eye, said what I meant, "I wouldn't miss it for the world. Absolutely turn down his invitation. Left Brain and I will both be there. You're not having that party without us!"

Toni's face lit up, and she broke into a big smile. "Good. Because we're thinking about having it at your house."

And they did.

No Ma'am. I Don't Smoke

May 2016, *Southeast Lifestyle*

May. Mother's Day month. Whether your mom is living or, like mine, has "passed," it's a nice time to think back to some of the good times and laughter you had together, even if that laughter came yearrrrrrs later.

I smoked once. I don't mean that I smoked during one era of my life. I . . . smoked . . . once. One afternoon. One time.

The afternoon I "tried smoking," I was in the seventh grade. I came home from school and found Mother napping. I went into the den and sneaked a couple of cigarettes and matches from her "pocketbook." Please don't think harshly of Mother because she smoked, which in today's world draws criticism from many. When I grew up, all of my friends' mothers smoked. They also covered their babies in baby powder, which today would bring in Social Services.[6] Just trust me, Mama was a good person who was smart and reflective, but she definitely smoked.

(An "aside." In writing this story, I asked my assistant Toni if her mother smoked. Apparently, it depended on where her mother was and who she was with. They lived in Chattanooga, but when Toni was a child, they drove south to visit older family members in New Orleans.

6 At one time, baby powder or Talcum Powder was made from talc, a substance that contained asbestos, a carcinogen.

While there, someone asked Toni if her mother smoked, and Toni repeated to me what she had overheard in the car. "She smokes when she's in Chattanooga, but not when she's in New Orleans.")

That day, with cigarettes hidden against my sweater, I hurried down the hall to the room I shared with my sister Katherine, who was two years older than I. At that age, we rarely spoke to each other, but we had to share a bedroom. We split the room right down the middle and cordoned it off with tape and rope. That let friends know we were forced to share the room, but we didn't like it. Boundaries were definite, and a sister or her friends didn't dare step on the other sister's side unless the other was absent. We had to turn sideways and go through our designated half of the doorway to enter or leave the room.

That infamous day, inside the room and definitely on my side of it, I put up a window so the smoke could escape and lit one of the snitched cigarettes. I took a huge breath, inhaled with all my might, and was thrown into a coughing spasm. Cough. COUGH! It was absolutely awful. So, for some reason known only to God, I did it again and got the same reaction. More coughing. Hacking. Pain. Even dizziness. That's when I heard Mother coming down the hall calling, "Jeanne?"

Panicking, I flung myself into action. I put out the cigarette and threw it in the trash can on my sister's side of the room. Because it was cold outside and there was no reason for the window to be open, I frantically tried to close it. After several hard pushes and almost breaking my hand, it finally shut. Bam! I scooped up my history book and jumped on my bed. All of this was accomplished within seconds, during which time Mother called again from the hall, "Jeanne, where are you?"

"I'm in here," I sang out, lightheaded, "doing my homework." Sure enough, when Mama came in the room, I was reared back on a pillow at the headboard, studying history.

Mother had been in the room for five seconds when she stopped talking mid-sentence, paused, and slowly started looking around. My heart sank when she crinkled her nose to sniff.

Seconds later, she did a slow turn in my direction and stared hard at me before finally asking the dreaded question. "Jeanne, are you smoking?"

Being in seventh grade, I looked her straight back in the eyes and said, "No, ma'am."

And the trash can burst into flames.

Mother grabbed a towel and started beating at the flames. By then, I was off the bed, dancing around, saying the only thing a sister could say at that age. "Katherine was going out when I came in! What did she do?"

When the fire was out, Mother turned her attention back to me. I thought she would say a comment we heard often, "We'll talk about this when your father gets home," but she didn't. She said calmly, "I've got an errand to run. When I come back, those cigarettes and matches had better be back in my purse and that trash can cleaned up." Then, she pointed to my allowance on my bedside table. "And that money had better be in my purse too."

I stood up and pronounced defiantly, "Mama, I didn't take any money out of your purse."

She smiled. "I know it. But that allowance is exactly what you owe me for the cigarette."

When she got to the door, I breathed a tiny sigh of relief, thinking she was leaving and I was safe for the time being. The loss of a week's meager allowance at that age was well worth getting me out of the situation. I should have known it wasn't the end of it.

She turned around one more time before leaving the room and, with a big smile, said something that became a commonly repeated phrase in our family through the years, even the day they took me to college.

"One more thing, Jeanne, when you're studying, turn the book right side up."

I never smoked again.

Happy Mother's Day to moms everywhere. Thanks for the memories.

What Size Does the Baby Wear?

September 2016, *Southeast Lifestyle*

Okay. Whew. We made it through a hot summer, and the "kids" are back in school proudly wearing their brand-new clothes. School starts in August these days, so by the time September rolls around, items are on sale in most stores, and mothers are searching for any remaining bargains. I don't have any young schoolchildren in my family at this point. (I now make all the peanut butter and jelly sandwiches for me.) But I always smile when I see the "Back to School" ads. They remind me of shopping with Mother for school clothes. See, Mother made shopping fun.

One shopping trip with Mother, in particular, stands out so much that I smile and laugh when I think about it. It's a good reminder to enjoy the "kids" stage of life and to make every day a "fun" day for young people by influencing them to keep a sense of humor.

The time I just alluded to was the day Mother and I went shopping for my seventh-grade Fall school clothes. Just the two of us. She had taken my older, five-foot-five sister shopping the day before and then turned her attention to her taller challenge, me. I had just gone through another growth spurt over the summer and, at age thirteen, was six feet, two inches tall. I towered over Mother, who, like her older daughter, was also five feet, five inches tall, standing on her tiptoes. We thought our size differences were funny, but looking back on it, we made an interesting mother/daughter combination.

To the clerk in the first store who asked, "May I help you?" Mother gave her a quick smile and used her Southern drawl as she patted me on the back, "Yea'uss. I'd like to get some shoes for thuh baby."

That stopped the clerk in her tracks, but she quickly got herself together, looked up at me, and said slowly, "What size shoe does 'thuh baby' wear?"

Mother drew herself up to the top of her five-foot-five height and said loudly, "She wears a seven and a half." Then she dropped her voice and mumbled, "But an eleven feels really good."

The lady didn't know whether to laugh or not, but I laughed because Mother was having fun. As often happened, the store didn't have any size elevens, and we moved to another store, a new clerk, and other items.

We did find a few things at the next store and, after a while, approached the counter to check out. Standing at Mother's side, I remember her telling the lady behind the cash register that she was glad to find a few things that would fit her daughter and nodded in my direction. I smiled. The clerk's response was to look down at Mother. Then up at me. Back down at Mother and then, a second time, back up at me. All without saying a word. Her eyes looked like a vertical tennis match. Up. Down. Slowly back up. Down.

Finally, with me standing right there and able to hear her, the clerk shook her head from left to right, looked down at Mother again, and said, "I can't believe you had a daughter that size."

Mother leaned in toward the clerk and explained sweetly, "She wasn't that size when I had her."

We were just getting started. We shopped all afternoon, and we laughed and laughed and laughed some more.

Mother made shopping fun, and I guess we should all strive to do the same. Unfortunately, I'm not sure I'm as good a person or as patient as my mother was. Our grown son Beaver still relishes telling about the time I apparently screamed at him in a store during a shopping trip. He swears I said, "Get in that dressing room and try it on right now, or you'll go to school naked!"

Oh, well. Some days are more fun than others.

What's in a Name?

June 2018, *SE Gazette*

"Why do you call your son 'Beaver?'" It's a question I'm often asked, especially if I've just told a story about him in a show or speech. Beaver is not his real name, of course, but it's what everyone has always called him. People in my age group know it indicates a "sidekick."

To answer why we call our son Beaver, we will separate younger adult readers from the older ones. Most younger adult readers think Son Beaver was nicknamed after the television show *Leave it to Beaver*. Remember it? The Cleavers? June and Ward? Sons Wally and his little brother Beaver? The show still airs today on one of the thousands of channels, but Left Brain and I can't figure out how to get it on our televisions. Once in a while, though, we stumble upon it. It may seem a little tame by today's standards, but it nails the personalities we still see today. Who hasn't met an Eddie Haskell or two? ("You look very nice today, Mrs. Cleaver.") If you think Beaver got his name from this once-popular TV show, please count yourself as one of the young adult readers. For you are incorrect.

No, Beaver did not get his nickname from *Leave it to Beaver*. Not at all. He got it from a character most likely known by us older adult readers who are of the generation that went to the movies every

Saturday afternoon to watch our favorite cowboys—Roy Rogers, Gene Autry, and the Lone Ranger, to name a few. I loved those Western stars. I even loved Roy Roger's horse, Trigger. (I believed Trigger could count! I saw it with my own eyes. My older sister said it was a trick, but I didn't believe her.) Paraphrasing a popular country song sung by Toby Keith, "I should've been a cowgirl / I should've learned to rope and ride."

In addition to the Lone Ranger, Roy, Dale, and Gene, the older adult readers probably remember another star from that era, Red Ryder. Mr. Ryder got his start as a comic strip character, but eventually, he became a real character in movies and on TV. If memory serves me correctly, a BB gun was named after him. (Oh, what different times we live in now.) And Red Ryder's sidekick? I bet a lot of people my age remember that . . . although it may take us a few minutes to think of it . . . his sidekick was a young boy with a bow and arrow named "Little Beaver." That is exactly where Son Beaver got his nickname. (I won't even go into the fact that years later, Beaver named his first son "Ryder." He swears they named him after a truck, but. . .)

People also ask if we're glad we called him Beaver or do we wish we had given him a different name or nickname. If we had, we would have missed a lot of fun.

There is a stage in every person's life—I believe it's when we're eight or nine—when our teeth are proportionally larger than our heads. We all go through it. If you question that statement, check out your elementary school pictures. Maybe look at your third or fourth-grade headshots—the photos taken before braces.

When Beaver was about that age, he, Left Brain, and I went into a restaurant. LB stopped to talk to someone, and I was giving motherly instructions to Beaver as I continued to a table. I guess others could hear me. "Put your coat on the hook over there, Beaver." He did. The coat fell to the floor. He hung it up again. It fell to the floor again. He hung it a third time, and down it went. I sighed and said, probably a little impatiently, "Hook it on the label that's at the neck inside the jacket, Beaver." He did. It finally stayed on.

"Sit down right there, Beaver," I instructed, nodding toward a chair. He sat. I sat, too. Left Brain joined us. LB was 6'6" tall. I was 6'2", and Beaver was growing like a weed. (He stopped growing at 6'8".) There were a lot of long legs under the table that day, but we got settled, and I said, "Here's a menu. What do you want to eat, Beaver?"

Out of the blue . . . an obviously upset, a woman eavesdropping at the next table, whom I had never seen in my life, grabbed my elbow and, through gritted teeth, practically hissed at me. "How would you like it if he called you 'Giraffe'?"

Epilogue. I know. I know. I've left you with another unanswered question. "What is your son Beaver's real name?" I'm sorry. I forgot to include that. It's "Muskrat."

Valuable Is in the Eye of the Holder

April 2019, *SE Gazette*

People around "these parts" might remember when Sheriff Andy Taylor has to evict Frank Myers from his home in the TV episode "Mayberry Goes Bankrupt." Andy winds up inviting Frank to come and stay with the Taylors. Frank brings along some of his important stuff in a little box:

- A brass medallion from the St. Louis World's Fair
- A spoon with the skyline of Milwaukee on it
- A "gen-u-ine" whalebone napkin ring
- A red, white, and blue sleeve garter
- A bond issued by the town of Mayberry in 1861

They're "valuables" to Frank, but he knows they "ain't worth a tiddly-boo."

Every time I see that episode, it reminds me of a friend of mine, Ira Hayes. It would have taken more than a small box to load up Ira's sentimental relics.

During a speaking trip to Florida, I had a chance to visit with fellow professional speaker/friend, Ira Hayes. Ira was older than I and had been a speaker for a long time. His tremendous success in the speaking profession was due not only to his talent but also to the fact that he was a "gen-u-ine-ly" nice person. People liked to be around him. He was humble and quiet and then hilarious on stage. He relished his travels and adventures and was thankful for the opportunities he had been given. That said . . .

Ira had the junkiest office I have ever seen. But it was organized junk with charm and a true monument to the word "memorabilia." When I visited him at his home that day, his wife Carol said the room was set aside just for Ira's "stuff." Smiling, she told me they had downsized, moved to Florida, and brought all of Ira's stuff with them.

I came to a quick stop when I walked into Ira's office. Whoa. What in the world? I've always had a lot of memorabilia in my office, but this was over the top. "Stuff" was everywhere, but as I stated, organized. Ira stood nearby and didn't say a word while I tried to take it all in. For starters, the walls were completely covered with more than four thousand name tags push-pinned into them. I didn't do a count. I took his word for it. The tags were actually layered on top of each other. As I stared, Ira pointed out specific items. "This one is a little unusual," he said in his low-key style. "It's from a convention in 1948. Way back that far. Can you believe it, Jeanne? And look at this one. Ever see a name tag that big?" I had not.

Plaques from audiences covered up some name tags in spots. Gimmicks representing thousands of meetings peeped out from available spaces. If a group gave it away at a convention and Ira spoke there, he had it. The word today is "swag." Framed photos overlapped the name badges in other places. Ira had been President of the National Speakers Association, and I noticed the plaque for that. I also noticed the statue presented when he received that organization's top honor, the Cavett Award.

"Remember this?" he quizzed with a glint in his eye. It was a 1978 photo of the two of us. We looked funny, not just because of the change in style and hair. Unlike gymnasts, for example, there is no "correct size" for professional speakers. Stretching and standing on his toes, Ira came to my shoulder. In the picture, I'm kissing him on the top of the head as he looks at the camera with a sheepish grin. Did I mention he also had perfect timing?

Standing there with Ira, staring at the walls, I could sense that he was happy in his room. I was also thinking that one lighted match would make the place convention history, but we don't always say what we think. Instead, I said, "Ira, this is . . . wonderful."

He must have known what I was thinking. He stood quietly for a few seconds and added with a smile, "The kids will toss it fast, but it'll take them a while to get it all down." Then he became serious. "These are memories of a lifetime, Jeanne. Everything in here is a reminder of one of the places I spoke and of the nice things people did for me."

I nodded because I understood, and then I noticed high on the walls was one shelf that encircled the room. On the shelf were tiny bottles lined up in a row. They looked like miniature whiskey bottles flight attendants hand out on some flights. Normally, a shelf like that would have had an electric train to circle the room. This one had miniature whisky bottles about four inches tall. "What's that up there, Ira?"

Ira fixed his attention on the small bottles for several moments before replying, "That is very special, Jeanne. That's my dirt collection."

I nodded again to give myself time to think. You'll be happy to know that I resisted saying, "I have dirt collected all over my house, but I don't display it in little bottles." Ira was serious about this, and he probably had heard that comment from others.

"Jeanne, those bottles hold dirt from each of the states and countries where I was privileged to speak," explained this leader who had been in the speaking profession for decades.

We stood there staring upward, admiring the collection.

I broke the silence. "You're saying those tiny liquor bottles are full of dirt?"

"Yep," he replied. "I took a sack and spoon on trips and would ask my client to pull over on the side of the road so I could scoop up a little dirt from their state. Then I brought the dirt back home in the sack, filled up an empty airplane miniature bottle, and labeled it." He smiled as he remembered gathering the dirt. "See. Montana, New Jersey. There's your state, North Carolina." We looked at North Carolina in silence. What does one say in this situation? I probably said, "I've never seen anything like this."

We continued to gaze from tiny bottle to tiny bottle: white dirt, black dirt, tan dirt, red dirt. Every tiny bottle was a little different. It struck me that I could go around North Carolina and gather dirt of various colors, put it in bottles, and say it came from far-off places, but I didn't mention it to Ira. Others had probably mentioned that. (I didn't even ask if he drank all the liquor in the little bottles. I figured he had heard that, too.) The mental picture of him bent over on the side of the road or in a field somewhere—spoon in hand while others waited in a car—made me smile.

More silence and gazing upward. "There's Hawaii," he pointed out. "Alaska's to your left. They're in alphabetical order by states and then countries."

"Ah," I muttered, nodding my head. "Sounds reasonable."

I continued to throw in comments such as, "Well, that is really something, Ira," and "It must have taken a long time to get all these different dirts." I didn't know what else to say. Then, eureka! Something dawned on me.

"You know what, Ira? You may have the only personal, fifty-state, and foreign country collection of dirt in miniature whiskey bottles in the entire world."

That's when Ira turned toward me and grinned. "Nope. I made a set for each of the children."

And I say, "Why not? He had the dirt."

Working the Desk

January 2020, *SE Gazette*

(Preface from Jeanne: Be aware. This one contains words you usually don't see here.)

Surprising how tiny nuggets of information pop up later to help us if we can only remember them.

Several issues ago, I wrote about my assistant of forty-plus years. We had both gone to Auburn, and we both worked at the Auburn University library during our college years. I was there after Toni, but basically, we both shelved books and did whatever we were asked to do. I worked there a summer, Toni, for more than two years. She had much more responsibility. She got to "work the desk." I was never asked to "work the desk."

After I sent a proposed Auburn story to the publisher, Marty Heim, for her consideration, Toni and I started reminiscing about those days. At one point, she said, "Actually, one of the funniest things that ever happened to me happened when I was working in the library. Don't know why I've never told you about it." Here is what she related to me—

One day, a young male student came into the big library and wound up on Toni's fourth floor. She was working at the desk when he approached and told her that he was looking for a particular book his girlfriend needed for a class.

"Be glad to help you," Toni told him. "What's the title?"

The young man tucked his chin a little and mumbled, "It's a book about whores."

He definitely had Toni's attention. "Whores?"

"Yes. Specifically, *The Whores of Orver*. I think that's the title.''

Toni had never heard of a place named Orver, much less *The Whores of Orver*, and told him so.

He admitted he hadn't either but added, "Well, that's the book I was sent to check out."

"And it was assigned by the professor?" Toni inquired, walking with him toward the Card Catalog, the "computer" of the era. It had all the information.

"I think so. I don't know why she would be reading about girls like that if the professor hadn't assigned it. My girlfriend is a very nice person."

"I'm sure she is," Toni said quickly, adding, "and the book is supposed to be on this floor?"

"Yes. The fourth floor. That's what she said."

Toni thought about it for a few seconds, then asked, "Do you know what she's majoring in?"

He did know that. "Home Economics."

There was not a book in the card catalog under "Whores" that included "Orver."

No, he didn't know the author's name. But just as Toni was to suggest he get the author's name or more information, he reached into his pocket and pulled out a little piece of paper. "My girlfriend wrote it down."

Toni tried to keep from laughing when she read the French word "Hors d'oeuvre." Good thing he asked Toni for help and not a student like me. I thought "appetizers" were spelled "orders."

Keep laughing in the new year!

Oh, wait. One more thing. Toni explained it all to me. The fourth floor was the Science and Technology floor. Home Economics was considered a science. That's why the cookbooks were on that floor. According to Toni, they were the only interesting books on that floor and the only ones she could understand, so she read cookbooks during her breaks and learned things. And, even at that age, remembered them.

Now you know why she got to work at the front desk while I spent all my time shelving books. I sat in the lounge during breaks and gossiped.

Don't Mess with
the Ladies' Book Club

May 2020, *SE Gazette*

How is it said? You can please some of the people all of the time. And you can please all of the people some of the time. But to please all the people all the time? It's not going to happen, especially with the Graham Book Club.

There is no question about it. When a woman grows up in a small town in the South like Graham, North Carolina, and the local book club members ask her to come to a meeting and "do one of your little programs," the only answer is, "When?"

Years ago, when I was President of the National Speakers Association, I was up to my ears in work. I had responsibilities that accompany the presidency of a national organization in addition to my regular speaking schedule. I had writing deadlines. It was our son's senior year in high school. I was way too busy. And that was the year the Graham Book Club requested I come to their monthly meeting, specifically in October.

My mother had been a charter member of the club when it formed in the fifties. This was pointed out to me when a friend named Sara called. Mother had passed away, but the membership had not changed much, and I figured I probably still knew every one of the members. One doesn't turn down an invitation such as this, not if she plans to continue living in the area.

The club had twenty-four members, each of whom purchased a book every two years. They met monthly to swap books through a complicated exchange system monitored by extensive charts with a conglomeration of lines on them. The charts were pretty, and watching the process was worth the afternoon—high tech on poster boards. The government should run a tenth as well.

Every meeting started right on time at 1:30 pm with a social gathering. They like for the author of the day to be there at the beginning because, according to Sara, that was the most important part of the afternoon for many. After coffee and cake and the mandatory discussion of the cake recipe, the day I wound up being there, a reminder was made to "puhhh leaase" make sure to send their books to the meetings if they could not attend. "That's how we lose books," the presiding officer chided, "and we lose several a year. As a matter of fact, ladies, I'm sad to announce again that *Annie Laurie* has still not been found, and we continue to look for her." I leaned over and whispered to Sara, "If someone loses a book, is she responsible for replacing it?"

"Oh, yes, it's in the bylaws," Sara assured me. Seconds later, she leaned back in my direction and whispered, "In all these years, though, no one in the club has ever admitted losing a book. Thus, we may never find *Annie Laurie*.

"Ah, I see."

The treasurer rose next to give her report. She had a Ball jar, and I could see dollars in it. "We have six dollars." Rolling her eyes in my direction, she added, "Of course, we usually don't have a treasurer's report, but we want our speaker to know we do not have any money so that she won't expect a fee."

It really was a delightful afternoon, and it was great to see so many friends from my past. Mother would have loved to have been there. But the highlight of the afternoon for me came with the reading of the minutes.

When Sara invited me, she suggested a specific Wednesday afternoon in October, a hectic time for professional speakers. I would only be home a few days that month, and I was already booked to speak in Winston-Salem late the morning of the day she wanted.

So, I responded, "Sara, I'd love to do this, but let's find another date. I'll be tied up an hour from Graham until almost 12:45. Maybe next year?"

Sara was adamant. It was going to be that October, just two months away. "All the other dates are filled for the year. We need a program for October, Jeanne. Plus, I won't be the program chair next year, and I want you for my year."

I thought about it and offered another solution. I would have to do some fancy driving, but I could make it back to Graham by early afternoon. "I probably can't get there by 1:30 when y'all start, but I'll get there ASAP. Go ahead and start the meeting, and I'll slip in."

There was a long pause. Finally, Sara said, "We don't do it that way, Jeanne. We want the author here when we start. The mixing and mingling time is very important to our members. We can't have it at the end of the afternoon because several of them have other important appointments. We start promptly at 1:30. We always have since your mother was a founder and we never vary our schedule."

I knew being there at 1:30 would be chancy, so I offered one final solution. The timing was so close that I asked Sara if the Book Club could meet at 2 pm rather than 1:30 which would assure me of being on time for the mixing and mingling that was so important to them. I could give my "little program" and then make a flight out of Raleigh-Durham early that night. It didn't seem like an unusual request for someone who was doing a "little favor" by giving a "little program," but Sara hedged. She would have to let me know after the September meeting. Again, she stressed that the members never changed the time. They would have to vote on it. I understood. Book Club ladies like to vote on changes, and some people are like Deputy Barney Fife; they just like things to stay the way they are.

I should have remembered Sheriff Andy Taylor's advice, "Never, ever mess with the Ladies Auxiliary."

After the September meeting, Sara called to report that the time had been changed. For this one time in the history of the Graham Book Club, the meeting would begin at 2:00 pm. "But you have to finish on time, Jeanne, because several people are getting their hair cut at four."

Again, I pleaded, "Just let me do it next year, Sara."

"No, it's all worked out. Everyone is on board. Every single one of them is so excited about you coming. They're your friends. You know, your mother was a charter member of this club."

"Yes, Sara, l know."

Therefore, it was interesting a month later to sit with the twenty-four women in a circle around the hostess's living room and hear the reading of the minutes from the month before. The secretary read, "It was moved and seconded that the meeting time be shifted thirty minutes later for our October meeting to accommodate the speaker's apparently busy schedule for that day. The motion passed, 21 to 3."

Apparently busy? Twenty-one to three?

I couldn't help but look around the room and wonder . . . who?

A few days later, when I was back home, Sara called to thank me for coming. I took the opportunity to apologize again for having to change the time and casually asked, "Who were the three members who voted against changing the time? I hope they weren't upset."

Sara hesitated a few seconds and said, "Aw, they just don't like change. I'll tell you their names the day we find out who has *Annie Laurie*."

P.S. My sister and I agree. Mother would have voted against it.

Mighty Good Memories

June 2020, *SE Gazette*

Want to get a conversation going with people my age from central North Carolina? Just mention Hurricane Hazel to a group sitting around, pontificating on whatever comes up. The comments and memories will flow forth like water from Niagara Falls. We "of a certain age" will practically fall all over ourselves to share our comments and memories of "the worst hurricane to ever hit North Carolina" to younger North Carolinians or people from other areas.

"Oh, if you lived around these parts in 1954, you'll never forget the day Hurricane Hazel hit us." (If someone just says that, others will nod in agreement and wait their turns to chime in.) "It came all the way from the ocean to right here in the middle of North Carolina and whopped us up the side of our heads."

"You're kidding?" a younger person might say. "Not just rain?"

"Noooo, not just rain. It whammed us. It was a full-blown, powerful hurricane when it got here."

"They still say it's the worst storm to ever hit North Carolina." (Everyone nods in agreement.)

Others begin.

"Oh, yeah. I was in the sixth grade. Biggest mistake ever made in Graham, North Carolina. They let out the school at the height of when Hazel came through. We didn't have a weather channel back then. When it calmed down during the eye of the storm, the school officials thought it was over. They told everybody to go home. We hadn't ever had a hurricane in Alamance County. We didn't get the word that it would get bad again after that eye went through."

"I remember it like it was yesterday. When they let school out, we all had to walk home, right there during the worst part, in a downpour. The wind was up to 150 miles an hour." (Note: The exact miles per hour have tended to grow through the years.) "Trees were falling everywhere." (As has the number of trees that actually fell, but it only takes one to fall across the street leading to the school to cause havoc. I can affirm falling trees were involved. Just not the number.) "It's a miracle we weren't all crushed or 'blowed' away."

"He's right. We didn't have any cell phones then. Parents couldn't get through the fallen trees to get us and didn't know where we were. People were looking for their kids. Many of us were huddled in Wrike Drugstore downtown, drinking cherry Cokes, far away from the windows.

"Mr. Wrike didn't even charge us," someone always remembers, and everyone nods in agreement. "He sure didn't. Not a single penny."

On and on and on.

Now, years later, Hurricane Hazel is way behind us. Still, those of us "of a certain age" sure do have some good stories and memories about going through "the worst hurricane in North Carolina history." We love to talk about it, shake our heads, and commiserate. Now, here we are in 2020 in the middle of a much bigger, much worse, much longer-lasting horrible mess—a pandemic. After three months, I guess it's time to ask . . .

Have you had your fill of sheltering in place by now? Is family getting on your nerves and then some? Have you grown weary of jigsaw puzzles and being in your children's homemade videos? Wish you had never heard of TikTok? Have charades run their course? Are you surprised to learn that siblings cheat at Monopoly? Spouses too? Maybe it's time to look at these sheltering-in-place situations another way. The whole thing might be a chance for some good memories in the future.

My sister Katherine named one of her daughters after me. This was smart, very smart. After all, I don't have a daughter, and my jewelry—pitiful as it is—has to go somewhere eventually. "Little Jeanne," as the family refers to my niece, and I, referred to as "Big Jeanne" by people in the family out of my earshot, are alike in many ways.

Our many similarities could go for paragraphs, but I'll just point out a few to illustrate my point. We both enjoy a sense of humor and laughing. At one family gathering, someone jokingly asked the younger Jeanne if she really did hope that I would leave her pieces of my already mentioned pitiful jewelry. A girl after my own heart, she glanced at me and grinned. "I've seen the jewelry. I prefer airline miles."

Niece Jeanne grew up in Graham, NC also, and pulled for the local high school Red Devils as I did. She also has a thick Southern accent. Both of us were told over and over that we sounded alike.

"Little Jeanne's" first year out of Auburn University (another similarity), she worked for Alpha Gamma Delta Sorority (yet another one) and traveled around the country as a Chapter Consultant. It was a way to eeeeease into the real working world after four years of college life. She didn't have an apartment, car, or even a closet other than a small one at her mother's house. She just traveled from university to university, eating dining hall food and staying on campuses, sending in reports to national headquarters. The traveling part sounds a little like my life as a professional speaker, except I'm generally in hotels.

Both of us, of course, travel with our thick Southern accents in tow.

In an airport in Michigan during that year, as "Little Jeanne" stepped away from the airline check-in counter, an older gentleman a couple of spots behind her in line got her attention. "Excuse me, miss. I couldn't help but overhear you talking to the agent. Would you be willing to say a couple of words for me?" He was smiling.

Small-town, savvy young women often have the knack of sensing when a situation is harmless, and niece Jeanne knew this one was. "Well, sure, sir. I'd be happy to. What couple of words do you want me to say?"

The stranger her grandfather's age explained, "I'll close my eyes, and you say, 'Hey, sugar. S-U-G-A-R.'" he spelled it correctly.

Jeanne knew exactly where he was headed. What he wanted was an H on the end of the second word. She put her arm around the man's shoulders, lowered her voice, and slowly drawled, "Hey, sug'ah."

The man opened his eyes and sighed. "Ah, that's it. Thank you so much. I was once stationed in the South, and you just brought back some mighty good memories."

Unfortunately, the last several months have been extremely tough and even life-altering for many due to the COVID-19 pandemic. Our thoughts and prayers go out to them. For the rest of us, it's been an unusual, difficult three months as we try to do what we've been told to do to help the overall situation. With all this sheltering in place and spending so much time with our families, I believe it's also a chance to create some mighty good memories for ourselves, our families, and especially our children. We just have to choose to do so.

"Big" Jeanne says, "What an opportunity!"

The Ruby Ring

August, 2021 *SE Gazette*

Well, here's another holiday I didn't know existed, but makes sense. National Sisters Day is the first Sunday in August. Sounds good to me. There were three sisters in our family. Therefore, I know firsthand there is a competitive element to the relationship between sisters. It never goes away.

Background. Everyone seemed to pass away out of order in our family. Parents first. Then their parents—my grandparents. This means that my older sister Katherine, younger sister Andrea, and I oversaw the funerals and closures of several houses and "debated" about every piece of furniture.

The last to pass was our Grandmother, "Grandbubba," who lived in Luverne, Alabama. It also meant three young women were about to divvy up—once again—a house full of furniture and get the pieces we wanted (which was all of them) transported to NC and Atlanta. We also were to handle all funeral arrangements and then gathered in Alabama to do just that. We met with the local funeral home people and felt quite comfortable planning the service.

The day arrived, and visitation was over. Grandbubba's remains were in an open casket at the funeral home, ready to be closed to the public and transported to her church for the service. The funeral home directors asked us three sisters if we would like a little private time with our grandmother before the casket was closed for good. It took us off guard. We had been in the viewing visitation room for about an hour talking to those who came by, but for some reason, "Would you like a few last minutes of privacy with your grandmother?" seemed like something we ought to do. We said yes, and the three people assigned to our funeral said they would be up the hall in the lobby. "Just let us know when you've finished."

They left. We moved straight to her casket. As we stood there patting her hand and saying, "We love you, Grandbubba," my older sister Katherine suddenly gasped and said, "She's got on that ruby ring." We all looked straight at her hands, and sure enough, hands folded together on her stomach, there sat the ruby ring she loved so much. As children, we had asked, "Are they real rubies?" She always shook her head and said, "No, but they are to me." Therefore, they were to us. Not far away from her hands was a small lavender silk handkerchief tucked into her lavender suit breast pocket. Very grandmotherish. Perfect for her era.

We all stared, and I will admit, I spoke next. "Grandbubba would die if we buried her in that ruby ring." At that came the first giggle. There was no discussion. We just stared. Younger sister said, "I'll get it off," and reached into the coffin while my older sister said, "I'll watch from the door. Hurry."

Important. All we had to do was ask the funeral home professionals if they would remove the jewelry and give it to us. This is what they do everywhere. But no. That didn't occur to us.

Within seconds, my older sister was standing guard at the door, peeking around the corner and rolling a hand around above her head like she was lassoing a calf. "Hurry up. They're still in the lobby."

Younger sister, "Uh oh. A problem. Her fingers are bent and won't move. I guess rigor mortis has set in. Unless I can get that finger straight, I can't get the ring off. I've got to get a better angle." She jumped up on the gurney and practically straddled the coffin. I thought I saw the gurney move a little and got at the head of the coffin to support the process.

Suddenly, "Good news! It's up! Her ring finger is sticking straight up. I can get the ring." She twisted the ring off and dropped it in her pocket.

Me, "Tell me you didn't break a bone."

Sister at the door, still circling her hand, "They just looked this way. Get back in place."

Then, we heard the bad news from younger sister, "Oh, no. Her finger won't bend back down. It's sticking straight up in the air. IT WON'T BEND."

Sister at the door, "They're walking this way. Do something!"

And I said, "I know what to do," and I did it.

Seconds later, the funeral home people walked into the room and saw three granddaughters standing at the casket, heads bowed. Our shoulders were going up and down, and they thought we were crying. We were holding back laughter. The finger was still sticking straight up toward the ceiling, but you couldn't tell it. Both hands were covered discreetly by a lovely lavender silk handkerchief, a little higher in its center, like a tepee.

Fast forward. During Covid, I have had a weekly show from my back porch and often have guests. I had forgotten this story until I asked author Jane Jenkins Herlong the name of her book. *"Bury me in my Pearls,"* she replied. That led to me telling thousands of people who tuned in that day what you've just read.

But there's just something about sisters. As we went off air, my phone was ringing. It was my older sister Katherine. You could have heard her across the room or from downtown. She bellowed, "Who has that ruby ring? Andrea has passed, and we didn't find it in her estate. I certainly don't have it, and that means you do, Jeanne. You kept it all these years. Does that seem fair?"

(*SE Gazette* readers, I don't have the ring. I have never had the ring.)

This happened in March, and I've been to at least twenty flea markets since then looking for a similar ring. When I find it, I'll buy it and put it on my finger. Then I'll call my sister Katherine. "Wanna go to lunch?" I'll ask.

Happy Sisters Day!

Section Two

Left Brain

[Editor's suggestion: If you are unfamiliar with Left Brain people vs. Right Brain people, you should start this section by reading "Hanging Pictures with Left Brain" first.]

The Word Nordstrom Perks Me Up

It's a Family Trait

April 2001, *City-County Magazine*

After traveling all week, I arrived at the hotel in Indianapolis around seven pm and immediately checked with Jerry back home. Most of the conversation consisted of me telling him how tired I was and how I really needed a good night's sleep. My speech was early the next morning, and I was heading straight to bed. I was worn out, completely whipped to a frazzle.

When I hung up, I noticed information on the bedside table that the new Circle Mall had opened in Indianapolis. It was accessible to my hotel through a walkway, and it had a Nordstrom. The word Nordstrom perks me up. It's a family trait.

When I returned home the next night, Jerry immediately asked how the speeches had gone, and I told him. Had I been able to get a good night's sleep Friday, he wanted to know. He had been concerned that I was so tired.

"Oh yes," I assured him, not mentioning the trip to Nordstrom. "I felt much better by morning. I just needed to crash."

"But you were able to get to bed early?" he questioned again.

"Yes," I lied, for no reason other than it seemed like the thing to do.

Jerry got that little smiley smirk on his face that husbands can get and handed me a piece of paper. "Well, here. You'd better call this number and talk to the people at Visa. Someone charged $332.47 to your card at Nordstrom around 9:00 last night in Indianapolis. Wonder who it was?"

At 11:00 pm the night before, Jerry had been awakened by a call from someone at Visa headquarters. Their computers had kicked out a red flag on my card because charges were being placed on the same card from three locations at approximately the same time. First, someone at Global Travel in Burlington had charged tickets on my card late that afternoon. Jerry explained that could certainly be possible. His wife's airline tickets were always charged to her Visa card.

Someone else had been charging on that same card number at the same time in Florida, the Visa representative told him. That could be possible too, Jerry explained. His wife's secretary was on vacation in Florida but was keeping up with business via long distance. She easily could have ordered something for the office late that afternoon and put it on that card.

Then, the woman wanted to know if someone could have charged $332.47 to that same card that evening at Nordstrom in Indianapolis. "That's when I became concerned," Jerry told me with a fake puzzled look. "I told her that my wife was in Indianapolis, but it couldn't have been her. I had talked to her earlier, and she was going straight to bed. She was absolutely worn out."

I said, "You were correct, but I took a drink of Nordstrom and felt much better."

Get Your Hearing Checked!

October 2006, *Alamance Magazine*

I'm here with important healthcare advice. When each of us has our annual physical, make sure to include a hearing test. It's just a suggestion, but an important one.

My husband Jerry says that I have started to mumble. That's flat-out scary for a professional speaker. You want to know the truth? Just between you and me? He doesn't hear as well as he used to.

I can't help but notice it. For example, something broke in the kitchen not long ago, and I walked within five feet of Jerry and said, "I need you, honey." He stood up and pulled out his billfold. "I've got some tens and a couple of twenties."

See what I mean? Therefore, not long ago, I suggested in a nice, loving tone, "Jerry, you need to get your hearing checked." There aren't many women from my era who don't know what he said, "I can hear as well as any man my age."

He's sixty-eight. Big deal.

Not long after that, we went down to Cumming, Georgia, for the christening of one of our wonderful grandchildren. Son Beaver (that's his name), our daughter-in-law, and the children went ahead of us to the church. Jerry and I went together in our car because we had to get back early and start lunch. We had not been to their church before that day. We entered the sanctuary together and sat together. We talked to the same people. When the time came, we went down front together and promised to do whatever we were supposed to do. In other words, Jerry and I had the same experience in church that morning. When it was over, we hurried to our car and left quickly to beat the crowd back to the house.

We were putting out lunch in the kitchen when Jerry said, "Boy, weren't you surprised at the number of men in their church who play golf?"

It was as though I had entered the *Twilight Zone*. [7] What in the world was he talking about? There was no way he could know how many men in that church played golf. I didn't see somebody hand him a church bulletin and whisper, "Seventy-three percent of the men in the congregation play golf."

"What are you talking about, Jerry? You've got no way of knowing how many . . ."

"Ah ha," he interrupted. "You nodded off. The minister asked all the men who are golfers to stand, and we did."

It's at times like these that I can't speak again until I can figure out what in the dickens he's talking about. It took a few minutes, but finally, it hit me.

"Honey, it's Father's Day. The minister didn't say, 'Will all the golfers stand.' He said, 'Will all the fathers stand.' And I wanted to ask you about that anyway. You stood up, sat back down, and then stood up again. What was that all about?"

Jerry started laughing. "I thought he said 'golfers,' so I stood up. And then I started thinking, 'I'm not really that good of a golfer. Here I am in the church—in front of God—implying that I'm a good golfer.'

7 *The Twilight Zone* is an American television series created by Rod Serling in which characters find themselves dealing with often disturbing or unusual events, an experience described as entering "the Twilight Zone." Wikipedia.org.

So, I sat back down. Then I looked over and saw Beaver was standing and thought, 'I'm a better golfer than he is,' and I stood back up."

I repeat: Get your hearing checked.

Men . . . You've Got to Love Them!

January 2010, *Southeast Lifestyle*

My Husband Jerry and I were watching a football game, and a commercial came on. The man in the little box said as clearly as anyone says anything, "Men think about women every 5.3 seconds," and then he went on to advertise soap.

Men think about women every 5.3 seconds? Well! I looked over at Jerry. He was just staring at the set, so I asked, "Do you do that?"

Every woman of any age knows what he said when he turned to look at me. "Do what?"

"What the man just said on television. You're looking right at it."

"Well, honey, I'll be real honest with you," he said. "I was looking at the TV, but I wasn't paying attention to it. There's a timeout because it's fourth down and three to go, and the coach has to either go for the first down or kick a field goal and go for an onside kick. Time's running out. I'm just sitting here trying to figure out what the coach ought to do."

"Oh." (One thousand one, one thousand two, 3, 4, 5) "So you're not thinking about women?"

"I *am* thinking about winning. I think he ought to go for it."

Don't Swat a Bat

January 2011, *Southeast Lifestyle*

For months, I suggested to my husband Jerry, a.k.a. "Left Brain," that he get his hearing checked because I was beginning to tire of repeating myself so often. Then finally, the proverbial straw appeared that broke the camel's back. Read on . . .

I had been away on an eight-day speaking trip. I usually don't leave town for that many days in a row, but I had to. This meant Left Brain was in the house for eight days by himself doing whatever it was that Left Brain people do. The night I arrived home, it was late, so I went straight to bed. He was in bed, too, looking at a basketball game on the TV over on the side of the bedroom.

I mumbled something about being too tired even to watch a basketball game. I was going to sleep. Right before I closed my eyes, I looked at the far end of our long room and thought, maybe a little disgustedly, "What has he done?" Something new was right there in the center of the ceiling. It was round and black. My shoulders sagged. What in the world . . .

"Did you put in a new smoke detector while I was gone?"

He never took his eyes off the television, "No."

Hum? "Did you put some sort of a sprinkler system?"

"A sprinkler system? No. I didn't put in anything new. Did you see that rebound?"

"No." My gaze stayed on the ceiling. "It's just odd, Jerry. We've been living here almost thirty years, and I've never noticed that black circle in the center of the ceiling over there. What is it?"

He finally looked up and then quietly clicked off the television. We both stared until he mumbled, "Something's in the house." Seconds later, as we were staring up at the ceiling, it hit us both at the same time. It was a bat! It is not hanging down like in the pictures but spread out in a perfect circle in the center of our bedroom ceiling.

There are people—we all know them—who, at that point, would pull a gun out from under their bed and start firing—bam, bam, bam—killing the bat (maybe) and putting a number of holes in the ceiling.

Others would get the baseball bat or rolling pin they kept under the bed and wham the bat off the ceiling, and knock it down, and beat it, and pound it until it was the size of an ant.

But we are not gun people. We are not pounding people. We are broom people—big difference.

If there's a bird on the porch, "Get the broom."

The washing machine overflowed, "Get the broom and sweep out the water."

There's an intruder in the house, "You trip him with the broom while I hit him with the dustpan." You get the idea.

Therefore, within seconds, Left Brain was back upstairs from the utility room. He had the dustpan in one hand and the broom in the other, and he was ready to do what we do.

I need to stop right here to make sure you know something. In our home, when we go to bed, we are not Victoria's Secret people. Trust me. There is not a thong in our house. In our house, a thong is a flip-flop.

For my last birthday, Left Brain went to Victoria's Secret to buy me a gift. Someone told him they had "pretty things." I wish I could have been there to see it. Apparently, a young saleswoman held up something skimpy and asked, "Would your wife like to sleep in this?" Left Brain said, "She might, if she can keep on her socks."

He did purchase something for me to sleep in from Victoria's Secret. It had strings and ribbons and things to tie, and quite frankly, I couldn't figure out how to get in it. When I finally did, I couldn't get out of it. With all the strings and ribbons, I felt like I was back in my childhood, playing cowboys and Native Americans—all tied up. What was he thinking? If I slept wadded up in a ball in that outfit, I'd cut off my circulation. If we had a fire, I'd have to roll out of the house. I took it back to Victoria's Secret the next day and traded it in for hand lotion.

But I digress. That bat night, Left Brain was standing there with the broom in one hand and the dustpan in the other. He had on white boxer shorts, a white T-shirt, and black socks. I had on white socks and a long flannel gown that I got at the Tall Girl Shop. It's white with little purple flowers all over it. The first night I wore it, Left Brain rolled over in the bed, saw those flowers, and thought he had "passed."

What we were wearing really isn't that important. What is important is that he was ready to attack. First, though, he said, "Get back, Jeanne. I'm going to swat him off the ceiling and hold him down with the broom."

We all have sayings and comments tucked in the recesses of our minds from who knows where. For example, "Don't wear white shoes after Labor Day." I also have tucked in my brain hundreds of comments from my all-time favorite television show, *The Andy Griffith Show*. When Jerry said he was going to swat that bat off the ceiling, something Barney Fife said popped into my brain, and I screamed, "No, don't swat at a bat! It's liable to come down here and get in my hair and lay eggs."

And that's what finally got Jerry to get his hearing checked. Because right then is when he said, "Jeanne, that's the most ridiculous thing I've ever heard you say. It can't get to the eggs if you don't open the refrigerator door."

"I'd like to make an appointment, please . . ."

The Helium Balloon Challenge

February 2012, *Southeast Lifestyle*

My husband, "Left Brain," and I don't exchange Valentine's gifts. Somehow, I got pulled into a thing years ago that involves one balloon each year with "I love you" written on it. That's correct—just one balloon for both of us. It's fun and creative. It's also cheap, which is why Left Brain started the tradition. I like the fun and creative parts, but the "cheap" aspect ticks me off a little when I occasionally remember that it was all his idea.

On February 14th, I'll find a helium balloon with the words "I Love You" written on it and tied somewhere in the house. Without saying a word, I would untie the balloon and put it in another place that Left Brain will probably see soon, such as his closet. When he sees it, he doesn't say anything, just moves it again. You see the pattern.

The helium lasts for weeks, and as long as it lasts, the balloon keeps reappearing. It can disappear for a few days, but if there's helium left, it continues to come back. In keeping with an unspoken rule, a spot can't be used twice, so after a few days, the creative part comes into play. We laugh a lot with this.

One of my "good hides" was in the refrigerator. Left Brain opened the door for mustard, and the balloon popped out. Two days later, it popped out at me in the rented storage unit where I keep my DVDs. I didn't realize we could go "off property."

One of his "best hides" occurred after I had put my rolling suitcase in the car before leaving for the airport. I went inside to tell him good-bye and went straight back to the car. Forty minutes later in the airport parking deck in Greensboro, I opened the trunk, and out floated the balloon. I still don't know how he did it.

One year, Left Brain didn't find the balloon for over a week. I was afraid it would deflate where I had tied it, so in the middle of the night, I nudged him and said I heard a noise downstairs. When he pulled the baseball bat from under the bed, the balloon was tied to it. He didn't say a word; just put the bat in its place under the bed and went back to sleep. The next afternoon, the balloon floated up at me out of the huge rolling trash can out back. On and on it goes every year until the balloon is flat. Well, I take that back.

There was that time when one of us got desperate, hid the balloon in the toilet bowl, and closed the lid. That pretty much ended the game that year. But in general, we play until the helium is gone. That's when Left Brain tries to throw it away, but by then, I've gotten attached to it, and being more romantic, I keep all of the flattened balloons neatly in a box. (Except for _that_ one.)

This all leads around to the fact that I don't expect a Valentine's gift other than what I get every year. It's O.K. Truthfully, I like the annual "I Love You" balloon and the weeks of fun and laughter it pops into our lives. Granted, it's cheap, but at least Left Brain is not like a husband I read about in Atlanta.

According to the article, readers were asked to send the newspaper their ideas for special Valentine's Day gifts. One man wrote that he wasn't giving his wife a gift for Valentine's. "Last year," he explained, "I took her out to eat in a nice restaurant, and all she did was complain, complain, complain. From now on, when I want to go to Hooters, I'll go by myself."

Red-Eye Gravy

November 2012, *Southeast Lifestyle*

I "took after" my grandmother, who didn't cook, rather than the one who did. My husband Jerry, a.k.a. "Left Brain," loves eggs, country ham, grits, biscuits, and that most southern of traditions—red-eye gravy. I like these dishes too, but I prefer to order them in restaurants. I know to ask, "Do you have real country ham or just city ham?" I save my breath if the restaurant is not in the South.

The first year we were married, I asked Left Brain what he wanted for breakfast during Thanksgiving weekend. (It was the last year I gave him a choice.) He chose a big Southern breakfast like the one outlined above and placed special emphasis on the red-eye gravy. He even added something like, "Do you know how to make it?"

"Of course," I assured him and immediately telephoned my "cooking grandmother" in Luverne, Alabama. Babies in Alabama are given directions for cooking red-eye gravy when they leave the hospital. Unfortunately, I wasn't born there. [8]

She shared her directions with me. "Leave the fat on slices of ham and fry them in your black cast iron skillet until the ham is brown on both sides. You do have a black cast iron skillet, don't you?"

---

8 Jeanne was born in Chelsea, MA.

"Yes, ma'am," I answered and jotted down, "Buy a black cast iron skillet."

"Good. When the ham is brown, cut off some of the fat, take the ham out of the skillet, and put it on a warm plate. Leave the browned drippings and fat in the pan. Add several tablespoons of coffee to the drippings in the skillet and maybe a little water. Cook it down until it starts smoking, and pour it into a bowl. In a few minutes, you'll see a difference in color. That's the red eye in red-eye gravy."

It certainly sounded simple, although her words "maybe add a little water" made me nervous. And what was "cook it down"? But it was the word she didn't use that caused the problem. If you read back over her directions, you'll notice she didn't say a word about first brewing the coffee.

I bought a sure 'nuff black cast iron skillet. (We now keep it under the bed to knock out intruders. It's the heaviest thing we can pick up and still swing.) I fried the ham until it was plenty brown and put it on a warm plate. Then, as instructed, I measured out several heaping tablespoons of ground coffee and dumped them amongst the drippings in the skillet. I threw in a little water and started "cooking it down." I still wasn't positive what I was looking for, so I just waited for it to start smoking. When it did, I scraped the gritty concoction out of the black skillet into a bowl. I sure didn't see any red eye. It looked like dirty grease. That said, I was right proud of myself when I plopped it all down in front of Left Brain and watched him heap gravy on his grits, eggs, and biscuits.

I'll say one thing for him. He tried. He truly tried to eat whatever it was that was all over his food. But he didn't rave, so soon I said, "Well?"

He chewed slowly several times and then held up a finger to signal, "Gimme a minute." Next, he took a big swallow of milk, chewed some more, and finally proclaimed, "It's different."

"Different, how?"

"I'm not sure," he mumbled, working his tongue around in his mouth. "But it's the first time I've ever had red-eye gravy stuck between my teeth."

A Penny for Your Thoughts

February 2013, *Southeast Lifestyle*

Being left-brained doesn't mean you can't give a "priceless" Valentine's Day gift.

My husband Jerry, a.k.a. "Left Brain," and I don't head to Hawaii on a routine basis for vacations, but my speeches do occasionally take us there. When we vacation on our nickel, we usually go to our place at the beach. The words "our place at the beach" might bring forth thoughts of a big, rambling house right on the water. One of those places with a long porch and a row of rocking chairs where people sit and watch schools of dolphin swim by.

In reality, "our place at the beach" is a single-wide mobile home in the Apache Campground at North Myrtle Beach. We've had it for more than thirty years, and we love it. Our friends jokingly refer to it as "Dumpity Dump Lane," but we've noticed they never turn down an invitation to go there. I'm just setting the record straight here. We're not mega-wealthy people who vacation all over the world. If we were mega-wealthy, we'd have a double-wide.

With that said, I booked a speech at the Ritz-Carlton at Kapalua on Maui, Hawaii, or as we say in the South, "Hi'wah'ee." Kapalua is north of Ka'anapali, Ka'hului and Lahaina and is way past Lower Hono'piliini

Road. From the little porch off your room—the lanai—you can see Molokai and Lanai, but you can't see Haleakala. (Now I'm just showing off.) Being able to write, much less pronounce, these beautiful Hawaiian words is pretty good for a Southerner. If I'm going to use them in a speech, I practice for days to get the pronunciations right. People take notice when someone with my thick Southern accent can repeat fast and correctly: Maui, Kapalua, Ka'anapali, Ka'hului, Lahai'na, Hono'piliini, Molokai, Lanai, Haleakala, Coconut and Ukulele.

Anyway, Left Brain went with me for my speech at the Maui Ritz-Carlton. The location was truly breathtaking. The first night we were there, I called him to come out on the lanai to see the view. Palm trees were blowing in the wind below us. Light from a full moon reflected on the water and made it possible to see the perfectly groomed golf courses on the sides of nearby mountains. When golf tournaments are being televised on those courses, an announcer whispers into his microphone, "This is one of the most beautiful views in the world." For the benefit of the left-brain people who may be reading this, what I have just described is romantic. I realize this fact may go over your heads, and I don't want you to miss it. Again, a scene such as this is romantic. Very romantic. Got it?

As we stood there, taking it all in, I looped my arm through Left Brain's and eased up close before asking the one question a person with a right brain should never, ever ask a person with a left brain. "A penny for your thoughts?"

What I wanted for my penny was something such as, "Jeanne, of all the women I've ever met, if I could choose over again, I would choose you." Not bad. Newly married young men reading this, especially if you're a little left-brained, you might want to make notes for sure. This is good stuff.

Or how about this for my penny? "You're more beautiful today than the day we married." Whoo. Another good one. "More beautiful today than . . ." Oh, me. Underline that one right now.

Or, a third possibility. "I know how important your career is to you, Jeanne. I've seen you go from speaking on flatbed trucks at county fairs across North Carolina all the way to the Ritz Carlton on Maui. I'm so proud of you." Oh, yes! Compliment what another person does. "Proud of you." Can't beat that.

Out on the lanai, I snuggled up to Left Brain and said in my sexiest voice (which sounds like all my other voices), "A penny for your thoughts." Left Brain looked around, took in all the beautiful scenery, and finally answered, "I was just wondering what they paid to get this piece of property."

Proving once again you get what you pay for.

Though, in all fairness, Jerry is not by any means the only Left Brain out there. I told an Ohio audience what happened at the Ritz a month later. A young, newlywed guy was sitting in the front row. I kidded him and specifically suggested that he take notes. Several weeks after the speech, he emailed me. "Mrs. Robertson, I'm the newly married guy sitting in the front row at the meeting in Cincinnati. (I remembered him.) "I tried what you told me to do and thought you would want to know the results. My wife loved the lines about choosing her all over again and being more beautiful now than the day we married. But she got confused on the part about the flatbed truck and Maui."

I have no idea what Left Brain will give me for Valentine's Day this year. Probably another balloon with "I love you" written on it, which will be great. Nor do I know what you plan to give your special person. But telling someone that they look as good to you now as the day you met or married, that you're proud of what they do every day and that you sure would choose them all over again . . . generally proves to be "priceless."

"Idle Hands are the Devil's Workshop."

August 2013, *Southeast Lifestyle*

By the time you read this, it may be as dry as toast in Piedmont, NC. That wasn't the case when I submitted it to the magazine in mid-July. At that time, the ground was soggy beyond words after weeks of daily rain and wind. If it didn't pour all day, it stayed cloudy until late afternoon, and then the bottom fell out.

One night, in the middle of this rainy stretch, a crack of thunder was so loud that I sat straight up in bed. My husband, "Left Brain," didn't move. So, as any good wife will do, I shoved his shoulder to wake him up. "Did you hear that?" It turned out he had heard it because he mumbled, "Someone's building an ark," and went back to sleep.

During this monsoon season, I became aware that Left Brain had begun to stand at a window for long periods, looking out longingly. I knew the problem. No golf. No tennis. He was in some sort of a rain-induced sports withdrawal.

Sadly for him, it went from bad to worse. The Fourth of July rolled around, and the indoor courts for badminton and pickleball were closed for the entire week. With no golf, tennis, badminton, or pickleball, he seemed to spiral further downward, going from window to window during the day to stare and make sure it was raining on all sides of the house. I had a list of things he could do inside the house, but I couldn't get him to stare at it. (I should've taped my list to the inside of one of the windows.)

By week three of the rain, I realized Left Brain was not only staring out the windows but at times, was also wandering aimlessly from room to room, a racquet in hand, practicing tosses and swings at imaginary birdies and balls. It's sad to see someone deteriorate so quickly.

All of this was of particular concern to me because (1) I truly love the guy, and (2) I had been told repeatedly as a child, "Idle hands are the devil's workshop." With all the rain, Left Brain clearly had some idle hands. What to do, what to do. Fortunately, that's when it hit me. Our trees! Our many trees! Those beautiful North Carolina trees have little sticks that break off and fall to the ground during storms.

The next morning, after standing with him a few minutes at a big window, I remarked casually, "Lot of sticks in the yard. When it stops raining, you might have to go out there and pick 'em Up."

'Nuff said! From then on, when there was a break in the rain, Left Brain announced with great importance, "I'll be outside picking up sticks." He was busy. He was happy. He was a man with a purpose.

He was also a man who didn't know I had quickly accumulated my own private stash of small wet sticks. When he was picking 'em up in the front yard, I was tossing 'em toward the back. No idle hands here.

I posted on my Facebook page what was happening with Left Brain staring out the windows and picking up sticks. One never knows when one's solution may help another person, and I do love to be helpful. My day was made when someone named Melody posted back, "It rained here for so long one time that my now ex-husband also stood at the window for hours, just staring! I finally opened the door and let him back in."

Don't Ask. He'll Tell.

September 2013, *Southeast Lifestyle*

It's September. All our little darlings should be back in school. That means . . . PTA.

When our son Beaver was 16, husband "Left Brain" and I went to the first PTA meeting of the year at his school. It's the one where you go from room to room with the other parents, meet all the teachers, and for us learn how well everyone else's son or daughter is doing in the classroom.

That night, we learned from every teacher that Beaver hadn't turned in a piece of homework since school started. Oh, he was going to school every day. He never missed a day of high school in four years because, as he often said, "School is where 'mah people' are." He was assuring us he was turning in his homework—waving papers in front of us every morning. Telling us he was making good grades. Unlike elementary school, where we checked every night, we had given him an element of trust in tenth grade. That trust was perhaps a little early because, according to every teacher that night, he hadn't yet turned in a page of assignments. We were not happy.

On the way home, I was mumbling phrases my mother used to say. ''I'm going to wring his neck like a chicken. I'm going to skin him alive." Finally, Left Brain said, "Two things here, Jeanne. Number one, you say those comments your mother said in today's world, social services will put you in jail. And Number two, you tell Beaver you're going to wring his neck like a chicken, and he and I will both burst out laughing. You've never touched a live chicken in your life, much less wrung one's neck."

The reason Jerry is called "Left Brain" is because he is. That means he's methodical. Analytical. Organized, etc. A couple of blocks later, he said calmly, "Jeanne, you're really upset. Let me handle this. I'm calm, and I've studied these types of situations. Don't forget, I've been a school principal. The important thing is we don't want to tell Beaver what we found out at school. Beaver needs to tell us—own up—to what he's done or not done. He knows he's not turning in homework. He should have to tell us. Trust me, this is the way to handle it." Then he had to add, "Honey, don't forget. I do have a doctorate in education."

A line from the greatest television show ever produced—*The Andy Griffith Show*—popped into mind. It's when Thelma Lou tells Barney, "Now you're throwing your education at me."

"May I remind you, Left Brain," I replied. "I have a physical education degree. I would prefer to handle this as some coaches on the sidelines and scream at Beaver when we get in the house."

After further discussion, we decided to put all of LB's education to good use. He would handle it calmly. He would get Beaver to tell us that he hadn't turned in any homework. I would sit there.

We got home and told Beaver that we wanted to talk to him in the living room. He immediately responded, "Oh no." One time, I mentioned to Beaver that the furnishings in the house would eventually go to him. He said he didn't want anything from the living room because he had never sat in the living room when he wasn't in trouble.

So, in the living room that night, Mr. Doctorate in Education, Left Brain, knowing it was best to have Beaver tell us that he wasn't turning in homework rather than have us tell him what the teachers had told us, opened the conversation and got straight to the point. "Beav, we saw many of your friends' parents tonight, and of course, we talked to all your teachers. Rather than tell you what we've learned at the school, do you have something to tell us first?" At that, Mr. Doctorate in Education sat back and waited to hear his son's answer as to why he wasn't doing his homework.

Beaver sat there, his mind racing, cutting his eyes back and forth between the two of us. I wanted to say something but did as I had been instructed. I kept my mouth shut and let the one amongst us with all the degrees handle the meeting. After what seemed to be an eternity of silence, Beaver finally cleared his throat and spoke. "Well . . . Britt bought the beer."

The beer?! We were stunned. I kept waiting for LB to say something, but no. Nothing. Total silence. Not a word. Finally, I leaned over and whispered through a fake smile, "Thank you, Mr. Doctorate in Education. Now, we have two situations to handle. I'm going to the kitchen. As they say in baseball, 'You're up.'"

In hindsight, and perhaps with a bit of advice for parents this year, it's obvious that Left Brain should have gone into law, not education. Or, for Pete's sake, at least he should have watched a few crime shows or trials on television. That's where normal, right-brain people with physical education degrees learn that in situations like this one, you don't ask a question if you don't already know the answer.

Y'all have a good time at that first parents-teacher meeting.

Fond Memories of Moving Days

October 2013, *Southeast Lifestyle*

Last month, I stood in the doorway of a university dorm room and watched with amusement the process taking place in front of me. It was "move-in day" for freshmen, and our grandson was one of them. He was attending Elon University. Due to our proximity to the university, this "let" Left Brain and me be involved in the move-in process. In truth, we were thrilled to be included and eager to help . . . at the beginning of the day. By the end, we were dragging.

The university had this big day organized to a "T." The government should run half as well. But a school can do only so much. We were watching two 18-year-old guys, one from Georgia and one from West Virginia, move into a dorm room with all their "stuff," from size 15 tennis shoes to X-Box 360s. While talking to the parents and older students there to help that day, I was reminded that young women rooming together color coordinate everything from bedspreads to curtains. They also arrive with everything ironed and on hangers. Guys don't color coordinate. They pack in sacks. But according to all parents and grandparents helping in our area of the campus that day, everyone left something they needed at home. "Sheets?" we heard a mom say.

"You forgot to pack the sheets?" The most often overheard comment was, "Didn't you get that box in the carport?"

When you're a grandparent, the best thing to do in situations such as this is to pitch in, do what you're asked to do, and keep your mouth closed. Of course, while I do that, I can't help but keep an eye open for humor.

Many of you have "been there and done that" and could most likely top anything I experienced. That said, I don't have to think long to smile at the funniest thing this grandmother remembers from that hot Friday. It was husband Left Brain, holding up the end of a single bed that had clothes and boxes stacked on top of the mattress while two tall, athletic young men on their hands and knees tried to move a carpet into place under that same bed . . . while they were kneeling on top of the carpet. You would have been proud of me. It was difficult, but I refrained from laughing, even when my own grandson, on top of the carpet, said, "Something's keeping it from sliding."

Meanwhile, their mothers were shaking their heads because they thought the carpet was being put down in the wrong direction anyway. Interestingly, no one was questioning out loud why the carpet was brought from the van last. At that point, I eased out of the already crowded room and went to sit under a big oak tree. My thoughts turned to another moving day.

My family often recalls when our Aunt Carolyn hired a moving company to take items to their house after my uncle closed the family drugstore in Auburn, Alabama. The largest pieces to be moved were a soda fountain and the wooden cabinets behind it, both of which had been in place since the drugstore opened. Carolyn intended to put them down the wall of a long room they had added to the back of their house. The massive pieces were gorgeous antiques, but they had to weigh a mega-ton. Moving these two pieces of history was going to be a monumental task, but there was no doubt about it. The soda fountain and cabinets were going home with Aunt Carolyn.

When the driver arrived from the moving company, he glanced at all the boxes and items stacked around the store and immediately nodded toward the massive fountain and cabinets. "Do they go?" Carolyn told him they did. Without missing a beat, he said, "We'll get them Monday."

"Do you have a special piece of equipment for extra-large furniture coming Monday?" Aunt Carolyn asked.

"No, ma'am," the driver drawled. "Monday, I'll be on vacation in Tennessee."

At the end of move-in day, Left Brain and I were heading home after dropping off supplies from our third trip to nearby stores. We really did appreciate being included in the process, but if you're of grandparent age, you will identify with our conversation going home.

After driving along in silence for a few minutes, Left Brain exhaled and said, "Well, that's the last time we'll have to do that. One of the fathers told me that after the freshman year, it's easy."

"But don't forget, honey," I replied, "Grandson #2 is in the eighth grade. If he comes to college near here in five years, we'll have one more collegiate move-in day to go."

Left Brain took his eyes off the road for a few seconds to glance at me with a grin. "Yes, but on that day, I'll be on vacation in Tennessee."

A Split Decision

May 2014, *Southeast Lifestyle*

It's Spring—prom time for high school students. Young women are buying dresses in the current style they've been dreaming about for many months. Moms, Dads, and other adults will be taking photos and wiping tears from their eyes. And young men will be figuring out how to "get into" their rented tuxedo. I hope they have more success with theirs than my husband Jerry, a.k.a. "Left Brain," had with one of his.

"Does your husband 'Left Brain' go with you to all your speeches?" It's a question I'm often asked. No, he does not. Not to all of them. Actually, he has never gone to all of my speeches, but he did go with me more often in the beginning. After so many years, he travels with me once or twice a month, although he's quick to add that he's glad to go anytime I need help at a show or driving to a speech. He is also the first to admit he likes to go places when we can stay a few days and there is a golf course. But the real reason he doesn't go with me all the time? I don't always ask him. Read on, and you will understand why . . .

I was to speak at a banquet in a huge ballroom on the campus of one of our major universities in North Carolina. I won't tell you which one, but it's in Raleigh. It was a formal occasion, but other than that, the agenda for the evening was fairly routine. First, there was a banquet, then I was to speak, and then there was a dance. Between my speech and the dance, little pickup desserts and coffee were served in the lobby to those who were interested. Some people just mingled around the ballroom during that time.

After I had spoken, I was doing my part, standing around with everyone else while the tables were cleared and the orchestra moved into place for the dance. I was smiling. Once you've been in the Miss "Amorica" Pageant (as we say in the South), you never forget how to smile. Some call it a "pageant smile." I also call it my "marriage & mother smile." Many of you know what I am referring to. Women, in particular, know how those of our gender can stand around at an event such as a formal banquet with broad smiles on our faces, and everyone there will think we are as happy as we can be. At the same time, though, we can talk to our husbands through our teeth and never break those smiles, and they will know we are not happy at all. It works with kids and teenagers, too.

I was standing with my big smile across my face, chitchatting with people who had just heard me speak, when six-foot-six Left Brain came up and whispered, "Get your things. We're leaving." Women reading this will be so proud of me. My smile never flinched as I whispered back through gritted teeth, "What do you mean, 'We're leaving?' We're not going anywhere. I told these people we would stay for the dance."

"I know that, but we can't, Jeanne," LB whispered. "We've got to go right now! Get your things."

Still smiling, I whispered back, looking straight into his eyes, "I don't believe you heard me. We have to stay for the dance. I promised my client."

Now Left Brain whispered back through his gritted teeth. "I understand that, but we have to leave. I've ripped my tuxedo pants right down the back of the seat."

I leaned back and glanced at the situation. Left Brain had a problem. Not only had he ripped his pants at the seam, but he must have been seated when it happened because the pants were wide open. But I had a problem too. I had told my client that we would stay for their dance.

I had on a gorgeous orange evening gown made out of three bolts of North Carolina textiles. Someone mentioned that I looked like the Great Pumpkin, but I thought it was pretty. In my little evening bag, I had a spool of matching orange thread and a needle. I wish you could have seen Left Brain's expression when I took the orange thread out of the bag and explained my solution. All we had to do was go somewhere where he could take off his tuxedo pants for me to sew them up with the orange thread. It took a quick, mumbled, frantic discussion, but I finally got him to realize this was what we had to do.

There was no way I could sneak my body unnoticed into the men's restroom. Not at 6'2" tall and dressed as a huge pumpkin. Then I thought about the ladies' room and the many stalls it would have. My thought was, "If I can get him in there and get him into one of those little stalls, we're home free."

Question. How many women do you think were lined up to get into the ladies' room between the banquet and the dance? That's correct—a lot of them. I couldn't take Left Brain in there.

However, I had spoken on that campus in that ballroom many times, and I knew that down the hall and around a corner was another ladies' room that most people didn't know about because they didn't walk by it.

Left Brain backed down the hall with me, his hands behind his back, trying to hold the gap in his pants together. We got to the ladies' room, and sure enough, it was empty. He hurriedly untied his black tuxedo shoes and took them off, followed by his tuxedo pants, which he handed to me. Then, being "Left Brained," he proceeded to put his shoes back on. (I can't explain it. I just report it.) You can probably get the picture: Left Brain, standing in the ladies' room, nervously looking around and wearing a white dress shirt, black tuxedo jacket, little black bow tie, black cummerbund, black socks, white boxers and of course, his black tuxedo shoes, back on his feet and tied perfectly.

At that point, he proceeded to make me nervous by hopping from one foot to the other as he pointed to the tiny hole in the needle. "Right there. Put the thread through there." He also felt inclined to say repeatedly, "Hurry up. Hurry up."

I'm a Physical Education major and a former coach. I don't sew. Even at this age, I might be able to get a basketball through a hoop, and I do well to thread a needle in good light, in a room by myself, but Left Brain's actions weren't making the situation easier.

That's when we heard female voices coming down the hall. It was evident they were coming into the restroom. We were at a dead end.

Left Brain started frantically racing around the room, bumping into towel dispensers and bouncing off sinks. I'd never seen him move that fast, but he wasn't getting anywhere. Frantic, I said, "Get in the stall!" He jumped in the stall. I looked down, and all I saw were two men's shiny black tuxedo shoes. I whispered to the door, "Put your feet up or get out of the stall!" He put his feet up, and his knees went up over the top of the stall door.

I said, "Get out of the stall! They're outside the door. I can hear them talking." He came charging out of the stall, and I ordered in hushed tones, "Get in the closet!"

He jumped into the closet and slammed the door. At the same time, I quickly wadded up his pants and put them behind my back as two women came through the door.

The women had been in the little room for about five seconds when we heard a banging on the closet door and a male voice frantically whispering, "*Open* the door. *OPEN* the door."

I wish you could have seen the ladies when they heard a man's voice. They looked at me quizzically. I shrugged to indicate that I hadn't heard a thing.

Then the pounding and the voice got louder. "*OPEN THE DOOR.*" Left Brain had never been afraid in the dark. What was his problem?

At that precise point, I heard in the loudest voice I have ever heard Left Brain use, *"JEANNE! PLEASE OPEN THE DOOR! I'm OUT IN THE BALLROOM!"*

Perhaps this story explains why Left Brain doesn't go to all my speeches now.

Enjoy your prom, young people. Guys, check those tuxedos carefully before you go.

Clueless in North Carolina

September 2014, *Southeast Lifestyle*

Left Brain—I love this man. He's my best friend. I wouldn't write about him if it hurt his feelings, but let's get everyone up to speed.

From time to time, I need to answer the question, "Why do you call your husband 'Left Brain?'" The answer could come in a long dissertation, but the short version is—"Left Brain" sounds classier than "Clueless." Occasionally, however, "clueless" is the best term for him. It certainly was one day last November.

Left Brain and I are currently in what we call "The Maintenance Stage of Life." I still travel more than twenty days a month, giving speeches. This means that when I'm home, I spend my time seeing doctors. I have so many doctor appointments that at Christmas, I feel as though I need to drop by each of their offices with a gift. (Maybe a 7-Up pound cake? [9]) Understand, I'm not sick. It's just . . . maintenance.

For example, this past year, I spent hours at the dentist's office having a couple of implants put in my left teeth. (That's the teeth on my left side, not the teeth that are "left.") With my schedule and the

---

9 The 7-up pound cake comment is in reference to Jeanne's story "Don't Send a Man to the Grocery Store" on YouTube.

stages of the procedure, it took months. Finally, the last appointment was scheduled late on a Monday morning during football season.

Left Brain and I love our alma maters. I went to Auburn, and he went to "Dook." That doesn't make him a "Dookie." He's a big fan, but if you ever see him shirtless with blue paint on his face, jumping up and down anywhere, "Call the EMTs!" The mere thought of Left Brain springing up and down in the air makes me burst out laughing. Did I mention he's 77?

But while we love our college alma maters, we are also both avid fans and supporters of Elon University. Elon has a football team, and during the season, there is a luncheon on the Monday after each game. The coach comes and brings a couple of players, and they talk about the game we just had and the one that is corning up. Left Brain loves going to these Elon luncheons. I do, too, and go if I'm in town. So, I was a little disappointed when that last dental procedure for the long ordeal had to be on a Monday after a game.

That morning, Left Brain said, "I'll be glad to go with you, Jeanne, and drive you home." He was a bit sincere, but I could see his fingers crossed. I assured him I could drive myself home. "Well, if you're sure," Left Brain said, then continued, "I think I'll go to the football luncheon. But I mean it, honey. I won't go if you need me." Gotta love this guy—Left-brained, clueless, and transparent.

Fortunately for me, my "bestest friend" Norma Rose, her husband Alan, and Left Brain were at the same table at the luncheon. If Norma Rose hadn't been there, I may never have known what transpired that day. You can count on your "bestest" friend". . . most of the time. There was a total of five men and three women at that table. The three women were all friends of mine. One was my "bestest" friend, but I also considered the other two to be good friends.

According to my "bestest," someone at the table said to Left Brain, "I saw Jeanne at the game Saturday. Tell her I said she's looking good." It was just casual table conversation until Left Brain said slowly, "Well, she works at it." A hush fell over the table while they continued to eat. The next person to speak was one of the women, who waited a few seconds, leaned across the table, and asked, "What does Jeanne do to work at it?" (Hearing this later let me know that one of the women might not be as good of a friend as I had thought.) It was also a reminder that if my "bestest" friend had moved a little quicker, or at all, she should have turned her plate over in her lap and ended that conversation.

Everyone kept eating, but they cut their eyes over at Left Brain, waiting for him to answer the woman's question, "What does Jeanne do to work at it?"

And being left-brained . . . and clueless . . . he did.

"She walks a lot, trying to keep her weight down," he told the attentive little group. "People don't notice it because she's tall, but she can balloon up. Pass the salad dressing, please."

No one said a word, but apparently, he didn't need encouragement to continue. That's the left brain in him; he had to give a complete answer. "She read somewhere that if she swings her arms while she's walking, it helps. That's how she dislocated her shoulder last spring."

Norma Rose said people nodded and continued to eat without talking. The only sounds were from forks clinking on the plates, sweet tea being poured, etc. They weren't willing to get into that conversation, but they were willing to listen. Left Brain kept right on explaining.

"She tried taking yogurt classes, but she kept getting pretzeled up and couldn't get loose on her own. It wasn't pretty. Pass the rolls, please."

Later, I said to Norma Rose, "Left Brain has a doctorate. Tell me he didn't say 'yogurt' classes."

"That's what he said, Jeanne. 'Yogurt' classes. But don't worry about it. The women knew what he meant, and the men didn't know the difference."

Because no one else was talking, Left Brain must have felt the need to continue. (Who was this man?) "Before she goes to sleep, she puts lotion all over herself, from her toes to her ears. One night, she's going to slide right out of the bed." They all chuckled, according to Norma Rose. She said that she thought the topic was finally closed. But nooooooo.

Seconds later, Left Brain added in his delightful, naive way, "And today, while we're here, she's getting two implants put in."

Clueless.

Ho. Ho. Ho. Mer' Ree' Christmas

December 2014, *Southeast Lifestyle*

Husband, "Left Brain," and l aren't much for playing practical jokes, but occasionally, one is in order. Such was the case after he told several friends at an Elon football luncheon that I had two implants put in but innocently forgot to mention they were dental implants, and the news got around town. (I related that incident in an earlier article.) I didn't know exactly what I was going to do after that occurred, but I knew I needed a mild, fun form of retaliation when he least expected it. I got my idea in an airport gift shop.

We've all seen motion-activated gadgets in gift shops. For years, the most popular of these items—especially in airports—were small stuffed toy dogs attached to ribbons, waiting on the floor for someone to "activate" them by walking by. Because people walked by all the time, the little pups were constantly rolling on the floor and laughing. The ribbon kept them from rolling away. The dog's laugh sounded the same as a human laugh. It could be startling.

Then there were the Halloween toys. Motion-activated goblins, witches, and other "creatsters" (as Ernest T. Bass would call 'em on *The Andy Griffith Show*) were all over stores during Halloween. I don't know how people work in these shops with witches screeching and crackling every time someone comes through the door. It would drive me bonkers, but that's where I got my idea for having fun with Left Brain about the "implants" comments.

My idea came when I saw a motion-activated Santa Claus in one of these shops not long after my dental work. I walked by, which caused Santa to say, "HO. HO. HO. Mer' Ree' Christmas." The voice didn't sound quite right. The person who did the voiceover for this Santa didn't understand that this time of year is a happy time. Whoever recorded the voice for this Mr. Claus was still in scary Halloween mode. When I waved my hand toward the little rotund Santa, a deep, scary-sounding male voice said again, deliberately, "HO. HO. HO. Mer' Ree' Christmas."

I was looking straight at this toy and had caused it to activate, but it still made me jump. This Santa sounded like Lurch on the old TV show *The Addams Family.* Remember Lurch? The huge butler who made us think of Boris Karloff as Frankenstein's monster? Lurch always appeared too fast when summoned and drooled, "You . . . Rang?" Just the tone of his deep, spooky voice sent shivers down our backs and made us howl with laughter every time he appeared, and we heard, "You . . . Rang?" The person who recorded "HO. HO. HO. Mer' Ree' Christmas" could have been Lurch's cousin.

Santa went home with me. We had work to do. I put my new Santa on the counter in a small bathroom down the hall from our bedroom. I made sure to position him right next to the light switch on the wall, and I didn't tell Left Brain about it. That night, we got ready for bed, and I was already chuckling to myself because I knew it would be just a matter of time until Left Brain went to that little room during the night.

We do that at our age. We get up in the middle of the night, wander around the house to do whatever, and then get back in bed—especially Left Brain. I wake up when his feet hit the floor. Sometimes, he goes to the refrigerator or the bathroom or to his "secret" chocolate stash. Other times, he checks to make sure we turned something off. A couple of times, he's gotten up in the middle of the night to move a car into the carport because a storm was coming. He knew that because too many acorns were hitting the roof. Thus, it's Grand Central Station at our house every night, all night.

One summer, we had reservations on the first-morning flight out of the "Greensboro, High Point, Winston-Salem, Regional, Triad, Piedmont, International Airport." (What local people my age still call "thuh new airport.") I told Left Brain we needed to set our alarm for 3 am. He thought a few seconds and announced, "I can't do that anymore. I could when I was younger, but now, I can't get up at 3 am."

"Of course you can, honey. Go to bed. Go to sleep. The third time you get up in the middle of the night, stay up."

I digress. Back to the motion-activated Santa Claus.

It's a matter of time, I told myself as we went to bed that night and cut out the lights. I was right. Around midnight, I sensed Left Brain's feet hit the floor. Eureka! I knew where he might be headed. The bathroom down the hall. FYI, we have a bathroom right off our bedroom, mere feet from our bed. But Left Brain is a nice person. A little naive sometimes and left-brained much of the time, but always a nice person. He never wants to turn on that nearby light and wake me up. So, that night, as usual, he headed in the dark to wherever he was going, and I was correct. This time, it was the small bathroom down the hall where Santa awaited his arrival.

I could hear Left Brain fumbling his way out of our dark bedroom as he moved toward the hall—right hand on his dresser, proceed across the room, left arm and hand extended, find the closet door with his left hand, feel along the wall with his right hand until he found the doorknob of the bedroom door. I took it all in, smiling under the cover because I knew what was going to happen.

I've been the mother of a teenage son. I know where every creak is located in the floorboards of our house. So, with every creak of a board, I knew exactly where Left Brain was as he maneuvered down the dark hall. My smile got bigger. Finally, he got to his destination. Once inside, he reached in the direction of the light switch, and his arm passed that motion-activated Santa. And in the middle of the night, in that pitch-dark bathroom, a deep, Lurch-sounding male voice said slowly, "HO. HO. HO. Mer' Ree· Christmas."

I wasn't there, but I knew. Left Brain froze. He stayed that way for several minutes. The light never came on. I was a hall and room away from him, but I could picture it. He was standing in the little bathroom like a statue in the dark—thinking. It was good he didn't have a broom with him, or he would have pounded Santa to smithereens and broken the big mirror swinging at air.

Finally, I heard him slowly start making his way back to the bedroom—still in the dark—where he got in the bed and turned away from me toward the wall. I waited an appropriate amount of time and then said, "What took you so long?"

From under the cover, Left Brain mumbled, "I was trying to hear him breathing so I'd know where he was."

HO. HO. HO and Mer' Ree' Christmas. When your phone rings during the holidays, just for the fun of it, think of Lurch and me and say, "You . . . Rang."

You Don't Know Garth Brooks?

I was to speak at a convention on a Friday morning in Scottsdale, Arizona. In an earlier conversation, my client told me that they were having a private Garth Brooks concert for their 500 attendees on Saturday night following my speech. If I wanted to stay over for the concert and even have my husband fly out for it, they'd love to have us come. I thought he was joking. Five hundred people in a banquet room for a private concert by Garth Brooks? I actually said, "Do you have a Garth Brooks impersonator, or are you going to play his music and put up a cardboard cutout?"

It turned out this group did indeed have Garth Brooks, backed up by his choice of a band, coming and for a good reason. At that point, this group of dentists had donated more than ten million dollars to Garth's charity for children. (They have now given more than 30 million.) The concert was a thank you from the great country music legend to them.

The instant I received the invitation, I knew I was staying over for that concert. I wanted Left Brain to fly from the nearby "Greensboro, High Point, Winston-Salem, Regional, Triad, Piedmont, International Airport" in North Carolina to Arizona and join me. I was bubbling over with the details when I went straight to his office. "Honey, you won't believe it . . . private concert. Garth Brooks . . . Scottsdale, Arizona. I'll already be there . . . My client will even pay for our room. I have *plenty of airline miles*, so flying you out there won't cost us anything. I know you're busy that Friday, but you can come on Saturday morning and fly back Sunday. I have to go somewhere else on Sunday for another speech."

After my excited explanation, Left Brain looked back at me innocently—almost like Gomer Pyle—and said, "Well, I've already been to Arizona."

I almost hyperventilated. "Oh, that's right, honey. I forgot. Five years ago, we did go there. How silly of me to think that ever in your lifetime, you might want to go back to Arizona."

"I like Arizona," he said defensively, nodding his head. "I'd like to go back sometime. But to fly from North Carolina to Arizona and back in two days to hear *just a singer . . .?*"

"JUST A SINGER! Garth Brooks is not 'just a singer.' You might as well call Coach K at Duke a playground instructor."

"What is he if he's not a singer?"

"He's Garth Brooks! He's sold over a 100 million albums, for Pete's sake. He's right in there with Elvis and the Beatles."

"He may be all that, Jeanne, but I don't know a song he sings.

(*Beam me up, Scottie.*) "Yes, you do. Garth Brooks, honey, cowboy hat?"

And I promise you, Left Brain said, "He sings a song called 'Cowboy Hat'?"

"Oh, stop that. You know, Garth Brooks, Left Brain. You just don't know that you know him, but you sing along with him in the car. Like on the word 'low' when he sings, 'I've got friends in low places.' You join in on 'loooow.' You're usually off-key a little, but you join in. A couple of lines later, you come in on 'Oh'o'o asis.' Both of your hands are on the steering wheel, and you turn it to the right and then to the left, swerving the car on the road while you belt it out. 'Oh'o'o asis.' There is no telling how many people you and Garth Brooks have run off the Interstate on that one word. So, you do know some of his songs. It's just that with your left brain, you never think, 'Who's singing that?'"

I think what he mumbled was, "Well, if you like the song, it doesn't matter who's singing it." I let it slide.

Then, Left Brain tried to take up for himself. "You know what, Jeanne? I'm not as left-brained as you go around the country saying I am, and I can prove it. If you have 'plenty of airline miles' and don't need to save them for something important, I would fly from North Carolina to Arizona one day and back home the next if I could go to a concert by Nat King Cole."

I was so taken back by what he said that I almost couldn't speak. Finally, I got myself together. "Left Brain, sit down, honey. I have sad, breaking news. I hate to be the one to tell you this, but Nat King Cole . . . is dead. He's been gone almost fifty years. I don't know whether he went *up* to Heaven or *down* to you-know-where, but either way—*up* or *down*—we don't have enough airline miles to get to a Nat King Cole concert now."

I didn't mention the trip again, but I figured he was thinking about it. He's that kind of guy. Give him time. He'll always do the right thing and likes to make me happy. Then that night in the bed in the dark, right before I dozed off and when I thought he was already asleep, Left Brain mumbled, "You know what we were talking about this morning? About Arizona?"

"Yes!" I thought. "He did think about it! He's going!" That's what I thought. But what I said in the dark was, trying to play it cool, "I hadn't thought about it much."

Left Brain said, "Well, I've thought about it off and on all day. I think he went . . . UP."

Caps, Gowns, and Brown Paper Sacks!

May 2017, *SE Gazette*

It's May! Graduation month across the United States! Let me be among the first to send congratulations to all 2017 graduates at every level, from kindergarten through doctoral programs. All these steps through life can be so happy. Or not.

Our son Beaver's college graduation stands out in my memory as though it were yesterday. This is because it was an unbelievably stressful time for me. To this day, I hyperventilate just thinking about it. Not because we were hosting our entire family for a complicated meal at our house later in the day or because we were all leaving for a wonderful family trip together at the conclusion of the ceremony. Goodness no. Those would have been simple compared to the real situation. Our challenge? As we approached Elon University that morning, we didn't know if Beaver was actually going to graduate. We had sent out invitations to close family members, but that didn't mean a diploma was guaranteed. Far from it. Oh, the stress of it all.

See, if Beaver graduated, he was not graduating summa cum laude, magna cum laude or even cum laude. The last month he was in school, he was in a group called "Please help him, laude." Beaver believed during his entire college career that any quality points over the exact number required to graduate were a waste of his time, energy, and personality. Nothing we could say or do to dissuade him from that opinion worked. Believe me, we tried everything. As the big day approached, we knew he was on a list of " Graduates—to be determined." Stress. Stress! STRESS!

This particularly drove my husband Jerry, a.k.a. "Left Brain," up the wall. LB went to "Dook" University on a basketball scholarship. He played basketball at "Dook" for four years and graduated in the exact same four years right on schedule. After that, he went to a school several miles away from "Dook." Now let's see. What was the name of that university? Um, um, oh, I remember The University of North Carolina at Chapel Hill. There, he earned a master's degree and a doctorate.

Simply put, he over-degreed himself. With this information, one can see how LB especially wasn't thrilled about Beaver's academic achievements or lack thereof. There were many conversations about the situation, but one stands out.

Beaver's fourth year in college, which was also his sophomore year, was the same thing—Left Brain called him aside for a parental/son conversation. "Look, Beaver. You've been in college for almost four years. You haven't made particularly good grades, and you've changed your major three, maybe four, times. You belong to a fraternity and seem to have social memberships in two more, and you're still listed as a sophomore.

Meanwhile, your mother and I have been to three freshman teas. The university thinks we have several students enrolled. Do you have any idea what you want to be?" Left Brain's expression was priceless when Beaver answered immediately and sincerely, "Yes, sir. I know what I want to be. I want to be a junior."

With this information, you can most likely sense that we finally approached Beaver's scheduled graduation from college with great trepidation. He swore to us he had cut it close but was going to graduate. "History" caused me to question his assurances, and I'm not referring to a history class. I am referring to his "history." We can't be the only parents who've been through this.

That fateful graduation day, ten thousand other parents, friends, faculty, and trustees were sitting under the beautiful oak trees on the Elon University campus on a Saturday morning in May, waiting for the orchestra to signal the beginning of the processional of the graduates. And because we weren't sure of the outcome of the day and maybe to get back at Beaver a little, there in the middle of this mass of people, Left Brain and I sat incognito with two big brown paper grocery sacks over our heads. This allowed us to pray in private inside our sacks that Beaver would indeed graduate and not be pulled out of line as he approached the stage. Yes, of course, people were laughing and pointing at us, but who cared? They didn't know who we were, and we weren't about to take off the sacks and be recognized.

As the graduates walked down the center aisle in caps and gowns, we bumbled our way to standing positions when we sensed that those around us had stood. It took groping to find each other, but somehow, we managed to get to our feet. It was then that I realized the little holes I put in my sack had gotten out of sync with my eyes. I couldn't see a thing. After several frantic pats around my sack searching for the holes, I gave up and leaned toward Left Brain. "Honey, can you hear me? My sack's gotten turned. I can't find my eye holes. Is Beaver still in line?" Several seconds passed before Left Brain leaned in my direction and bumped his head into my sack, almost knocking me to the ground and the sacks off both our heads. "I don't know if he's there or not," he finally whispered. "My sack's twisted too."

Suddenly, a man's voice startled both of us when he said, "I'm behind you. Your four eye holes are looking at me."

Congratulations to all the exceptional graduates from the many outstanding institutions. You worked hard. You deserve much praise.

Congrats also to the many students who completed their studies even though they were not at the top of their classes. You made it! We're proud of you. And, kudos to all the students like our son Beaver, who squeaked out of college by the skin of their teeth but will tell you to this day those were six of the best four years of their lives.

The world awaits you all!

Hanging Pictures with Left Brain

June 2017, *SE Gazette*

Betcha, I know something you don't know. May is National Moving Month. That means June has to be National Unpack-Those-Boxes and Hang-Those-Pictures Month. Actually, the month following any move is always an Unpack-Those-Boxes and Hang-Those-Pictures Month. Most of us put off both tasks. They require a lot of time, and I can testify that the hanging pictures part can be really tough if you're doing it with a left-brain person. (It can be funny, too.)

I mention my husband Jerry, a.k.a. "Left Brain," in my stories, so it's only natural that readers ask, "What's the difference In being 'left-brained' and 'right-brained?'" The short explanation revolves around one word: Order. Left-brain people want their lives—and our lives—in order. The difference? Right-brain people hear the word "order" and think, "Food!"

Because there will be so many people unpacking boxes and hanging pictures this month, I'll use the following story to illustrate this LB/RB thing another way.

Let's say Left Brain and I want to do something simple together such as . . . well, such as hanging a picture in the middle of a blank wall in our home. Left Brain feels the need to measure. He's happy measuring. He's got a thirty-foot, locking steel, made in the U.S.A., tape measure, and he loves it.

Left Brain can hold his tape measure case in one hand and pull out the long "inches and feet" ruler part or use his thumb to push it out as far as he wants it to go. It remains stiff unless he pushes it too far. When that happens, it suddenly bends downward, which means he gets to snap his arm up and down and fight it like straightening out old window blinds. Eventually, though, he gets the ruler the length he needs and locks it in place. When the tape measure is locked, it is so stiff that he can slice his arm through the air and cut lamps in two.

Left Brain can also push a button to unlock the tape measure, which means that the "feet and inches" part comes flying back inside the case in his hand. Whoosh! That's when he usually glances at me and nods with that look that says, "Did you see me do that?" I have an iron that has a button to push to make the cord come flying back into place inside it. Mine never comes back more than halfway on its own. I have to shove the rest into the hole and usually wind up wrapping it around the iron. This could be because the iron is so seldom used. But Left Brain's tape measure is used often and always comes snapping back. Whooooosh! He probably oils it when I'm not looking.

Back to hanging pictures. He then begins to measure. That's when I pull up a chair. I know how long this will take. He measures from the ceiling down and then the floor up, taking notes as he goes. Then he measures from the corners of the room inward and from the other pictures hanging in the room. When all this measuring is complete and where all the lines mysteriously intersect, Left Brain takes out a pencil—not a pen!—he may need to erase it. And on the wall, he makes a . . . dot.

Nodding at the dot and then at me, he returns the tape measure and pencil to his toolbox and turns back around to face the wall, but he can't find that dot. His brow wrinkles, and he moves the palm of his hand along the wall, searching for this tiny pencil dot. It would be painful to watch if it weren't so funny. "Come over here, honey," he'll say. "Help me find this dot! It's right here somewhere. It's small. And gray."

"Sort of like a pencil dot?"

"Yes! Exactly like a pencil dot." (May I remind you—this man has a doctorate.)

After a while, he gives up and measures a second time. If that second dot doesn't fall right on top of the first dot, he goes for two out of three.

When the dot location is finally established, he takes a hammer and a small nail out of his toolbox. The reason it's a small nail is that in this story, we're going to hang a small picture. We don't have enough space in this article for me to tell you about hanging a large, heavy picture. No. If I were to tell you about hanging a large, heavy picture, I would have had to go into finding the stud, asking friends to help borrow a truck, etc. While I don't have that much space, let me briefly explain one tiny detail.

There's an app now for finding studs in a wall. There's also a gizmo now that we can place in our homes. It will go around corners and find everything in the house but your teenagers. But I live with and love a true left-brain person. True left-brain people do things the way they learned them—the old-fashioned way. Left Brain will not use an app or a gizmo. He locates studs by hammering a nail into our baseboard every few inches and then pulling it out, repeating the process until he locates a couple of studs. This lets him calculate exactly where to put nails to hang big, heavy pictures. Bam! Nail into the baseboard. (Pull out the nail.) Bam! Nail in. (Pull out.)

"Back up, Jeanne, I'm going to find these things!" Bam! Bam! Bam!

My sister Katherine dropped by once and saw a straight row of holes in the den baseboard. "You've got organized termites."

"No. Left Brain was looking for a stud."

She grinned. "I've got friends who've been looking for one for 25 years."

I digress. In this story, we're hanging a small picture. No studs. After all his measuring, LB puts a nail exactly where it needs to be and hangs the small picture. Anyone with a right brain like mine could glance at it and tell him whether or not it is level. He wouldn't believe you. Left-brain people need verification. He pulls out that tool with a bubble in it and balances it on top of the picture. Now we're sitting there as a family, waiting to see if the bubble moves. ("I'm going to fix a sandwich. You watch the bubble.")

I'm right-brained. Right-brain people don't need to measure. Right-brain people eyeball it. We guesstimate. I back away from the empty wall and glance at the picture we want to hang and the other pictures in the room. I lay my palm out and say, "Gimme a nail and a hammer." Seconds later, I announce, "It goes right there." BAM! (Nail into the wall. Picture hung.) "No, it's a little low. Move it up a tad."

The word "tad" drives a left-brain person up the wall. LB actually says, "You show me in the dictionary exactly how much to measure for a 'tad.'"

Anyone with a right brain like mine was born knowing information like this. A "tad" is a teensy bit more than a smidgen.

When Left Brain pulls out the nail to move it up a tad, thereby leaving a tiny hole made by a tiny nail, he goes outside and comes back with spackling to fix the hole. I get a tube of toothpaste and squirt some in there—same thing. And your house smells better.

I have valuable information for you. First of all, if hanging pictures is a problem, reverse the situation. Hang your pictures first and THEN move in the furniture. Moving a sofa an inch or two is much easier than moving a picture already on the wall.

And secondly. If you have friends who come into your home and when they go into your kitchen, they make a beeline to your picture and lift it up to see if there's a small hole back there . . . get some new friends.

Now. Go unpack those boxes.

Oh, wait—one more thing. I'm sure some are thinking, "Jeanne sure has moving on her brain. I wonder if they're changing locations?" No. But I've got a little time between theater shows in the next few weeks. It might be a good chance to unpack the boxes we moved with us to this house forty-four years ago. After all, it's June.

Left Brain, Is It Funny or Not?

September, 2017, *SE Gazette*

People often ask where I get my humorous stories. It's simple, really. I seldom write stories from scratch. I just keep my eyes and ears open and let "the world" write them for me. The trick is getting what I see or hear into "tellable" form. To do this, I follow a short formula. It's not rocket science.

When something happens, I get to my computer or paper tablet and pen (which is always in my purse) ASAP and jot it down. Then, as soon as possible, I write it out in a longer version. If grammar is important, I figure I can always work on that later. The main thing is to quickly get the story down in rough form before the humor in the idea "evaporates." Or I plain out forget what happened.

Next, I may try it out in conversation with a seatmate on a plane or a friend on the phone. If they laugh, I keep working on it. After all these years, I have friends who interrupt me from time to time and ask, "Are we talking, Jeanne, or are you trying out material on me?" Guilty. Of course, those same friends are great about calling to say, "I heard something you might can use."

Affirmation is the point. When ideas come along, and I'm working on a story, I want someone to affirm that it's funny. I may think it's hilarious, but I do love those affirmations. Toni, my assistant for all these years, is the best person for that. We think alike. She has a great sense of humor, and she'll be honest. I get excited when she says, "Now that's funny, Jeanne. You have to tell that." She has just as often said, "I don't get it" or "It's funny, but you can't tell that on stage." Usually, I already know I can't, but one hopes. In the long run, I try to go by the rule, "When in doubt, leave it out."

Once in a rare while, I've asked my husband "Left Brain" what he thinks of a new idea—maybe when I'm working on stories early in the morning before Toni comes, and I'm eager for that aforementioned affirmation. With that in mind, I now have an announcement to make. Hear me now. For the record. Write it down. The day I again ask Left Brain to read a story will be the day I am run over by a herd of stampeding buffalo coming down my street in Burlington, NC. It ain't gonna happen.

I recently got a new idea I thought was funny. Something that might work in one of my theater shows. I was home, so following my little formula, I got to my computer fast, typed in the rough beginnings of the story—punch line and all—and ran it off, chuckling to myself the entire time. Toni wasn't coming for a couple of hours, and I couldn't wait. So, I went straight upstairs to Left Brain's little home office with papers in hand—a mistake.

"Honey, I've got a story idea here. Do you have time to read it and tell me if you think it's funny?"

It was a silly question. Left Brain always has time for me. Ask anyone who knows him. He's a nice guy. He set his work aside. "Sure," he said.

"It's not long. Two pages," I explained. "Just read it and tell me if you think it's funny. If you do, I'll keep working on it. In the meantime, I'll go make some coffee."

He nodded, already looking down in deep thought at the first page. Halfway downstairs, I heard his office door close. He can do that with his foot from his desk chair. It means, "Do not disturb."

Right there, a thought flitted through my brain. Maybe I should have waited for Toni. Too late.

I cleaned the coffee pot, made twelve new cups, and waited for enough to drip through to fill two mugs. Then, coffee in hands, back upstairs I went. Left Brain's office door was still shut. His television was off. I put my ear to the door. Not a sound. No chuckles, much less guffaws. Maybe he was reading it for the second time. Perhaps he laughed out loud when I was downstairs.

Because I had asked him to stop what he was doing and read my story—in essence, do a favor for me—I stood there for another five minutes, hot coffee mugs on the floor at my feet. Ear still to the door. No sound.

Then, I began to think and shift my weight from foot to foot. He was reading two pages, for Pete's sake. Big Type—Font #14. Double-spaced. Wide margins. All I needed to know was if he thought the idea was funny or not. I glanced at my watch. It had been at least twelve minutes since he shut the door. Surely, he had finished. Maybe he didn't know I was back? Finally, I couldn't stand it. Without knocking, I opened the door, picked up the coffees, and sang out, "Fresh coffee."

Left Brain was bent over the two pages at his desk, pen in hand. All of his earned educational degrees were framed on the wall to his left. A BS degree from Duke. A master's degree and a doctorate from Carolina. Frankly, he over-degreed himself. How long should it take such a smart man to read two pages?

"Hon'ey," I almost pleaded. "Is it funny? What do you think?"

Sure enough. Left Brain glanced in my direction and said, "What do I think about what?" (Sigh.)

"The story, honey. The story, on your desk, under your hands. Is it funny or not?"

I love this man. He's my best friend. I wouldn't write about him if it hurt his feelings. But in the "Patience Department," this was a test.

He turned back to the papers, made a mark with his pen, and explained, "I haven't read it for 'funny' yet. I'm trying to get these commas corrected."

~!^<#^ . . . I have learned.

(PS There are no buffalo herds in Burlington.)

First Date

May 2018, *SE Gazette*

My husband, Left Brain, has developed a little "following" of his own. He doesn't quite understand it because, well, he's left-brained. He honestly is amazed when strangers come up to him and ask, "Are you Left Brain?"

This recognition has come about because I tell many stories about LB in my shows, speeches, and, yes, in my articles. Many of my stories involve living with a person who is not only left-brained but also frugal. I suspect readers know what it means to be frugal. In the South, another term for frugal is "cheap." This all leads to the fact that I'm often asked, "When did you first notice Left Brain is, well, 'left-brained?'" I know exactly the first time I noticed it. It was on our first date. I just didn't know what I was seeing or what to call it. The terms "left brain" and "right brain" weren't used in the sixties, or, if they were, they weren't in my vocabulary. I just noticed he made odd statements from time to time or gave extended explanations that didn't make a lick of sense to me. Without any terminology or definitions, I couldn't quite put my finger on what to call it. Whatever it was, I thought it could be overlooked and eventually repaired. Wrong. As the years went by, I realized it's far more fun to stop trying to "repair" him and enjoy being with him.

Below is what I noticed on that first date. What he noticed on that first date leads to a common term we hear nowadays. Stick with me.

Our first date—a blind date—was to play bridge. On the way, we stopped to eat at Jim's Tastee Freeze in Graham, NC, my hometown. It was 1963. After he picked me up that night, we made what I call "first-date, blind date, chitchat conversation." It can be so painful. I'm surprised there was a second date.

"Why did you go to Auburn?" Left Brain asked, driving toward the Tastee Freeze.

"Because it's an excellent academic school," I said quickly.

He seemed surprised. "Really? I didn't realize that. I've always thought of Auburn as a football school."

"Well, of course, football is important too," I explained. A long block later, I added, "They're in the Southeastern Conference, and they went undefeated and won the national football championship a few years ago." (I'm not sure what that had to do with anything. Chalk it up to first-date nervous chitchat.)

Almost defensively, I added proudly, "But I went to Auburn because it's strong academically."

"I'm sure it is. What's your major? "

"Physical Education."

"Ah."

(Silence) A couple of blocks later, I mumbled, "Plus, my grandparents live in Auburn, and my parents met there. My sister and all my cousins go there. I grew up wanting to go to Auburn." I resisted, adding, "I was hoping there would be some tall boys there," because Jerry was tall. (Hence the reason a mutual friend set up the blind date. I was 6'2, and he was taller.) To keep the conversation going, I asked, "Where did you go to school?"

"Duke."

Having spent the previous years of my life in Alabama at Auburn, I didn't know much about Duke. I had been busy, busy in high school and hadn't paid much attention to colleges in NC. Plus, I already knew where I was going to school. After a somewhat awkward silence, I asked, "Is Duke strong academically?"

The future "Left Brain" paused—perhaps in disbelief—and finally nodded. "Yes. Duke has a reputation as a good school. I was proud to go there. Now I'm in graduate school at Carolina."

Graduate school? Oh, brother. Where was this conversation going? Not knowing much about graduate school, I switched back to his first comment. "Why did you go to Duke?" And I admit, I smiled and added, "You couldn't get into Auburn? "

He smiled and answered in a quiet voice. "Duke offered me a scholarship. I played basketball there for four years and then graduated."

"Oh," I answered and thought, I bet he's been in the newspaper. He's so cute. I should have checked this out a little better. But I hadn't read about him down at Auburn. All I could think of to say was, "I bet it was fun to be on the team."

He didn't mention being Co-Captain at Duke. He didn't mention playing in the ACC. He simply grinned and nodded slowly. "Yes, it was fun."

We rode a couple more blocks in silence while I thought of my next thing to say. "Do you have any brothers or sisters?"

"I have a twin sister."

"Really? Are you identical twins?" (More grinning on his part.) "No. She's a girl, and I'm a boy."

"Oh."

See what I mean? First-date, blind date, chitchat. I probably wasn't at my sharpest. It was good that I knew how to play bridge.

At the Tastee Freeze, I ordered a cheeseburger. Younger people will find it difficult to believe, but the cheeseburger costs 35 cents. Jerry, destined to be dubbed "left-brained" and "frugal" in future years in my stories, ordered a hamburger, which was 25 cents. Making further conversation as our order was being prepared, I said, in a cutesy first-date manner, "You don't like cheese?"

LB said, "Oh, I love cheese. I just don't think a slice of cheese is worth ten more cents." To my amazement, he then went on to explain that ten cents made the cheeseburger some sort of a percentage more expensive. Percentages are not one of my strong suits. I didn't take that class at Auburn. It was all gibberish to me. Absolute gibberish. But I looked into his blue eyes and nodded as though I understood what in the world he was talking about. Actually, I was thinking, "I wonder if he's going to try to kiss me?"

When he finished his extended explanation about percentages, I smiled and said, flirting a little, "Well, maybe if you ask me out again, I'll get a hamburger to save money and bring my own piece of cheese."

To this day, he remembers sitting there thinking that I was frugal, which impressed him. After all, I had just said I'd save money and order a hamburger next time.

Summarizing this information after years of marriage—Left Brain sat in his car at the Tastee Freeze in Graham in 1963 and thought his blind date didn't talk much, but he thought she understood what he was explaining about percentages and she was willing to save money.

In today's world, we call this—"Fake News."

Keep laughing!

And the Rain Goes On

July 2018, *SE Gazette*

There's a lot of news these days for "Royal Watchers." I admit I'm one of them, somewhat. I've always followed the British Royals from afar, and to be honest, I've been especially intrigued lately by those "fascinators" the royal women often wear sticking off the sides of their heads. Not sure they're my style. Eight to ten inches of feathers and/ or flowers sticking off the side or top of my head would scare even me when I passed a mirror and saw myself. Say nothing of the effect it would have on small children and dogs.

That stated, I would have been glad to wear a fascinator if we had received an invitation to the recent wedding of Prince Harry and American Meghan Markle. I actually thought there was a slight chance of that happening. After all, as I've admitted right here, I do keep up a little with the Royal activities. I know that Prince William and Princess Kate's new baby is named Prince Louis. I even once stood outside Buckingham Palace one afternoon during a trip to London, hoping to see "someone."

On that same trip, I saw many of the Crown Jewels on display in The Jewel House at the Tower of London. Everything was gorgeous, especially the crowns and tiaras. But hey, I still have my Miss North

Carolina crown, and it's also pretty. Yes, it is covered in rhinestones, but it holds its own and ought to count for something toward getting into a royal wedding. What else would one have to do to get an invitation?

I told our postwoman to be on the lookout for a special, exquisite envelope, maybe padded, but alas, no wedding invitation arrived.

After much thought, I think I've figured out why husband, Left Brain, and I weren't included on the big list for this huge Royal event. (We would have been happy to stand outside, me in my fascinator.) Apparently, one could be dropped from the "Approved list" due to any number of little picky reasons. I think we were dropped from consideration because I told a specific story about LB in a speech or two. It involved the Royal family, and word travels quickly these days. I certainly didn't mean to hurt anyone's feelings, but between you and me, sometimes the Royals are a tad bit thin-skinned.

The story—
Not long ago, Left Brain told me that I had started to mumble. That's scary for a professional speaker. The truth is (just between you and me) that Left Brain doesn't hear as well as he used to. Therefore, the time came when I suggested in a nice, loving tone that he get his hearing checked. There aren't many women my age of life who don't know what he said in response, "I can hear as well as any man my age." Oh, brother. Big deal. He was in his seventies!

"Honey," I replied, "I wouldn't brag about that if I were you. Not at your age."

"I'm not bragging. I'm stating a fact. I can hear as well as any man my age."

Soon after he ignored my suggestion of getting his hearing checked, we hit a period of weather in Piedmont County, North Carolina, when we had six weeks of almost solid rain. It poured daily. The ground was saturated. Puddles of water were everywhere. Left Brain and I were in the kitchen one morning when I looked out the window to discover that it was pouring yet again. Water was literally gushing through the backyard. I got a cup of coffee and commented, "I don't think the ground can take much more."

From across the kitchen, Left Brain nodded nonchalantly from the kitchen table as he opened the newspaper. "That's why Queen Elizabeth won't abdicate the throne."

Queen Eliza . . .? !?*!#**?/! Won't abdicate . . .

I turned to stare. He was sitting there, oblivious to having made a comment that didn't make sense. I love this man, but sometimes he has to be interpreted. I was looking through the window at the pouring rain and had just said the ground couldn't take much more, and Left Brain had launched into a conversation about Queen Elizabeth.

"Honey, what in the world are you talking about?"

"Queen Elizabeth," he answered as he took a swig of coffee and glanced up from the paper. "It's that boy of hers." ("That boy," meaning Prince Charles.) "She's not going to abdicate the throne." Back to the paper.

I wiped a counter, took another sip or two of coffee, and tried to figure it out. Finally, I walked over to where he was seated and pulled down the paper. "Jerry, honey, listen to me." I pointed to the window. "I am talking about rain. R A I N."

He looked up and said, as he turned the page of the paper, "I'm talking about reign too, Jeanne. She's not going to give it up."

Sometimes, people who need to get their hearing checked do hear a word correctly, and confusion still ensues. And, of course, in this case, I just had to retell this story about what happened in the kitchen, from the stage whenever the British monarchy was in the news. The story is not even that funny. It was just cute and true. Looking back, I realize that the Royals must have heard about it.

It's the little things that keep you off a list.

It's the Thought That Counts?

December 2018, *SE Gazette*

When my husband, Left Brain, and I were dating, I noticed what I considered to be his slightly odd ways of thinking and little "quirks" in his personality, especially when it came to money. He was quite frugal. Not that my family didn't watch spending, but not getting cheese on a hamburger because it costs ten more cents wasn't on our radar. On my birthday in 1963, when we were first engaged, he gave me one piece of stock. Brunswick. Five dollars. I still have it.

He loves to point out that fifty-five years later, it is now worth $6.20.

I glossed over the quirks and honestly thought he could be repaired. (Ah, youth.) So why was I surprised when Left Brain said, after we were married, "Let's just swap $5 gifts at Christmas and give mostly to others?" I liked the part about giving to others and certainly wanted him to think I was a good person, so I agreed. The five-dollar gift part got caught up in the deal.

At first, it was fun. Sort of. We were both creative in our gifts and stuck to the agreement. Then, I began to find things for him that I believed he needed, but that cost more than five dollars. I used Christmas as an excuse to get them. New T-shirts. A coffee cup with his name on it. Golf balls. He often questioned me on Christmas morning.

"You got this for less than five dollars?" My response was always the same. "Found it on sale."

Meanwhile, I was getting junk on Christmas morning. The agreement had been for up to five dollars, and I declare, sometimes, he spent about $1.50. The year he gave me several packs of chewing gum was the proverbial last straw. The fact that it was "Big Red" made it personal because I like that brand, and I guess it showed he put a lot of thought into it.

As the next Christmas rolled around, I brought up the five-dollar agreement and told Left Brain I thought we could afford to spend a little more on each other and still give to others. We both had jobs. He was a principal. I was a teacher, so we were pulling in the big bucks there. (That is an attempt at humor.) I was also being paid to give speeches. I thought we could allot more than five dollars and told him so. He listened carefully to what I said, brow wrinkled, which indicated he was thinking. I'll never forget his reply. "So, you want to go to $7.50?"

"No, I do not want to go to seven-fifty."

We went to ten dollars.

That year, for Christmas, Left Brain gave me three placemats. Three! To have given me four would have thrown him over the ten-dollar limit. I knew the fourth placemat was hidden somewhere in the house, and for the next twelve months, I kept an eye out for it. It was in his filing cabinet, but I never found it. I actually did check the filing cabinet, but it wasn't under "P" for Placemat. It was under "E" for Eat.

The next year, I got the fourth placemat and a pepper shaker.

I let this slide until the following Fall and then mentioned that I wanted to change the Christmas gift deal. He said something that many have heard. "Honey, I would be happy to pay more for your gift if I knew what you really wanted, but I have no idea what that would be."

We were in the kitchen when this discussion took place. I'm not in the kitchen much because I'm not a kitchen person. That day, I was trying my best to "fix" supper. Therefore, I was trying to open a can.

If I'm going to cook, I have to get into a can. I was using one of those can openers that you clamp down with one hand on the top of the can, breaking into the tin. Then you turn something like tiny blades on a helicopter. Turn. Turn. Turn to cut around the top of the can. My wrist was hurting as I did that, and said, "Okay, Left Brain. I'll drop a hint of exactly what I want. Listen up. Pay attention. Our electric can opener is broken. Let me repeat. The electric can opener is broken. I have arthritis in my hands. Using this old butterfly, helicopter-looking thing hurts my wrist. If I had a very nice electric can opener—maybe even one with a lid lift magnet—my wrist wouldn't hurt so much. I might even cook more. Do you understand?"

Everyone reading this story knows I could have gone out and bought an electric can opener myself. How much is one these days? $14.95? Even with the magnet. But at that point, I considered Left Brain in Gift-Giver Training and used what was in my hands as a training tool. I continued to make my point about the old opener as I pointed to it.

"Plus, see that little black spot there? That's rust. We're going to get botulism from using this opener. I keep using it because—are you listening—I say again, The ELECTRIC CAN OPENER is broken." He slowly nodded his head. I smiled. By Jove, I think he got it.

Let's cut to the chase. Women reading this already know what I was blatantly hinting that he could give me for Christmas. Sure. An electric can opener. As I said, he was in training. He's a smart man. My gosh, he has a PhD. By the way, this means little when one has a left brain.

On Christmas morning, I had a beautifully wrapped box from Left Brain, not the usual little sack. I smiled as I opened it. And ta'da! In front of my eyes was a brand-new version of exactly like what I had: the manual can opener with the helicopter/butterfly-looking turn thing.

I looked up at Left Brain in disbelief. You gotta love this guy. He said proudly, "Merry Christmas. No rust. No botulism. Will you be cooking more?"

Tis the Season, y'all. Remember, it's the thought that counts. I guess. Happy Holidays!

Prom Date

May 2021, *SE Gazette*

My husband Jerry graduated from Walter Williams High School in Burlington in 1955. I didn't know him then. I was younger and went to school in nearby Graham. But I know that era. It was a "different time."

Left Brain dated once in a while his senior year but didn't have a steady girlfriend. He was primarily interested in playing basketball and was hoping for a scholarship to play ball in college. His dream came true, and he signed with Duke and played there for four years, even serving as Co-Captain his senior year. It may seem almost impossible in the Atlantic Coast Conference today, but he actually played four years and graduated exactly on time. For that, he didn't have to pay to go to college. He was most grateful, and so were his parents.

In January of '55, as soon as school started back after the New Year's break, the principal of W.H.S. sent word to Jerry to "come by the office." He needed to talk to him about something. Jerry was President of the Senior Class and assumed it had something to do with that. It did, but he never could have predicted the purpose of the conversation.

Principal Calvin C. Linnemann asked Jerry if he had a steady girl-friend. Jerry's answer was, "No, sir. I'm mainly just playing basketball and studying right now," and he related that he was hoping to get a scholarship.

"Well, that's all fine and good, but do you have a date yet for the Junior-Senior Prom in May?"

Left Brain was a little bewildered. It was the first week in January. The Junior-Senior prom? In May? He answered honestly.

"No, sir."

At that time of the year—in the depth of basketball season—Left Brain wasn't thinking about the prom in late Spring. But he thought about it quickly when Mr. Linnemann continued.

"Well, as President of the Senior Class, if you'll go ahead and get your date, it might start things rolling and others will start lining up their dates too." It turned out that he had received several calls from mothers who explained that their daughters needed time to line up their dresses for the big event. In many cases, the dresses had to be made. The earlier their daughters were invited, the better for all concerned.

Apparently, Mr. Linnemann had agreed to do what he could do. Approaching the President of the Senior Class was his big step. It quickly became clear to Left Brain he was supposed to do as requested, especially when Mr. Linnemann closed the meeting with, "Be back in here Friday, Jerry, to tell me whom you asked. If you haven't asked anyone by then, I'll have several names that you can choose from."

See? Another era, a different time. Can you imagine that happening today? Today, students go to prom with a date, by themselves or in groups. But the principal telling a student to get a date in five days? To be back in his office by Friday with that date's name? In today's world, it would be on cable news by sundown. Left Brain left the office a little shaken, but he thought and thought and finally decided whom he would call by Friday to ask. He even said later that he was going to ask her by Wednesday, so if she turned him down, he'd have time to ask someone else.

But there was a big problem. Quoting Deputy Barney Fife, "Aw, big ain't the word for it." In those days, telephone party lines existed. Jerry's family was on a party line. My family was, too, over in Graham, and many of you remember party lines also. Truly, about everyone I knew was on a party line. For those much younger people reading this, families shared a telephone line with strangers. Often several different strangers. I mentioned this story to a friend who said, "We were on with thirteen other people." That seems like a lot to me, but that's what he said. Well, whether sharing with one or thirteen other homes, you could usually eventually figure out who was on your party line if you listened in enough. To do that, when your mother wasn't watching, you picked up the receiver ver'ry care'ful'ly, not breathing into the mouthpiece and . . . oh, never mind. The point is that those "other people" could pick up their phone receivers and listen to your conversations anytime they wanted to. That's when people stopped talking mid-stream and said, "This is a private conversation. Please stop listening in." Click.

Left Brain didn't want anyone listening in if the young woman turned down his prom invitation.

So, he gathered up his dime—yes, a dime—after a basketball practice that particular week and left his house, walking. He knew of a pay phone several blocks away. No party line. No one's listening in. He dialed the number, swallowed, and waited. Someone in the girl's family answered. Oh no, it was a man's voice. Her father! Her father was home! He swallowed again and said, "May I speak to . . ." and he asked for her by name.

"Just a minute," her father said on the other end of the line and put the phone down on a table. Clunk.

Sure enough, several long seconds later, the girl said, "Hello." Left Brain had his words memorized. "Will you go to the prom with me in May?"

There was a slight pause, and then it sunk in. Left Brain told me it sounded as though she squealed and said, "Yes! YES! Thank you for asking me. I would love to go to the prom with you in May."

Then, after another pause, she added, "Who is this?"

Another era. A different time.

An Unusual Request

June 2021, *SE Gazette*

The conversation as it occurred . . .

My first paid speech was in July 1963, and I've been speaking professionally since then. I'm a fortunate person, and I know it. One of the nice things about a career as a professional speaker is getting to travel to so many places, especially in one's own country. From a big convention on Maui to a banquet in Climax, NC, I've enjoyed them all. My husband Jerry and I have tried to take advantage of the many nice opportunities. For years, when possible, we arranged to stay over in places we had never been. Of course, it can get expensive, although my travel expenses are always paid by my client. Left Brain's come out of our pocket. It's always worth it to see even the tiniest places. We love going to a local diner for lunch in a little town and chitchatting with strangers.

One day, my assistant Toni came bustling into our small office. Obviously, she had something to tell me. "I told these people on the phone that Left Brain won't do something, but they made me agree to at least ask. But he's not going to do it. I can tell you that right now, Jeanne, he's not going to do it."

It turned out that the prospective client wanted me to speak, and they wanted Left Brain to come with me. To California. All expenses paid. Yes, there was a catch. They wanted to put a big, overstuffed, comfortable chair on stage while I was speaking and have Left Brain sit there for the entire speech. They wanted to watch his reactions while I told stories about him. This was a first.

I said to Toni, "Let me get this straight. He's just supposed to sit there the whole time I'm speaking while they stare at him?"

"That's what they said. All expenses paid. Airfare, food, a nice hotel on the water."

"You and I both know Left Brain's not going to do that, Toni."

She replied, "I know. I know. But they made me promise I would at least ask you to ask him, and I've done it."

"Are they a group of psychiatrists?"

"No, they just think it would be fun. Will you at least ask him so I can tell them that we did, and he said no?"

I went upstairs to Left Brain's little office and interrupted him while he was in the middle of reading the newspaper to explain that a group was willing to pay all of his expenses to have him accompany me to California for a speech. I explained that he didn't really have to do much when we got there, but they truly wanted him to come, avoiding the actual request. Being frugal as well as left-brained, he perked up at being "willing to pay all expenses."

He gave it some thought and began to recite what stood out in his mind. "I always go to your speech, but I bet they'll want me to go to their reception, and I don't guess that would hurt. I do that all the time. I meet nice people. Can we stay a few days?"

"Yes, apparently so. They probably get convention rates at this hotel."

Left Brain still found this invitation to be too good to be true. "They're willing to pay all those expenses, and all I have to do is sit in the back of the auditorium like I always do while you speak?"

Right there, *right there,* is where our conversation got tricky. "Well, honey, you won't actually be sitting in the *back* of the auditorium."

"Why not? That's where I always sit."

"I know that."

"Well, if they want me to sit down front with the dignitaries, I guess I could do that for a free trip. If we go to the reception, I will have met a lot of them."

"Well, um." Nothing to do at that point, but lay it out there. I confessed, "They don't want you to sit in the audience, honey, up close or way in the back. They want you to sit on stage for the entire one-hour speech in a comfortable chair so they can watch your reactions to me telling stories about you."

Don't ever think being Left Brain means a person is not a quick thinker. No, not at all. Left Brain didn't bat an eye. He folded the newspaper and smiled. "If it's important to you, honey, I'll be glad to sit up there on stage for an all-expense paid vacation to California."

I couldn't believe my ears. "You will?"

Left Brain said, "Sure. Because I know in my heart that I wouldn't be on stage five minutes before several married men in the audience came up there and untied me."

Keep Laughing!

Don't Snap an Elephant To A Tree

Published posthumously

Left Brain and I are still trying to learn to sign to deaf or hard-of-hearing people. It's the most difficult thing I have ever learned or tried to learn. Left Brain said, "Well, if you're gonna learn it, I will too; that way, you'll have somebody to chitchat with." He attacked learning sign language. He made 1,800 flashcards, and he memorized them within two weeks. It took me months, and I still get confused. He memorized them with that left brain of his, but he memorized them while staring right at the palm of his hand; he never mastered the art of turning his hand toward a deaf or hard-of-hearing person. This means that if we attempt to communicate with one of our friends who needs signing, they must walk behind us.

It's always been my belief that a sincere smile is a powerful asset, and I've got a good one. My smile is one of those "pageant smiles" people joke about, although I had it way before I was ever in the Miss America Pageant. It's big, and I flash it often. I can pull it out in the busy Atlanta Airport while trying to walk through a crowd. All I have to do is stop, pose, and flash that pageant smile, and people will miss me. They will go out of their way to bypass me by a mile.

A smile can also be reassuring to others and may even be helpful in getting through a crisis. If the person is in charge of whatever, and something goes wrong, people around her know it and are watching. If she can keep smiling, others will believe she has whatever it is under control. They think, "It's going to be OK. She knows what she's doing." Of course, if they don't know something has gone wrong, and the person in charge can keep smiling, she might be able to get it solved before anyone finds out. That's always fun, too.

I have to practice the reassuring power of the smile in every presentation. If you are in my audience, and I am up there on stage being funny and smiling up a storm, you would think I didn't have any problems—none at all. Seeing me smiling, you wouldn't know it, but I've been covering up something. If I didn't tell you, you would not know that my pantyhose are at my knees.

They don't make pantyhose for 6'2" women. So, before every speech or show, I duck out of sight into some closet or dark corner and pull them up. It's an inch-by-inch process. I start at the toe and work up—all the way up my tall frame. Then, the instant I stand to speak, those pantyhose start working their way down.

One night, I lost track of time and forgot how long I had been on stage. When I took a big step, my hose reacted like a rubber band— whoosh! They snapped my back leg right up next to the front one, which threw me forward and forced me to take a bunch of quick, short steps toward the edge of the stage. The audience was startled, so I produced an extra big smile. And do you know what the audience did? They smiled back, and I continued.

A couple of years ago, my longtime assistant, Toni, came in the office on a mission. "Jeanne," she said. "Sit down. I need to talk to you, and this is serious."

I replied, "Whoa, we're never serious in the office. What are you talking about?"

Toni replied, "Your friends, including Norma Rose and I, have something important to tell you. You need help with your clothes!

Sometimes, when you're speaking, you look like a rumpled sheet. You need some advice in the dressing department. The consensus is we think you ought to hire someone to help you."

Easy for Toni to say. She's five feet nothing and can buy clothes anywhere and just cut them off. There are only a few places where I can buy clothes that fit. When I find them, I have a tendency to buy outfits, stylish or not.

Toni continued. "And another thing. What are you doing in the middle of your speeches when I see you pulling and tugging at your clothes at your waistband?"

"Ohmygosh, Toni. I didn't realize I was doing that. But I guess if my hand lands on my left hip, for example, I think . . . well, as long as I'm here . . . and the audience can't see it over there to my right . . . I might as well give my pantyhose a tug."

"Is that what you're doing when I see you gouging your thumb into the top of your skirt in the middle of your talks?" Toni asked.

"Tall men and women will tell you. They don't make shirttails long enough for us tall people. I guess I'm subconsciously tucking in my blouse."

"Well," replied Toni, "since you seem to have an excuse for everything, I'll be blunt.

"I think you have already been right blunt."

Ignoring me, she continued. "Jeanne, you keep your clothes long after they've gone out of style. I think you're waiting for them to roll around again. I have news for you. They're not coming back, not at this age, not in this lifetime. Now, get some help!"

So, I got some help. I hired a woman from New York City named Jane Tucker to come down to my house in North Carolina, go through my closet, and "Tuckerize" me.

Her first question was, "What are your wardrobe concerns?"

I figured honesty was the best policy. "Well, my friends think I have three. Number 1, I can't keep my pantyhose up. Number 2, I can't keep my blouses tucked in, and Number 3, some of my clothes from high school are getting tight."

Jane told me she could solve number three over the long haul, but she could solve numbers one and two just like "that," and she snapped her fingers.

"Like that?" I was impressed.

Jane continued. "Jeanne, anytime you wear a suit that requires a blouse, don't wear a blouse; wear a bodysuit instead. It will hold your pantyhose up and can't possibly come out at the waist."

"Whoa. A . . . a bodysuit? Is that the thing that the tiny gymnasts wear? It's elastically? Snaps between your legs?"

Jane nodded in the affirmative.

I shook my head. "Unhuh, Jane. You may be from New York City, but I can tell you right now those snaps aren't going to hold—not on a 6'2" woman."

She said with New York authority, "I'll have you know—those snaps will hold an elephant to a tree!"

"Nooooo, Jane. I don't think so."

"Well, if it's too tight," Jane responded, "we can buy a four-inch piece of the same material with those same elephant-strength snaps on either end and add it to the bottom of the bodysuit. That way, you'll have more room."

She was a consultant, and I was paying for advice, right? So, why wouldn't I at least try what she suggested? I ordered a black bodysuit with the extra piece. It came in late one afternoon when Left Brian and I were getting ready to drive to Asheville for me to speak. I tossed the thing in my bag.

The next morning, while Left Brain was still sound asleep in the bed with the covers over his head, I struggled into my pantyhose. Next, I pulled the pantsuit out of the bag. It looked like a large headband. I found the elephant strength snaps at the bottom of the suit, put them on the floor, stood on them, and leaned backward to stretch the bodysuit as far as I could. When I pulled the suit on, the collar came just to the top of my waist. With a great deal of effort, I pulled the thing off, got out the four-inch extension piece, and snapped it in place with those elephant-strength snaps. When I put the body suit back on, it was longer and fit better, probably from having been pulled on twice. But now I had this four-inch extension piece of black material hanging down in the back that had to come up through my legs and snap to the bodysuit in the front.

I inched my feet until they were several feet apart, and then I started trying to thrust my hips forward to swing the four-inch piece through my legs to the front. "If I could . . . just . . . catch . . . it!" I thought, but every time I saw the tail end and reached down to grab it, it would swing back behind me.

I tried to lean backward, grab the material from behind, and push it through my legs so I could grab it with my other hand, but I got nowhere. Leaning sidewise and stumbling around the room, I looked like a sand crab running sideways on the beach.

My last option was to bend forward as far as I could, reach through my legs from the front, and grab hold of that extra material—but at my age, I had no flexibility, so I got nowhere, and I wound up chasing the thing while going in a circle—like a dog trying to catch its tail.

Right then, Left Brain said from under the covers, "You're going to slingshot yourself into the wall."

I said to Jerry, "Get out of bed; get on the floor and help me get in this thing. Fast!" I further instructed, "Now, look between my legs. I don't have time to tell you why; just look between my legs. See that piece of material hanging down there with the snaps? Reach through my legs, pull it up here, and give it to me so I can use those elephant snaps to attach it to the material up here."

Left Brain looked up at me from the floor and said, "These snaps aren't gonna hold."

"I'll have you know," I replied, "These snaps will hold an elephant to a tree!"

Right there, his left brain kicked in on him. He looked up, shook his head back and forth, and said, "Why would you want to do that? We don't know anybody who owns an elephant."

"Just help me get the thing snapped!" I replied. "There. . . That's it. But man, this thing is tight. Move me over to the television," I instructed.

There I stood for several minutes, nearly bent over double. I figured I had two choices in order to stand up straight. (1) I could inch my way up slowly, or (2) I could inhale and stand up in one fell swoop. I elected to inch my way up into a standing position. Then I told Left Brain, "Just turn me toward the door. I'm going down and make my presentation."

He said, "I'm coming down and sitting in the back. I've got to see this."

I remember this speech well because it was at a national convention. They had evaluations, and so many people wrote that the speaker had such good posture. Speaking is what I do for a living, so from my opening words, I was in control of my message, but I was in a personal battle with that bodysuit.

I'd take a few steps on stage to make my point, and out of the blue . . . bam! . . . The thing would grab me and pull me forward. When it happened, the people in the audience reeled backward in their chairs and exchanged funny glances—what's wrong with her? I remember thinking, "Practice what you preach, practice what you preach," and I gave them my biggest pageant smile, and, reassured, they smiled back.

I tried to get a read on the suit. For example, did it grab me every 23 seconds? If so, I could be ready and bow my back. I thought things were under control, but halfway through the speech, my pantyhose, uninvited and on their own, decided to jump into the fray. I suddenly had the pantyhose pulling me under, the bodysuit pulling me over, and everyone in the audience smiling back at me because I was confidently smiling at them.

Then I stepped to the front of the stage to ad-lib with a man in the front row, and when I leaned just the slightest amount in his direction, at that precise moment, my pantyhose and my bodysuit got in sync. Whoosh! I know that aging eventually brings shrinking, but I had just dropped from 6'2" down to 5'2"—right there on that stage.

I was thinking, "OK, now what am I going to do?" I knew I wasn't going to shimmy my way up right there on stage. There really was nothing else to do . . .So, I gave the man on the front row my best pageant smile, inhaled, and stood up!

And those snaps? Those snaps that will hold an elephant to a tree? They broke loose! And the thing came shimmying across my stomach and came up and knocked me in the face.

When people stopped screaming, I looked down, and that four-inch extension was waving to my audience.

All of a sudden, Left Brain stood up in the back of the room, put his hand right in front of his face, and started moving his fingers all around.

What is he . . ??.

His fingers moved faster.

Later, I said, "Honey, what were you doing?"

He said, "I was trying to sign to you—The snaps didn't hold."

Section Three

On Stage

Where's Miss North Carolina?

August 2001, *City-County Magazine*

It's August, which means that a hoard of tiny people in Alamance County will be entering the educational system for the first time. My opinion is that God has a special place in Heaven for those who teach them.

My speech was scheduled for high school students in Port St. Joe, Florida. The school superintendent and I were standing in the "gymatorium" waiting for them to arrive when he said, "We got so excited about having a speaker from out of the county that we decided to bring in all the students, kindergarten through grade twelve." I had a hot flash—or, as we say in the South . . . a little personal summer.

Kindergartners are four and five-year-old people. Quite frankly, they're not really people yet. Well, that is not fair. Of course, they're people. They are just not real people. Not yet.

"What do you want me to talk to kindergarten students about?" I finally managed to ask. "Assertiveness? Leadership? Time management? My hat goes off to those who teach this age group, but the best thing I say to a five-year-old is, 'I'll give you some money if you will go away.'"

The superintendent said, "We knew this would be a challenge. We told the high school students you would talk to them about the steps to developing a sense of humor. But with the little ones, we played up the Miss North Carolina angle. We showed them dozens of pictures of young women holding roses, wearing crowns and long flowing gowns."

I was about to hyperventilate, but as the morning would prove—if shown enough pictures, five-year-olds can be made to understand the words "Miss North Carolina." Unfortunately, there is no picture for the word "former."

They came off the buses looking for her, teachers herding them along like city slickers on a cattle drive. They travel in little clumps at that age. One entire class was holding on to the same long piece of rope, moving along like a giant centipede. At the front of the line, the teacher had complete control over them. If she felt like it, she could pop that rope, and tykes would ripple like a wave, up and down until the end of the line.

One teacher led her tykes around the gymatorium three times. I used to teach, so I knew she was trying to tire them out.

After a while, one of the teachers led the line into the stands, and before she knew what was happening, one of the little five-year-old girls broke loose. Within seconds, she was standing by my knees, where she looked up and said, "Where is Miss North Carolina?"

We all know the importance of truth and honesty at all times, especially when dealing with young, impressionable children. I looked straight down at her little cherubic face and said, "She's sick."

She stared up at me and asked, "Are you her mother?"

The Baton Story—on Sabbatical

September 2002, *City-County Magazine*

I have a story that I've told in speeches since the early '70s, which I call the "Baton Story." It's become a signature story for me in some circles. In other words, the "Baton Story" is what many audiences and speakers think of when they hear my name. "Oh, I've heard her. She tells that funny story about the baton twirler."[10] People call my office and ask, "Is this the speaker who tells that story about the baton twirler?" If new speakers attempt to use the story in their programs, other pros rise to my defense and tell them outright, "Hey, that's Jeanne's story. Don't even try to tell it."

Being associated so strongly with one story is both a blessing and a curse. The blessing part is that it is 15-20 minutes of surefire, guaranteed-to-grab-'em, funny material. The variance in time comes from the fact that there are shorter and longer versions, depending on if I need to stretch time or save it. It can't get much shorter than 15 minutes without leaving out some really good lines.

The curse is that, well, it's 15-20 minutes. This takes up a lot of time in, for example, a 30-minute program. It's almost impossible to

10 If you are not familiar with the "Baton" story, keep reading.

squeeze in the "Baton Story" unless I'm booked to speak for at least 45 minutes. Sometimes, people book me for a 25-minute speech and want "that 'Baton Story.'" It won't work. There has to be introductory and closing material. "Baton" needs a buildup. All of this may be of little interest to people who have no desire to be speakers, but it's important if I'm going to tell you something that happened. And I'm going to.

After telling the "Baton Story" for more than 25 years, I got tired of it. I would start the story, and in the back of my mind—right while I was telling it—I would be thinking, "Sixteen more minutes until I finish this thing." I had developed other material that I thought was stronger, but as long as I told "Baton," I couldn't work in newer stories, especially longer ones. The solution? Put the "Baton Story" on sabbatical. Like a college professor, let it go away for a while and rejuvenate. I had the perfect place to send it out on a high.

My plan proceeded right on schedule. We taped the story as part of the video *Here she is . . .Jeanne Robertson*, in 1998, and I stopped telling "Baton." Went cold turkey! It was tough. Sad, too. It's like not seeing a good friend for a long time. But I knew that when I brought it back, it would be fresh for me and, thus, for my audiences.

It's now 2002. Since the taping in 1998, I can report that I've told this story only once, and that's because the client insisted. Other clients have asked if I was going to tell the "Baton Story," but when I assured them the newer material was just as good, if not better, they always said to do what I felt was best. But not this one client.

This one company had to have the "Baton Story." Never mind that I was hired for a banquet speech where shorter, crisper material would have been better. Never mind that they only wanted 30 minutes. Never mind that I thought I could make the point they requested better with other material. No. They were adamant. I had told the "Baton Story" at one of their meetings several years earlier, and it had made a great impact. They wanted it for this smaller group. They were having problems and thought the "Baton Story" was perfect for their situation. It would set them on a new path. It was why they had brought me in. They must have the "Baton Story"!

My goal is to make my clients happy. I told the story. I had to practice it in the hotel room that afternoon because it had been so long since I had thought about it. But never let it be said that I won't do my part to help a company that is having problems. I'm just proud to be in a profession where I can make a difference. The speech was for a division of Enron. [11]

Note: My husband says I did make a difference with the "Baton Story." I should think about how many companies I helped by not telling it.)

---

11 Enron was an energy company based in Houston, TX. In October 2001, the company filed for bankruptcy, the largest bankruptcy in US history. As a result, its accounting firm, Arthur Andersen, one of the top five audit and accountancy partnerships, was dissolved. https://en.wikipedia.org/wiki/Enron_scandal.

Don't Forget to Wear a Crown

March 2008, *Alamance Magazine*

Before I spoke to the Women's Club in Wheeling, West Virginia, I called my contact and asked if a friend who lived near Wheeling could accompany me. She agreed and was thrilled to learn that the friend I referred to was former Miss America Jackie Mayer Townsend.[12]

Six years later, I scheduled a return engagement with the same organization. When we booked it, my efficient administrative professional, Toni, remembered a woman who had called the office months earlier. The caller wanted to hear me speak and asked Toni to let her know when I would be in her vicinity. She lived near Wheeling and was a friend of a friend in Alamance County, so Toni called the club hostess to ask if I could bring a guest, having totally forgotten that we had made the same unusual request of this group six years earlier.

My client was thrilled! "Oh, yes! The last time Jeanne spoke here, she brought a former Miss America. Who is she going to surprise us with this time?"

Minutes later, Toni called the guest to tell her it was all set up, and naturally, the woman asked what she should wear. Toni thought a few seconds and was honest, "Look the best you can, and if you have one, wear a crown."

---

12 Jacquelyn Mayer was crowned Miss Ohio in 1962 and Miss America in 1963.

In Texas, We Don't Ask Women Their Ages

May, 2010, *Southeast Lifestyle*

Several weeks after I signed a contract to speak at what I thought was to be a women's luncheon in Irving, Texas, on Mother's Day weekend, I found out it had been changed to a Mother/Daughter Tea. My first thought was, Oh, No. Mothers and daughters? A tea? Teas are great, but I instantly started worrying about the ages of the daughters. The truth is, I don't enjoy speaking to young children and visions flashed in my mind of five-year-olds dressed in ribbons and bows walking in holding their mom's hands. Trust me on this. The best thing I can say to a five-year-old is, "I'll give you some money if you'll go away." But the contract was signed, and I was locked in, five-year-old daughters or not. I put on a happy face about it, but for months, it was in the back of my mind. Five-year-olds . . . .

Then, a couple of weeks before the trip, I called the client to go over details and, at some point in the conversation, I asked, "How old are the daughters who'll be there that day?" The pause was so long that I started to say, "Hello? Hello?"

Finally, she answered in her delightful Texas accent, "We'll, I'd guess, thirty to forty years old. But the truth is, in Texas, we don't ask women their ages."

The Cartwheeling Flautist

August 2011, *Southeast Lifestyle*

The heat of August means that Fall—and football can't be far behind. It's a matter of weeks before we hear the sounds of clanking helmets on high school fields across the Triad. [13] Other signs that Fall is on the way? Marching bands practicing and majorettes twirling. It all reminds me of the time . . .

A woman came up to me after a banquet speech to tell me that she particularly enjoyed a story I told about a pageant contestant I had seen twirl a baton for her talent. It truly is a funny story, and people often comment about it, but this woman added something that I had never heard.

Laughing and shaking her head, she said, "I wish my mother had been here to hear that baton story. That would have shown her."

"What?"

"Jeanne, that story would have shown my mother that if she had just let me be a majorette, I might have won a pageant, and I could have been a professional speaker."

I started to say, "Well, it takes a little bit more than just winning a . . ." but she was laughing and went on to explain, so I didn't say anything.

---

13 A reference to the north-central Greensboro–Winston-Salem–High Point region of North Carolina.

Apparently, when she was a child, she spent her afternoons in the yard twirling the baton. In summer, she twirled all day, or at least that's the way she recalled it. She also recalled that she was the "best in the neighborhood," and everybody knew it. "I could toss the baton way up in the air, do a cartwheel, and be standing upright in place in time to catch it."

I found that difficult to believe, but I let it go because I don't know much about twirling the baton, and every time I tried to do a cartwheel, it took forty-five seconds to get my legs all the way over. I spent my childhood afternoons playing basketball.

As the woman's story unfolded, it turned out that twirling in the backyard as a child was fine with her mother. Twirling on the football field "in front of the town" as a teenager was another matter.

When high school rolled around, this woman naturally wanted to try out to be a majorette, but her mother wouldn't let her. My new friend could even imitate her mother. "No daughter of mine is going to prance around in front of the town, flipping up a short skirt and doing cartwheels. You've taken flute lessons. You are a 'flautist.' If you want to be on the football field, it will be in the marching band."

The whole thing had become one of those running mother/daughter battles that most of us know about. Mother won all four years. "And that's why I wish Mother could have heard your baton story," the woman explained. "It would be funny now, but we weren't laughing when I was in high school. For four years, my friends—who couldn't twirl as well as I could—strutted around the football field in cute little majorette outfits, twirling their hearts out. And for the next four years," she continued through gritted teeth, but smiling, "I marched around the football field behind them, in long pants, playing the flute and looking like a toy soldier in a chin strap."

At that point, this woman, who was dressed in a professional business suit and heels, dropped her briefcase to the floor and started marching in place right in front of me in the banquet room, working her wrist back and forth as though she were twirling a baton. I backed up. This was a person who needed space, and I gave it to her. Cartwheel incoming?

Suddenly, she switched her demeanor to portray a determined teenage girl. Still marching in place facing me, she slung her arm to her right, pretending to twirl the imaginary baton in that direction as she announced to me with pride, "But, Jeanne, I never marched off the field in the band without finding my mother in the stands, flipping up the bottom of my uniform coat and twirling . . . that . . . flute right in her direction!"

I burst out laughing, and she picked up her briefcase to leave. But I truly "lost it" seconds later when she wheeled back around and announced proudly, "Homecoming of my senior year? I knew it was my last chance. I stepped away from the band and, just once, tossed my flute up in the air and did a cartwheel. And when I caught that flute and the crowd erupted into cheers, I made eye contact with my mother sitting in the stands. We both smiled, and I got back in line and marched off the field with the band."

Bring on football, marching bands, and cartwheeling "flautists" who know how to twirl!

Have You Heard the One About . . .

August 2014, *Southeast Lifestyle*

Well, looky here. National Tell A Joke Day is celebrated on August 16th each year.

You might think that as a speaker who makes her living being funny, I would know many jokes. Not so. I rarely tell a joke. My specialty is telling true stories from my everyday situations. Exaggerated some time? Yes. I agree with Mark Twain, who said, "Never let the truth get in the way of a good story." But while I primarily tell about life experiences, having a few jokes stored in the back of my mind can pay off.

Although I rarely tell a joke, it might seem strange to you to learn that I collect old joke books. Hundreds of them from the past 150 years are stacked around the house. First of all, I like old books. Secondly, I read these old joke books, and I study them. Sometimes, I mark in them lightly with a pencil. I know this is a sin, but I just can't help myself.

Why do I study them? Because I never know when an old joke will trigger an idea or remind me of something that happened in my own life—something that I hadn't thought could be a possible story. Last but not least, if I study enough, an old joke might even stick around in my mind and pop up when I desperately need it. Like one did that day in Nevada . . .

The client had booked me to be the "Keynote Speaker" during their Opening General Session at a convention in Reno. The session started promptly at 9:30 am. I was to be "on" at 11 am and close out that session before the lunch break.

We immediately started running behind when the president had to pound the gavel eight times rather than once to get the meeting started. From there, it went downhill. Every person introduced felt obligated to "say a few words" whether they were scheduled to or not. Within minutes, people were looking at their watches. When you're the last speaker, you tend to notice things like that. I sat there and did what I do well. I smiled and at least pretended to listen intently as committee chair after committee chair gave reports and as people in the audience began to slip out.

Running behind happens more than you might think at meetings, but since we are invited guests, speakers usually just smile and mentally start cutting their material. It goes with the territory. Unfortunately, this event wasn't just "running behind." It was backing up into the previous month.

By the time I was introduced at 12:15 rather than 11:00, more than three-fourths of the audience had fled. Watching the slow, steady exodus (and wishing I could go with them), I also started sifting through my material, searching for something to say or a story that might fit the situation.

As a humorist, I viewed this as an opportunity. You have to understand I sit at banquets and hope the banner peels off the wall so I can use a piece of material I have for when that happens. One of my favorite things is when PowerPoint stops working. Oh, a humorist loves it when PowerPoint won't work. It's almost as much fun as when slides used to come on the screen upside down. I certainly had time in Reno that morning to sit there and try to pull up something to say when they finally got around to me. That's when studying old joke books suddenly paid off. One of those old jokes popped into my mind and made me look a lot sharper that day than I actually am.

When I was finally introduced in Reno, I stood on stage quietly for a few seconds and then opened with the following, still smiling:

Sitting here this morning, I was reminded of an old story. A man was waiting to be introduced to deliver the keynote address at a convention, but apparently, the script called for the emcee and officers to introduce and thank everyone they knew in the room. To make matters worse, almost everyone who was introduced for any reason strode to the microphone and delivered an impromptu mini-speech. Award recipients thanked the world and told us about their lives. Outgoing officers reminisced and introduced their immediate and extended families. Foundation fundraisers begged for money. That's when most of the people in the audience slipped out—in droves. Finally, only three people were left in the ballroom: the keynote speaker, the emcee, and one other man sitting out among the empty chairs.

After his introduction, the keynote speaker stepped toward the front of the stage and said to the one lone fellow still there, "You don't know how much I appreciate you staying for my remarks."

The guy said, "Could you hurry it up? I'm the next speaker on the program."

It was the first time I received a standing ovation after telling only one piece of material, and that piece of material was a joke.

August 16th is National Tell A Joke Day. Go tell one! And remember, even an old joke is new if it's the first time someone hears it, and it usually works if it fits the occasion.

The Governor's Wife Knows What She's Doing

February 2015, *Southeast Lifestyle*

Well, here we are again. Smack dab in the middle of the collegiate basketball season. Next month are the annual, much anticipated NCAA Basketball Tournaments for men and women, leading up to the "Final Four" for each. Basketball fans worldwide almost hyperventilate at the mere thought of "March Madness."

But this is February, the month when teams work hard down the stretch to make the national tournaments, each known as the "Big Dance." It's also the month when most universities play their arch-rivals at least once, often twice. Arch-rivals are usually in the same Conference and are formed through years of victories and heartbreaks. Duke/Carolina. Clemson/South Carolina. Auburn/ Alabama. Husband "Left Brain" and I follow Elon University which has been beaten way too many times by Davidson College. We don't like 'em, in a friendly sort of way, of course. Elon/UNC Greensboro games also stir emotions. It's that proximity thing. I say, "Great!" College rivalries are part of the fun of sports.

There is a huge non-conference rivalry, however, that you may not think about until I call it to your attention. It involves Duke, in the

Atlantic Coast Conference, and a university that is not in the ACC—Kentucky. The people who pull for the University of Kentucky simply do not like "Dook" and never will. Does the name Christian Laettner ring a bell?[14] 'Nuff said.

Several years ago, I was invited to speak at a "Celebration of Hope" luncheon for breast cancer survivors in Kentucky. My invitation came from Jane Beshear, the First Lady of Kentucky.[15] As the date approached, Mrs. Beshear's assistant called "my people." "My people" means Toni Meredith, who has run my office by herself for over 35 years. The young man explained that the Governor's wife would like to present me with a gift when my speech was concluded. Toni told him that was nice but certainly not necessary.

He continued. "I'm calling to double-check something about the gift. Didn't Jeanne's husband play basketball at Duke?"

"Yes, he did. A long time ago, but that's correct."

"Okay. The Governor's wife thought so. When Jeanne's speech is over, Mrs. Beshear would like to tell the audience about the Duke connection and then present Jeanne with a Duke shirt."

Toni is an extremely savvy sportsperson. She was once asked not to participate again in a trivia contest at an Auburn Piedmont Alum Club meeting because she had won the first five prizes. A Duke shirt? Her antenna went up. "Whoa, wait a minute. Jeanne will have just spent an hour getting the audience to like her. Many of them will be UK fans. If the Governor's wife comes out on stage and tells them Jeanne's husband played at Duke and gives her a Duke shirt, you'll hear mumbles and grumbles from the crowd. I'm sure they're too nice to boo," she added quickly, "but they won't be happy about it. Jeanne likes

---

14   Christian Donald Laettner is an American former professional basketball player. His college career for the Duke Blue Devils is widely regarded as one of the best in National Collegiate Athletic Association history. In 1992, Laettner hit a jumper in the final second of overtime to defeat Kentucky, sending Duke to the final four and sending Kentucky home.

15   She served as first lady of Kentucky from 2007 to 2015.

funny and getting a Duke shirt in front of a Kentucky crowd won't be funny. What would be funny is if Mrs. Beshear told the people Jeanne's husband played at Duke and then gave her a Kentucky shirt."

The assistant hesitated a few seconds before replying, "Let me check with Mrs. Beshear and call you back."

Within minutes, our phone rang. "We're going to stick with what we've planned. Mrs. Beshear likes funny too. Trust me. The Governor's wife knows what she's doing."

Toni hung up and shouted to me, "You're in trouble!"

The comment "The Governor's wife knows what she's doing" became an often-repeated line in our office. When I said, "Where am I staying in Kentucky?" Toni answered, "I don't know, but I'm sure the Governor's wife knows what she's doing."

"Well, if they do give me a Duke shirt, I hope it fits."

"I'm sure it will. The Governor's wife knows what she's doing."

The day of the luncheon rolled around, and it turned out—in my opinion—that they really didn't need an "outside speaker." Head Coach of the University of Kentucky Wildcats, John Calipari, walked into the huge hall, and that was all the meeting planners needed to ensure the event's success. Oh, the excitement. There was spontaneous applause when they realized he was amongst them. I could hear comments passing through the crowd. "Coach Cal is here." "Look! At the door! It's Coach Calipari." "I'm going to see if I can get a photo of Coach Cal and frame it for my son." Cell phones were flashing everywhere. UK had won the NCAA Tournament a few months earlier, and "Coach Cal" was mobbed. Autograph seekers lined up to watch him eat.

Right on schedule after the meal, I was introduced. I gave my speech and couldn't have had a more responsive audience. Everyone was upbeat, having fun, and supporting a good cause. They laughed at the right places and clapped at the end. A humorist can't ask for more. But the entire time I was on stage, I had a funny feeling in the pit of my stomach because I could see a young man named Mark Krebs, a

Kentucky graduate and former basketball player, standing off stage. He was holding what was clearly a Duke blue shirt. Mrs. Beshear was standing next to him.

As the audience applauded at the end, the Governor's wife walked out on stage, grinning. Her expression made me think, "Something's up here." Her assistant's words bounced around in my head. "Mrs. Beshear likes funny too."

Indeed, she did. Mrs. Beshear announced to the crowd that my husband had played basketball at Duke. That's when I found out that Toni was wrong when she said, "I know they're too nice to boo." They booed. But it was nice, friendly booing. This means they were also smiling. After all, they had just won the national championship.

The First Lady then introduced Mark Krebs, who the audience knew. They cheered when he stepped onto the stage. He walked toward me, holding the Duke shirt in front of him as though it were a silver serving tray. But instead of handing it to me, he flipped it open and held it in front of me for all to see. There was a brief pause while what was written on the shirt registered with the crowd of a thousand. Then, they erupted in laughter and applause.

Written in big black letters on the front of the Duke blue shirt was:

D U K E #1. But the D and E had been X'd out, leaving the big letters proclaiming U K #1.

The shirt got more applause than Coach Calipari.

My cell phone was ringing when I got in my rental car. It was Toni. "What happened? What happened? What happened? Will you ever be able to speak in Kentucky again?"

"I'm trying to get out of the parking garage, Toni. I'll call you when I get to the airport. For now, suffice it to say . . . the Governor's wife knows what she's doing."

When You Walk Through a Storm . . .

May 2015, *Southeast Gazette*

It's May! Graduations are popping out all over. As in the rest of the country, students will be lining up in caps and gowns in droves across North Carolina to "go forth" into the next stage of their lives.

Here's one grandmother who is thrilled that she doesn't have to go to a graduation this year. I've been to my share, and I've got several more coming my way, but not this year. Whee. I'm free!

Attending high school graduations started for me in the ninth grade because I was in the Glee Club at Graham High School. We sang every year, and if memory serves me correctly, we sang the same song, "You'll Never Walk Alone." It was a show tune from the Rodgers and Hammerstein musical *Carousel*. In the production, the cast sang it during a graduation scene. Perhaps that planted the seed for graduations for years to come.

Many of you will remember this classic. It starts slowly with, "When you walk through a storm / hold your head up high / And don't be afraid of the dark." It then moves along, slowly working its way to the crescendo of "WALK ON THROUGH THE WIND! / WALK ON THROUGH THE RAIN!" Etcetera. It could be inspiring if sung correctly; trust me, the Graham High School Glee Club sang it correctly.

I don't think "they" sing the same song at graduations every year now. Recently, I read that seniors often write their own graduation songs or vote on a contemporary hit. Another popular option in today's world is for the choral director to write a song for each class. That's all fine with me. Quoting my grandsons, "Whatever." However, I don't think of graduation that the refrain "Walk on. Walk on / With hope in your heart!" doesn't pop into my mind.

That's probably why I once caused a little commotion before a banquet. Telling you about it gives me an opportunity to toss a little piece of advice to those graduating this year.

It happened at a big convention. I was the after-dinner speaker . . .

The convention attendees gathered in the hall outside the banquet room for a reception before a dinner at a large meeting in Washington, DC. The area was abuzz with the usual excitement that accompanies old friends seeing each other annually. (Another "buzz" was in the air due to the drinks being served at the reception, but there is no need to "go there" in this story.)

The real activity, however, was on the other side of the huge convention banquet hall doors, where dozens of hotel employees made last-minute preparations before the doors opened and the people poured in. I had slipped into the big room to check the microphone for my speech later that evening. The "wait staff "—composed of waitresses and waiters dressed in crisp black uniforms with white collars—gathered at one end of the big room for a head count and final review of table assignments. Each held a white sheet of paper with information pertinent to his/her job that night. When I arrived on the scene, they had evidently just received these sheets. All had glanced down to read their instructions. The Captain of this group stood in front, facing the group and checking uniforms. When he spoke, the ensemble snapped their heads up and looked in his direction. From where I stood at the other end of the room, they looked like members of a big choir, each holding sheet music, waiting for the director to wave his arms for them to begin singing.

I had the microphone in my hand and was standing at the far end of the hall. The group was oblivious that I was there. I could have slipped out, but quite honestly, it was too good of an opportunity for me to let pass. Maybe the Choral Director in several episodes of *The Andy Griffith Show* popped into my mind. You might remember him—Choral Director John Masters? A man who knows, "You can't have a concert without a soloist."

Standing tables away from the "choir," I put the microphone up to my lips and slowly started singing. Dozens of performers have recorded this song through the years. I chose to imitate the version sung by Elvis. "When you waaalk through a storrrm . . ." I didn't realize the volume was turned so high. My voice literally boomed throughout the room. "WHEN YOU WAAALK THROUGH A STORRRRM . . ." Most of the waiters and waitresses started to laugh but stifled it quickly when they received a no-nonsense look from the Staff Captain.

"Excuse me," he shouted in my direction. "No one is supposed to be in here at this time. You need to leave. Now!"

In hindsight, even years later, I can report that he didn't see the humor in the situation. Many in the "choir" did, but not "Mr. Director."

"I'm sorry," I said into the microphone, and I meant it. "I'm the speaker for the banquet. I just wanted to test the sound. I didn't realize it was turned so high." My sincere apology got me nowhere. After all, I had interrupted his instructional meeting, and he was in a time crunch. I turned off the microphone, put it down, and left immediately. The Captain watched me leave while the entire "choir" cut their eyes at each other and awaited further instructions.

Thirty minutes later, a thousand people came through the doors and found their assigned tables. I was on stage at the head table with the officers of the organization. Two people were in charge of serving our table. Out of habit, I leaned to one side when I sensed a waitress was behind me and heard her say, "Excuse me." She bent forward to place the salad down, and when she neared my left ear, she sang in perfect tune, just loud enough for me to hear, "Hold your heaaad up hiiiiigh."

Go forth, graduates. The world awaits you. Have wonderful lives. And whatever you do, stay in the group that keeps a sense of humor.

Your Cue is "Baton"

August 2017, *SE Gazette*

Do you remember that sick feeling you had inside when you were in a high school or a church play and it was your turn to say a line . . . and the line was gone? Your family and friends instantly knew it and almost fell into the aisles. They knew all the lines. (My mother used to come wearing an identical costume. Just in case. You never know when you'll get your "big break.") Then, right before you literally passed out in front of your hometown, the prompter—standing on a stepladder behind the curtain and holding the script—whispered a cue to you, and you were back on track.

I'm going to give you a cue word from this month's story, and from this day forth, it can be your cue to see the humor in stressful situations, and your cue to stay "cool." Why? Because the word will remind you of an eighteen-year-old young woman I saw in a small town in North Carolina. If she could see the humor in what I saw happen to her, the rest of us should be able to see the humor in most situations. Your cue is "Baton."

I was in a small town in eastern North Carolina in the early seventies (in the last millennium) to emcee the annual local beauty pageant.

The night of the rehearsal, I asked one of the contestants, "What do you do for your talent?" She said, "I twirl the baton."

All I could think was, oh no, not another baton twirler. Can you imagine how many baton twirlers I had seen while emceeing pageants, even at that early point in my speaking career?

I don't know anything about twirling the baton. Growing up, I spent all my spare time playing basketball in Graham, NC, and shooting hook shots. We asked if I could shoot hook shots for my talent in the Miss America Pageant. My Daddy told pageant officials, "We'll bring a portable basketball goal and sandbags to hold it in place to New Jersey in our truck. When talent rolls around, you put it on stage, and Jeanne will come out and shoot hook shots for three minutes. She can hook right-handed. She can hook left-handed. If she hits them, you might want to name her Miss America. If she misses, we'll put the ball, the goal, and the sandbags in our truck and come home."

Pageant officials politely said it wasn't possible. They politely explained that we didn't know how long it takes contestants to perfect talents such as singing and dancing. This told us that someone in New Jersey at the Miss America Pageant didn't know how long it takes to perfect a good hook shot. I think my Daddy told them that. Politely.

Now I'm older and wiser. I've even judged at the Miss America Pageant three times, and I understand these things. They were afraid I would win. The headline would have read: "Hooker Wins Miss America!"

Let me take back something I just wrote. A few lines back, I told you I didn't know anything about twirling the baton. That's not exactly true. I know two things. No.1, a baton doesn't just fall in your hand and start twirling itself and pulling your arm through the air. It has to go in and out of your fingers some way. And No. 2, twirling the baton is like most things in this world. It takes years of practice to get it just like you want it. Years. Unfortunately, this contestant had only two weeks.

She decided to be in the pageant at a late date and almost backed out when the officials reminded her that she had to have three minutes' worth of talent. But she thought about it and remembered that her sister had a baton in the second grade. She would borrow the thing and twirl it.

The music she had selected was a hit of the day—"The Hustle." Remember it? Dun, dun, dun, ta-dun, ta-dun, dun, dun. The night of the rehearsal, she got out in the center of the stage, and she didn't twirl the baton at all. She held it smack dab in the middle and twisted her wrist back and forth, back and forth, back and forth as fast as she could move her arm, trying to make it look like from a distance—in a dark auditorium—that she was twirling the baton.

When I saw what she was doing, I quickly stepped backstage to one of the sponsoring Jaycees and said, "I've got to talk to someone. She's not twirling the baton."

He said, "Well, we know that," and added, looking out at the contestant in the center of the stage, "But isn't she purty?"

I swallowed hard and said, "You don't understand the world as it is today and pageants in general if you think being "purty," as you called it, is the main thing. She's going to embarrass herself tomorrow night in front of her hometown!"

I'll never forget his response. "No, Jeanne, I think you're the one who doesn't understand the world as it is in this town. You just breezed in here tonight as an out-of-town expert. We've been working with her for two weeks. Don't you come in here and mess her up. She's got more personality than most of the other contestants put together. She just doesn't have any talent! Leave her alone and let her do what she can do."

Then he said something about her that I want people to say about me after every speaking engagement. Something I believe most of us want people to say about us. He said, "After working with her for two weeks, all of us backstage have decided that we want her to win. She's so pleasant, and we know we'll enjoy working with her for the coming year."

What a compliment. He didn't say, "She'll be Miss North Carolina." He said, "She's so pleasant. We know we'll enjoy working with her for the coming year."

This contestant had one teensy, tiny hope of gaining any points in the talent competition. A minute and fifteen seconds into her three-minute routine, she reared back and got ready to toss that baton up into the air. Once. She had no control over where it went. People who had been at rehearsals for two weeks knew to duck when she got ready to throw the baton! Some started coming in old football helmets. Wherever the baton went, the contestant went after it. If she caught it and she happened to be facing the back of the stage, that's the way she faced until the music ended, moving her wrist back and forth, back and forth, back and forth.

You were not there. I was there. But let me describe the situation, and you think back and see if you haven't "been there." We've all been there.

It was summer, and it was hot. It had been almost a hundred degrees that day—outside. We were in one of those old, wooden elementary school auditoriums—no air conditioning. Sticks were holding open all of the windows down the sides of the auditorium, which I thought was interesting because all of the windows were broken out!

Eight hundred people were jammed inside, and the place only seated six hundred and fifty. People were everywhere. A woman in the front row had one of those curved, Popsicle-stick, cardboard, funeral home fans—with a picture of Heaven on the backside—and she was fanning her chest. She never missed a beat. I could barely emcee the pageant for watching her bionic arm beat her chest.

This was before cell phones, but someone had come through town selling walkie-talkies, and every Jaycee working the pageant had one on his hip. Jaycees stood four feet from each other backstage, saying into those walkie-talkies, "Can you hear me? Can. You. Hear. Me? Let up on the button, Bubba!"

The stage hands rolled a piano out on stage for one contestant who stood next to it and announced to the crowd, "I'm going to play a medley of Gershwin tunes that I wrote." (I can't make this up.)

During the years I emceed pageants I normally stood at a lectern on the side of the stage, introduced each contestant, and then got off stage. This night, I wouldn't have left the stage for anything. I had to see with my own eyes if our baton contestant could fool anyone.

"The Hustle" started. Dun, dun, dun, ta-dun, ta-dun, dun, dun. Dun, dun, dun, ta-dun, ta-dun, dun, dun. She started her routine—back and forth, back and forth, back and forth, back and forth.

Eight hundred people sat in total disbelief. I knew they were in shock because they all leaned forward in their seats at the same time. It was an 800-person jaw drop. Out of the corner of my eye, I saw the woman in the front row slowly put down the funeral home fan.

But did they burst out laughing? No. See, they didn't know what they were supposed to do. It was as though all those people said, "We'll help you, but what do you want us to do? Give us a clue. Is this comedy? Tell us now. Is this comedy?"

I maintain that in every situation, when something happens that is a little unpleasant, stressful, awkward, or embarrassing, people stand around and wait for a cue. If the cue is to get angry, people can sure do it. If the cue is to fall apart, they can do that too. But if the cue is to see the humor in the situation, they'll pick it up and run with it.

For one minute and fifteen seconds, this contestant stood in the center of the stage with the baton in her hand, twisting it back and forth, back and forth, and the people in the audience held back their laughter. It wasn't easy. Judges broke their pencils. Mothers slid their hands over their children's mouths. They had mentally told themselves they could hold back anything for three minutes.

But they didn't know about the big toss. At a minute and fifteen seconds, the twirler reared back. The Jaycees, backstage, started mumbling prayers. "Let her catch it. Please. Don't let her knock somebody out." And in front of all those people, she tossed that baton up in the air . . . and it didn't come back down. It just did not come back down.

The music didn't know it hadn't come back down, so the music never missed a beat. "Dun, dun, dun, ta-dun, ta-dun, dun-ta." And can't you see her? Sure, you can. The young woman is looking all around the stage. She looked over at me. I mouthed, "I don't have it." She looked out at the audience, and it was as though everyone in the auditorium at the same time shrugged, "We don't either." The baton was lodged up in the curtains, and it wasn't coming down!

Pageants take a lot of criticism. Some of it is justified, but much of it isn't. But if you're eighteen years old and have made the decision to be in one, and if you are on stage twirling a baton in front of your hometown and you don't have a baton? Well. You tell me what could be more important?

Remember, this happened in a small town, the kind of town where when this contestant is eighty years old, she could be leaving the grocery store, and someone would say to her, "Do you remember the night you was twirling that baton? "

If it had been me, I would either have fainted, or I would have pretended to faint. A group of people would have had to drag my body right off the stage. But at eighteen, she had what I love to remind people and myself. She had the ability to see the humor in a stressful situation, stay cool, and keep going.

She also had to make some choices right then and there that we have to make every day. She could have stomped off the stage in anger, and right before disappearing behind the curtain, she could have turned to the audience and spat out, "Those Jaycees!" People pick up on clues so quickly that half of the audience would have immediately assumed that the Jaycees had done something. The Jaycees had not done a thing. They certainly didn't have a man up in the curtains who reached out and grabbed the baton as it went by.

Our "purty" baton twirler could have burst into tears and run off the stage. Remember, she was only eighteen. Everyone would have shaken their heads and said, "What a shame, what a shame." But they would have had that sick feeling we get in our stomachs when we know a person didn't handle a situation the best way possible.

But this young woman decided to see the humor in it. When she did, I stood on the side of the stage all those years ago and watched her literally influence eight hundred people to see the humorous side of the situation with her.

She looked up and saw that the baton was caught in the curtains, and it wasn't coming down. She jumped up and down on the stage a couple of times—Boom! Boom!—trying to jar the auditorium enough to free the baton. Sticks fell out of the windows. Dirt fell on the floor. But the baton was not coming down.

She looked out at an audience of people who were about to explode but were doing their best to hold back their laughter. She heard the music, knew she had about a minute left, and made a snap decision to see the humor in the situation. She suddenly gave her best beauty pageant smile and started pantomiming a baton routine, the likes of which you have never seen in your life. She pretended to toss a baton up into the air and faked catching it behind her neck when it supposedly came back down. She pretended to twirl it around her waist. People went berserk!

She had them in the palm of her hand. Why stop? She pretended to toss the baton up a second time, and when it was supposedly in the air, she rolled her head around and mimicked watching the baton take loops in the air. I looked out, and eight hundred people were looping their heads as though watching the same thing. Just before it would have hit the stage, she reached under her leg and pretended to catch it.

By now, mothers were throwing their babies up into the air! But did she leave well enough alone? Seldom when you're on a roll and never when you have 'em in the palm of your hand. Still pretending to twirl the baton in one hand, she danced to the edge of the stage and acted as though someone off stage threw her a second baton, which she faked catching with her empty hand. When the music ended, she was back in the center of the stage, pretending to twirl two batons as fast as she could.

A man in the back row said to his wife, "She's twirling 'em so fast, I can't see the batons!"

Write down the word . . . Baton

And stay cool.

The Word Is "Sandbagged"

February 2018, *SE Gazette*

Although I've heard all my life that there is more than one way to skin a cat, the comment is probably no longer appropriate. I heard the comment often because Mama used it repeatedly. But it never occurred to Mama that she was politically "incorrect" and obviously "insensitive" to cats and cat lovers. If she had, in fact, been privy to this information, she would not have used the phrase because Mama was kind. Just uninformed.

Today, we understand these things. We are an "informed population." Cats have unionized and hired a PR company. I, for one, am truly sorry for any pain I may have caused them with this phrase. Therefore, until the world "rights itself," I won't state again that there is more than one way to skin a cat. I'll find another way to express the same advice in the following story.

Several years ago, a cooperative booked me to speak at five banquets during their regional annual meetings across several states. Each night, their voting members and spouses entered a big banquet hall, went through buffet lines, ate, and then voted on directors for the coming year. While the vote was being counted, they listened to an "after-dinner speaker." That particular year, I was it. I've lost count of the number of these types of meetings I've been a part of over the fifty-four-plus years of giving speeches. Usually, these programs go off without a hitch. The group I'll tell you about this month wasn't so lucky.

The people arrived early and moved quickly through the food lines. When everyone was served, the emcee began the "business" portion of the evening. This was to consist of brief remarks from their new Board Chair before the candidates were introduced and the voting took place. The "brief remarks" were where it all broke down.

I'll call the new Board Chair "George," which conceals his real name in case he should ever read this. He would definitely recognize himself, but others don't have to.

The people from the "main office" had prepared George's remarks and sent them to him to use. It was some sort of an anniversary year, and, therefore, they had prepared a doubly-dull speech full of facts, numbers, and historical information about the group. I glanced at my watch when he started and then sat in disbelief along with everyone else as he read—READ!—an hour-long speech to the group.

From time to time, someone would go to the kitchen for a pot of coffee and return to serve everyone at their table. But they did not leave. They were part of the required quorum. They came to vote. They were needed. It was important.

I believe I was the only one awake when George finally stopped reading and sat down. I've seen plenty of folks read dull speeches, and I've seen my share of speakers go overtime. Combine the two, and it's the perfect storm to ruin a banquet.

The next morning, the little group that was to travel to all five events gathered for breakfast. George was one of the last to come because the others had passed the word to come early and had excluded George from that invitation. They had a problem to solve and knew it. Someone had to tell George to cut his remarks in half, and they were going to decide who among them would do so. For some reason, they included me in the instructions to arrive a little early. I agreed with their comments that George's speech was way too long but kept my mouth shut. I certainly wasn't on their staff and didn't want any part of offending the new Board Chair.

George finally arrived, and all conversation ceased. After a few awkward minutes and shifting of eyes, taking extra sips of coffee, etc., one of the men—the leader at that point—cleared his throat and stated, "Um, George. We need you to cut your speech some tonight. We think you lost 'em a little." Another guy chimed in as though he was hearing the suggestion for the first time. "You know, I think you may be right. Many of our members have to drive long distances to get home. We need to get them out a little earlier." Everyone nodded in agreement and took sips of coffee, waiting for George's response.

Finally, George spoke in his defense. "I thought the speech was a little long, too, but it's what the staff sent me from headquarters. I only did what they told me."

"Oh, we know that, George," everyone quickly agreed. "It's not your fault."

"No, George, it wasn't your fault at all," a woman in the group chipped in kindly. Others around the table continued to nod but avoided eye contact with George.

I didn't nod or say anything. It wasn't my dogfight, and I wasn't getting in it. I hoped to work for them again, so I just watched it unfold.

The leader cut to the chase. "George, you've got to cut it in half tonight. At least by thirty minutes."

"Cut it in half? Thirty minutes?" George asked as he reached into his briefcase and plopped a copy of his speech on the table. It must have been forty single-spaced pages. "How do I cut it in half? Here it is. The numbers all line up. The history of the co-op is in chronological order, matching the numbers. I was told to read it as is. It's a special speech for the anniversary. It won't make sense if I read only the first or the last half." (No one said what all of us were thinking. It hadn't made much sense the night before.)

The leader was kind but serious. "It has to be edited, George. Cut it by thirty minutes, at least. Most of us are playing golf after we check in at the next hotel today. We suggest you spend the afternoon working on your speech."

"And miss the golf?" George said, his shoulders sagging.

"Yes, miss the golf. Get the speech cut in half for tonight, and you can forget about it and play golf with us every afternoon for the rest of the week."

I sat there taking it all in and felt a little sad for George. Then, to my utter disbelief, the group leader added, "But don't worry. You'll have help. Jeanne's a professional. She's going to stay at the hotel and help you." I almost spat out my coffee.

The word is "sandbagged."

I had not intended to play golf. I planned to sleep. I was looking forward to it. But George looked at me with such desperation in his eyes that I truly felt sorry for him. At first, I said, "Look, guys, I'm a humorist. I make people laugh. I am not a speech writer or a speech coach. Nor do I want to be. I'm not sure I can help." Then, I looked at George with all that "hope" in his eyes, shrugged, and changed my tune. "Sure. Sure, I'll try."

The leader then reached into his briefcase and plopped down a second copy of the speech in front of me. "You and George ride together today. We had this copy run off late last night. You might want to start going over it in the car." I took the copy, but I believe I mumbled, "If I get carsick, I'm getting out of the car and throwing up in your direction."

Let me remind you that I gave them clear warning. I distinctly reminded them that I'm a humorist, not a speech writer. But being a humorist doesn't mean that one isn't smart or creative. But I am a problem-solver. I finally acquiesced and said, "Give me your pen and the copy. Don't expect miracles."

George and I rode to the next location together as instructed; we were the only two people in our car. It took me five minutes to explain to him what he needed to do and the remainder of the trip to convince him to do it. Upon arrival, I went to my room and went to sleep. George played golf, assuring the co-op staff that he had the speech under control, stating, "Jeanne edited it for me."

Ta Da! That night, George's speech went on for exactly thirty minutes. He had cut it in half, with my direction. At the end of the banquet, the little group that worked the event each night gathered around to slap him on the back and tell him the speech was perfect. They congratulated me on helping him. George and I exchanged glances and smiled.

We had edited his speech exactly in half as a humorist would edit it. That's why, on the second night, George had walked straight to the lectern and read . . . every other paragraph.

They never knew. The speech made as much sense as it had the night before—maybe more.

George cut it to fifteen minutes the third night and winked at me when he returned to his seat.

Forget the skinned cat. There's more than one way . . . to slice an onion.

Don't Forget Your Wire Cutters

November 2018, *SE Gazette*

As I've said many times, there's more than one way to skin a cat. Wait! Strike that! "Skinning a cat" is not politically correct. It's awful sounding. How about ". . . to spill a cup of coffee." I broke my femur a couple of years ago, right above my knee. I'm "all better" now, but the whole process was a bear. During that winter and spring, I had to postpone twenty-six theater shows and miss many convention speeches. (Conventions can't change their dates like theaters can.)

I won't go into the whole ordeal. Suffice it to say that, like most things of this sort, we get through them. Then, after all the operations (there were complications) and hours of rehab, one day, I realized I was well enough to travel again, and I wanted to, but there were some teensy, tiny details that needed to be worked on. I knew a friend could travel with me and do the wheelchair pushing, I rationalized. The airlines and airports are good about having someone push people through the concourse and onto a plane, rolling by passengers shifting their weight and looking at their watches. I couldn't yet walk or stand for the length of a show, but I knew I could figure that one out. Truth be told, I wasn't excited about sitting in a wheelchair out there on the stage near the front. Even locking it in place, there was that nagging concern about the chair rolling off.

About the time when I realized I was ready to get back on the road, my husband and I were watching a basketball game on TV. I was sitting in a rocking chair, and it hit me like someone making a basket from half-court. Wow! A rocking chair! The solution!

I waited until halftime and then called "Thuh Nashville People," who booked my theater shows. That's the way Toni, my assistant of many years, and I refer to the people in Tennessee who approached me several years ago about doing theater shows rather than just conventions and banquets. When they first talked to me about it, I was hesitant. I wasn't sure people would come. Convention speakers don't sell tickets. People go to their respective conventions, and the speakers are there. Professional speakers market to meeting planners, and don't worry about tickets.

Theater shows are a whole different ball game. Theater shows mean drawing a crowd on one's name; usually, the tickets sell two at a time. That's why I was apprehensive, but "Thuh Nashville People" convinced me to give it a try. They were "big city." They knew about theater marketing. If they thought I could do theater shows and wanted to promote me, well, maybe I could. Now, I do mostly theater shows and love it. I wouldn't have known how to get into the theater world without "Thuh Nashville People's" help. They're out there in Music City. They handle "advancing the shows" but always seem happy to hear my ideas. If I do say so myself, this small-town Graham "girl". . . I know that's not politically correct, but I'm 75, so I can say it the way I want to . . . this small-town Graham "girl" might not be from the big theater world, but I come up with some good ideas from time to time. You get my drift, though. Nashville folks know all about it. That's why, even after all these years, Toni and I still whisper—as though they might go away—"Thuh Nashville People called."

So, I called "Thuh Nashville People" at halftime of the game. "I'm ready to go back on tour, and I've worked out most of the logistics. I can get someone to travel with me, and then, since I can't stand up for even a few minutes, much less for a 1½ hour show, I can do my show sitting down. I think it will work from a rocking chair."

"Are you sure, Jeanne? Really? A rocking chair? Great idea!"

I assured them it would work and told them my next idea. "How 'bout this? We can change the name of my tour to "The Rocking Chair Tour!" They loved the idea. I felt so clever. We agreed to think about how to set it up.

After the call, I thought about it for a few more minutes and came up with another "brilliant" idea. I called 'em again. Right then.

"1 know where we can get the rocking chairs! Cracker Barrel!" Pretty good idea, huh? We've all seen those rows of rocking chairs in front of Cracker Barrel restaurants. Wires looping from rocker to rocker? People rocking as they wait for a table or rocking after they've eaten while someone in their group shops inside?

"Thuh Nashville People" were even more excited. "Wow! That's another great idea, Jeanne! They're good rockers, and Cracker Barrels are everywhere!"

At that point, I came up with my next Alamance County, North Carolina, marketing idea. "Why don't we give away the rocking chair after each show?" They loved it and said they would work out the logistics. As Sheriff Andy Taylor might say, "I was feeling right proud of myself."

Later, many people in my audience asked, "Giving away a rocker after every show seems expensive, Jeanne. Why don't you get one good chair and take it from show to show?"

Well, duh. You can't get a rocking chair in an overhead bin on an airplane!

Anyway. After all my phone calls that afternoon, "Thuh Nashville People" were so excited about figuring out how to give away the chairs that when I hung up, I kept thinking and came up with what I thought was my best idea in this discussion. Yes, I called them back once again, hurrying because the second half was starting. If they didn't want me calling, they shouldn't have given me their cell phone numbers.

"Listen to this! Why don't we get Cracker Barrel to sponsor my Rocking Chair Tour? It could be the 'Jeanne Robertson Rocking Chair Tour—brought to you by Cracker Barrel!' I'll sit on stage and rock away in their chairs."

"Thuh Nashville People" got very excited. It turned out they knew some of the prime players at the restaurant chain and said they would contact them immediately to see if they were interested. They would handle everything. True to their word, they planned their pitch and contacted the company within days. Yes, sir, "Thuh Nashville People" know how to do all that stuff.

And Cracker Barrel said, "No."

Please know that I'm sure the management team at Cracker Barrel is very nice across the board. It is, though, a huge company. I chose to believe they just didn't know what we were proposing. Perhaps "Thuh Nashville People" didn't explain it correctly. Perhaps they just don't know marketing skills like I obtained growing up in Graham and from my year traveling as Miss North Carolina.

But I'm never one to give up. When I heard the turndown news, I hung up and started thinking again. I might not be from Big "Music City" Nashville, but "Thuh Graham Person" figured it out on her own.

I don't need Cracker Barrel! All I have to do . . . is slip out there late at night with some wire cutters.

Epilogue. I do hope you know that I haven't stolen the approximately seventy-five rockers we've given away thus far. If I had, Cracker Barrel would have me on video, and I would be heading to a place that didn't have rocking chairs.

Not long ago, I told the above story in Montgomery, Alabama, at The Alabama Theater. I said the exact same line at the end, "All I have to do is slip out there late at night with some wire cutters." It got a laugh.

After the show, I was in the lobby meeting and greeting folks when a man handed me a tiny piece of paper with his name and phone number. It wasn't a business card. It looked like the torn-off top of a popcorn box. With a grin and then a wink, he said, "When you get back anywhere near Montgomery, Jeanne, bring your wire cutters and give me a call. I know where you can get a good gas grill."

Snookered at the Hay Show

June 2019, *SE Gazette*

Many of you may recall an episode of *The Andy Griffith Show* titled "The Church Organ." In this particular show, the All-Souls Church needs a new organ, and Sheriff Andy Taylor tries to squeeze the financing the old-fashioned way—business leaders chipping in. They need a lot of money. Cake sales, raffles, kissing booths, and charity bazaars won't do the trick. I think they need the best money squeezer I have ever seen—a fellow named Byron Leewright from Mineola, Texas.

I met Mr. Leewright years ago at the annual Mineola Hay Show banquet, where it's a tradition to auction off the thirty-five top-grade bales of hay at the Hay Show competition. The proceeds go toward Future Farmers of America scholarships, so people come ready to contribute under the friendly guise of bidding against one another.

Byron Leewright, the emcee/auctioneer, reminded me of Mayberry's Mayor Pike in *The Andy Griffith Show*. A short, rotund fellow, Mr. Leewright proudly told me that he had conducted the auction for all twenty-five years it had been held. Before the banquet started, he explained the process to me and added with a distinct east Texas twang, "Now see here, Ja'neen, I may need yo' help during the auctioning, so stay sitting on the stage after your little talk."

I told him my name was "Jeanne" and that I would be happy to help in any way I could. Seconds later, I overheard him tell someone, "Ja'neen's gonna help out if we need it."

Before the bidding started, Mr. Leewright was by my side again with more instructions. "Now look, Ja'neen, we're just a bunch of hay farmers down here, and sometimes folks are shy about shouting out at an auction. If the action slows down, I want you to throw in a bid on the low side to get things rollin'. They'll jump in if somebody gets it started. They just don't want to be the first one to speak up."

"You can count on me, Mr. Leewright," I assured him with a smile. "And by the way, my name is pronounced 'Jeanne' as in the old TV show, *I Dream of Jeannie.*" He thought about it for a couple of seconds and said, "Whatever you want, Ja'neen, but help me out when I need it."

The bidding started quickly, with the top-graded bale selling for close to a thousand dollars, and progressed rapidly through the next several bales, each bringing in slightly less money. Then, around the six-hundred-dollar level, folks suddenly seemed to get frogs in their throats. Everything slowed down. Waaaaay down. Bales started selling for five and then four hundred, and a lot of bales were still on stage. Folks were keeping their bidding hands in their pockets until the prices dropped even further. Mr. Leewright was at the microphone, beads of perspiration gleaming on his forehead, cajoling the crowd to bid on the remaining bales. "Come on, folks. Don't sit on your hands. It's for a good cause." He even called out friends. "I see you back there, Sam. You gonna bid this year or what?" Sam jumped into the mix and bought a bale.

I was seated at the head table right on stage near all the action. After one particularly long, drawn-out sale, Mr. Leewright whispered to me, "They've gone quiet on us, Ja'neen. Throw in a bid on the next bale and get things started." With that said, he turned back toward the audience. "What do I hear for this next fine bale of hay?" he boomed and cut his eyes in my direction.

Right on cue, I raised my hand and shouted, "A hundred and fifty dollars!" There was a distinct gasp as every head in the place turned toward me. But before they, or I, had a chance to think further, Mr. Byron Leewright slammed down his gavel on the lectern and shouted, "SOLD, TO JA'NEEN FOR A HUNDRED AND FIFTY DOLLARS!"

The crowd applauded wildly and laughed at my shocked expression. Mr. Leewright looked me straight in the eyes and almost dared me to say anything as he proudly threw back his shoulders and rested his hands on his stomach. I sat there a few seconds, considering my options, and then slowly smiled back. When all the hay was sold, I wrote out a check.

I still had the fountain pen in my hand when Mr. Leewright came up to tell me goodbye. I know a town character when I see one, and I was already trying to imagine how many years local folks would chuckle about the out-of-town speaker who got snookered at the Hay Show. He quietly but firmly took the check out of my hand and said, "Thank you, Ja'neen, you're sumpin' else."

(So were you, Mr. Leewright. So were you.)

Epilogue. Speakers often receive newspaper articles about events after they've spoken at them. After the Mineola trip, I received a copy of the local paper in Wood County, where Mineola is located. It contained a write-up about the Hay Show. I still have the paper. My friends and family often accuse me of making up stories, so I never throw away proof of a good story or memory. That paper is still in our house somewhere. I just can't put my hands on it right now. Actually, I don't have to. I'll never forget reading, "As usual, auctioneer Byron Leewright tricked the speaker into making a contribution."

He Hit the Proverbial Nail on the Head

November 2019, *SE Gazette*

Professional speakers are usually outgoing, gregarious type folks. A ballroom packed to the walls with them might be a little overbearing, so just imagine a hotel full. By "full," make that 2000+ speakers in the same hotel at the same time. It gives new meaning to the slogan we sold on a T-shirt at our convention several years ago. "Help! I'm speaking, and I can't shut up!"

During a National Speakers Association Convention in Washington, D.C., several of us filled an elevator in the J. W. Marriott. Typical of professional speakers, we were all talking. It had been a year since many of us had seen each other, and the hugs and the catch-up conversations flowed.

Wedged into the corner of the elevator was a man who was not talking, a man whom I didn't recognize. I figured however, that if he were in the hotel, he was attending our convention. He must be a speaker! Probably a "First Timer." Speakers love to make First Timers feel welcome.

I was also the President of NSA that year and felt I should be the first of our talkative group to acknowledge the quiet man. I thrust my hand in his direction. "Hey, I'm Jeanne Robertson. Are you here for the speakers' convention?" Everyone else in the elevator stopped talking and turned in his direction.

The man cautiously extended a hand, shook mine suspiciously, and stepped back even further into the corner of the elevator without saying a word, shaking his head slightly. Okay, maybe he was not one of us.

"I'm sorry," I explained. "I figured you were attending our convention. A national meeting for professional speakers is here in the hotel. About two thousand of us."

He grinned. "No, ma'am. I'm not one of you, but I know who you are." Assuming the stranger was referring to them personally, each speaker on the elevator stood a little taller and smiled. (My husband says that people need to move quickly through the lobby at the speakers' convention, or they might catch ego.)

"I'm in town by myself on business," the man we didn't know explained. "Last night, I was standing in front of the hotel trying to decide where to eat dinner. Several of your members came out and did exactly what you just did—walked right up, stuck out their hands, and asked if I were a speaker. When I told them I was not, they said it didn't matter, to come on and eat with them anyway. And I did."

Then he flashed a broad smile and hit the proverbial nail on the head regarding my profession. "It took me about twenty minutes to figure it out," he said. "What you people need . . . is an audience."

Sing to Your Own Tune

April 2020, *SE Gazette*

With this stress about the pandemic, I remind all of us—myself definitely included—to look for the humor around us every day. Yes, especially now.

Try this. If you don't see any current humor, think back at some of the humorous incidents from your past. Enjoy them again!

The tone for an annual Dupont banquet, I'm remembering, is always set the year before.

At the end of each banquet, club officers for the next year are announced, and I do mean "announced." The current committee selects some folks for positions, from flag bearer to president and an odd assortment of offices in between. The new slate of officers is a total surprise. And those selected are pushed to the stage by laughing people who are relieved they were not on the list that year. Then, these surprised elected officials are sworn in before they can get off the stage. It's all in fun. The only assignment for these new officers is to plan next year's banquet. At the banquet the following year, they get the thrill of surprising another group of friends by naming them the new officers. The only rule? People may not reappoint those who appointed them.

After the officers are announced, two people are also tapped to the prestigious positions of Song Leaders at next year's banquet. They don't have to have musical backgrounds or be the same height to ensure that their voices will blend better. In fact, being able to carry a tune is *not* a prerequisite. Not even a tiny bit. The only criterion for the "honor" of being named Song Leaders is having someone on the previous slate of officers think it would be funny if you were named one of the two Song Leaders for the next meeting. In other words, they set you up.

The evening I spoke, the two Song Leaders, holding up the obligatory Dupont signs, led the group in "You Are My Dupont," sung to the tune of "You Are My Sunshine." The Leaders said the tune was "You Are My Sunshine," so I guess it was, but it was hard to tell. The guy next to me had one of the worst voices I had ever heard. He had a knack for hitting a note just enough off-key to make anyone's skin crawl. I'm sure he was a nice person, but he couldn't sing. Not a lick. Of course, not everyone can sing, so we should be tolerant.

Their rendition of "You Are My Dupont" sounded much like the Mormon Tabernacle Choir compared to what followed. That's when one of the song leaders announced it was time to sing the "Dupont 25-Year-Club Alma Mater." The humorous lyrics were printed in our programs. After five hundred people located their programs and fumbled to the correct page, laughing the whole time, the second leader announced, "The Dupont Alma Mater is supposed to be sung to the tune of the Cornell Alma Mater. If you have no idea what the Cornell Alma Mater sounds like, just sing it to the tune of your high school or college alma mater or fight song."

Five hundred people in the ballroom of the Grove Park Inn in Asheville, NC, then sang the same words at the top of their lungs but to the tunes of several hundred different school songs. It gave a heightened meaning to the word "caterwauling," and it was so much fun.

It was one of the funniest events I've ever seen or participated in. I knew the Graham High School fight song and read the words in the program. I'm not sure about singing on key, but it didn't matter. The group never found a common key.

I sure laugh when I remember singing at the top of my lungs the "Dupont 25-Year Club Alma Mater" to the tune of the fight song of the Graham High School Red Devils. I was also doing a little cheerleader step, as were many others.

Keep laughing! It's a choice, especially during stressful times.

Who's the Squeaker?

September 2020, *SE Gazette*

The Darlington 500 Race has been back in place for the last five years and kicks off in September on Labor Day weekend. It gives me a chance to thank NASCAR for getting their act together and getting some form of their sport back into play during this COVID-19 mess. This particular race always brings back a good memory for me. It's when Donnie and Bobby Allison helped me greatly and etched their way into my memory forever.

I met Bobby and Donnie Allison at the Unocal-Darlington Record Club banquet before a Southern 500 race years back. Past winners, their pit crews, other members of the "racing family," and media were in attendance. It was a swanky affair down to liqueurs and cigars after dessert for those who were feeling especially "sporty," as Sheriff Andy Taylor says. To say that it was a macho event is an understatement.

The event planner had already warned me that it might not be an easy speech, and I was a little apprehensive. Looking back on it, he was the one who took the real chance. The people invited—all men—were drivers and their pit crews, who were all past winners of this race. Not only had they never had a woman speaker at this particular event, but a woman had never been permitted even to attend the banquet unless she was a part of the wait staff.

"I'm not telling these guys you're coming," my contact added. "They'll probably get right quiet when you arrive at the reception."

Right quiet? Does Aunt Bee put a pinch of nutmeg in her apple pie?

A hush spread through the room when the fellows realized that, for the first time, a woman who was not serving hors d'oeuvres was walking among the good ol' boys. They weren't rude by any means. They were stunned. I hoped my smile concealed my nervousness about the whole thing, but to be honest, it was one of the few times in my career that my stomach was churning. As a speaker, I felt like I might be in big trouble. Eyes squinted suspiciously every time I stuck out my hand and said, "I'm Jeanne Robertson. I'm the speaker for the banquet." My nervousness made me say "squeaker for the banquet" to one pit crew early in the evening. They just stared at me until someone finally questioned, "The squeaker?" When I walked away, I could hear the story spread throughout the room. "She said she was the squeaker." Of course, everyone was polite. Their mamas had taught 'em right, but even that didn't prevent the awkward silence as I moved through the crowd.

Suddenly, there was a slap on my shoulder, and I turned to see two wide, mischievous smiles looking upward at me. Donnie and Bobby Allison of "The Alabama Gang" from Hueytown, Alabama, had stepped forward to meet the speaker or the squeaker. Whatever. I have always read the sports pages and recognized them immediately.

"You don't have to tell me who you are," I began. "I'm an Auburn graduate, and I have followed your careers . . ." My sentence was interrupted in midair. "An Auburn graduate? An Auburn graduate!" they shouted for everyone in the room to hear. "Everybody, get over here. What is the world coming to? An Auburn graduate! Somebody has gone and let an Auburn fan in the banquet." (Notice the fact that I am a woman wasn't a concern, but an Auburn fan was another thing.) One of them pulled a chair over and stood on it. The crowd packed in around us. In this group, when the Allison brothers wanted your attention, they got it.

"You couldn't get in the University of Alabama?" one of 'em shouted for all to hear, me standing there smiling. "Not smart enough? Not from good enough stock? What was the problem?" Again, they laughed uproariously, basking in the attention of the crowd. I heard someone in the back mumble, "The Allison boys know the squeaker."

I was with "ma people" and opened my mouth to attempt to hold my own in traditional Auburn/Alabama banter. Before I could say a word, though, one of them turned to the on-looking crowd and proclaimed, "Listen up, everybody. LISTEN UP! Hey! You guys at the bar, be quiet! This lady is our speaker tonight, and she's a friend of ours. She went to Auburn, so she hasn't had a happy life. As a favor to the Allison boys, we want all of y'all to be real nice to her."

He jumped off the chair, and the brothers melted into the crowd as it surged forth, hands extended to welcome me.

In the speaking world, we call that "being home free." And this "squeaker" has never forgotten why she was.

Epilogue. Remember, it was a long time ago. So, no one got upset. In my conversations with my contact for this event, I was a little surprised they wanted me for an all-male event and said something such as, "Their wives and dates don't come?" He said quickly, "No, but we're not like the other racing events. No, sir. Here, we bring the wives and dates to the country club. We don't leave them sitting in the hotel, finding something to eat on their own." He paused, then added, "Now, we feed 'em in another room." I always thought that was funny. He didn't realize how it sounded. As I said, it was a long time ago. That night, while the guys ate, I went down the hall and did a fifteen-minute set for their wives and dates, who were indeed "eating in another room." And quite happily, as I recall. Same menu. I checked. I might need to cut them some slack. Both groups together wouldn't have fit into either room. It just sounded funny.

Too Much Junk

October 2020, *SE Gazette*

Lines from *The Andy Griffith Show* pop into my mind at the oddest times. They have nothing to do with what's happening or being discussed. It's just boom—there's a line, front and center. I don't always say the line out loud when that happens, but I think it. For example, someone might say, "It was a big wedding." I think, "Aw, big ain't the word for it." See what I mean? I bet many of you do the same thing.

You might have seen in the last several articles that I've written another book, and it's out. The title is *DON'T BUNGEE JUMP NAKED and Other Important Stuff.* "Thuh Nashville People," who book my shows, expressed concern about using the word 'stuff' as part of the title. It didn't sound "highbrow." But my longtime assistant Toni summed it up. "Oh, for Pete's Sake, why are you concerned about that, Jeanne? It's the way you talk. Plus," Toni continued, "the name of the book is *Don't Bungee Jump Naked.* Use of the word 'naked' indicates it's not real 'highbrow.' It's funny, but it's not highbrow." I digress.

We're promoting the book in many places, but to be honest, I'm not pushing it to you. If you've read my monthly stories here for the past eleven years, you've read much of what's in the new book—bits and pieces for sure. (I've been practicing on y'all. Thank you.) So, I'm not being pushy here; I'm being honest. Much of it will ring familiar to you.

But since y'all are my "bestest" friends after all these years, I must share that publishing a book is thrilling but can also be humbling. I already knew this, but I did it anyway. Maybe I wanted to be like Helen Crump in *The Andy Griffith Show*. Helen was Andy's main girlfriend in the series. She wrote a book titled *Amusing Tales of Tiny Tots* in the episode "Helen, the Authoress."

Many people also remember Elinor Donahue, who played Andy's girlfriend, Ellie Walker, for a year. There was another well-remembered girlfriend too. Peggy McMillan is a nurse played by Joanna Moore. That relationship was one of the few times Andy acted like the rest of us—a mortal human.

When one of Peggy's high school friends came through town, Peggy chose to spend time with him over Andy. Our wonderful Sheriff became a little disgusted. One might say jealous. It showed up in telling Barney the man's name. Andy practically spats out, "Don. Wouldn't you know his name would be Don?"

Back to the subject of books. One of my clients bought copies of another book I wrote (out of print) titled *HUMOR: The Magic of Genie* to give as favors at a spouse event during their convention.[16] It was back when most spouses at a spouse event were women, but that had begun to change, and more and more men were attending in the spousal role. Today, it's fifty-fifty. My assignment was to make everyone laugh. After I spoke, people lined up to chit-chat and get their gift books autographed. I was having a ball. Maybe you can tell that I love my work.

Many of the attendees asked where I got my speech material. Did I write it from scratch? I told them the truth. "I don't have to write it. I just have to keep my eyes and ears open so I'll notice it when it comes

---

16 We are happy to report that her book has been retitled *HUMOR: The Magic of Jeanne*. It has been reprinted and is currently available for sale.

along." I refrained from adding a famous line from Deputy Barney Fife. "I'm a trained noticer."

Right then, a man stepped up to shake hands and commented that he enjoyed the speech and was glad he came. Others were gathered at the table within earshot. "Oh, you don't have a book," I pointed out, noticing that he was empty-handed. "The association has provided them for you as a gift."

"That's okay," he responded. "If I take one of your books back to the room, my wife will have a fit. We're in the process of downsizing, and that's exactly the kind of junk we're throwing out."

His name badge told me his name was Don. That's right. The man who just referred to my book as "junk" was named Don. I gave him a big smile because, after all, I was Miss Congeniality.

But my brain was on the inside of my head trying to spit out, "Wouldn't you know his name would be Don?"

There's a line for everything.

Section Four

On the Road

The Secret of Success—Showing Up

June 2000, *City-County Magazine*

Graduating seniors will hear a hodgepodge of advice this month from an array of speakers. I'll add my two cents worth here. The first rule for success? Show up.

I checked into the hotel in Casper, Wyoming, after a long trip and immediately called room service. It was the middle of the afternoon, and I feared the restaurant was closed. A young-sounding male voice answered. "Do you have baked potatoes this time of the day?" I inquired, figuring, like most places, they did not. His answer surprised me. "Not usually, but I'm the executive chef. I can get you a baked potato if you want it."

Within thirty minutes, he delivered my order and couldn't have been much older than twenty.

"How does one get to be an executive chef at your age?" I asked.

"You get to be executive chef," he explained, putting my tray down, "when three people don't show up for work."

Sometimes, it's as simple as that.

Don't Mess with Philadelphia

July 2001, *City-County Magazine*

My suitcase on wheels acted like a young child pulling against me when I arrived at the Philadelphia airport. The plane was late, and my clothes were so wrinkled that I looked like I had just spent five days in flight. I was tired. My feet hurt. My bursitis shoulder ached, and my bags seemed to have doubled in size. The steady drum of airport announcements was getting on my nerves.

There were few passengers in the halls as I trudged toward the escalator. "Oh, great," I thought in disgust when I arrived at the top of what should have been moving steps. The small sign said, "Turned off." My shoulders sagged. I was going to have to pick up that heavy rolling cart and hanging bag and carry them down the steps.

Then I remembered. Near every escalator, there is an elevator.

Almost tripping myself when rearranged the wheels, I walked around the corner, dragging everything behind me. Yep, there it was, complete with a sign that reported, "Out of order."

My attention was diverted to a man who was leaning against the wall, watching me make these discoveries. The words on his shirt told me he worked at the airport.

"Well," I began. "I have just arrived in the City of Brotherly Love, and your escalator is turned off, and your elevator is out of order."

He did not alter his position against the wall as he snapped his fingers, pointed in my direction, and said, "The Liberty Bell is cracked, too."

Big Brother's Not the Only One Watching

October 2005, *Alamance Magazine*

When I was in one of my shapeup crazes, I put on my warm-up outfit the afternoon of a banquet in Minneapolis and went to check the meeting room before heading out to walk. The large facility was empty, and after seeing it, I had a question about the setup. Someone in the kitchen told me to wait in the ballroom while he contacted the person in charge.

Back in the large hall, I passed the time by counting tables, checking silverware, and straightening centerpieces. It's not in a speaker's normal contract, but it seemed like the neighborly thing to do.

Unbeknownst to me, I had a couple of companions. Two guys working on the spotlights were behind a one-way glass up in the audiovisual room at the back of the hall. Apparently, they had me under constant surveillance. (It's a good thing I don't take silverware.)

Minutes ticked away, and I was getting antsy because my exercise time was dwindling. I started stretching a little, reaching for my toes, if not actually touching them every time. Still, no one came.

In a few more minutes, I moved out of sight of the main doors, got on the floor, and started doing sit-ups. Up, down, up, down. I hit my limit quickly, struggling on the last ones— thirty-eeeeight, thirt-tee-ninnnne, forty!— and fell back onto the floor, exhausted.

Suddenly, a spotlight clicked its full beam directly on my body, sprawled out on the floor. A voice boomed through the sound system, "Come on, ma'am. You can do five more."

He Is Too a Nice Boy

September 2008, *Alamance Magazine*

And people ask where I find my speech material . . .

I was seated in a gate area at an airport, waiting to board a flight, when I became aware of a heated argument several rows behind me between a teenager and her mother. Having been a teenager albeit years ago and having had a teenager at one point, I recognized the tones immediately. Actually, I could have filled in for either of them and continued the argument without missing a beat, and I thought about it—just step over, tap one of them on the shoulder, and say, "If you want to take a break, I can handle this for you for a few minutes."

The situation was awkward. On purpose, I looked in another direction and faked disinterest, but I couldn't help but hear that they were arguing over a boy. No surprise there.

Suddenly, the teenager spat out, "You can take me on this trip, and you can take away my cell phone, but when we get home, I am going out with him. You can't stop me!"

I glanced around to see if anyone else was eavesdropping on this little scenario as I was and discovered that everyone in the gate area had become interested in anything in the opposite direction. People were gazing out the big windows, staring at books, looking at the ceiling, examining their fingernails. One man was untying and retying his shoes—anything to avoid looking over at the ugly scene.

A few seconds later, I discovered that we were all listening because we all burst out laughing at the same time. It was when the teenager hissed to her mother through gritted teeth, "He is too a nice boy! Why else would he be doing two hundred hours of community service?"

Searching for Final Four Tickets

March 2010, *Southeast Lifestyle*

The NCAA basketball tournament, known as "March Madness," never rolls around that I'm not reminded of a speech I gave in New Orleans on Tuesday morning, March 30, 1982. The date means nothing to you unless you are an avid basketball fan, as I am, or unless you are a fan of the basketball teams at either Georgetown University or UNC-Chapel Hill. My speech on that date was given the morning after the finals of the NCAA tournament when those two teams met for the championship.

The way the tournament is set up, of course, fans don't know if their team will be in the Final Four until the weekend before the games when the Elite Eight games are completed. When it became apparent the Tar Heels would be making the trip, thousands of Carolina fans in NC were trying to get transportation from North Carolina to Louisiana. Plane tickets were scarce, as were hotel rooms. Even more scarce were tickets to the final two games.

I had an airline ticket because my speech had been booked for months. I also had a room reservation at the convention hotel. I did not, however, have a ticket to the final game. All that week, friends who knew I would be in New Orleans asked repeatedly, "Have you gotten a ticket to the game?" "Are you going to the game?" "What are you going to do?" I was straightforward and told them like it was. "I've got an airline ticket to New Orleans. I've got a hotel room. And you don't know me very well if you think I won't get there and find a ticket to the game."

Take it from one who has been there. You don't know what awkward is until you stand on the streets of New Orleans. . . . in the French Quarter . . . a woman . . . by yourself . . . and shout, "Name your price!"

She Can't Do Anything Right

April 2010, *Southeast Lifestyle*

Administrative Professionals Day, previously known as Secretaries Day, will be celebrated this month. The actual day is always the Wednesday in the last full week in April. Consider yourself reminded. If applicable, it's not something you want to forget. It's one day a year when bosses honor the people who make them look good all year round.

One day won't be enough for a businessman I observed on a trip.

I had already boarded a flight out of Fort Lauderdale when the gate agent came down the aisle to talk to the man seated across from me. The agent told the passenger that upon checking his ticket, they discovered his reservation was for the twenty-fifth, the next day. The man reacted instantly and slammed his laptop shut. "That secretary! She can't do anything right!" His voice and his expletives carried halfway through the plane. "This is the last straw!" he finally spat out, stuffing the laptop in its case.

The gate agent assured him there was no problem. Seats were available on this and his connecting flight, just not the seats that he thought he had been assigned. He would need to step outside and talk to the agent. She left.

Out of the corner of my eye, I could see this fellow sitting there, staring at the seatback pocket in front of him, thinking. In a few minutes, he quietly gathered all his things and headed for the front of the plane. As he passed the door, the same flight attendant said, "Everything is being worked out, sir. Just leave your things on board while the gate agent switches your ticket to today."

Passengers within earshot fought back laughter when the man mumbled, "Well, actually, I've thought about it. I'm not supposed to be going until tomorrow."

His administrative professional could have told him.

Packing for a Family Trip?

Don't Forget Your Patience and a Sense of Humor

June 2010, *Southeast Lifestyle*

School is out. Family vacations are in. So, here is great advice about what to pack for your family trip. Heed . . . my . . . words.

If you're traveling with small children, pack a sense of humor and a large amount of patience. It's guar'an'teed. You'll need both.

The nonstop flight to Honolulu was almost nine hours, which is long for adults and a lifetime for children. Thankfully, my husband and I were in first class because of coupons and sat next to a window in a row that had six seats across. Two. Two. Two. A nine-year-old girl and her seven-year-old brother sat in the center, two seats across from us. Their parents had two seats on the other side of them and held their third child, a toddler, whose only seat was on someone's lap or on the floor of the plane.

The "someone's lap" changed constantly for nine hours. The family squirmed, played games, mumbled at one another, and took turns holding the toddler. Twice, the young child broke loose and ran to the back of the plane, his mumbling father in hot pursuit. All that time, the toddler didn't sleep a wink, despite the fact that mom had given him a big spoonful of cough syrup right before we lifted off. Obviously, he needed a bigger dose! Six hours into the flight, the passengers behind us tried to buy the rest of the bottle.

The flight was a constant fruit basket turnover with lots of that under-the-breath mumbling already mentioned. Every member of the family sat in every seat at some point and took turns trying to placate the baby. I mentioned to my husband that I was going to offer to hold the child for a little while. His look gave advanced meaning to the word "horrified."

As we approached our destination, several of us overheard the flight attendant ask the seven-year-old boy if it was his first trip to Hawaii. We all burst out laughing when he answered innocently, imitating words he must have heard several times. "No, ma'am. It's my second trip. And it's my Daddy's last trip."

The Cowboy Hat

October 2010, *Southeast Lifestyle*

A routine commuter flight changed into something more when an attractive, young, college-aged woman exited through the plane door. Her attire included a black cowboy hat with a feather, cowboy boots, and an extremely short skirt. (The "extremely short" assessment may be my age showing.) The baggage handlers working the flight cut their eyes in her direction as she started down the steps. One of them dropped a duffle bag.

Suddenly, the wind pulled the black hat off the beauty's head and sent it to the tarmac at the bottom of the steps. Before she could get to it, a stronger gust picked it up and sent it tumbling away.

Finally on solid ground, the passenger took off in the direction of her hat, but airline personnel quickly stopped her and escorted her back to safety, hatless.

Seconds later, a muscular, good-looking "hunk" of a guy on the ground crew came walking up, grinning, hat in hand. She was so grateful that she flung her arms around his neck and kissed him on the cheek, bringing hoots and whistles from his buddies and smiles from other passengers.

Not to be outdone, the rescuer suddenly dipped her backward and laid a big kiss right on her mouth. It reminded me of the famous Times Square photo of the sailor and nurse when World War II ended. Apparently, that nurse hadn't minded, and neither did this passenger. Louder hoots and hollers arose from all. Several applauded.

A woman about my age, standing next to me, whispered, "I'll think I'll drop my purse and see if I can get him over here."

Where Is the Cajun's Wharf?

November 2010, *Southeast Lifestyle*

The flight to Little Rock was pre-Blackberry, iPhone, and all the rest of them. Directions and information weren't instantly available by moving your thumbs around, and as we approached the airport, I could hear two flight attendants discussing where they wanted to eat dinner that night. They had heard of a restaurant called Cajun's Wharf but didn't know where it was located.

A nearby passenger chimed in that he had heard it was great, but he couldn't help them with directions. Realizing the passengers near them had overheard their conversation, the attendants looked from one to another of us, eyebrows arched in question. When they looked at me, I shrugged and mouthed, "Not from here." I could have told them where to get good barbecue in North Carolina, but we were landing in Arkansas. They asked several other people for the information to no avail.

Finally, one of the flight attendants clicked on the intercom and said, "Attention, ladies and gentlemen. If anyone on board knows the location of the restaurant in Little Rock named Cajun's Wharf, please raise your hand."

People chuckled, and several hands shot up. "Thank you," she said and proceeded up the aisle to get the information.

A woman in the row behind me touched the attendant on the arm when she passed and said, "Excuse me, Miss, but would you mind asking if anybody knows the name of a clean, cheap motel?"

A Quick Valentine U-Turn

February 2011, *Southeast Lifestyle*

Some men don't make a big deal over Valentine's Day gifts. Others do. Then, there are those who surely need to make a big deal. A dozen red roses wouldn't begin to help a man I heard about on one of my trips to Arizona.

A taxi driver in Phoenix was still chuckling when I got into his cab at the airport. It didn't take much prodding for him to tell me why. On an earlier airport run that day, he had picked up a couple with a lot of luggage. The man quickly got into the backseat, and the woman started telling the driver how to arrange the luggage in the trunk. Her husband wasn't interested in the process. He was already preoccupied looking at papers he had pulled from his briefcase.

The cabby went on to explain to me, "I put luggage in my trunk and out of my trunk all day long. I know my trunk, and I know luggage, but I did what she told me to do even though I knew it wouldn't work. I'm married, and I follow instructions well." He then caught my eye in his rearview mirror and grinned. "Of course, I loved it when we eventually had to take it out of the trunk and put it back in like I had it the first time. But just the two of us were working on it. Her husband never said a word. He just kept reading those sheets of paper."

When the luggage was finally stored in the trunk, the woman asked if she had time to run back and get something in the airport gift shop. Wouldn't take but a minute, she insisted. The husband, engrossed in his work, didn't seem to hear her ask, so the cab driver told her she had time. She took her billfold out of her shoulder bag, tossed it in the back seat next to her husband, and left. The driver returned to the front seat. The husband must have been aware that she had gone because he mumbled, "Go ahead and start the meter." The driver did.

Several minutes later, the back door slammed shut, so the driver eased away from the curb and drove off. As they approached the hotel twenty-five minutes later, the husband suddenly shouted, "Oh, no! My wife's still at the airport! We left without her! Turn around! Turn around!"

Can you say, "Fast, Gigantic U turn?"

Apparently, when the cab had been at the curb, the man had noticed the back door was partially open, and he slammed it shut. Bam! The driver thought the woman had returned and pulled away. Obviously, she hadn't.

They headed back to the airport as fast as the speed limit would allow, and the husband quickly started punching his wife's number into his cell phone, mumbling the whole time. "She's going to kill me. I'll never hear the end of this." Within seconds, her phone rang in her big purse on the back seat next to him. It was in the big shoulder bag. "I mean it. She's going to kill me. We ought to just start driving for the border."

Miles later, the passenger was still wringing his hands as he explained to the driver, "My mind was on a huge, important business deal. I didn't even notice she wasn't in the cab when we left. I can't believe this."

I wish I could have been there to see the "return." The driver said the woman was standing in the same spot where he had pulled up at the airport. Her arms were folded. She was not smiling. Her husband opened one of the back doors, but she slammed it shut, opened the front door, and got in beside the driver, slamming her door with authority.

"Not a word was spoken then or all the way to the hotel," the cabby went on to explain. "Not a word—probably not the case once they got to their room."

My opinion? That "huge, important business deal" would pale in comparison to the size of the Valentine's gift the guy would have to buy his wife that year.

Three Checked Bags

June 2011, *Southeast Lifestyle*

It's summer—vacation time. For many, that means air travel. Take it from a person who flies 20+ days a month—pack light, or take a credit card that is way under its limit. You'll need it if each member of the family checks several bags. Having to pay to check luggage is just another sign of the times.

During a recent trip, a flight attendant with "seniority" and I (also with "seniority") were discussing all the changes we've seen in air travel, especially in the past several years. When the new luggage policies came up, she was reminded of something that happened "pre-9/11" when she worked in reservations for the airline.

She explained that she left reservations to become a flight attendant because, in reservations, she gave the same information over and over and over. "Be at the airport at least an hour before your flight . . . No, there is not a movie shown on a thirty-five-minute flight." And, back then, "You are allowed three pieces of checked luggage."

My thought was that flight attendants also say the same thing over and over. "Have a nice day. Watch your step. Thank you for flying with us." I didn't mention it because she went on with her story.

One day, just when the reservation job got boring, an obviously angry passenger-to-be called and announced, "I wanna speak to your supervisor. Now!"

My new friend explained that part of her job was to try to ward off transferring callers to her supervisor, so she responded with what she had learned in reservation training. "Why don't you tell me the problem? Perhaps I can help you."

"No. I want to speak to someone in charge. You gave me the wrong information once, and it cost me a lot of money. I'm not talking to anybody but a supervisor!"

Still trying to head off directing the call to her supervisor, the reservationist-now-flight attendant asked, "What wrong information? How did it cost you money?"

"Well, here is exactly how it cost me money! I'm going on vacation next month. I called y'all last week and asked how much luggage I could take on my trip, and the woman told me plain as day, 'Three checked bags.' And I went out and bought three expensive red and black checked bags! Now my friend says I didn't have to do that at all. And that's why I want to talk to a supervisor!"

"At that point," the flight attendant said to me, "I transferred the call. That's why supervisors get paid more."

Have a good vacation. If you're flying, pack light.

The Delightful Mr. Breeney

June 2012, *Southeast Lifestyle*

Traveling by air this summer? Be aware that many things have changed in the last year.

Airlines are charging for everything from overhead space to particular seats, as well as what used to be routine snacks. Most of them are also charging us to check a bag, which simply means that most passengers are trying to carry more of their "stuff" on board. The result? If your boarding pass indicates that you are boarding in Group 3 or higher, get ready to check your carry-on bag at the plane door. I know this for a fact. I usually board in a group called "All Remaining Passengers."

It's a new day in airline travel, and as one who flies more than twenty days a month, I have some advice for you—keep a sense of humor and make it a priority to look for the delightful people around you. They're always there. You've just got to look for them.

Meet Mr. Breeney.

The passengers were already seated and ready for departure on a flight from Atlanta to Greensboro when two female gate agents escorted one more person down the jetway. I had noticed the elderly gentleman in a wheelchair in the gate area, but with their help, he was walking onto the plane. Slowly. Somehow, he had missed the preboarding time for those needing special assistance. He had a cane, which helped a little as he slid his feet along. The two gate agents helped even more. All three were smiling, and the elderly gentleman was clearly enjoying the attention.

At the door of the aircraft, the gate agents turned him over to the flight attendants. "Mr. Breeney needs a little help," one of them said. Just because the airlines have changed many policies doesn't mean the airline employees aren't still nice.

Two flight attendants immediately stopped what they were doing and turned toward Mr. Breeney. "Well, we're the people who can help him," one of them announced.

Mr. Breeney turned back toward the agents and said, "So, you're turning me over to them?"

"Yes sir, Mr. Breeney, they'll take care of you now."

"Oh'kay," Mr. Breeney answered nicely, emphasizing the "o" and sounding a little like someone from Minnesota. He said it with the rhythm of a slow "O'key Doe'key." Then he turned slowly toward his two new assistants with a big smile. "Whoever is supposed to take care of me . . . here I am." He was in hog heaven, grinning from ear to ear. Friendly, sharp-looking women were hovering around him, and he was basking in the attention.

"I'll GET IN FRONT OF YOU, MR. BREENEY," one of the flight attendants said, raising her voice as we often do around elderly people. She maneuvered into position while the second attendant stayed behind him. Mr. Breeney continued his tiny steps, slowly inching forward, still smiling. It quickly became evident that in the crowded conditions in the aisle of the plane, his cane was in the way, so one of his "helpers" adjusted. "WHY DON'T I HOLD YOUR CANE, MR. BREENEY," the flight attendant in front of him said. "AND YOU PUT YOUR HAND ON MY SHOULDER."

"Oh'kay," Mr. Breeney said again as he moved one hand to her shoulder. Then, the flight attendant behind him said, "OR, MR. BREENEY,

I'll PUT MY ARM UP HERE BY YOUR SIDE. YOU MIGHT WANT TO HOLD ONTO MY FOREARM OR MY ELBOW."

Mr. Breeney never broke his shuffle or lost the twinkle in his eye when he answered to the delight of all seated within hearing distance, "Oh'kay. You girls just show me the part . . . and I'll grab it."

Have a great summer. When you're traveling, be on the lookout for the delightful Mr. Breeneys amongst us.

Playing Zigzag Golf

July 2012, *Southeast Lifestyle*

When you're making summer vacation plans, don't forget all the great places we have in North Carolina. Our tourist dollars fit in as well here as they do in other states. Having traveled this state for years, I guarantee we've got it all, including an especially large supply of terrific golf courses.

The van driver from a resort in Florida picked up four men with golf bags and me at the Tampa airport. The golfers were chit-chatting because they knew each other, and I was just riding along, headed to the resort to speak at a convention. As we approached our destination, the driver gave us his usual general instructions about the resort. "Shuttle vans were available to take us from the lodging to the convention building. Complimentary coffee was in the lobby every morning. Room service was available if we preferred to eat in our rooms." At the end of his spiel, he added nonchalantly, "If you play golf, be careful of the alligators on the course."

He had the men's attention. Mine, too, and I wasn't even planning to play golf. After a few moments, it was evident the golfers weren't going to speak up, so I did. "Excuse me, did you say there are alligators on the golf course?"

"Oh yes, ma'am. You'll see them out there almost every day. Big ones, up to twelve feet long."

Twelve-foot-long alligators? On the resort's golf course? The four golfers still didn't say a word, but I sure did.

"Are you making this up?"

"No, ma'am. I most definitely am not. I'm warning y'all."

"Won't they attack people? In the movies, they run fast."

He nodded. "They do run fast, but only for thirty or forty yards. After that, they tire out."

I mumbled, "It would be the fastest fifty-yard dash I'd ever run."

At the next stoplight, the driver twisted around in his seat to tell me quite earnestly, "Well, you wouldn't really want to try to outrun 'em, ma'am. If an alligator is chasing you, the best thing to do is to zigzag. Cut left to right. Right to left. Left to right and so forth. Keep it up, and you'll be okay. Alligators don't zigzag well."

I couldn't believe his advice didn't produce comments from the four men. They were the ones who might be zigzagging, but they were just staring out the windows as though alligators weren't being discussed. I hadn't planned to step foot on the golf course anyway, and after hearing that information, you couldn't have pushed me out there.

The light changed, and he turned back to his driving, but by then, I was thinking about this whole thing. The driver's exact words were, "Alligators don't zigzag well." One doesn't have to be a rocket scientist to figure this out. They don't have to! All they have to do is run straight! If the humans are zigzagging from left to right, right to left, left to right in front of them, alligators can just stay on a straight path and, before long, snap! They win!

I had to speak up again. "I'm getting a mental picture of a man running lickety-split across a golf course, trying to get away from a twelve-foot alligator. His friends up at the clubhouse are screaming. 'Cut back and forth, Charlie! Zigzag!'"

The driver made eye contact with me in his rearview mirror. "Well, that's when the headline reads, 'Zigged when he should have zagged.'" No one laughed.

Minutes later, standing in line to check in at the resort, one of the golfers stepped up, tapped me on the shoulder, and said, "I'm praying for rain."

Yep, do consider vacationing right here in the great state of North Carolina. But if you don't . . . y'all have a good time playing golf in Florida, now. Ya hear?

Just Coffee, Please

September 2012, *Southeast Lifestyle*

Where do you get your material?" is a question I hear often. The truth is that sometimes I work on a story for years, and then other times, one falls out of the blue when least expected. All I have to do is be on the lookout for it—like the night I decided to order only a cup of coffee for dinner even though I wanted food.

I was seated by myself in the hotel's restaurant when a gum-chewing waitress, tablet in hand, sauntered up to my table. She produced a pencil from out of her hair and said without eye contact, "Whut you want?"

Those were her only words. Not "Good evening" or "Welcome. How are you?" Certainly not, "My name is Whatever. I'll be your server tonight." Just three words. "Whut . . . you . . . want?" Obviously, this person missed the training session on good customer service. But the way to my food was through her, so she had my attention. And, although I hadn't been specifically looking for a piece of material, I could sense one coming, could feel it in my bones.

I smiled and closed the menu. "I'll have the big Caesar salad, and I look forward to watching you prepare it at my table as the menu indicates you'll do."

She shifted her weight and looked off at some faraway place as she shook her head back and forth. "We don't do that anymore. We fix the Caesar salad in the kitchen now."

I nodded but wasn't about to let that pass.

"Why?"

Taking my menu and putting it under her arm, she finally looked me right in the eyes. "They told me that if we're fixing the salad at the table and we're mixing everything around in that big bowl, and some of the lettuce falls on the floor, and the customer sees it . . . there's nothing we can do with it then but throw it away."

Out of the blue. When you least expect it. Just coffee for supper.

Don't Walk in the Plaza After 9

October 2012, *Southeast Lifestyle*

Concerning any election cycle, let me paraphrase the line so many of us keyed in repeatedly in high school typing class, "Now is the time for all of us to come to the aid of our country by keeping a sense of humor."

Will Rogers, arguably the greatest humorist of all time, spent a lifetime illustrating a line that doesn't need paraphrasing, "The more things change, the more they stay the same." For example, he summed up the political conventions in 1928 by saying, "I tell you, if we got just one-tenth of what was promised to us in either the Democratic or Republican acceptance speech, there wouldn't be any inducement to want to go to heaven."

I ran into a fellow in Colorado who isn't a humorist by profession, but he sure was good at using humor to "sum up" what many were thinking as we watched the election process play out.

It was late when I arrived in Denver, and the cab ride to the downtown area was a long one. At one point, we rode by a park in the center of a number of large, white buildings. I didn't know where we were when we passed it, but a few minutes later, we pulled up in front of my hotel. Early the next morning, I asked the bellhop at the hotel about walking in that area.

"Oh, you're referring to Civic Plaza Park," he told me. "Civic Plaza is a small park surrounded by government buildings. It's not far from here, and it's a good place to walk."

You'll remember that Will Rogers also said, "He never met a man he didn't like." Well, he would have loved this bellhop. Being a small-town person in a very big city, I asked if it would be safe to walk in the Plaza so early in the morning. He glanced at his watch and nodded. "Sure, it's O.K. to walk there now." Then he gave me a great big grin and added, "But to be absolutely safe, ma'am, you'd better be gone by nine. That's when the politicians come in."

The next time you pass the house of good friends and see signs in their yard for "the other candidate," remember, "Now is the time for all of us to come to the aid of our country by keeping a sense of humor." Or, you might also recall the words my Daddy would have mumbled in the same situation. "Get some new friends."

Special Delivery to Cowpens

March 2013, *Southeast Lifestyle*

There's a commercial on TV right now that features a pig sitting on an airplane waiting for it to take off. He's buckled up in his seatbelt and is studying his cell phone, so he looks like any ordinary traveler, except—well—he's a pig. Actually, he's Maxwell, the pig seen in GEICO ads. I like him better when he's sitting on an airplane rather than squealing endlessly at the top of his lungs.

In the ad, two flight attendants come over, and one tells the pig sweetly, "It's time to power down your little word game." The other one says that she's sure his friends will understand. It's a cute commercial, but GEICO keeps its eyes on the prize—getting us to use their app.

Maxwell politely tells the flight attendants that he's just paid his bill using the GEICO app. He then proceeds to tell them all the things he can do with the app. As the flight attendants walk away, one says to the other, "I'll believe that when pigs fly." This commercial is airing often, but if you've missed it, the pig turns to a man across the aisle and says incredulously, "Okay. Did she seriously just say that?"

The mere sight of a pig sitting with other passengers on a plane is funny, but it's not farfetched to me. Sometimes, pigs ride in cabs, too. And taxi drivers also know how to keep their eyes on the prize.

I asked a taxi driver in Spartanburg, South Carolina, what was the funniest thing that had happened in his cab. He mulled the question around in his mind a few seconds and drawled, "It coulda been that time I had a hawg as a fare."

"A hog? As in . . . a big pig?" I asked.

"Yep, a hawg. H-A-W-G," he spelled. "Hawg."

He had my attention.

He told me that a fellow needed to get a "hawg" down to his brother in Cowpens, South Carolina. His truck was broken down, and a cab seemed like the best solution.

My driver "hadn't much wanted to do it," but then he started thinking and decided that "a fare's a fare."—sort of like GEICO keeping their eyes on the prize.

Apparently, it took the two men working together to get the huge hog into the backseat. It had a typical big snout and pointy, floppy ears. It also had a stubborn streak and didn't want to ride in a cab. The animal spread its feet up against the door frame and fought them as both men pushed from behind. Getting nowhere, one of the men went around to the other side and tried to pull "Porky" into the cab, holding on to what, I don't know. But with one pulling from the front and the other pushing from the rear, the men finally got the hog on the floor in the backseat of the taxi and, as my driver put it, "Me and the hawg was off to Cowpens."

Once they started moving along, the hog managed to bumble up onto the backseat. Perhaps it wanted to see the passing scenery. It alternated between breathing on the back of the driver's neck and looking out the windows. People in other lanes were hitting their brakes and veering toward ditches. After a few miles, the driver pulled up to a traffic light and stopped.

A woman in the next lane rolled down her window and started pounding on the outside of her door to get the driver's attention. "Hey, mister! Mister!" When he looked her way, she pointed and shouted, 'There's a hog in your backseat."

"I wanted to shout back, 'Are you sure?'" the driver told me. "But the lady wasn't being funny. She honestly didn't think I knew where the hot air being snorted on my neck was coming from."

I asked him if he would do it again, and his response was quick.

"Nope. Never again," he said, shaking his head. "I don't want any more hawgs in the backseat of my cab or up front with me either."

I leaned forward and put it as delicately as I could. "It messed up your cab, didn't it?"

"Naw, that wasn't it at all," he explained. "The thing is . . . hawgs don't tip."

Then, this clever driver caught my eye in the rearview mirror and grinned. "But ladies do."

Keep your eyes on the prize!

Trouble on the Panama Bridge

May 2013, *Southern Lifestyle*

The driver of the resort van at one of the Florida beaches was a young man I'll call Sam. I was his only passenger to the Panama City airport early one morning. We struck up an immediate conversation, and he told me he liked the job because he was basically outdoors and he was meeting interesting people. Then he grinned and caught my eye in the mirror. "But I won't do this job forever. My mother says I need to learn responsibility and patience and grow up a little before I go to college again." (I caught the word "again," and as a mother who's "been there," I smiled.)

When we crossed over the long bridge that connects the beaches to Panama City, we passed a car that had just stalled on the opposite side. Cars were beginning to pull up behind it. The minute he saw the situation, Sam picked up his two-way radio.

"Fifty-two to base."

After a short pause, a woman's perky voice responded. "Good morning! Come in, 52."

He cut to the chase. "We've just passed a car in trouble on the bridge. Please call the Highway Patrol and let them know."

She was hesitant. "Call the Highway Patrol?"

"Yes. Stalled car. The Highway Patrol will take care of it," he responded matter-of-factly, explaining to me, "We're not allowed to use our cell phones, so we contact the office on the two-way radio."

"Ten-four," the woman suddenly said through the little box, startling both of us. Sam shook his head and caught my eye in the rearview mirror. "She's new. The drivers have told her a hundred times not to say 'ten-four,' but she's seen too much television." (I thought maybe she'd seen everybody's favorite deputy, Barney Fife, speak into a microphone, "Mayberry unit No.1. Uh, all units. Roger and over. Over and out. Over and under. Ten-four. Four-ten. Ten-four. Bye." But didn't say anything. The driver was too young.)

He went on to explain. "We always call for help in this type of situation. A stalled car on that bridge will back up traffic for miles. And this time of morning? With everyone going to work? It'll be a mess."

I nodded. Seemed reasonable to me. A few minutes passed, and "Base" returned, almost in a frenzy. "Base to 52! Base to 52!" Come in, 52!" Sam attempted to respond, but she interrupted him. "Are you there, 52?"

Sam sighed but said politely, "I'm here." He bounced the heavy receiver in one hand as he drove along, waiting for her to speak. "I've got the Highway Patrol on the other line. They want to know which side of the bridge the stalled car is on."

"The side toward the beaches, from the airport."

"Ten-four." Click. She was gone. Sam shook his head and mumbled. "She just can't get it."

We rode on, but in a few minutes, "Base" was back again. "Fifty-two! Come in, 52!"

Sam reached toward the dashboard. "I'm in."

"The Highway Patrol says it's not their responsibility. It's the city police's."

Sam rolled his eyes at me and exhaled. "Then please call the city police," he said, his patience beginning to waver slightly. "And remember, we don't say 'ten-four.' Just say, 'O.K.' or 'Got it.'"

A few seconds passed, and then she said, "Oh, darn. I'm sorry. I keep forgetting. From now on, 'O.K.' or 'Got it.'"

On we rode. But before long, the sound of the two-way system again filled the air. "Fifty-two? Are you still there?" Sam smiled and mumbled, "Where else would I be?" but said, "I'm here."

"I hate to bother you, Fifty-two, but the city police want to know what kind of car it is. I guess they want to make sure to help the right people." Sam opened his mouth to answer, but before he could, she blurted, "If you don't know what kind of car it is, do you know the color? That might help 'em find it."

Sam's shoulders drooped slightly, and he rolled his head toward his window for a split second, continuing to bounce the receiver in his hand before moving it back toward his mouth. At that point, he again exhaled deeply, calmed himself, and said deliberately, "Tell them . . . that on the bridge, there will be a line of traffic that is not moving. The car in trouble . . . will be at the front."

There was no response, and Sam said to me, "She's thinking." And as sure as I live and breathe, seconds later, the woman said, "O.K. Got it! Ten-four!"

When we arrived at the airport, I gathered my luggage and tipped Sam, of course. But before I rolled my little suitcase away, I had to say, "Tell your mother you're doing fine."

Relax. In most cases, they're doing just fine.

Don't Talk to Strangers

July 2013, *Southeast Lifestyle*

It's what we all preach repeatedly to our children and grandchildren. "Don't talk to strangers." We do so because it's good advice. As a matter of fact, after watching all the regular news stories on TV, I'd say "excellent advice." But as a person who makes her living traveling day after day from one side of this country to another, I would miss out on a lot of fun if I didn't talk to strangers. As a humorous speaker, if I keep to myself during travel, not only will I miss out on fun but also on great material for speeches.

I was seated next to a cordial, yuppie-type young man on a flight back into what I refer to as "The Greensboro, High Point, Winston-Salem Regional, Triad, Piedmont, International Airport." (Local people my age still call it "thuh new airport.") I'll call him Dave. During polite chit-chat, he told me he grew up in nearby Asheboro, but at that time lived in Forsyth County. I asked him a typical airline conversation question. "Who are you with?" He named one of the biggest companies in the nation, based in Winston-Salem.

"Wow," I said. "That's great. What do you do there?" He recited his title with the company. My jaw dropped. All I could do was nod my head up and down. I had no idea what he was talking about, but

I know a little humor when I hear it. After a lull in our conversation, just to make sure I had heard it correctly, I asked, "Would you repeat what you do slowly so I can write it down?"

That brought a big smile because his small-town upbringing knew where I was headed. I got out a pen and tablet, and he slowly repeated what he did while I wrote.

He said, "I'm the senior technical manager of corporate information systems audit, responsible for microcomputers, decision support systems, and data communications network audit."

By then, I was attempting to stifle my laughter, and to be honest, he was chuckling a little too. An episode from the *Andy Griffith Show* also flashed through my mind. The one titled "Goober the Executive." It is the one when beloved Goober is overly impressed because a salesman's title is Vice President in Charge of Regional Sales for Northeast North Carolina for the Emblem Oil Company of El Paso, Texas. At least that title could be figured out.

I looked away from Dave and out the window while I mulled his answer a little longer. Then I put up my tablet and turned back in his direction. "Tell me something, Dave. When your mother goes to her church circle meeting down in Asheboro, and her friends ask her what little Davy is doing now, what does she say?"

He grinned and nodded in understanding. Then he answered in a clear, small-town North Carolina way of talking. "She smiles and says with great pride, 'Little Davy has a reaaaal gooooood job in Winston-Salem.'"

If you're traveling this summer and it's appropriate, talk to strangers. I'll guarantee ya'll have a reaaaal gooooood time.

Wise Like Will Rogers

November 2013, *Southeast Lifestyle*

"This country has come to feel the same when Congress is in session as when the baby gets hold of a Hammer." Will Rogers

Will Rogers sure had a humorous way of putting into words what the American public was thinking. Most of his quotes still ring true today. I met a young man in Washington, D.C., who might not have the talent of Will Rogers, but he got to the point in his own style and with his own words.

One of the challenges of submitting a story for a magazine is that much can happen between when the column is submitted and when it's published. The due date for this particular article was the middle of October. At that time, the country seemed to be falling apart. The government was shut down. Political name-calling had gotten way beyond ugly. Paraphrasing Sheriff Andy Taylor in *The Andy Griffith Show*, people weren't "acting right," and most of us had been taught, as Andy taught Opie, to "Act like somebody."

Here's my take on the state of the country. Will the country have defaulted by the time you read this? I don't know. Will one political party have "defeated" the other and declared victory in words that will ensure further long-term division among Americans? I have no idea. Will many of the current politicians be "turned out" by voters in the 2014 elections, or will they be re-elected in landslides? Well, for Pete's sake. I'm a humorist. A physical education major. I have no idea what will happen in the next election, which means I know about as much as the "experts." But as sure as the proverbial statement, "A twenty-five pound bag of flour will make a big biscuit" (as we do love to say in the South), whenever the current crisis in Washington. D.C. is "solved," another one will take its place.

But wait! Good news! Each political crisis ensures you and I will have at least a few chuckles when kernels of humor pop through the manure spread in the political garden. I like that last sentence. Husband Left Brain said there ought to be a better word to use than "manure." I told him there is, but the reader could substitute it. Maybe "fertilizer?" Maybe not.

I'm reminded of the time I gazed upward at nine clocks on the wall behind the registration desk of the Sheraton Hotel in Washington, D.C. I'd seen similar clocks in other public places. Each gave the time from a different location around the world, with the hour hands varying according to particular time zones. Washington, D.C., five o'clock; Chicago, four o'clock; San Francisco, two o'clock, etc.

That day in the Sheraton, the hour hands on all nine clocks were correct to the best of my knowledge. I had to guess what hour it was in places like Shanghai and Dubai, but in general, the hour hands looked correct. With those looking accurate, a person might have expected the minute hands to also be correct. Chicago, four fifteen; Los Angeles, two fifteen, for example. They weren't. The minute hands on the clocks behind the registration desk weren't "in sync." They gave times that were not possible, such as "Washington, five fifteen," "Dallas, four twenty," and "San Francisco, two forty-five." Say what?

While I studied the clock "situation," the young desk clerk was busy checking me in on his computer. When he handed me my room key, I smiled and nodded toward the wall behind him. "You might ask the maintenance people to check your clocks. The times aren't right."

As noted, I love the quotes of Will Rogers, arguably the country's greatest humorist. If ever a person had a way with words, it was he. But this young man at the registration desk in the Sheraton also had a way with words. When I told him the clocks were wrong, he didn't even glance over his shoulder. He just grinned back and said, "Ma'am, you're in Washington, D.C. Everything's screwed up here."

Amen, brother. The baby's got the hammer!

Hand It to Michigan

January 2014, *Southeast Lifestyle*

By now, I suspect that all the usual New Year's resolutions that are going to be made have been made and possibly even broken. If you're still thinking about making some, here's a simple, easy, cost-efficient resolution you may want to consider: Look for humor every day. It's everywhere, it's free and it's fun. I'll start the ball rolling . . . .

Michigan is like a hand!

The state of Michigan is shaped like a hand. Most of us know that. It's the way we learned it in grammar school. I speak in the state often and have noticed they also take this "hand thing" to the next level. Any time I ask people from Michigan where they live in the state, the response is the same. They shift their weight, hold up a hand, palm facing outward, and patiently explain, "Michigan is like a hand. I live over here in the little finger," they might say, pointing to the exact spot on that little finger. Or, "I live in the middle of the palm, right here." (Tap, tap in the palm.)

I mentioned this in a show in Kalamazoo. When the show was over, a woman came up and said, "Jeanne, you hit the nail on the head about us saying 'Michigan is like a hand.' We all do that."

"Oh, I know. But in your defense," I told her, "the state does look like a hand, and when you point to a place on your hand, we know exactly where you live. It works." Then I bent my left arm at the elbow, taking my forearm straight across my body from left to right . . ."I live in North Carolina. North Carolina is like a forearm. I live right here." I pointed to where I thought the Triad might be located. She started smiling, so I kept going.

"My grandsons live in Georgia. Georgia is like a pot roast." We made eye contact and, at the same time, pointed toward our hips and started laughing.

"Then she continued, "But let me tell you something funny that happened in connection to this, Jeanne. I grew up in the thumb of Michigan." And I'll be doggone if she didn't raise her right hand and point to the bottom of her thumb. "Right here." (Tap. Tap.)

"One time, I went down South to visit a college friend of mine," the lady continued. "She had to work and took me to her club to spend the day. I was in a chaise lounge by the pool, under an umbrella, reading, when two women whom I think belonged to that club came into the pool area. They had all sorts of paraphernalia to spend a day by the pool. From behind my sunglasses, I saw them spot me when they came in and then watched them raise their eyebrows and shrug to say, 'Who is she?' 'I don't know.'"

She continued. "With all the empty chaise lounges around the deck, they chose to set up headquarters for the day with one empty chair between us. We all nodded cordially. They lathered up with sunscreen, got out their books, and, before long, settled in, but they kept cutting their eyes at me, trying to figure out who . . .? I could see all this from behind my sunglasses. I kept reading.

Finally, lack of information got the best of them. The one nearest me leaned in my direction across the empty chaise lounge and started chit-chatting. With my Michigan, non-Southern accent, it didn't take her long to say, 'Well, you're not from around here, I can tell. Where did you grow up?' I had a book in my hands, Jeanne, so I just said, I grew up in the thumb of Michigan. No hand up. No pointing toward my thumb."

"Oh, noooo. I'm soooo sorry," the woman gushed with her thick Southern accent, her brow wrinkling in obvious, great concern. "But I'm soooo proud of you for getting out."

"Jeanne, I had no idea what she was sorry about," my new friend said. "Maybe she thought Michigan was frozen year-round. We went back to reading, but in a few minutes, I heard the one on the end away from me, lean to her friend and whisper, 'Where'd she say she's from?'"

"The first one said, 'Shsss. Don't mention it again. Poor thing grew up in a slum in Michigan.'"

Need a New Year's Resolution? Look for humor. It's everywhere. It's free, and it's fun.

You're Gonna Shrink

March 2014, *Southeast Lifestyle*

It's March. For those of us who love college basketball, that means it's time for the NCAA men's and women's basketball tournaments, known as March Madness. It also means several weeks of watching young men and women play their hearts out, trying to advance with each win. I know only the Elon University student-athletes personally. All other teams' players I meet via television. But I share a common bond with many of them. No, not athletic skills. At this point in my life, I'd need a good running start to jump over a pencil. My common denominator with many of these young men and women is height. Though we may never meet, we have many of the same experiences on a daily basis. I hope they enjoy all the predictable "tall comments" as much as I do.

"How tall are you?" "How's the weather up there?" "Were you born tall?" Trust me, I've heard my share of the comments people say to those of us who are taller. As a matter of fact, I've included funny stories about these comments in my speeches for more than fifty years. If I had to, I could actually give an entire program on being 6'2" in the seventh grade at age thirteen. The amazing thing is that I'm now seventy, and even at this age, height comments still pop up. Maybe it's because I smile a lot, and people sense I'll enjoy their comments.

I can be walking in airports, and strangers call out, "Lady, who do you play for?" I know who they are talking to. "Can you dunk the basketball?" And my all-time favorite, "How long does it take you to sit down?" I have a tall friend who got so tired of people asking him if he played basketball that he started saying, "No, I didn't. I used to be a jockey, but the big horse died."

However, I know better than to say I've heard every comment about being tall. Once we say we've heard every comment, it's a matter of time until we learn we haven't.

I'm now seventy and, quite frankly, enjoying the attention. I also enjoy crossing paths with all types of personalities, and I make it a point to like them all—even the blunt and grouchy.

After a speech not long ago, two shorter women made a beeline up to me, practically moving others out of their path. We all know people like the one who spoke first. Miss Personality, as I'll call her, had no hint of a smile. Instead, she had a "bulldog" expression that said, "I'm going to speak my mind, and you're going to listen." She opened the conversation with a raspy voice and drawled, "Jean'neee."

I can sound as Southern as anyone else. I drawled back, "Yea'uhsss."

"We loved your speech," she said quickly, her wrinkled brow telling me there would be a "but" coming. She was just getting the "We loved your speech" part out of the way. I was correct. She continued. "But we don't want you to worry anymore about being tall." The second woman seemed more pleasant but nodded in agreement.

The comment surprised me, and I couldn't help but smile. "Wait a minute. Wait a minute. If my speech came across to you that at 'this age,' I'm not worried about being tall, it's not going over as I thought it was. If I woke up short, I'd have to write a whole new routine."

I thought that was a cute enough comeback, but Miss Personality didn't react at all. Clearly, she was not amused. She had something to say, and by golly, she wanted to get to it. "We don't know anything about routines, Jeanne," she responded matter-of-factly. "What we came up here to tell you is (shaking her finger in my direction) any day now, you'll start to shrink. You live long enough, and you'll be a normal-size person."

As though I were not standing there and couldn't hear them, they began to discuss in front of me how long they thought I needed to live to be a "normal-size person."

The quieter friend lowered her voice and gave her opinion, glancing at me but talking to her buddy. "I think she'd have to live to be a hundred and seventeen to ever work her way down to normal size." Miss Personality didn't agree. She shook her head and continued to stare right at me. "Noooo. I don't think so," she said. Then she stepped back and sized me up and down slowly from head to toe before she settled the matter and announced for all to hear, "I think if she lives to be ninety-five, she'll be five-foot-two."

Five-two? Um, that's a big drop. A person goes from six-foot-two down to five-two? I'd say a very big drop. At that point, I felt I needed to insert myself into their conversation. "Excuse me, but for my own information, I have to know. Could it happen all at once? Could I be walking in a mall and, whoosh, drop down twelve inches? Could my clothes appear to move along without an apparent person in them? Or will I wake up one morning and my clothes won't fit at all? The sleeves on my jackets will be way down below my hands?"

Miss Personality seemed taken aback for a split second, but she recovered quickly and snapped, ''That's not the way it happens at all. Your body shrinks . . . but your arms stay the same."

Good luck to all basketball players at every level who make it to their respective "Big Dances," especially the tall players, a.k.a. "the bigs." I'll be watching y'all with special interest because we share a bond of similar experiences. Play your hearts out and enjoy the month. And laugh the first time someone shakes a finger at you and says, "Any day now, you'll start to shrink."

You gotta love people—even the blunt and grouchy.

My Achy, Breaky Heart

April 2014, *Southeast Lifestyle*

April is National Humor Month. Most people don't know that, but relax. There's no gift-swapping associated with it. National Humor Month is a reminder that humor is everywhere and can be found daily, year-round. All we have to do is be on the lookout for it. If this month's story doesn't illustrate that, nothing ever will.

The background music in a major airport had just started playing "Achy Breaky Heart" when I went into the women's restroom. You know the song, "Don't tell my heart, my achy, breaky heart . . ." Love it or not, most of us recognize the song that was written by Don Von Tress and made famous by Billy Ray Cyrus. (Yep, *her* daddy.)

This particular airport ladies' room was typical. A long line of sinks stretched in front of an equally long mirror. Stalls lined up on the opposite wall. What was not typical was that the restroom was practically empty—usually, women had to wait in line. This time, there was only one woman about my age, which made her possibly a grandmother. She was at the far end of the room, at the last sink, and was dancing to the music as she watched herself in the mirror.

Having been to more than my share of Southern wedding receptions in the preceding ten years, I saw that she was line dancing by herself in front of the last sink. "You can tell the world you never was my girl / You can burn my clothes when I'm gone." Step forward, step back, forward and back, skip, turn. "You can tell my arms to go back to the farm / You can tell my feet to hit the floor." She was adding extra wiggles and hand movements with her dance steps and was waving her arms here, there, and yonder, keeping time with the music and all the while continuing to watch herself. She was oblivious to the fact that I had come into the room.

I didn't know whether to rush over, grab her shoulders, shake her, and comfort her, "Get a grip! Don't let airline travel get you down!" Or, go back to the concourse and find more women to join us for a group line dance. I did neither. I stood there and kept watching. The music continued, and so did she, puckering up her mouth at the mirror on, "You can tell my lips, to tell my fingertips / They won't be reaching out for you no more."

Several times in this song, there are places when Billy Ray Cyrus and the backup group sing, "Whooooooo." When that rolled around, this lady put her hands on her waist and shook her hips. Then, she started turning to her right, still dancing, as she looked over her left shoulder at the mirror. The song and her gyrations continued, surely with more exaggeration than if she had known she was being watched. The song kept going. "But don't tell my heart, my achy breaky heart / I just don't think he'd understand." By the time she got to another "Whooooooo," she was shaking her backside full speed toward the mirror. I thought she was getting ready to "moon" herself in the mirror and started to leave.

No "mooning" occurred, thank goodness. After that short stop, she started turning to her right again, suddenly saw me and screamed. I screamed back because she startled me, and then we both went into the "Oh my gosh, you scared me to death!" phase, both of us laughing.

"Are you okay?" I finally asked.

"Oh, sure. No problem. I'm just trying to get the water to turn on."

My thought was that she didn't travel often, so I proceeded to give her the benefit of my travel savvy. "Its motion activated. Put your hands under the faucet. That triggers the water."

Her look back at me was priceless. She could have said, "What do you think I've been doing?" But she simply smiled and swept her hand toward the sink as she stepped out of the way. "Be my guest. You do it."

The music kept going in the background. "You can tell your ma I moved to Arkansas / You can tell your dog to bite my leg."

I stepped over, balancing my big purse on my left shoulder, and waved my right hand under the faucet. Nothing. I tried it again with longer, bigger circles. It was then that I understood what she had been doing with her hands. Still, no water. "You have to hit it just right," I explained, putting my purse down in the sink to the left so I could use both hands. The water at *that* sink cut on immediately and gushed into my purse! We bumped into each other, trying to get my purse out. She quickly put her hands under the spout in that sink, but by then, the water had cut off and wouldn't come back on.

With my purse draining on the floor, I turned my attention back to the first sink, determined to make it work. As I circled my hands around in the sink bowl, I started dancing too. I couldn't help it. Catchy tune. "Or you can tell my eyes to watch out for my mind / It might be walking out on me today." No water.

That's when this savvy traveler assured her new friend, "I deal with this all the time when I travel. Sometimes, you have to back away from the sink and approach it again, full-on. So let me get as far away from the sink as I can," I explained and backed into the stall behind us until my legs touched porcelain.

"Here I come! Get out of the way!" I shouted and started marching out of the stall with exaggerated stomps toward the sink and mirror. After three stomps, the toilet behind me automatically flushed.

That threw both of us into gasping for breath laughter. Just then, two women came into the restroom, saw us, and backed out!

"But don't tell my heart, my achy breaky heart / I just don't think he'd understand."

The song was winding down when I got back to the sink, and by then, I was dancing as much as she had been. "And if you tell my heart, my achy breaky heart / He might blow up and kill this man."

She was bent double laughing, so I began to show off—I have a tendency to do that—really wiggling my hips in time with the music. When the song hit the last "Whooooooo," I shook my whole body like a dog getting out of a pond and threw my hands up in the air.

The woman almost fell over my purse as she stumbled and grabbed my elbow. "Don't throw your right arm up! The paper towels will shoot out!"

Happy Humor Month!

You Don't Sell Vanilla Milkshakes?

July 2014, *Southeast Lifestyle*

It's July. It's hot. Most of us are consuming sweet tea, ice water, lemonade, iced coffee, and an assortment of other cold beverages. May I suggest that it might also be time for a good, old-fashioned, honest-to-goodness milkshake? I had one not long ago, and I'm still smiling about it. Of course, it's the way we choose to look at things, and I looked at what happened through humorous eyes.

My travels put me on a toll road between South Florida and Orlando. In Florida, their toll roads have Service Plazas between the two directions of traffic. This is so travelers can pull off, get whatever they need, and get back on the road without going through another toll. These plazas are the size of small towns. If you need something, it's usually there. On this trip, I pulled into one such place to get gas and a bottle of water. (I was dieting a tinsy bit.)

Inside the plaza was an assortment of fast-food chains, most with people waiting in line. One place didn't have a line, and I could see from a distance that it had "MILKSHAKES!" Forget the water. Forget the diet. I made a beeline in that direction and stepped up to the counter. At the same time, a family of four got there. The young couple's children were about five and six. We did the "You go ahead" thing until the father said, "It's going to take us a few minutes. Please go first." I thanked him and stepped forward.

When the young woman behind the counter asked if she could take my order, I didn't hesitate. "I'll have a vanilla milkshake."

She said, "We don't sell vanilla milkshakes."

I glanced up at the sign above her head that clearly touted, "MILKSHAKES!" "Oh, you're out of vanilla milkshakes?"

"No. We're not out of vanilla milkshakes. We don't sell vanilla milkshakes." She saw me glance up at the sign again and explained. "We sell chocolate milkshakes. We sell strawberry milkshakes. But we don't sell vanilla milkshakes."

"Okay. I'll have a chocolate milkshake." I paid her and happened to glance over at the father, who nodded slightly. He said, "That sounds good."

Our eyes followed the teenager as she stepped over to a workstation and pulled out one of those typical tall stainless-steel cups used to make milkshakes. She put it in place on a piece of equipment, pulled down a handle, and out came what appeared to be a vanilla milkshake. The father and I exchanged quick glances. He commented, "Looks like you're going to get your vanilla shake after all."

"I guess so. They must have changed the machine when she was on break."

When the tall cup was filled with vanilla, she stepped to her left and put the cup under a handle that she pulled down. Out came a big squirt of chocolate. She did this twice, but the second time, it sounded like sucking through a straw at the bottom of a drink. The chocolate was almost empty.

The man and I exchanged glances again and smiled slightly. The young woman stepped to her left, put the tall cup under a tall milkshake mixer, and turned it on. Whirrrrrrr. Seconds later, she poured out my chocolate shake and put it on the counter in front of me. "One chocolate milkshake."

I cut my eyes toward the young father. By then, he was grinning from ear to ear and shaking his head. We were both wondering, "Why . . .?"

I shook my head, smiled, picked up my chocolate shake, and turned to leave.

Then I remembered. One of the reasons people my age are still here is to enlighten the youth! I turned back to the counter. Making sure to smile as I spoke, I got her attention. "Excuse me." She stepped back in my direction.

"Have you ever thought," I began slowly, being as nice as possible and glancing at the machine with all the vanilla. "And please know I'm not criticizing. I'm just wondering. Have you ever thought that if you filled the cup with vanilla and then—right then—stopped!—that you would have a vanilla milkshake?" She shifted her weight a little and practiced patience. "Ma'am, as I have said several times, we don't sell vanilla milkshakes."

"I know that. You've told me that, and I understand what you said, and you said it very nicely. But the next time you're on break or have some time on your hands, think about it. If you don't squirt chocolate or strawberry flavoring in the vanilla, you will have a vanilla milkshake. It's just the difference of a squirt or two."

Our eyes locked for a few seconds, and then I saw the lightbulb turn on in her head. Looking back on it, I think a little glow even came out of her ears. She got it! By Jove, she got it!

But there are always two sides to every issue. She leaned over the counter toward me to explain hers. "Ma'am, it's all computerized now. You're correct about the squirts, but there is no place on the cash register to mash down for a vanilla milkshake. So, we don't sell vanilla milkshakes."

As Kenny Rogers sings, "You gotta know when to fold 'em." I whispered, "You're certainly right. I didn't take that into consideration. In my day, if someone wanted a vanilla shake, we would have just charged the same as the chocolate shake and left the chocolate squirts out. I see why it won't work now. Thank you for explaining it."

I took my chocolate shake and turned to go, making eye contact with the father. He was holding back a chuckle as he stepped to the counter. I could sense she was watching me as I walked away.

A few feet later, I stopped to take the paper wrapper off the top of my straw. By then, the two children were chanting, "We want a chocolate milkshake! We want a chocolate milkshake! Daddy, please, get us a chocolate milkshake." He and his wife nodded in agreement, and he said to the young woman, "We'll have four chocolate milkshakes."

And I'll be doggone if she didn't say, "We're out of chocolate milkshakes."

Then she stood a little straighter, looked past him at me, and announced proudly with a smile, "But I can get you four vanilla milkshakes."

Don't Take the Hotel Key or the TP

August 2015, *Southeast Lifestyle*

As a person who makes her living traveling year-round, I feel obliged to offer a couple of pieces of advice for this last month of summer travel. Here's the first one: Wherever we travel, we represent the great state we live in. In my case, it's North Carolina. Please be careful what you take out of hotel rooms. It comes back to reflect on all of us. Little soaps? Tiny shampoo bottles? A shower cap or two? Sure. Toss 'em in your bag. Hotels expect those to be gone. (From your room. Not the carts in the halls.) But rolls of toilet paper? Really, people. Quoting Sheriff Andy Taylor, "Act like somebody."

Waiting to go through airport security recently for a flight back to NC, I saw a TSA person open a lady's rolling cart, and wah-la! There, squeezed in next to her clothes, were two unopened toilet paper rolls from her hotel.

I'm not saying for sure that she "took," as in "stole" the TP rolls. There's always the chance that she went to the front desk and said, "We're out at home. It would save me a trip to the store if I could purchase a couple of toilet paper rolls from the hotel." Sure, she could have done that. But none of us in line behind her at security thought that to be the case. Not the way we were exchanging glances when the

TSA agent put each roll out on the table for all to see while she poked around in the passenger's bag. People laughed and started nudging others as they nodded toward the rolls on display. The passenger was obviously embarrassed but laughing as well. She was caught red-handed and knew it. A man in line mumbled, "Think she's a toilet paper salesperson?" I talked to her later. Yes, she was coming home to NC. How embarrassing? More embarrassing was when I told my husband about it. He said, "She should know better than to take toilet paper from the hotel room unless she's driving home." I think he was joking.

Here's another piece of valuable advice. If your hotel still uses a key that goes into a hole and has to be turned as opposed to a computer card, don't take the hotel room key. It can come back to haunt you.

I was at the Executive Inn Riverfront Hotel in Paducah, Kentucky, to speak at a luncheon. After the event, my client was to take me to the nearby airport. That morning, I asked the hotel people for a late checkout time so I could go back to my room and change clothes after my speech. They couldn't give it to me because another group was checking in. They had to clean the rooms. Not a problem. I would have been happy to check my bags with a bellhop and change them at the airport, but my client suggested that I store my bags in her room and change them there before we left. Sounded good to me.

The Executive Inn Riverfront didn't have electronic key cards at that point. They still had those older, beautiful, flat brass keys alluded to earlier. My client was more southern than I was. When she gave me the brass key to her room, she drawled, "Now, puh'lease, don't lose this key, Jeanne. I've already lost two of 'em, and I would be mor'ti'fied—ab'so'lut'ly mort' ti' fied—if I had to go back to the desk and get a third one." I assured her I wouldn't lose the key. I didn't want to be responsible for throwing anyone into an "absolutely mortified" state.

After the luncheon, I quickly changed clothes in her room, got my bags, met her in the lobby, and we headed to the airport, talking nonstop. A short time later, I was sitting on a packed commuter flight. The door of the plane was shut, and we were waiting to pull away from the gate.

Suddenly, someone started banging on the airplane door from the outside. The flight attendant looked through a little window, turned the big handle, and opened the door. A gate agent came on board, picked up the PA system, and announced with authority, "Will passenger Jeanne Robertson ring your flight attendant call button. Jeanne Robertson." Since that's my name, I reached up and pushed the button, thinking I had left something in the gate area. "Ding!"

When my bell sounded, the agent boomed through the PA system, "Mrs. Robertson, the people at the Executive Inn Hotel want their room key back!"

Everyone on the plane started laughing, including me. I knew what the situation was—my client had asked him to get the key, which I had forgotten to give her. She probably went to high school with the guy. Who could have predicted he would use the opportunity to break into a comedy routine?

I stood up to get my purse and hit my head on the overhead bin. By then, the gate agent had come down the aisle and was standing next to me with his hand open flat, bouncing it up and down, implying impatience while he waited for the key. "Any time, Mrs. Robertson." The more passengers chuckled, the more he "milked" it, and the more I couldn't find the key. I was rummaging through my suitcase-size purse, trying to feel it. (Women know the situation.) I finally had to slant the purse sideways and shake everything down into a corner. He was still standing there with his palm open, rolling his eyes at other passengers, when I finally put it in his hand. "Here. Sorry."

The agent began to walk away, but he had a laughing audience and everyone's attention. After a few steps, he turned in my direction. "Mrs. Robertson, if you're going to do this type of thing, don't come back to Kentucky." A few passengers applauded and high-fived him as he walked up the aisle. It was fun. When he was gone, the flight attendant shut the door.

Right there—right there—is where I should have zipped it up. But nooooo, I'm a professional speaker. I felt the need to explain to the people around me what had happened. "See, I couldn't get a late checkout, and a lady lent me . . ." etc. Everyone within earshot was listening at first. But slowly, one by one, they began to peel off and turn back to their magazines.

Finally, the only two people who seemed the least bit interested in my explanation were a man and a woman straight across the aisle from me. They were willing to listen, so I kept right on explaining, lowering my voice as I leaned into the aisle in their direction. "I knew what had happened, but when he boomed into the microphone, 'The people at the Executive Inn Hotel want their room key back,' it made me nervous." The woman leaned even closer toward me and answered in a hushed tone, "Made you nervous? We've got a couple of their towels."

It's August. It's hot. Many of us are traveling. But as proud North Carolinians, let's try to "act like somebody." Stick with taking the tiny shampoos.

From Fan to Fanatic

February 2016, *Southeast Lifestyle*

A man came up to me after a show this past Fall and, within earshot of others in the crowd, announced that he loved my work. I would be less than honest if I didn't admit that I enjoy hearing that type of comment.

"I've listened to you so much," he continued, "that I know by heart every one of your stories. If you ever get sick, call me. I can fill in for you."

''I'll do that," I responded tongue-in-cheek.

"I mean it, Jeanne."

"Well, I have more than a hundred funny stories out there, on DVD's and . . .

"And I know every one of 'em," he inserted again quickly.

At that point, he started to recite my punchlines to me and the crowd, laughing as he said, "I laughed so hard my water broke, and I wasn't even pregnant." Then, "She's twirling them so fast I can't even see the batons."

I was beginning to feel awkward, so in order to cut to the chase, I said, "Stop, stop, stop. Tell us which is your most favorite of all the funny stories?"

The crowd grew quiet as we awaited his choice. He thought about it for a minute, and finally, he answered. "My favorite funny story is . . . Jerry Clower's coon dog story."

I burst out laughing. The crowd burst out laughing. Other people came over to see what was so funny. And I'll be doggone if this guy didn't start telling Mr. Clower's coon dog story.

Two Miss North Carolinas

December 2016, *Southeast Lifestyle*

I was Miss North Carolina in 1963 and in the Miss America Pageant. Fifty-some years ago. That stated, it's important to me that you know something. I am not traveling around the country at my age, walking up to random strangers in airports, and opening a conversation with, "I was Miss North Carolina in 1963." They might look at me strangely and say something such as, "I scored a touchdown in junior high."

That little piece of pageant trivia helps explain why I smile a big smile often and also laugh every time I see one thing in particular. Just can't help myself. My reaction to "this one thing in particular" stretches back to the year we had two Miss North Carolinas at the same time. In case you lived in a cave that particular summer and missed it, let me refresh your memory. It may dawn on you as you read this because, unfortunately, it became a national and then an international story.

I didn't know either of the young women involved when it was happening. I have since met one of them and the family of the other. I choose to believe now what I chose to believe then. As we say in the South, "They are fine young women who got caught up in something." I also choose to believe, "They come from good people."

Here's what happened—

An outstanding young woman won the title of Miss North Carolina and was getting ready to go to the Miss America Pageant. Something came up. It's immaterial to my story, so there's no reason to go into it, but she resigned. The first runner-up, another outstanding young woman, was then crowned Miss North Carolina. Soon, her family had all their new clothes, airline tickets, and hotel rooms, and they were getting ready to go to the Miss America Pageant. Somewhere during this time, the first one decided she wanted the title back. Anyway, you cut to it. This was going to be a problem because the second one wasn't going to give the title back.

Is it coming to you now? Remember all this?

The lawsuits started. These people went after those people and vice versa. People heavily involved or even slightly involved talked way too much to the media. All over the state, North Carolinians took sides. The whole thing became a running front-page story every day.

Deputy Barney Fife would have said, "It was a royal, first class, Grade A mess." We sat in the state of North Carolina and prayed, "Don't let 'em hear about it in Virginia." I'm sure many of you know the following, but just in case you don't—people in Virginia have always thought they were better than the people in North Carolina. You know it's true. They always have, and they always will. But it doesn't bother the people in North Carolina because we know we're better than those in South Carolina. If you're from South Carolina, don't get upset about that. You've got Georgia. Now that I've kidded or downright insulted several of the states in our region, let me get back to the story.

Even though we hoped other states wouldn't hear about the two Miss North Carolinas situation, the late-night comedians—as we also might say in North Carolina—got "holt" of it before long. Every night on the late-night shows, people like David Letterman and Jay Leno began bringing it up. "What's going on down in North Carolina with the two beauty queens?" they would ask the nation. Or, "It's another day and another Miss North Carolina story." The saga was perfect for late-night TV, and sure enough, within a few days, the whole country knew what was happening. People mentioned it to me everywhere I traveled, especially with my Miss North Carolina history.

While this all went forward and the publicity grew, the Miss America Pageant drew closer and closer. Each Miss North Carolina "winner" was adamant that she would be on stage in Atlantic City, New Jersey, representing the Tarheel State. A decision had to be made. The whole thing finally landed with a judge somewhere who would handle the situation. As a state and nation, we waited to hear what this learned person, so much smarter than the rest of us, would decree. The judge studied all the paperwork and finally announced, "Let them both go." Well, duh. We hadn't thought of that.

So, at the Miss America Pageant that year on national and international television, one young woman walked out on stage, looked straight into a camera, and announced to the world that she was "Miss North Carolina!" after which she gave her name and walked off. Next, another young woman walked out on stage, not looking anything like the first one. (We're not talking about a set of twins.) She looked into the same camera and announced to the same world, by golly, that she was "Miss North Carolina!" and gave her name and walked off.

I mention all this because the week of the Miss America Pageant, I was flying out of a place many of you know well. The "Greensboro, High Point, Winston-Salem, Regional, Triad, Piedmont, International, new airport." (That's what local people my age still call "The new airport.") The two Miss Carolina story was on the front page, and I was reading it before takeoff. Soon, I became aware that the man sitting next to me was reading over my shoulder. In a few minutes, he leaned over, thumped the paper on the story, and said, "Now that thar's sumphin, idnd't it?" I knew he was from North Carolina, too. He sounded like I do.

I will admit that at that precise moment, I turned slowly to a perfect stranger and said with immense pride, "This is particularly interesting to me because some forty years ago, I was Miss North Carolina."

Quick as a flash, he said, "Miss North Carolina's gettin' to be like Santa Claus. One on every corner."

Y'all have a great December, and smile extra big every time you pass a Santa. Look on the corners. Happy Holidays!

Proud to Be an American

November 2017, *SE Gazette*

Lee Greenwood gets it right in his song, "Proud to be an American."

For the first time, I am not attempting to be funny in my monthly article. I am, however, sharing something that happened during one of my trips this Fall. It is my hope that over the Thanksgiving holiday, it will remind us to take a few moments to be thankful we live in this great country. Also, I hope that on November 11th, the official Veterans Day (eleventh month, eleventh day, eleventh hour), we will all pause to remember those who have served to keep us free, especially those who are also remembered on Memorial Day, designated to remember those who made the ultimate sacrifice.

Friday, September 29, 2017. Delta #1814 Atlanta to Pensacola. A packed plane. On the plane with us was an American who made the ultimate sacrifice. And was going home. A coffin draped with the American flag was in the underbelly of the plane. It was being escorted home by a member of the military, in full dress uniform, carrying a folded American flag and other special items for the family. A passenger in first class gave up his seat for this escort. People politely applauded. We all would have done the same.

When we landed, the Delta crew asked that we let the military escort deplane first. He was to meet the family. Not a person on the plane moved. No one even stood to quickly retrieve a bag from the overhead bin in order to be ready to hurry off the plane. I heard no one talking on a cell phone. After the escort deplaned, we all stood quietly to gather our things and leave. The plane emptied without anyone saying a word.

In the gate area, with no instructions to do so, the passengers turned as a group and walked to look down through the windows as members of a military guard walked slowly in perfect time toward the plane and waited for the fallen warrior. None of us headed toward baggage claim. When people from other flights saw what was happening, they stopped walking and joined our group at the windows. Then, slowly, so very slowly, a coffin—draped in the American flag—appeared and began to move down the conveyor belt of the plane into the hands of the white-gloved military escorts. At the first sight of the flag, passengers from our flight and many others, without instruction, put their hands over their hearts as they stood in respect. Many, I'm assuming former or current military, saluted. No one moved until the remains were carefully placed in the back of the white hearse by the honor guard. The vehicle left the tarmac, and the military team walked quietly away in unison and disappeared.

I glanced around. People of various races, ages, and religions had stood in respect because they wanted to. They took time to honor a fallen warrior because they wanted to. They honored the American flag because they wanted to. Many had tears streaming down their faces. I was one of them. None of us knew the race, religion, gender, sexual orientation, or politics of the fallen American. It didn't matter. It just didn't matter. An American had come home.

Thanks to all who have served, and let us especially remember those who "gave all" for the rest of us. God bless America.

Would You Like Some Grey Poupon?

January 2018, *SE Gazette*

Happy New Year! It's a great time to make a resolution to look for humor this year. If you make such a resolution, let me offer a tip on one way to stick to it.

I have a little 3-step Humor Formula that helps me find the humor around me every day, which makes my life fun. This formula has worked well for me for years, and if it appeals to you, give it a try. It might make your day, too.

The three-step process involves using some form of three statements or questions. It especially works in what I call "lag time." When I travel, my lag time comes when I'm in a cab, or when I'm with people at a banquet, and we've run out of conversation, or when I'm sitting next to a talkative person on a plane. While I'm not a Chatty Cathy, I enjoy talking to people, so when the time is right, I make it a point to engage them in conversation. The tricky part is that I want to lead them toward telling me something that makes us both laugh and maybe gives me an idea I can develop later for a show. For example, let's say I'm in a taxi. That's definitely lag time. I could use that time to chitchat on my cell phone, but that means I might miss an opportunity to engage with the potentially interesting person behind the steering wheel. What a loss. So, Step No.1 in the Humor Formula is to open the dialog by saying some variation of "How long have you been driving people around?" (Or, ". . . worked in this restaurant?" Or, ". . . been on staff in this hotel?") I've never met anyone who wouldn't answer that.

Then comes Step No. 2. My second leading statement is, "I bet you've seen a lot of funny things dealing with the traveling public." I drop that line casually. Often, that's all I need to say. The person will begin to relate a funny incident or one they think is funny. It doesn't matter if they're not funny. I mainly just want to enjoy the day. If a new story develops from what they say, it's a little bonus.

Honestly? When I try to "lead" someone with that second comment of "I bet you've seen a lot of funny things happen," they say they have and then go right back to what they were doing. In the taxi scenario I'm using here, that means they keep quietly driving. That's when I pause a few seconds before Step No. 3.—my clincher—it's a simple follow-on question. In this case, it would be, "What's the funniest thing you've had happen driving people around?"

This doesn't always work in places like New York City. When I ask drivers in NYC something in my Southern accent, they start laughing, practically turning in their seats to ask, "Where ya frum?" That's okay. It gets a conversation going. NYC aside, when the 3-Step Humor Formula works, it's truly fun. Granted, I hear good and not-so-good stories, but at times, I've laughed out loud at a response. Take that day in Louisiana . . .

My convention speech was to be at the Hyatt Hotel in downtown New Orleans. The group arranged for me to be met at the airport by one of the Hyatt bellhops/drivers in the Hyatt's stretch limousine. Therefore, minutes after I left the coach class airline seats where I couldn't move my legs, I found myself in the back seat of one of those long, black, Godfather-looking cars, about a block behind the driver. While maneuvering out of the airport, I noticed people in other cars were looking at the limo, peering straight in my direction. They were trying to see who was in the back seat but they couldn't see anything because the windows were tinted. Only people "of a certain age" will "get" this next part. When I'm occasionally in limos like that one and people are staring straight at the tinted windows, I've always thought it would be fun to lower my window at a stop light, reach in my purse for a certain item I had put in there and then extend my arm out the window in their direction. "Would you care for some Grey Poupon?" (Younger people, Google the ad. You'll love it.)

My driver that day in New Orleans was named Stewart. He was young. I jotted down a note to get a small jar of Grey Poupon mustard for future trips and then waited a minute or so after we pulled away from the curb before I started my little 3-Step Humor Formula. Stewart had to have experienced funny incidents in The Big Easy, as New Orleans is now called. I was so far away from him that I practically had to shout when I went to my first step. "Stewart! How long have you been driving people back and forth to the airport for the Hyatt?"

Stewart was looking in his side mirror and over his left shoulder as he eased the stretch limo into another lane, but he answered, "A couple of years. I'm a student at Tulane. It's a good way to pick up a little spending money."

"I bet so," I answered. Then, in keeping with my often-used plan, I let that rest, but in a few seconds, I followed with the second step. That's when I planted the seed with Step No.2, "I bet you've seen a lot of funny things happen driving people around New Orleans."

Stewart answered, "Yes, ma'am. I sure have." He didn't offer anything else. He was doing his job working us through airport congestion and construction toward the Interstate. I probably should have let him drive, but nooooo, I kept going with my standard plan. It's what I do and have done for years. I let the statement about seeing a lot of funny things sit there for a few seconds. I was calm. Step No. 3 was coming up.

When we were safely on course and in the traffic flow, I finally went to that last step and asked my clincher question. I must have done this a thousand times, and I'm not exaggerating. In all my years of doing so, I have never had a response like Stewart's. I leaned forward toward the front of the limo and asked, "What's the funniest thing you've had happen driving people around?"

Stewart cocked his head to one side and looked at me through his rearview mirror. Studying me between glances in my direction and the traffic in front of us, he finally answered, making eye contact through the mirror. "Mrs. Robertson, the funniest thing I've had happen is . . . that's the same question you asked when I drove you about a year ago."

The next morning, I told my audience about Stewart and his good memory. They loved it. Later, I saw several of them gathered around him in the lobby at the bell stand. They were smiling and laughing. I knew they had been in my audience because I could see their convention badges. To say the least, Stewart was enjoying the attention. He was leaning back, resting his elbows on the bell stand, and had a big grin on his face. There must have been eight or nine people standing around him, giving him attention. And as we say, "He was eating it up."

I watched this scene from afar for a few moments until Stewart suddenly realized I was across the lobby. Without shifting his weight, he threw up a hand in my direction as though waving to the masses from a balcony. He then shouted, "Hey! Mrs. Robertson! Thanks!" And then, sweeping a hand toward the small crowd, he shrugged and added, "You made me a star!"

Okay, dear readers—go forth and look for humor in 2018. When the situation is right, follow the 3-Step Humor Formula. It can be loads of fun, and who knows? It might make someone a star!

My Hawaiian Fashion Advice

August, 2018 *SE Gazette*

August. One more summer month for many to lounge around in their favorite swimsuits, daring the "rays" to get through the sunscreen. One more month for a final quick vacation, maybe down to the beach for a long weekend. It's also possibly a great month to buy a new swimsuit for next summer at a good price. Maybe even on sale. Therefore, it's time for me to offer sage advice. Here it is: A "good price" should not be the deciding factor in buying something. Not even if it's half off the original price. Let's take that a step higher, not even if something is two-thirds off the original price. Or, as I heard a man say in Hawaii about an item he didn't like, "Not even if they give it to me."

I've seen people do it over and over and over again. I've even done it. I'm referring to purchasing local outfits that seem perfect where you're vacationing, especially if they're on sale. Then, when we're back home? Uh, no.

My speech in August was in the Aloha State, where swimsuits are in style and in demand year-round. The gift shop in a big-name hotel on Maui was crowded with conventioneers—mostly women—from all over the United States. I knew that because I had just spoken at their luncheon. Most of them wouldn't need swimsuits year-round, but the shop in the hotel had such a large, colorful, island-looking selection of swimwear that it was hard to walk by and not browse a little. The convention was ending, people were leaving the next day, and the swimsuits were "On sale! Half price and more!"—"Katy, bar the door!" I was right in there with the rest of the tourists, looking for a swimsuit—in a tall size.

Among the shoppers was a couple whose name tags indicated they were from the Midwest. Due to the great sales prices, I assume the wife had persuaded her sixty-ish, slightly balding, little bit pudgy husband to try on a swimsuit made of tight, elastic, stretch material—the teeniest bit of material. All of us had seen so many of these suits around the island that week, and I suppose we had become acclimated to them. We sure have skimpy swimsuits in Piedmont County, North Carolina, or down at the beach, but "skimpy" took on a new meaning in Hawaii.

The man protested when his wife thrust a piece of stretchy material in his direction and said, "Try this on."

He turned it over in his hands a few times. "What is it? A handkerchief?" He went on to tell his wife he didn't want "that thing" but finally acquiesced to her plea when she used those magic words that have worked on all of us. "Just try it on. I bet it will look great on you. What have you got to lose?" Then the clincher, "It's on sale. They're practically giving it away."

He sighed and disappeared into the small dressing room, a tiny piece of material in hand. His wife hovered at the door. Shoppers exchanged glances and smiles because we had heard the conversation. Several minutes ticked by.

Finally, she could wait no longer and rapped her knuckles on the door. "Hey. What's taking you so long? Do you have it on?" she said, loud enough for all to hear. People all over the store turned to look. Most of them chuckled.

The man's response was hushed. "I guess it's on."

There was a long pause. Buyers exchanged little smiles, pretending disinterest, but all of us were waiting for the outcome.

"I don't want to come out there," was the guy's next response. "I don't like all the Hawaiian flowers on it. I like solid colors."

"Well, let me see if I can find the same suit with solid . . ."

"No! It's not the flowers. It's the swimsuit. It's about the silliest thing I've ever seen. I don't care if they give it to me. I'm not wearing it. Period. I'd feel like a fool." Several women stifled laughs.

I thought the man had made his opinion rather clear, but his wife persisted, brushing over his comments. "You can't tell in that little, dark dressing room whether you like it or not or how it looks on you. Come out here in the better light, and let me see it on you."

There was no movement. The door didn't open. I wondered if there was a window he could escape through. She lowered her voice to a more persuasive level—but we could all hear—and she leaned toward the dressing room door. "Just let me see what it looks like on you, honey. No one else is looking. No. One. Cares."

My thought was that if she had to coax him out of the dressing room in that tiny suit, she would never get him down to the beach in it. But I let it ride. After all, he was her husband to do with as she pleased.

Suddenly, like a jailer's key turning in a hollow dungeon, we heard the sound of the man fiddling with the latch. Chitchat around the small shop subsided. I found myself nonchalantly pricing a ship-in-a-bottle that l didn't want to buy. I wasn't going to miss this.

Finally, the door slowly opened, just wide enough for his wife to peer inside the little cubicle. "Oh, for crying out loud," she spat out quickly. "You wear that at home. They'll laugh you right out of Kansas!"

Proving once again: A good sale price doesn't make it a good buy.

Stay cool.

"Young and Efficient" Meets "Old and Tired"

March 2019, *SE Gazette*

I was to speak in Carbondale, Illinois, for the local school system on Southern Illinois University's campus. It wasn't my first trip to Carbondale, and I had stayed at the Ramada Inn the other two times there—speaking for the same group on both of those previous trips. So, without reading my paperwork carefully, I flew to St. Louis from another speech, rented a car, and drove straight to Carbondale the day before the school event. It was a long travel day that started early and came after several other long travel days. I was worn out by the time I got there. When I saw the Ramada Inn, I pulled into the parking lot out of habit. It was all familiar. Same lobby as before. Same front desk. Another young, personable student employee from the University was efficiently smiling as I approached. "Welcome to the Ramada Inn."

"Thank you. Glad to be back," I stated. "I've stayed here a couple of times in the past. My name is Jeanne Robertson. I believe you have a reservation for me made by the school system."

"I'll be happy to check that for you, Mrs. Robertson," the clerk responded with another big smile as he started typing. After a few seconds, he stopped typing, and I detected a little frown.

"Uh oh. Is there a problem?" I asked, handing him my ID and credit card.

"Oh, no, not at all, Mrs. Robertson." (He was good at repeating the customer's name.) "We were expecting you. Let me just step into the office for a minute. Your assigned room has not been cleaned, but I may be able to get you a better room that's ready now."

"Great. Thank you. I know I'm here before check-in time. It's been a long several days of travel. I'd love to get in the room now if at all possible and go to sleep."

He disappeared and, within minutes, returned with papers in hand. "Here we are. Your room is ready now, and I was able to upgrade you at no extra cost. Just sign right here, Mrs. Robertson." I did. He gave me a couple of keys and returned my ID and credit cards. "Call the front desk if there's anything we can do to help you during your stay, Mrs. Robertson. We want you to come back if your plans bring you this way again."

I couldn't help but think, "Wow. He's young and efficient." At that point during that particular trip, I was feeling old and tired.

Minutes later, I was in the room. He had indeed upgraded me. I fell in the bed and slept all afternoon.

Later that night, after dinner, watching a ball game on TV, and getting ready for bed, I pulled out my paperwork to double-check what time I was to meet my client in the lobby of the hotel the next morning. We had chatted by phone several times, but I needed to review my notes. I was to be picked up at 8 am, as I remembered. But wait! What's this? Meet in the lobby of the Holiday Inn! The HOLIDAY INN! I was at the wrong hotel! There it was in black and white. My reservation was at the Holiday Inn!

I got my clothes back on and hustled down to the lobby. The young and efficient clerk was behind the counter and flashed a big smile as I approached.

"Hello, Mrs. Robertson. I trust your room is satisfactory."

"Oh, the room is great. Thanks for the upgrade and for getting me in early. I slept all afternoon, but now, I'm confused. You won't believe this, but I've just discovered that I'm in the wrong hotel. When I checked in, do you remember me saying, 'I'm Jeanne Robertson. I believe you have a reservation for me?'"

"Yes, of course, I remember, Mrs. Robertson."

"It's my mistake, and I'm feeling old and tired about now, but I'm supposed to be at the Holiday Inn, not here. Thinking back about it, I don't think you really did have a reservation for me."

He thought a few seconds, stood a little taller, and said with pride, "Actually, you're right. We didn't have a reservation for you." Then he grinned and leaned in my direction to almost whisper, "I covered very well, didn't I?"

I paid for and slept at the Ramada Inn, where I had already settled into the room. I called the Holiday Inn, and amazingly, they didn't charge the school system or me for that room.

The next morning, I was dressed up and sitting in the lobby of the Holiday Inn when the client arrived at 8 am. I was smiling and ready to go and never saw the need to mention the mix-up. When my client asked, "How was your room?" I answered truthfully, "Great."

"Old and tired" covered very well, didn't she?

San Quentin and Church Bingo

May 2019, *SE Gazette*

I often comment that when it comes to stories, the true ones are usually the best. We just have to look at the world through humorous eyes, and we'll see them. Let me emphasize that again this month. I'll tell you a story, and you tell me how in the world I could have fabricated what happened?

A friend and fellow professional speaker from San Francisco, Patricia Fripp, frequently tells of an inmate she met during several pro bono speeches inside San Quentin State Prison. I'll say that the guy's name was Sparkey.[17]

In reality, the name is changed here to protect the writer.

I've heard Patricia's Sparkey story so often I feel as though I personally know Sparkey. Apparently, he was a personable fellow and well-liked by the other prisoners. That's something to write home about, I suppose. It's a terrific story that I'll leave for Patricia to recount because, through my friendship with her, I have my own Sparkey story.

On a speaking trip to Lake Tahoe, Nevada, the last portion of my travel was on a small commuter plane. I struck up a conversation with

17 Jeanne used the monikers "Treetop" and "Sparkey" to identify the character when telling this story. The editor decided to use Sparkey in this version.

another passenger, a woman who was frantic about flying in that size aircraft. In trying to reassure her, I discovered that this was her first trip from her small Midwest town since her husband's death the previous year. She had never been to Nevada, and her only gambling experience was church bingo. (She explained, "The prizes were donated, so it wasn't really gambling.") The anticipation of seeing a childhood friend faded after a hard day of travel. "I don't know why I let her talk me into this," she mumbled, shaking her head. "My husband always took care of everything when we traveled. I don't know if I'll even be able to get to the hotel."

I assured her that traveling could be fun and added, "Just wait until you tell your friends at church bingo about your trip." She smiled. Slightly.

Her words about her husband popped into my mind when I saw her standing empty-handed at the baggage claim. Her luggage hadn't made it. This woman needed me, so I stepped into the role of her deceased spouse. I helped her start a trace on her bags, assured her that she could get toiletries at the hotel, and called us a cab. Before long, we piled in the back seat of a taxi and headed for the hotel/ casino where we both happened to be staying. As we pulled away from the curb, she laid her purse between us in the back seat and slowly exhaled. It had been a long day for her, and I tried to influence her outlook by saying, "When your bags don't arrive, it's another story to tell at church bingo."

"Maybe so," she replied, halfheartedly.

The cab driver was a big, rough-looking man with long hair, but he greeted us with a smile and seemed friendly. My new friend gazed out the window at unfamiliar surroundings as we rode along, so I turned my attention to the driver, engaging him in conversation, hoping to hear something humorous.

"How long have you been driving a cab?"

"Oh, about a year in Tahoe. I used to drive in San Francisco."

The woman continued to stare out the window, content to let us rattle on.

"I love San Francisco. Are you from there?" I asked.

"No, ma'am. To tell the truth, I worked in San Quentin a long time and drove a cab when I left there."

At the mention of San Quentin, the lady snapped her head around so fast that I'm surprised she didn't crack her neck. She mouthed to me, "San Quentin?" But by then, I was leaning forward, resting my arms on the back of the front seat. "You won't believe this, but I sort of know a guy who was in San Quentin for a while. Did you, by any chance, know a prisoner named Sparkey?"

The woman's jaw dropped three inches! She was in the backseat with a woman who was asking the taxi driver about a possible mutual friend, a prisoner in San Quentin.

The driver banged his hand on the steering wheel and turned in my direction, grinning from ear to ear. "Know him? Everybody knew Sparkey! He was a terrific guy! Really, he was in prison but had a great personality."

Out of the corner of my eye, I saw the woman slowly pick up her purse and then quickly clutch it to her chest as she wedged herself deeper into the corner of the seat. She didn't speak for the remainder of the ride. Quite possibly, she never exhaled.

The driver and I exchanged Sparkey information for the rest of the way to the hotel. How did I know him? Did I know that he had gotten out? What was he doing? Was he still married? Did they have children? Had he stayed out of trouble when he got out? (FYI. No, on that last question about staying out of trouble. Sparkey was back in some prison somewhere. A good personality can take one only so far.)

The motor was still running in front of the hotel when the woman slapped a twenty-dollar bill on the seat and bolted for safety. When she slammed the cab door, the hem of her jacket caught in it, but she didn't open the door to free it. She frantically yanked, yanked, yanked at the material until I leaned over and cracked the door open. One final jerk, the jacket was loose, and she disappeared into the hotel crowd. Then, the strangest thing happened. After all my help with her lost bag, transportation to the hotel, calming her fears, etc., every time I saw her in the lobby over the next few days and tried to approach her, she scurried away. I don't want to be paranoid, but I guess some people just don't like Southerners.

I've thought about her often. There she was, meeting an old friend on her first solo trip after a horrible year. She was in a gambling town, miles away from the sanity of familiar surroundings, riding in a cab with two people who were discussing a mutual acquaintance: a prisoner in San Quentin.

I wish I could have heard her tell it at church bingo.

You can't make "stuff" like this up.

Obey All Rules!

July 2019, *SE Gazette*

The Andy Griffith Show has been a part of my life since it first aired on October 3, 1960. Since then, like my many readers, I've watched all the episodes over and over. I know and love the characters. I've studied them and even written about them. Mostly, I've just enjoyed them. Therefore, to this day, something will happen in my travels, and it will trigger not only a situation from an episode but also quotes that are embedded in my memory.

For example . . . I can hear Mayberry's Deputy Barney Fife say these words in an episode titled "The Big House." He practically shouts at a couple of prisoners in a cell as he walks back and forth and back and forth in front of them. "Now, here at the Rock, (pace, pace) we have two basic rules. (Andy rolls his eyes.) Memorize them so you can say them in your sleep. (Pace, pace.) The first rule is, OBEY ALL RULES! Secondly, do not write on the walls as it takes a lot of work to erase writing off the walls."

The man who checked me into a hotel on Maryland's Eastern Shore told me the restaurant was closed for the afternoon, but room service was available. Well, his exact words were, "It's not exactly open, but they're back there in the kitchen. Just call 'em. They'll pick up." I had missed breakfast and lunch, and airplane peanuts can only carry one so far. I knew before I got to the room and checked the menu that I would indeed call them.

The room was fine, but I couldn't find the menu. After searching all the usual places that housekeeping people put them, I punched the button on the phone for room service. A lady who answered was adequately chipper for someone who might have to take an afternoon order.

"What can I do for you?"

"Hey. This is Jeanne Robertson. I've just checked in. The man at the front desk told me y'all are still open for room service. Is that correct?"

"Well, sure. I guess it is. But the restaurant's closed."

"I understand. No problem. I'll just order from here—I'll even come down and get it—but I can't find a room service menu in the room. Any idea where it might be?"

The woman on the other end was silent for a few moments, then said, "There ought to be a menu on the dresser, but I hear most rooms don't have them."

I resisted saying, "Don't have a dresser or don't have a menu?" I knew what she meant. No need pretending I was a grammar teacher or irritating a person who was going to prepare my food. "Well, let me look around again," I said. "It's probably here somewhere. I'll call back."

"Nah, don't worry about a menu. It doesn't matter," the woman explained quickly. "I'll just tell you what we fix for room service, and you can tell me what you want."

The choices she gave me reminded me of another of my favorite episodes on *The Andy Griffith Show*, the one titled "Convicts At Large." Remember it? Three women escape from prison and wind up holding Floyd and Barney as hostages. They turn on the radio to find dancing music. Seconds later, an announcer interrupts the music to tell of the prison escapes. He then proceeds to give the aliases of the ringleader, a convict known as Big Maude Tyler. He says Big Maude Tyler is also known as "Clarisse Tyler, Maude Clarisse Tyler, Annabelle Tyler, and Ralph Henderson." That's a laugh-out-loud line to me, and so were the options the room service woman reeled off to me in the hotel that day.

She said, "This is what we fix. You can have a shrimp boat, fried shrimp, boiled shrimp, shrimp salad, or . . . a hamburger."

Thinking she would laugh, I said, "Can I have shrimp on my hamburger?" (And people ask, "Where do you find your material?")

There was total silence on the phone at first. Really, the woman said nothing. I thought she had gone away.

Finally, her serious voice informed me politely but bluntly, "We. Don't. Vary. The. Menu!"

And you probably can guess my immediate thought. Correct. "Obey. All. Rules."

Keep looking for humor, y'all. It's out there—And don't even think about writing on the walls.

An Ego That "Hertz"

March 2020, *SE Gazette*

Famous TV Sheriff Andy Taylor puts it well when he suggests, "There's more than one way to pluck a buzzard. Yes, sir."

That particular quote comes from episode #11, "Christmas Story," when Andy was dealing with Ben Weaver's "Bah, Humbug" attitude. Or, as Mr. Weaver puts it, "Christmas, Ha!" But Sheriff Taylor's sentiment can be applied to a situation on an airplane trip a few years ago in the days before passengers could make telephone calls, send email, and text in mid-flight.

The rude, pompous passenger insisted to one of the flight attendants that he be allowed to use the "private telephone" on board reserved for airline personnel. He needed to rent a car at his destination. The flight attendant told him several times that there was no such telephone, but he was adamant. He knew the plane had a secret phone that passengers weren't supposed to know about, but he, of course, did. After all, he was a "million miler at the platinum level, by golly." Passengers near him could hear the conversation. As Sheriff Taylor would probably also say, "He needed some 'niceness' lessons."

After repeated confrontations, the young woman realized that she had a super-ego buzzard on her hands. Creative plucking was in order.

Finally, she lowered her voice, but just slightly. I think she wanted the people around him to hear her. "Actually, sir, you are correct. We do have a private, secret telephone on board," she told him. "You must be very important to know that. It truly is just for airline personnel, but if your car reservation is that important, I will let you use it. Which rental agency do you want me to call?"

Puffing out his chest and cutting his eyes to several passengers around him, he nodded as if to say, "I knew I was correct," and responded, "Hertz." The flight attendant walked toward the back of the plane to supposedly place the call. He gave the passengers around him a "they know better than to fool with me" look.

Minutes later, the professional attendant (with a sense of humor) returned. "I have put that call through to Hertz for you, sir. They're on the line. Please come with me." He followed her to the front of the plane, and she handed him the intercom, which did resemble a telephone of sorts. She had clicked it to private communication. It's how the flight attendants talk to one another, when necessary, in flight.

Putting the "phone" to his ear, he heard a flight attendant in the back of the plane say, "Hertz Rent a Car." He made his reservation—he thought—and, with a smug smile, returned to his seat.

Proving that, once again, the great Sheriff Andy Taylor is right. There is more than one way to pluck a buzzard. Yes sir.

Don't you love people?

Two flight attendants in the back of the plane and one at the front laughed and giggled until the end of the day, probably even for months.

I'm not sure about the people at the upcoming Hertz counter.

Rattling Wrappers

January 2021, *SE Gazette*

Opie: "Can I have my nickel for milk?" Aunt Bee: "Um, hum. Now, remember, this is for milk, not another piece of apple pie. You need that milk to make your bones hard."

Aunt Bee certainly knows the correct order of eating and takes pains to remind her nephew in "Opie and the Bully." In this episode, the writers have Aunt Bee point out that milk makes our bones hard and sandwiches come before apple pie—two important pieces of advice. More than likely, we all had "Aunt Bees" to tell us what they believed to be important information. But even when we know better when those who remind us are not around . . .

I shared the forty-minute shuttle van drive from the Savannah airport to Hilton Head Island in South Carolina with four men from a food company. They were part of the group I was to address, the Southeastern School Foods Association.

We were all hungry, and the driver must have overheard our conversations about it. We had flown in on the same commuter flight. No snacks. The group of four had barely made the flight due to a tight connection in Atlanta, and I was out of breath behind them. There was no time for the food we ran by in order to make our flight. A couple of miles from the airport, the driver said he had eaten lunch, but he offered to stop at a little "groceteria" near the airport if we made it snappy. He had to stay on schedule.

The five of us hit the ground running and descended on the little store like a busload of hungry teenagers after a ball game. Inside, we scooped up the first snacks that met our eyes, threw down our money, and, within minutes, scurried out with our arms piled high with an assortment of chips, candy, beef jerky, and popcorn. All five of us bit down on the brims of cups filled with soft drinks on ice. The liquid jostled in and out of the cups as we ran. After we settled back into our places in the van, the only sound was the rattling of wrappers.

On the road again, the driver eventually asked why we were going to Hilton Head. No one answered at first because our mouths were full. Then, too, maybe we didn't want to respond. Finally, one of the men mumbled the truth through chocolate and nuts, "A conference on school nutrition." The rest of us almost choked from laughing. The driver belly-laughed the loudest.

The next day, I was seated on stage, waiting for the introductions of officers to be concluded. I wasn't an officer. I was the guest speaker, waiting my turn while the outgoing president gave her remarks. Out of the corner of my eyes, I saw an employee of the hotel come to the front of the room and pass an envelope to the woman on stage seated to my far right. She glanced at what was written on it and handed it to the next person. The note continued up the row of people until it reached me and I saw what was written. "Please pass to the speaker, Mrs. Robertson."

That exact note is why I'm encouraging all my readers to not only look for humor in the coming year, but create a little of it when it doesn't hurt anyone else.

The message was, "Looking forward to your remarks on nutrition and eating wisely. We won't tell if you won't." Signed, "The four guys in the shuttle van."

I looked around the audience until I made eye contact with them, sitting out there grinning like Cheshire cats. I grinned back, folded their note, and put it in my purse. And we all smiled.

Happy New Year! Make 2021 a humorous one.

Rule Bending at Its Best

March 2021, *SE Gazette*

For the most part, I follow rules. If I forget and someone reminds me to wear a mask, I put one on ASAP. If someone reminds me to stand six feet from others, I find the little circle and try to squeeze my size 11 feet right on it. These people are just doing their jobs. I always quickly comply and thank them for the reminder. If the state tells me that I can only have, say, fifteen people to my house for dinner, I respectfully ask, "Do I have to have any?"

But don't let these comments suggest I don't believe in rule-bending when the occasion calls for it. No siree. Sometimes, it's the best thing to do. I might have gotten that from my parents, but more than likely from Sheriff Andy Taylor of Mayberry.

In episode #4, "Runaway Kid," of *The Andy Griffith Show* series, Opie befriends a runaway boy. Eventually, he shares the information with his father, who agrees not to tell. Of course, Andy has to tell and quickly calls the boy's father in a nearby town. Opie doesn't understand why his Pa broke a promise. Andy explains it as follows, "You see, son, rules are very important things. But sometimes, they seem to get in the way when we're trying to help somebody. So, what we do in a case like that, we don't exactly break 'em. We just bend 'em a little bit."

It may be one of the big secrets of getting along in life: knowing when to bend the rules and when not to. In Mayberry, Sheriff Andy Taylor always seems to sense which way to play it. Fortunately, others in the world do, too.

When I arrived at the Bangor, Maine airport in May 1991—yikes, almost thirty years ago—it was like an explosion of color because of the impressive display of red, white, and blue ribbons around the terminal. This was not unusual a few months after Desert Storm; most airports proudly displayed the national colors, our flag, and the popular yellow ribbons. But Bangor was decorated to the hilt—way over the top. Something was going on. While I was waiting for my ride to the hotel where I was going to give a speech the next day, I went over to an airport employee to find out why.

It turned out that every military plane returning from the Gulf made its first stop on U.S. soil at the Bangor airport. There, the personnel deplaned for a few minutes while the aircraft was refueled. The employee telling me all this lowered his voice and said, "You'd be surprised how many of these young people get off the plane to stretch their legs and drop to the ground to kiss this U.S. soil." I will never forget that comment as long as I live. It brought tears to my eyes.

The military officer who met me proudly pointed out that the people living in the area turned out to greet every single military plane that arrived. Vets, teenagers, and families came in droves. They waved flags, cheered, and applauded as the soldiers deplaned. Local radio stations and newspapers spread the word of incoming arrival times, and the locals poured forth over and over and over again.

Knowing the non-drinking policy in the Gulf and trying to make casual conversation, I asked if a beer was the first thing most of them wanted after many months away from home.

"Well, ma'am, the officer said, tucking his chin slightly, "it's against the rules to have beer at the airport to give to military personnel. But amazingly," he added with a grin, "there are always a few cases around. Unauthorized, of course."

Of course. Go for it. I'd bet those returnees stepping foot on their homeland after being away so long called it "rule bending at its best!"

Once again, thanks to all who have served, their families, and those serving today.

Section Five

Just Jeanne

How Does Delta Know?

April 2000, *City-County Magazine*

The word "progress" certainly seems to get people excited. Like most things, though, it has a downside. Now, take the computer, and many people wish you would. It offers all sorts of high-tech advantages, but let this be a warning: it sure makes it easy for a "big brother" to happen.

My Executive Assistant, Toni, bounded into the office early one Monday morning and wanted to know how long I planned to be on a diet.

What in the world? How did she know I was dieting?

Sandra, down at Global Travel, told her she explained.

"Sandra? At Global Travel?"

"Yep, Delta Air Lines told Sandra."

Gigantic conglomerate Delta Airlines tells my travel agent, who tells my Executive Assistant that I am on a diet. And how did Delta know?

There is always an explanation, and this time, it could be attributed to what would have to be called "progress." Toni had whipped by Global Travel that morning to pick up a ticket. When Sandra pulled up my record in the computer, she saw that the night before, I had changed all my Delta airline meals for that week to salads and figured it was because I was dieting. She told Toni, and Toni asked me.

"Alright, I'm dieting. Put it on the World Wide Web!"

Stuff like this leads me to agree with the man who bought his first computer and bargained for a thirty-day trial period. If it didn't work out, he could return it in a month. After fifteen days, he called the company and asked two things: (1) Did he have to keep it for thirty days? and (2) Did he have to return it in one piece?

Progress. Humph!

Stuffed Shoes

May 2000, *City-County Magazine*

A home improvement craze is sweeping the country. It seems like everyone in the neighborhood is adding on, building out, or knocking down something in an attempt to have more space. I could double the space in our house by just throwing things away. Sounds easy, but . . .

I save stuff. Not valuable stuff in the financial sense of the word. Just things that bring back happy memories. I throw away nothing. My packrat habits have brought on much ribbing through the years, mainly from my husband. But his objections have never fazed me. I've continued to stash as though on a mission, and the day of the mission has finally arrived.

Exonerated! It feels good. Real good.

After speaking to the Graham Historical Society, Gail Knauff showed me an eight-by-ten framed photograph from my Miss North Carolina days. She and her husband had recently written the history of Haw River. Now, they and others in the community were actively involved in putting together the Haw River Historical Museum.

She had run across this photo and thought the gown I had on was made of corduroy. If I remembered the dress, and it was indeed corduroy, did I know if it was Cone Mills corduroy? That would mean it had been made at the Cone Mills plant in Haw River and that they wanted to hang the picture in the new museum. [18] Could I help her?

Oh boy, could I help her. It was the day I had been waiting for. Yes, I told her. The dress was made of corduroy. Yes, the material had been made at the Haw River Cone Mills plant. Yes, put the photo in the museum and—ta-da!—did she want the gown? How about the matching shoes?

Around 2 am, I located the 34-year-old corduroy gown piled in with some psychedelic-looking bell bottoms. Forty-five minutes later, the matching shoes fell out of my college physical education uniform.

Of course, things don't ever run as smoothly as they sound. In preparation for the big donation, Gail had discovered that the Haw River Historical Society's mannequin had only half a body. If she had the bottom half of the thing, the bosom and shoulders of the gown would fall over to one side. If she had the top half, the skirt would bunch up around the waist. Either way, the mannequin would be shorter than six-foot-two.

By the time the donating night rolled around, however, Gail had obtained a whole-body mannequin from Margaret's Dress Shop in Burlington.

To be accurate—and I certainly strive to be—I must report that the mannequin's feet were a little smaller than mine. When we eased her down into my shoes, ever careful not to knock off her blonde curly wig, the mayor of Haw River got on the floor to steer the feet into place. Seconds later, he looked up and said, "Bring me a bunch of rags. There's a whole lot of space to fill in these big shoes."

You'd think my husband would have been excited about my donation, but no. Jerry said he'd get excited when somebody took all my high school clothes—a definite "home improvement."

18 The Cone Mills plant in Haw River became the largest producer of corduroy in the world. In 1981 it employed over 1,000 people. See a full history at https://www.carolana.com/NC/Towns/Haw_River_NC.html

If you're looking for something to do in Alamance County, please do drop by the museum in Haw River. If the mannequin looks tipsy, stuff some papers in the shoes. The Historical Society would be thrilled if you used dollar bills.

Queen of the Game

September 2001, *City-County Magazine*

My husband and I were sitting in the stands during an Elon College football game when a voice over the loudspeaker got everyone's attention during halftime. It was time to announce the Queen of the Game!

My good friend Norma Rose, also the Elon athletic director's wife, leaned over to tell me this was something that would happen at every game that year. A local florist donated flowers, which would be brought to the Queen by a student.

By then, the announcer was saying that the Queen of the Game was in such and such section. It was ours. I had a sinking feeling in my stomach.

Sure enough, seconds later, the voice boomed, "And our Queeeeeen of the Gammmmme is . . . Jeanne Robertson!" Everyone around me laughed. When the flowers arrived seconds later, I stood and waved and blew kisses.

When the game was over, the Athletic Director, Dr. Alan White, came to where we were talking. I, of course, was still holding the large bouquet of flowers. "O.K. Alan," I began. "Where are my prizes? Do I get a scholarship?"

A sly fund-raising smile crept across his face. "No, Jeanne. You don't understand. The Queen of the Game isn't someone who *receives* a scholarship. The Queen of the Game is someone we think might *give* a scholarship."

Jeanne Floats the Bill

December 2003, *Alamance Magazine*

At an Arts Council meeting in my hometown of Burlington, NC, we were discussing how much it would cost to have a float in the upcoming Christmas parade.

One of my friends, looking at the parade information, said, "Oh, look. We don't have to pay. Jeanne, you can ride for us for free. It says, 'There will be no charge for beauty queens and cars over 35 years old.'"

Saran Wrap and Mayonnaise

February 2003, *City-County Magazine*

Several years ago, my sister Katherine and I attended a spouse's program during a convention in Atlanta. The speaker was from the Total Woman, an organization that had sprung up after the publication of a book by the same name. Their philosophy was that the best in a woman centered on doing anything to make the man in her life happy. Needless to say, the concepts in the book were being greatly debated.

When I learned that the *City-County Magazine's* theme this month would be "The Best in You," I was reminded of that earlier era when some people thought that being "the best in you" meant being the Total Woman. I am probably not the only one who is glad the idea didn't catch on.

At the convention, Katherine and I sat there along with 500 other women and listened as the speaker said, "Ladies, every marriage needs a little spicing up now and then." Katherine whispered, "I told you this would be better than the tour of Stone Mountain."[19] "For example," the woman continued, "one day before your spouse gets home from

---

19 Stone Mountain is a city close to Atlanta and is the gateway to the popular Stone Mountain Park.

work, take off all your clothes and cover your body in Saran Wrap and mayonnaise. You'll surprise him."

Well, I guess so. My mind wandered to a mental picture of Jerry walking in the house to find me covered in Saran Wrap and mayonnaise. The speaker was right. He'd be surprised.

Another picture also popped into my mind. How much mayonnaise would it take to cover a 6'2" body? Word spreads quickly in Alamance County, and as I said, the Total Woman concepts were being widely discussed. Tongues would start wagging the instant I checked out of our Harris Teeter grocery store with 17 quarts of mayonnaise.

That night, several women were making fun of the mayonnaise and Saran Wrap bit, but one lady believed that the speaker had a point. Every relationship did need a little shocker every now and then. She didn't know what hers would be, but she would know it when she saw it. Apparently, she saw it the next Halloween.

At the next year's annual convention, she couldn't wait to tell us her shocker, which she swore was true. All of her children were out trick-or-treating, and her husband was sitting in the den, reading the paper. She tiptoed upstairs to the bedroom, took off all her clothes, and put on her raincoat. Then she crept back downstairs to the kitchen, where she pulled out a big, brown grocery sack. Exiting through the back door, she went around the house in the dark to the front porch, slipped the bag over her head, and rang the doorbell. On the third ring, her husband put down the paper and ambled toward the front door. When he opened it, she stepped forward—the bag still over her head—flung open the raincoat and shouted, "Trick or Treat!"

How much trouble do you think the man was in when he looked right at his wife's nude body and said, "Who is it?"

Speechless

July 2011, *Southeast Lifestyle*

I'm seldom speechless, but it can happen . . .

An extremely attractive woman about my age (meaning "on up there") waited to talk to me after a recent speech. Every time I turned toward her, she indicated I should talk to others first. She would wait.

Finally, when everyone else was gone, the woman stepped up. "Jeanne, I'm Burma Davis Posey." (I made a quick mental note that I could remember her name because of those Burma Shave signs along highways when I was growing up.[20]) She then leaned in and whispered, "I was Miss Georgia in 1968."

Being two Southern women with a common experience, we immediately hugged like long-lost cousins. Then, because the whole pageant experience was terrific for me, I said, "I hope you had as much fun at the Miss America Pageant as I did." She nodded to indicate she had and then whispered what all former pageant contestants ask each other. "How'd you do?"

---

20 "Burma-Shave was an American brand of brushless shaving cream, famous for its advertising gimmick of posting humorous rhyming poems on small sequential highway roadside signs". Wikipedia.com

In the pageant world, "How'd you do?" is code for "Did you get into the Top Ten?" I didn't, and since she could look it up, I was honest. "I was Miss Congeniality, but I didn't make it in. How about you?"

Burma didn't "make it in" either, and then she said something strange. "But Jeanne, I felt as though I was in the Top Ten because my roommate for the week made it in, and I was an intricate part of her talent."

Her statement made no sense to me. She was an "intricate part" of another contestant's talent? Someone she had met that week? Burma went on to explain in a continued hushed tone.

"Jeanne, you know how it is. I sang in the talent competition. I was classically trained and went on to have a career in voice. My roommate, with just a little dance training, danced the Charleston. She put the routine together herself and made it into the Top Ten doing the Charleston. Can you believe that?"

We both laughed at the thought of it, but Burma still hadn't answered my question, so I asked again, "But why were you part of her talent?" Her answer stopped me cold in my tracks.

"Because, Jeanne, she didn't just do the Charleston. She presented the Charleston. It was a production like no one had ever seen, and the audience and judges loved it. The other contestants did, too. She had a big, double wad of bubble gum in her mouth that she had chewed and chewed and softened up. On stage, not only did she chew the gum in time with the music as she danced, she worked it into the entire routine. She would slowly pull the gum out of her mouth and stretch it way up in the air, all eyes following her movements. She did this over and over in various ways as she sprinkled in a series of bubbles that she blew and then popped, each bigger than the previous one. The gum became the focal point, and we could see what she was leading up to. It was genius.

She ended by slowly blowing a bubble that slowly got larger than her head, her eyes growing bigger and bigger until the bubble covered them up. And still, she danced. When the bubble finally popped for her big finale', she ran off the stage to thunderous applause. The audience had been mesmerized, and so had the judges. The place went wild. With her little bubble gum/Charleston act, she won the preliminary talent competition, so we knew she would probably make the Top Ten. The judges and the audience wanted to see her do it again."

"But how did that involve you?"

"Because," Burma Davis Posey explained, leaning in as though revealing an important state secret. "On national television, they named the Top Ten, and sure enough, she made it in. She hurried to the dressing room with the others to change into her talent costume. While she changed clothes, I stood at the dressing room door and warmed up the gum."

. . . Speechless.

Oh, My! Times Have Changed

August, 2012, *Southeast Lifestyle*

The 75th anniversary of the Miss North Carolina Scholarship Pageant was held earlier this summer. No, I was not the first one crowned. But when organizers asked us two years ago to please hold the date, I knew I would be there. It stretched into a several-day event for us, including a gala at the North Carolina Museum of History, where a six-month exhibit on the Pageant opened that weekend. Most of my pageant "stuff" is already in the Graham Historical Museum. I gave 'em everything: gowns, trophies, ukulele.

I didn't miss any of the reunion weekend—the gala, exhibit opening, and red carpet walk that we thought was funny but loved. And, of course, the 75th Pageant. Everything was special. But spending time with forty-four women who shared a similar experience? Priceless. And oh, the stories . . .

My favorite was hearing Miss NC 1946 Trudy Riley, who is in her mid-eighties and smiling away, tell us about a picture of her in a swimsuit still on display in a hot dog restaurant in Wilson. She noted that because metal was in short supply after the war, her crown was made of tinfoil, cardboard, and roses. Someone said teasingly, "They'd probably take it down, Trudy, if it bothers you." Trudy's eyes opened wide. "Bothers me? Are you kidding? I love it." We already knew that because we're all alike. Once a Miss NC . . . .

All the "formers" were hosted at a luncheon at the Governor's Mansion. Taxpayers shouldn't be upset, as the luncheon was funded by people in Raleigh who had supported the Pageant through the years. I had never been to the Governor's Mansion. It's absolutely gorgeous, and North Carolinians can be proud of it. Of course, this is being written by someone who loves history and antiques. The similarity of all the "antique" Miss North Carolinas being around the antique furniture and having the gala at a museum did not go unnoticed by this particular "former."

The invitation to lunch came from the Governor herself, but she wasn't there. Not a problem. It made it easier to sneak upstairs and go through her jewelry.

What to wear on a big weekend like that was a challenge to someone my age. I'm 68. Let's see. Gotta hide the upper arms. Can't be too tight at the waist because I'll want the dress to zip. I certainly don't want anything too low-cut. Of course, at 68, "too low cut" would be lower than it used to be. (Younger women won't "get that" now, but they will in time.)

Before the big televised show, I got on an elevator at the hotel with another woman about my age. We exchanged pleasantries, and I learned that she was going to the Pageant, too. On the next floor, a much younger woman got on with us, and we knew she was also going to the Pageant. She had on a gorgeous beaded gown that fit her thin body perfectly. As she "mashed" one of the elevator buttons, I noticed that the back of her gown swirled on the floor behind her. When she turned toward us, she knew exactly how to use her hand to flip the swirly part in place. That's when I saw the front of the gown. Oh, my! Times have changed.

The front of this beautiful gown was cut in a V shape from her shoulders down to her waist. My first thought was that she had the gown on backward. But then I realized that would put the swirly part in the front, and she would trip. My second thought was that her bosoms were going to pop out. I looked away. Seconds later, the other woman asked her something, and when the younger woman diverted her eyes to her, I sneaked another look. No, she seemed to have it under control. Tape? Glue?

As we descended toward the lobby, I held off as long as I could, but it was a losing battle. About the third floor, I just couldn't resist saying with a straight face, "I love that gown. I almost bought the same one."

Ah, youth. It went right over her head, but the other woman turned into the corner of the elevator as though she were in timeout. She was trying to suppress her laughter, but I could see her shoulders bouncing up and down.

Suffice it to say, I'm glad I went to the reunion. If the names Lu Long Ogburn, Elaine Herndon, Betty Lane Evans, Ann Herring, Maria Beale Fletcher (who became Miss America), Sharon Finch, Patricia Johnson, Susan Lawrence, and even Jeanne Swanner sound familiar to any of you . . . I hope you remember us with a smile.

Oh, and if that last name on the list seems slightly familiar to people in Guilford, it could be because I didn't win in Raleigh. I won in Greensboro when the Pageant was sponsored by the Guilford Jaycees. They were raising money for a stoplight at Guilford College.

We all wished the 75th Miss North Carolina, Arlie Honeycutt, well and the best of luck at the Miss America Pageant. Mostly, we hope she enjoys traveling around our state as much as we did.

One more thing. Don't call the police about the Governor's jewelry. They stopped me at the second level.

Southern Ham From a Southern Ham

November 2012, *Southeast Lifestyle*

The "Big Holiday Eating Season" is upon us, and that means food. Heaps and heaps of food, including special dishes, we often have only at this time of year. Comparing it to a football game, I'd sum up the forthcoming Big Holiday Eating Season like this: Thanksgiving weekend is the kickoff, and we hit the ground running. The kickoff is followed by the three steady quarters—Christmas, Hanukkah, and the entire month of December—when we plod along steadily stuffing calories in our mouths for days in a row. The fourth quarter frenzy takes place over New Year's because it's our "last chance" before we have to diet. Then, the game's over. We collapse and start getting ourselves back in shape by starving until the Super Bowl. The process repeats itself every year.

As the "Big Holiday Eating Season" approached the year I was president of the National Speakers Association, I sent each of my eighteen board members what I thought was the perfect gift from a Southern humorist: slices of country ham. Real country ham. Country ham trimmed with enough fat to make red-eye gravy. My gift card proclaimed, "It's the Holidays! Time to eat! Enjoy Southern ham from a Southern ham." It seemed clever to me.

The Southern board members raved. Well, of course. Receiving real country ham is like finding gold for the Southerner any time of the year. But heaven help me, the responses of speakers from "somewheres else" revealed that they had no idea what to do with real country ham. A seminar leader in Arizona used her country ham during Thanksgiving weekend and cooked her slices in the oven for hours. When she finally took a bite, a cap came off her tooth. A motivational speaker in California saved his ham for Christmas, mainly because he didn't know what to do with it. Then he beat it with a mallet and cooked it in a microwave until it was inedible. A sales trainer in Minnesota boiled his ham for New Year's to the point where even his dog wouldn't eat it. In general, most thought the ham had spoiled in shipping. So sad. So very sad.

Directly from Our Worldwide Headquarters

December 2012, *Southeast Lifestyle*

The Holiday Season is busy for all of us. In my little office, we go into triple time, not because I book extra speeches. I don't. Actually, I cut back on speeches to enjoy time with my husband, "Left Brain," and watch my grandsons play basketball. But my office is in overdrive because we don't use a fulfillment house.

You might not be familiar with the term, but I'm betting you know what fulfillment houses do. They receive and fill orders for companies or individuals. If I used one, they would handle all my CD, DVD, and book orders. In that case, I would never see the orders or my products. I would just get a check when all was said and done, and our house wouldn't be so cluttered.

It would certainly be easier to take advantage of this type of outsourcing, but we don't do it that way at the "Worldwide Headquarters of JSR, Inc." which is located in a spare bedroom of our house. JSR stands for my name: Jeanne Swanner Robertson. It's not a Fortune 500 company. We "insource."

Our little team has perfected the task of filling orders from years of practice. "Left Brain" brings items from storage every few days and keeps up with the inventory and check depositing, paying taxes, etc. "Bestest friend" Norma Rose runs the Packaging Department, which is located in our game room. ("Game room" is a fancy name for a garage with a ping pong table.) She boxes up items and has them ready to go. My longtime assistant, Toni, takes all orders and then fills them in the JSR Branch Office, which is located in her spare bedroom. Toni has a BIG JOB. She went to the Elon post office so many times last Christmas that someone there asked if she was running a fulfillment house.

"And what does Jeanne do?" you might ask. Well, for Pete's sake, I sign the orders! That's the reason we still do the shipping. I can't personalize those autographs if orders are outsourced. I autograph items all year, but over the holidays, it's almost around the clock.

I guess I'm still a small-town "girl" from Graham, NC, who also loves Mayberry humor. Sheriff Andy Taylor might say that autographing when requested seems like "the friendly thing to do." Of course, you can carry "friendly" only so far. We don't gift wrap. There would be a mutiny if I even suggested it.

In truth, doing it all ourselves is a little more profitable and heaps more fun. People we don't know personally brighten our office every day. It's impossible to autograph "Happy Anniversary, MeMaw and Pap Pap" without smiling. I appreciate the cleverness of "Please sign the DVD 'Happy Birthday to Suzie Q on State Road 2.'"

If you see a light on in my house in the wee hours, know I'm as happy as I can be, sitting there signing to people named, for example, Aunt Fannie, Aunt Thursa, Uncle Glover, Aunt Veenie and Uncle Fleener.

Work came to a stop the time an order arrived requesting, "Please sign to Dolores Faye, from Dolores Mae, Dolores Kay, Dolores Gay, and Susan." We figured Susan must have been the first wife's daughter—the one before Dolores Faye.

This year's favorite request thus far was a bit unusual, but we figured it out. "To Sue and Bill. See, the Mayans were wrong. Merry Christmas 2012." (If you don't understand this, ask around.)

Every year at this time, I smile when I recall the request from a sweet Southern lady who wanted a holiday gift for her sister. According to her, both were in their eighties. Toni received the call and asked if she wanted me to autograph her sister's item. "Oh, that would be so nice," the lady drawled. "My sister will love it. What will Jeanne write?"

"I'm sure she'll put your sister's name," Toni explained. "Then, unless you request specific words, she'll put something like Merry Christmas or maybe Happy Hanukkah."

The lady thought about it a few seconds and then said, "Well, Happy Hanukkah will certainly be O.K. if that's what Jeanne wants to write. But my sister's not Jewish."

Merry Christmas and Happy Hanukkah to you and all your Aunt Veenies and Uncle Fleeners!

Where's Jeanne?

February 2016, *Southeast Lifestyle*

"Break a leg." People have been telling me this for years before speeches and theatre shows. I've told others the same thing many times. Supposedly, good luck, whereas saying "Good Luck" brings bad luck. Got it? Sadly, I took it literally on 12/17/2015. I fell before the neighborhood hot dog supper at our house. I was rushing, hands full, etc. Broke my femur. Ambulance. (Leaving the neighborhood shouting, "The party's off! Spread the word! The party is off!") Six days in the hospital, then a rehab place where I spent Christmas and New Year's and still remain. I no longer like "Break a Leg." But please don't start saying, "Go Jump in a Lake." It would be so cold. And, oh yes, I found humor in all of it. Why not? Keep laughing! PS. Don't worry, I'll be back on stage, rocking away and telling stories.

What happens when one is in hospital and ortho rehab for weeks? I don't know about others, but as for me, I've watched every episode of *Property Brothers*, *Chip & Jo Gaines* in Texas, *Fixer-Upper*, and *Love It or List It*. I've mumbled over and over to the TV, "Don't go over your budget!"

What I want to do right now is get out of this place, get home, find a sledgehammer, and start whacking out walls. I know popcorn ceilings are out. I've heard it repeatedly every single day. "The first thing is to get rid of these popcorn ceilings." I can't do anything about it until I'm set free! Free!

What happened to *The Swamp People*? I didn't want to do that, but it was fun to shout at the TV, "Shoooot it! Shoooot it!" Alligator Rights people, please don't fuss. Not today.

Thanks, and keep laughing!

Silver Alert

June 2016, *Southeast Lifestyle*

I broke my femur in December 2015. Smack dab in two, right above my left knee. Yes, it has been mentioned to me by many well-wishers, "It's hard to break your femur. It's the strongest bone in your body." That may be true, but trust me, it's breakable. With the break and complications after surgery, husband "Left Brain" and I agreed with the physicians who suggested I get inpatient physical therapy. We were lucky to get a room in Edgewood Place at the Village of Brookwood retirement living community not far from our house in Burlington. I spent Christmas, New Year's, the Super Bowl frenzy, Valentine's Day, two snow storms, and most of the NCAA basketball season under the care of capable folks doing their best to help me. At one point, they even saved my life. That's a story for another day, but suffice it to say, I am blessed.

In Edgewood Place, I was mostly with folks I thought were the "older generation." In that area of the facility, if one's not careful, one could get her wheelchair tangled up with another person's cane. The fact that they were the same age as me was something that did not go unnoticed by me or my grandsons when they visited and whispered, "NeNe, most of these people are old."

"Yes, we are. Thank you for coming. Now turn the TV back to *Fixer-Upper*."

After several months, I wanted to leave, but since I couldn't yet put any weight on my left leg, it made it difficult. Friends who said repeatedly, "Let me know if there is anything I can do for you," didn't mean organize a breakout or dig a tunnel. They meant to bring a milkshake. I did my best to follow my own advice and find the humor in the situation.

After almost three months in rehab for me, I wanted to get off my floor, even if for just a little while. When Left Brain came to visit that day, I was waiting in my wheelchair. Would he mind pushing me to the other section of The Village? Maybe we could go over to the lake or drop by the library. I had heard rumors of a lovely gift shop. Lots to do and see "over there." Away we went.

We didn't know that I had to check out with the nurse in charge before leaving my section. We just left. I was wheeled right out of there as though we had good sense. It was so refreshing to be "out" that we meandered through the other side for almost an hour before heading back to my section. When we exited the elevator, staff members were standing there, getting ready to spread out through the buildings. One quickly shouted to others gathered at the nurses' station, "We've found her! Cancel the alert!"

Then, to me, "Where have you been? We have a Silver Alert out on you!"

I could tell they were upset. By then, I was too. A Silver Alert? Couldn't they have at least said, "Dirty-blonde?"

Basic Etiquette

April 2017, *SE Gazette*

The 80th anniversary of the Miss North Carolina Pageant will be on statewide TV on Saturday, June 24, 2017. (No, I didn't compete in the first one. Y'all are so funny.) That's more than two months from now and certainly not on most of our "radars" at this point or, for some, never. I understand. Just so you know, though, around the state, young women are working their heads off to be ready to compete in June. They're fine-tuning their respective talents, studying world events for their interviews, and walking in heels with sheets tied around their waists, dragging on the floor like evening gowns. Having "been there," I strongly suggest they also bone up on their etiquette.

The week after I won the title of Miss North Carolina in the last millennium (some 50 years ago), two women with the Pageant began working with me to prepare me for the Miss America Pageant. Or, as many say in the south, the Miss "Ahmur'ica" Pageant. They said that I was the most raw material they had ever started with. (I told Mother that, and in horror, she said, "They ended a sentence with a preposition?")

It was too late to do much about my talent. I only knew four chords on the baritone ukulele and accompanied myself as I sang an original song. Some news reports listed it as comedy, but I was singing the best I could. There wasn't enough time to switch to playing something like the harp, and anyway, while it might have scored points, no one had ever seen a singing harpist. The two women put talent aside and hoped the judges in Atlantic City might nod off when I was performing. (They also discussed causing a diversion in the lobby at that time.) Instead, we worked on walking and talking and similar things that they believed needed improvement and were "doable" within the time frame. In the middle of all this training, they accompanied me to a reception in my honor, after which they quickly turned their attention toward improving my etiquette skills to "cover all the bases."

The reception occurred soon after I was crowned Miss NC in Greensboro. I remember the occasion as though it were yesterday. It was the first time I met cheese surrounded by thick, red plastic. As the guest of honor at the reception, I was smiling and conversing with a small group when a wait staff member extended a tray in my direction, offering some type of hors d'oeuvre shaped in small red triangle wedges. It looked like cheese with maybe a tomato around it or pimento. It didn't dawn on me the red part was thick plastic. I simply nodded. "Thank you," I picked up one of the red "whatevers" around cheese and placed it on my little plate. Minutes later, I nonchalantly put the wedge in my mouth, thick red plastic cover and all, and started trying to chew. On the first bite, the plastic stuck to my top teeth and embedded in the bottom ones, holding them together almost shut tight. If I tried to open my mouth, I feared my teeth would be pulled out of my gums. That would not do. Mama and Daddy had spent a lot of hard-earned money on braces for those teeth. I went to work, chewed off a small piece of the plastic, and stored it on my right cheek. After repeating the process over and over, I looked like a squirrel with nuts in bulging cheeks and a crown on its head. Being young and determined to hide this sort of thing, I slowly chewed away while trying to appear interested in the conversation, smiling from behind my locked jaws. I was thinking, "This is tough cheese." Others must have been thinking, "She's going to the Miss America Pageant?" A kind woman slipped me a napkin and whispered, "Don't swallow it."

After that reception, the powers-that-be decided to go over a few areas other than walking and world events. "Etiquette school" moved to the top of my daily list. This bothered my mother because she thought she had done a good job teaching me about such things. When she heard about the plastic, though, she sighed and told the women, "Do what you can." Being nice, they told Mother it was best to cover all the bases. In a matter of weeks, I learned more etiquette than I ever cared to know. It wasn't enough.

It is not that growing up in the wonderful small town of Graham, NC, I had never heard of a finger bowl. I had heard the term "finger bowl" somewhere, sometime. It was just that we didn't use them every day in Graham. To be truthful, at that point in my life, I had never seen a finger bowl. I guess if I had ever thought about it, I would have thought a finger bowl would be about the size of somewhere to put your fingers. I would have never dreamed it's a bowl 4-5 inches across that's filled with warm water so people can wash their fingers at the table during very formal meals. Quite frankly, in Graham High School Home Economics, we were taught not to eat with our fingers. (If we had done so, Aunt Bea would have come out of nowhere and hit us on the hand with her spoon.) I certainly wouldn't have thought this bowl would have a lemon slice in the water to help cut the grease off one's fingers.

Several weeks after this etiquette push began, I was back in Greensboro as the guest of honor at a formal banquet at a country club. As the honoree, I sat at the center of the head table with people to my right and left. As soon as I saw the situation, my head started working like a computer, and computers hadn't been invented. Etiquette. Etiquette. They had taught me something about this exact situation. Now, what was it? It came to me. I had been taught that as the guest of honor and the person at the center of the head table, everyone would wait until I began to eat before they started.

As mentioned, it was a formal banquet. During the first food courses served, I tried out what I had learned. Each time a course was brought in, I sat right there at the center of the head table, smiling my pageant smile and chitchatting, but I was watching the rest of the table out of the corner of my eye. You would have been proud of me at that point. With each served course, I smiled at the people on my right and the people on my left, and when all were served, I picked up the correct utensil and started eating. Sure enough, the others at the head table then followed suit. The women helping me were correct! Everything clicked along smoothly through an assortment of courses, and then, my Graham stomach told me it was time for dessert. This is where you wouldn't have been as proud.

At that point, the waiter brought in a bowl about five inches wide and put it right down in front of me. Well, for Pete's sake. The liquid in the bowl looked like water to me, but it had a lemon slice floating around in there. I thought to myself, this must be some new type of lemon dessert.

I smiled patiently and watched while they served the people on my right. Then I turned my head and smiled my pageant smile while they served the people on my left. And when everyone at the head table was served, I picked up my spoon and dove right in.

Three people at the head table picked up their spoons and dove into their finger bowls, too. I've always wondered if they were as clueless as I was or if they were trying to make me feel better. After several spoonfuls, I finally saw others washing their fingers. It hit me, and I froze, spoon in my mouth. They didn't say anything in etiquette school about delicately getting a spoon out of your mouth and back in place on the tablecloth.

My career as a professional speaker for fifty-plus years has allowed me to attend literally thousands of meal events. In all my years of travel, I have encountered only one other finger bowl. It was at The Greenbrier in West Virginia. I almost fell asleep before I was introduced to speak. They served an eight—not a seven—but an eight-course meal. At one point, I remember thinking the next time they brought in food, it would be bacon and eggs.

Contestants. You've got a little more than two months to be ready for this year's Miss North Carolina Pageant. It's crunch time. Please remember that many of us out here truly know how hard you're working. I'm one of them. That lets me offer a piece of advice. Cover all your bases. When you're on those treadmills, slap an etiquette book on the shelf in front of you and read. It might help you get to the Miss "Ahmur'ica" Pageant. Good luck!

Where Do You Go to Church?

January 2019, *SE Gazette*

Happy New Year!

You read it here first. My New Year's Resolution is to attend church more often. There are many reasons my husband "Left Brain" and I need to do this, but here's what sparked making it a Resolution.

Left Brain and I are Christians, but we just don't go to church much on Sunday mornings. There's an easy explanation, excuse, reason, whatever one wants to label it, for our lack of attendance. Here it is: I'm not home on the weekends, and he won't go without me. I think my excuse is better than his.

As most of you know, I've spoken at conventions for fifty-five years. Those meetings can occur any day of the week, and often, that means I'm gone on weekends. My weekend work went into overdrive about ten years ago when I started doing theater shows. One doesn't need to pay for a research study to know that theaters sell more tickets for shows on the weekends than during the week.

My regular routine now is to fly out of the "Greensboro, High Point, Winston-Salem, Regional Triad, Piedmont, International Airport" on Thursdays to do shows on Friday and Saturday nights and often Sunday afternoons and evenings.

Put another way, I'm on the road all weekend. So, see, that explains it. I can't get to church on Sunday mornings. It's my story, and I'm sticking to it. If I don't have a Sunday show, I'm flying home on Sunday morning. I know what you're thinking. Believe me, I know these seem like excuses, excuses for not getting to church, but I'm going to do better this coming year because . . . .

Last March, I taped my 9th CD/DVD at the Paramount Theater in Burlington. We've used this location for many of my filmed shows because local people like to come, and we enjoy working with students and staff at Elon University. Just for the fun of it, we put down a red carpet on the sidewalk outside the theater, leading up the street and around to the corner flower shop.

Here we were in Burlington, North Carolina, acting as though we were walking the Red Carpet in Hollywood, and everyone got in the flow. It was funny, and we had fun. My tapings are open seating. People have free tickets, and once inside, they can sit anywhere. This means they tend to line up early to get good seats. As many friends have told me, "We like being near the front in case a camera picks us up."

Before the show last March, I went outside while people were waiting for the doors to open and "worked" the waiting line of people. It felt like "old home week" because I knew almost everyone. About fifteen feet from the front doors to the theater, however, a friend indicated he wanted me to meet a couple that came as his guests, a couple I did not know. My friend explained they were new to Alamance County, having moved from eastern North Carolina. We shook hands, and I said, "Thank you for coming to my show, and welcome to Alamance County. How long have you been here?" "About nine months," the husband said, smiling. His wife Sarah was in conversation with someone behind her, but he touched her shoulder. She turned and stepped in our direction so I could meet her, also.

I told both of them what I sincerely believe. "After nine months, I'm sure you already know, you will love this area. What brought you here?"

The man responded, "I'm a minister. We were transferred here."

I reacted positively, but of course, I had to try to be funny. (There was a crowd around us.) "A minister? Great. You're just in time. We've got some heathens around here. Maybe you can save a bunch of 'em. Which church?"

And Reverend Ross Carter of Front Street United Methodist Church in Burlington broke into a big grin and said, "Yours."

Well, of course, the crowd around us burst out laughing. I did, too, but I couldn't help but defend myself. "Wait a minute. Now, y'all just wait a minute. Cut me some slack here."

I turned back to explain to my new minister, who was enjoying my sudden befuddleness, "I make my living doing theater shows, and I'm not in church on Sundays because I work on weekends."

Rev. Carter smiled even bigger as he nodded. "I certainly understand that. I work on weekends, too."

Happy New Year. See y'all in church.

My 'Scuse Me—Go Ahead People

September 2019, *SE Gazette*

I've been blessed to travel this great nation, giving speeches and theater shows for the last fifty-six years. But make no bones about it. As the song says, "I like calling North Carolina home."

The greatest television show ever produced is *The Andy Griffith Show*. Period. Don't even try to argue with me about that statement. The show owns my heart. I like *American Picker* on the History Channel because it makes me think the junk in our house might be worth something. I also can get caught up in *Fixer-Upper* with Chip and Joanna. After one show, though, I tore out a wall, which took us months to fix. I remember my husband looking at the mess and saying, "Now What?" While in a hotel room on a speaking trip, I might even find myself staring at *The Swamp People*. "Thuoot him! Thuoot him!" But I stand by my statement, "The greatest television show ever produced is *The Andy Griffith Show*."

In doing research for a project on *The Andy Griffith Show*, I attended Mayberry Days in Mt. Airy several times. Twice, I even perched on a convertible as the Potato Queen and tossed out potatoes during the parade. (Some former Miss North Carolinas just can't move on.)

Tourists poured into town for the weekend. We lined up to eat porkchop sandwiches at the Snappy Lunch and crowded into the movie theater to hear a cockatiel named Chipper whistle the theme song from the show. ("The Fishing Hole" if you're a trivia person.) Getting through the song took a little time because Chipper wasn't a deep thinker. If he stopped anywhere during the song, he couldn't go back and pick up where he left off. His brain just wasn't that strong. This meant that if anyone coughed or shuffled their feet or opened the door in back in the middle of his performance, Chipper stopped whistling and snapped his little head in the direction of the noise. After a few seconds of total quiet, he had to take it from the top. The problem was that when he snapped his little head in the direction of the noise, people turned purple, trying to be quiet but generally burst out laughing. When this commotion finally died down, Chipper took it from the top. The whole scenario was hilarious, and the longer it went on, the funnier it got. Sheriff Andy Taylor would say, "Don't that beat all?"

When Chipper finally made it through the song uninterrupted, all of us in the audience were about to "bust our gussets." That session ended, and many of us moseyed over to the jail to see a goat that was tied up out front. Remember that episode? Blewey! It's amazing how long people will watch a goat chew grass, raising his head every so often to stare back at the onlookers while he chewed. I was just relieved he wasn't eating dynamite.

One store proprietor that weekend stands out in my mind. I told him we were having fun, and he said, "Oh, we love the Mayberry crowd. I call y'all the 'Scuse me—go ahead people.'"

"The what?"

"It's just something I've noticed," he explained. "During Mayberry Days, when Mayberry Days people arrive at the store door at the same time, they always stop, smile, and say, 'Scuse me. Go ahead.'"

I'll be the first to admit that North Carolina has its share of unfriendly old goats like Ben Weaver from Mayberry, whom we'd like to tie up somewhere. But my travels throughout our state for more than five decades tell me that the majority of North Carolinians are nice, polite, and friendly 'Scuse me—go ahead people.

And living right here "amongst them" as they would say in Mayberry, is one of the big reasons I love calling North Carolina home.

"Aw, BIG ain't the word for it."

Call It Like It Is!

February 2020, *SE Gazette*

Sometimes, it's good when people cut to the chase. Be blunt. Call it like it is. Then, other times . . .

Who amongst us hasn't looked in the mirror, put the palms of both hands on the sides of our face, and pushed the skin slightly upward just to see how much better we would look with a little plastic surgery? I certainly have, and truthfully, I look better. The problem is that we can't rest our elbows on a table or the arms of a chair and keep our hands in place, pushing up for the day. I tried it on a cross-country flight, and both arms went to sleep. Eventually, I couldn't move my fingers. And when the man in the window seat wanted out, it was awkward to stand up and step into the aisle without moving my hands away from my jowls. Several passengers around my seat did a double take. It was as though I was holding my head in place on my body.

Not long ago, I was looking at new photos I had made for my work and, to my horror, realized my left eyelid was drooping. I got out a magnifying glass to check it out. Yep, in the photo, that left eye was shut far more than the right one. The magnifying glass only made it more alarming.

Immediately, I went into the office where my longtime assistant, Toni, was working. "Toni," I stated, "My left eye is drooping. It looks horrible. I'm thinking about having it fixed, and while the surgeon is in there for the eye, maybe have him or her pull up the rest of my face."

Toni always calls it like it is. "You're going to have a facelift?"

"I didn't say I was going to have a facelift,' I replied. "I need to get my left eye fixed, and while someone is moving around that eye doing repairs, I see no harm in having the rest of my face pulled up. You call it 'having a facelift.' I call it 'multitasking.' It's a 'two birds with one stone' type thing. Eye and face at the same time, thank you very much. Now, go home."

Toni, who truly does cut to the chase, gave a classic response. "Jeanne, you can pull that eye up and your face straight if you want to, but your elbows are going to give you away."

I snapped my elbows to my waistline and held them there so they couldn't be seen.

At that point, I told Toni I needed her to get me an appointment with a plastic surgeon to check out my left eye and anything else that needed a little "work" on it. "But for Pete's sake, Toni, don't call anyone in this county. Get an appointment with someone far, far away."

She got me an appointment in Durham, only thirty miles east of Burlington. I call that an "office misunderstanding" or poor communication on my part.

A few weeks later, I was ushered into a plastic surgeon's office in Durham. He was at his desk and most professional. I sat in a chair across from him. After the cordialities, he asked politely, "Why are you here, Mrs. Robertson?"

"You can't see why? Look at my left eye." I turned my head slightly so he could see my left eye straight on. "It's drooping and showing up in photos that way. I'd like to have you fix it, and while you're in there rooting around on the eye, pull up the rest of my face a little."

The doctor frowned slightly while staring at my left eye. Soon, he came from around the desk and, with a penlight, checked out that eye thoroughly. Then he cut off the tiny light, went back around the desk, and sat down. It was awkwardly quiet until he spoke.

"Mrs. Robertson, there's nothing wrong with your eye. One eye always looks a little more shut than the other in a headshot that is photographed straight on. If that may have caused your concern, try to turn your head a bit in your photos."

"But I'm afraid it's going to close completely," I protested. "I don't want that to happen."

The doctor took the time to explain. "Mrs. Robertson, you might recall that when you were in the lobby filling out paperwork, you were not asked why you were here. I prefer not to know what area a prospective patient thinks needs work. I prefer to look at you when you come into my office and see where I think can be improved."

It made sense to me, but I didn't say anything.

I didn't have to wait in silence very long. Soon, he said kindly, "The truth is, Mrs. Robertson, that when you came in here today, I didn't even notice your left eye."

Right there is when it would have been best for him to stop talking. But nooooo. He added, "I thought you were here about your neck."

"Calling it like it is" is not always a wonderful thing. I got in the car and drove back to Alamance County.

An hour later, I was standing in front of a mirror at home with the palms of both hands on the sides of my face, gently pushing my skin up from my neck and thinking. "Hmm? Maybe if I try to always keep my chin tilted slightly, it will smooth out that sagging neck. Yeah, that works!"

Oh, look. The overhead light needs dusting.

The Senior Trip

February 2021, *SE Gazette*

As many of my readers know, homeschooling during this pandemic is tougher than people might think. There's all that strict "book learning" to be taught to various age levels while also trying to balance social interaction between their children and their children's peers.

During one stage of my life, I taught physical education and speech in a small school in Alabama. I loved teaching and my students. Being young and eager to please, I almost worked myself to death. Why? Well . . .

As is often the case in smaller schools, the teachers sponsor extracurricular activities. I coached all the sports that girls were allowed to play at that time. (Title IX had not yet passed.) I also sponsored the JV and Varsity cheerleaders, coached the debate team, chaperoned the Junior-Senior Prom and football dances, took up tickets at ball games, coordinated May Day events, and directed the senior class play. I could go on and on, but you get the picture. In addition, I was giving humorous speeches on the weekends any time I could work them into my schedule. At that point, I hadn't yet realized that speaking could develop into a full-time career.

In my third year of teaching, I was the senior class advisor. Thus, it fell to me to organize and accompany the seniors on their much anticipated "educational" Senior Trip. They didn't want to go to Washington, D.C., to our state capital, or even to Disney World. No siree. They had been planning their trip for three years. They were going to New Orleans. Period. It was a long but doable chartered bus ride away.

The parents and the principal of the school gave in to the students' dream trip by the time they were juniors, and the students looked forward to the trip for a year. By the time the bus pulled out heading south, all of the seniors were eighteen years old, the drinking age in New Orleans. And I am not referring to sweet tea.

None of the parents were going. Three other adult chaperones and I would be in charge. I was the only one connected to the school and felt an enormous responsibility. I met with the parents to get a better understanding of the rules they wanted to be enforced on the trip. My mouth dropped open when it became apparent that all the parents really wanted was for their teenagers to have someone to call if they got in big trouble. (As in, bail them out?)

The principal instructed me to make sure there were plenty of educational activities and to keep them busy. Being the typical overly eager young teacher who wanted to do what the principal instructed, I threw myself into the planning, especially the part of the trip that made it "educational." Let us never forget, however, that there are different types of educational experiences.

We were to be in New Orleans for almost a week. What. Were. We. Thinking? I filled the days with tours, cruises up and down the Mississippi River, museums, bus trips throughout the city, etc. They especially enjoyed seeing the above-ground cemeteries, although they finally said to me, "When you've seen one, you've seen them all." One night, we dressed up and went to a sit-down dinner (cloth tablecloth and napkins!) in a big hotel, where we saw a live show by Frank Gorshin. Mr. Gorshin was a well-known impersonator and actor in that era. You may remember that he played the Riddler in the Batman television series. He was terrific that night! The students couldn't stop talking about the experience. I was happy because it was educational to dress up for a nice meal in a large ballroom and see a family entertainer.

Another night, we went to Jackson Square and ate beignets covered in powdered sugar at Café du Monde. Then we squeezed into Preservation Hall, where we sat on the floor to hear true New Orleans jazz. Did I mention touring historic churches? You won't believe how many historic churches are in New Orleans. One of the students finally asked, "Are we trying to see them all?" I was trying to make sure the young people under my care learned the city's history and area. I also was trying to tire them out during the days.

Several nights, the students were on their own for "free time" with a set curfew to be back in the hotel, where the chaperones checked them in and went back to bed. I figured what you don't see, you don't know. I did notice that by the third day, the students were sleeping on the daytime bus tours. They couldn't seem to keep their eyes open. All in all, though, it was a grand trip. We didn't have any real trouble, and I thought we had a good mix of planned educational side trips and free time.

A few weeks after returning home, I ran into the mother of one of the senior boys who had been on the trip. Laughing, she filled me in. It seems that when the senior returned home, she let her son sleep as long as he could. When he finally surfaced and was hungry, she made him sit down at the kitchen table to talk to her about the trip. Getting teenagers to tell parents all the details of a Senior Trip can be like pulling teeth. (From experience, I can tell you the parents shouldn't want to know all the details.) Apparently, the young man recalled every "educational" tour we took and explained them to her in great detail. She listened patiently until he said, "And that was about it."

Throughout his long explanation of the trip, she had two items hidden in her lap that he couldn't see. She was very patient.

"You didn't mention going down to the French Quarter or walking up and down Bourbon Street," she inquired, as mothers would. "Did you at least get to take in those sites or maybe eat some Cajun food in the Quarter?"

She told me that her son shifted his weight in his chair at that point while he mustered his best look of innocence before answering. "Bourbon Street? Oh, yeah. Yeah. I remember it. We went down there. Our hotel was nearby, so we walked around in the French Quarter a couple of times. I think that included walking on Bourbon Street. But the truth is, Mama, there wasn't much to do on Bourbon Street except look at the interesting people."

Mama had him. Caught him like a small fish on a big hook. "I'm sure there were interesting people on Bourbon Street, but guess what?" she added with a smile. "Nice people are in the French Quarter, too." At that point, she pulled out the two hidden items in her lap and pushed one of them across the kitchen table. It was a letter inviting her son to return to a certain establishment on his next trip to New Orleans. Then, she pushed the second item across the table. "I know there are nice people there," she continued, "because one of the nice people at a Bourbon Street strip joint mailed your billfold back to you."

Dontcha love people?

You go, Mama!

Plus, Other Important Stuff

Here's One That Tickles
My Funny Bone

October 2000, *City-County Magazine*

Coffee breaks. Exercise breaks. Breaks to meditate. You name it, the American people can take some time off to do it. So why not humor breaks? Those times each day when you take a few minutes to sit by yourself . . . and laugh. It's good medicine, and it doesn't cost a penny.

In order to pull up laughs when you need them, I suggest keeping a personal file of stories, cartoons, and memories that make you laugh. Then, feeling the need for a humor break, take the top item, get by yourself, and read it. As your collection increases, the humorous items will roll around less frequently. Before long, they'll surprise you. I have a huge personal collection of stuff that tickles my funny bone, and here's one of 'em.

As the doctor made a house visit, the sick person's entire family gathered around, so the physician asked the private duty nurse to step into the bathroom with him to keep all the ears from hearing the discussion. They stepped into the small room and shut the door. Naturally, the family gathered around outside, trying to hear.

Inside, the doctor put down the lid of the toilet and sat down while he and the nurse went over the patient's condition. When they finished their discussion, he stood to leave and, out of habit, reached over and flushed the commode.

The family, eavesdropping outside the door, scattered . . . but exchanged quizzical looks as the doctor and the nurse emerged from the bathroom.

"Don't Forget to Zip"

March 2001, *City-County Magazine*

Among the passengers on one of her flights, an airline flight attendant told me, was a lady with a small boy and girl in tow. Shortly before lunch was to be served, the lady and her charges visited the toilets in the rear of the cabin. The lady sent the little boy into one of the restrooms and accompanied the little girl into the other one.

The little boy finished his business, left the toilet, and headed back to his seat. An elderly man, who had been waiting, went to the cubicle the little boy had vacated.

In a moment or so, the woman and the little girl came out of the other toilet. The woman, thinking the little boy was still engaged, rapped sharply on the door across the aisle and said, "When you're finished, don't forget to zip your pants."

In a few moments, the elderly man emerged, stopped by the flight attendant, and said, "Thanks, Miss. When you get old, you forget some-times, and it's nice of the airline to have you girls remind us."

Make Me an Offer

May 2003, *City-County Magazine*

The door prizes at a September meeting in Atlanta were two sets of tickets to a Braves baseball game and one set of tickets to a local theater production—winners' choice. The Braves were in a pennant race, so the room buzzed in anticipation of possible game tickets.

The first winner leaped to his feet at the sound of his name and shot both arms straight into the air. People glanced at one another in disgust. Well, he didn't have to scream so loudly. They watched as he knocked over two chairs while running to the front to grab the baseball tickets from the emcee's hand. "Give you $200 for them," a voice shouted as the winner returned to his seat, shaking his head to indicate they were not for sale. The masses settled. There was still a chance at the remaining set of game tickets.

The next name drawn was a fellow who had left the room. Without even checking in the hall, the emcee immediately declared, "You have to be present to win. Draw again." The audience applauded—friendly bunch of buzzards.

A moan spread through the room when the next name was announced. With no fanfare, a woman walked slowly toward the head table, her brow wrinkled in thought. Although every individual in the room would have done questionable deeds for the remaining set of baseball tickets, it was not a clear-cut choice for her. People sat up and took notice when she looked back at her friends, shrugged, and mouthed, "The baseball tickets or the theater tickets?" Sensing this slight indecision, the vultures around the room rose from their chairs and shouted, "Theater tickets! Take the theater tickets!"

She bit her lip, looked from one set of tickets to the other, and then lifted her head toward the audience. The chants grew louder. "THEATER TICKETS! THEATER TICKETS!"

Spinning abruptly, she snatched the baseball tickets from the emcee's hand, thrust them into the air, and screamed, "I have a child in college! Make me an offer!"

One of the vultures shouted back, ''I'll give you $5 for your child and $250 for the tickets!"

Trading Apple Juice for Coffee

June 2003 *City-County Magazine*

In my search for humor, a flight attendant told me something about a female streaker who had been on one of her flights. A woman?

"Yes," the flight attendant said. "The passenger was sitting in the rear of the plane, and she just went into the lavatory, took off all her clothes, and streaked to the front of the plane and back."

Imagining the passengers' reactions, I started laughing. "What did you do?"

"Well, obviously, we cut off her drinks, but that's not the funny story." The flight attendant leaned closer. "A little later, an older man who had been drinking apple juice pushed his call button and ordered a cup of black coffee. "No sugar. No cream. Just strong, black coffee," he said. He needed something to wake him up. With a wink, he explained, "My wife tells me I slept through something very exciting, and I don't want to miss it if it happens again. Which one of you girls was it?"

No Singing at the Prison

December 2007, *Alamance Magazine*

A family acquaintance of mine, Pearl Jean, was an active member of her small church's choir in South Alabama. As far as she was concerned, they were as good as the Mormon Tabernacle Choir.

After months of preparation for the annual Christmas performance, she approached her brother and asked if the choir could sing during the holidays at the prison where he was the warden. She extolled the group's hard work and accomplishments to her sibling. Wouldn't it be wonderful, she gushed, for the inmates to hear the joyous music made by her friends from the church during the Christmas season?

When she started talking, the warden began to shake his head, but she continued to plead her case for several minutes. When she finally let him get a word in edgewise, he said emphatically, "No, Pearl Jean. It's not a good idea. The choir is not going to sing at the prison."

She was indignant. "And just why not?" she asked.

"Because," he answered, having heard the choir on several occasions, "some of the prisoners might not be guilty."

Dealing with Bad Potatoes

September 2010, *Southeast Lifestyle*

The first rule in business? The most often heard response to that question might be that the customer is always right. And then there are times. . . .

I asked a flight attendant to tell me something funny she had seen on a flight, but she answered that she couldn't think of anything. Her next words were, "Not a lot of humor with the flying public these days." Was she kidding? I watch the flying public constantly to find funny speech material, and they never let me down. Within minutes, though, she returned, grinning from ear to ear. She had "rethunk" and yes, something funny had happened that might be of interest.

During boarding for a cross-country flight, a woman came on the plane who was demanding and obviously angry about something. She was seated in first class, but nothing suited her. With each complaint, she hit her loud, irritating flight attendant call button.

Ding! There wasn't enough overhead space. Please find a place for her luggage.

Ding! She didn't get the seat she wanted. What could be done about it?

Ding! Ding! Ding! The plane was too hot. Have the captain turn down the heat.

Passengers were staring, rolling their eyes at each other. A few were chuckling. The flight attendants were taking turns waiting on her, and the plane hadn't even left the ground.

When they were finally in the air and halfway across the country, dinner was served. It consisted of a salad, a piece of chicken, and a baked potato wrapped in aluminum foil. Before the flight attendant could return to the galley, the woman pushed the button yet again.

DING! And pronounced to the flight attendant and everyone else within earshot, "This is a BAD potato."

The attendant picked up the potato and spanked it three times. "BAD, BAD, BAD potato!" and put it back down on the woman's dinner tray.

Thank You for Serving

November 2011, *Southeast Lifestyle*

Last November, on Veteran's Day, I spoke in Bristol, Tennessee/Virginia. That's how they say it, "Tennessee/Virginia." Or, depending on which side of the street someone lives on, "Virginia/Tennessee." The state line runs right up the middle of the town on the appropriately named State Street. If you cross State Street, you change states. Walk straight up the center of State Street, and you can have a foot in each state. Some people seem to do that for the fun of it and take a picture. I understand it can create a traffic jam, but the Bristol Chamber of Commerce loves having visitors standing just about anywhere they want.

A Bristol matriarch and friend named Ruth King had recommended me to speak at an event for Veteran's Day in Bristol, and I asked Ruth, "Let's say you were driving on State Street on the Virginia side and police behind you had on their blue lights to pull you over for speeding or running a red light. Could you quickly do a U-turn and change states? Maybe roll down your window and chant, 'Can't get me, I'm in Tennessee,' like Ernest T. Bass?" Ruth's opinion was, "It might work, but you could never go home to Virginia."

My speech was at The Paramount Theater at an event honoring veterans, women veterans in particular. It was a big deal, and it was a sellout. It was also the first time I had a sandwich named after me for the day, "Jeanne's Silly Hillbilly Philly." I called my husband, Left Brain, to tell him, and he said, "Please bring a couple home with you. I can't find a thing to eat in the house."

Ruth and I were finding plenty to eat for lunch at a little restaurant downtown—I never knew whether it was in Virginia or Tennessee. A young woman came up to the table, said she was excited about the salute to veterans, and told us she would be there that night.

Naturally, I asked, "Are you a veteran?" She replied, "No, and I really don't have anyone in my family serving in the military right now, but I support our troops. As a matter of fact, Jeanne, many times when I see someone in the military—I know who they are because usually, they're in those camouflage uniforms—I go over to them and thank them for serving."

This young woman was after my own heart. I quickly said, "Great! And guess what? I fly a lot, and on several of the biggest airlines, the flight attendants announce when there are members of the military on a flight—they recognize the camouflage uniforms as well—and they say, 'Such and such airline welcomes you aboard and thanks you for your service.' The other passengers always applaud. It's wonderful."

The young woman nodded in agreement but then hesitated slightly. "Well, it's usually wonderful, Jeanne. But it can be a problem. Last summer, my husband and I were shopping, and I saw a man in the military in his camouflage uniform, and his wife and young son were with him. I told my husband I was going over there and thank him for his service.

My husband can be a fuddy-duddy. Actually, Jeanne, he might be left-brained like your husband is. He said, 'Don't go over there and bother them. He obviously just returned home, or maybe he's leaving. He's with his family. Leave 'em alone.' No, that's the point, I told him. I want to thank him in front of his little boy so his son knows that many of us appreciate his dad. If you don't want to go with me, don't. But I'm thanking him. And I walked straight over to the family.

I tapped the man on the arm with my left hand, and he turned toward me. Then his wife turned toward me, and his little boy turned and looked up at me. They all turned so fast that I was startled for a second or two. And before I could speak, my husband pulled my other arm and whispered, 'He's a hunter.'"

Thanks to all who serve and to their families. We appreciate you.

Timeless Southern Etiquette

Mother's Day rolls around every year, and as I'm a mother, I'm expecting a big day. Well, at least a phone call. I'll be in Mississippi speaking, but I've got a cell phone (as most mothers do nowadays), and Son, Beaver, has the number keyed in. There will be no excuses—and he won't again make the mistake of texting.

Those of us who no longer have our mothers still think of them fondly on this special day. My sister and I sometimes recall with laughter the variety of "rules" that Mother instilled in us. 'Til the day I die, I will not wear white shoes after Labor Day or velveteen after April 1. Of course, I don't wear a whole lot of velveteen any time of the year, but if I did, you can bet your bottom dollar that I wouldn't after April 1. Mama may have "passed," but she would know. Mothers always know. Some of Mother's rules and sayings transcend areas of the country, but I do declare many of them are uniquely Southern in nature.

A good friend of mine, Suzanne, lives in California but grew up in the South. We were commiserating about this not long ago. Suzanne said her mother would have been a casting director's dream of the "traditional southern lady." Her Mother never quite understood why her daughter chose to live "out there" on the West Coast. For that matter, the older woman never understood why her daughter chose to run her own business and had once owned a motorcycle.

When her mother was terminally ill, Suzanne came home to stay for a few weeks. She was needed to help out, and truthfully, she was hoping for last-minute bonding. Suzanne said she and her mother certainly weren't estranged, but neither were they really close.

Suzanne stayed at the hospital around the clock during her mom's final days. Toward the end, the woman slipped in and out of consciousness, but Suzanne knew her mother still recognized her from time to time. Imagine how the daughter felt one morning when her mother motioned for her to draw nearer. Some final words of love or approval? Prophetic words to live by? Where had she hidden the silver?

Suzanne fought back tears as she leaned over the bed to better hear what her mother was trying to say. That's when mom reached up, weakly clutched her daughter's arm, and whispered, "Don't forget to write each of these nurses a thank-you note."

A Tribute to Andy Griffith

June 1, 1926–July 3, 2012

January 2013, *Southeast Lifestyle*

A few years back, I wrote a book comparing humorous situations I find traveling as a professional speaker to the humor on my favorite television show of all time, *The Andy Griffith Show*.[21] In a nutshell, even though the series first aired decades ago, it pegs human nature to a "T," and human nature has basically stayed the same. Generations have enjoyed—and still enjoy—spending time in the town of Mayberry. We can all identify with its characters and how they live their lives.

When I was in the middle of writing the book, an episode from *The Andy Griffith Show* came on TV in an airline club in Atlanta. I whipped out a tablet to jot something down. A passenger seated nearby observed me continue to scribble ideas as I glanced back and forth to the TV.

After a few minutes, he spoke up. "Are you taking some sort of notes on Andy?" He said Sheriff Taylor's first name as though Andy Taylor was his best buddy from high school. Don't we all? Andy, Barney, Floyd, Aunt Bee, Opie, Gomer, Goober, and all the Mayberry residents

---

21 Jeanne's book *Mayberry Humor Across the USA* was recently updated and republished.

are our good pals. We call good pals by their first names in the South. Of course, "Aunt Bee" is considered a first name.

"It's a project on a type of humor that I believe is still prevalent today," I explained, eyes focused on the small screen. Andy, Barney, and Opie were trying to eat some of Aunt Bee's kerosene cucumber pickles rather than hurt her feelings. It was a labor of love. (We do the same thing today with a casserole a cousin makes every Christmas.) The man and I watched the screen for a few seconds, puckering our lips at the thought of how the pickles must taste, and then I added, "The project involves research of *The Andy Griffith Show*."

"Research?" the guy repeated, breaking into a wide smile. "Well, if I could get credit for watching *The Andy Griffith Show*, I'd have a Ph.D."

So would I, Mister. So would many of us. Thank you, Andy. Rest in peace.

What Are You Doing in Evergreen?

June 2016, Southeast Lifestyle

Actually, new stories and memories flowed forth while I was in rehab following my broken femur. For example . . .

In order to see her mother daily and oversee her care, a friend of mine in Auburn, Alabama, moved her mother from the small town of Evergreen to a nearby retirement community in Auburn.[22] The older lady's daily telephone calls became predictable, and one morning, the daughter's phone jingled before breakfast. Would her daughter drive her back to Evergreen that day? She had "a little business to tend to."

The daughter had a full schedule but promised she would call back if she could work in the trip. She put it on her list and then proceeded with her day. She didn't think about the request again until lunch when the telephone rang, and her mother sang out proudly, "I'm in Evergreen."

"Mothhherr! What are you doing in Evergreen?"

"I told you. I had a little business to do here today. When you didn't come, I got another ride."

The daughter was dumbfounded. "Ah-another ride?"

---

22 Evergreen is approximately 130 miles southwest of Auburn, AL.

"Yes. During breakfast, I mentioned that I needed to go to Evergreen. A gentleman living here said he thought he could find the keys to his car, and if it would start, he would be happy to drive me. So here we are."

Visions of some of the men who shuffled through the halls near her mother's quarters came to mind. "Mother, who is the man?"

"Just a minute, darling," her mother replied, then turned away from the telephone to inquire, "What did you say your name is?"

Several hours later, residents of the retirement community were out front watching when the couple slowly drove up, their white heads barely visible, bobbing above the dash of his car. They especially loved it when their fellow resident told her daughter, "I don't know what the fuss is about. We had no trouble at all. People seemed to stay out of our way."

Toomer's Corner

April 2020, *SE Gazette*

Looking for humor in stressful situations won't solve problems, but it sure helps us get through them. So where are we with COVID-19?

I certainly can't answer that because I have to turn in my monthly story several weeks before you read it. Unfortunately, I believe it will still be an issue when you read this. To what degree? Who knows?

I do know that I'm determined to look for some humor in connection with the virus situation that has affected all of us while at the same time remembering that many people are suffering much more than most of us during this time. I hope you'll join me in keeping them in our thoughts and prayers. But finding any piece of humor will positively affect our attitudes, so let's do it.

For example, at my Alma Mater, Auburn University, it's a tradition to roll the beloved Toomer's Corner after each sports victory. Literally thousands of fans run to Toomer's (or at least walk briskly) ASAP after any sporting event the Tigers win to watch and/or participate in the "rolling." It took only a few hours after the NCAA called off the March Madness Tournaments because of COVID that someone posted, "They had to call off sports at Auburn because they couldn't find enough toilet paper to roll Toomer's if Auburn won anything."

If we don't see any small pieces of humor in what the country is going through right now, maybe it's because most of us are staying at home a great deal lately—doing what we've been asked to do—but having fewer chances of seeing humor when we can't interact with others face to face.

Try this. If you don't see any current humor, think back at some of the humorous incidents from your past. Enjoy them again. Maybe even call an old friend who will remember the same funny things you remember. "Hey. I was just thinking back. Do you remember the time we . . ."

Neal Steel and the Morning Show Crew

December 2020, *SE Gazette*

Background: Since March, I've had a free event on my back porch every Saturday at noon. It's a way to keep the people who follow my work engaged during Covid. It airs on Facebook and later on YouTube. To my amazement, thousands of people joined worldwide. Many of them are still staying at home. It's free, funny and they can win prizes. I also answer the questions they post during the week, and most weeks, I have a fun guest. Y'all are certainly invited to join in and post questions or "lurk."

That info explains why three "radio guys" from Gloucester, VA, were on my back porch one Saturday in November. They were guests on the Saturday noon "event" just described. The head guy was Neal Steele, host of *The Morning Show* on Xtra 99.1FM.

The other two men were part of his large cast of characters that appeared regularly on his show. What impresses me is that Monday—Friday, they're on live about four hours a day and keep the show going with their music, news, and especially their humor. Whew. Local radio people are talented and a different breed of cat.

I have appeared sporadically on this show for more than ten years. They play clips from my humor CDs and, for all these years, have called me every month or so to be a guest. It's always fun for me and, hopefully, their listeners. To let you know of their following, I had a show at The Ferguson Center in Newport News, VA, which seats 1700 people. The Center sold all the tickets without advertising except for Neal Steele announcing it on his show. Powerful.

Last March, the week everything got canceled for COVID-19, I was on with Neal one morning. During the live conversation, I told him that all my theater shows had been postponed. Neal quickly asked if I would come on *The Morning Show* every Friday until the Covid was over. With the thought of guaranteeing that I would be on anything or anywhere once a week early in the morning, I hesitated. That was all Neal needed. He quickly said—on live radio with thousands of people listening in—"Why not? You just said all your shows are postponed. What else are you gonna be doing on Friday mornings?"

"What will I talk about?"

"You'll think of something funny." He had me.

As I write this, I've been on *The Morning Show* for an hour a week for thirty-five weeks. The show is streaming, so I get up at five in the morning every Friday to be tuned in at six am. I listen for two hours, making notes so I can coat-tail on what they've talked about when I come on from 8:05-9. We jokingly call it my "show prep." I've loved every minute of it, and the truth is, it's made me stretch to be better at what I do.

With the above background information, you can understand that sometime in September, I asked them to come to NC to be on my *Jeanne Live from the Back Porch* show any Saturday they could come. I didn't really think they would come down here, but they did on November 7.

Now that I've gone into that explanation, let me share with you the surprise from that day that will forever stand out for all of us involved.

My show ended at 1 pm and they were heading back to Virginia. First, though, we all went to Zack's Hotdogs in Burlington for lunch. The restaurant was appropriately spread out for COVID-19, but we waited and got a table for six. The nearest booth to us was a family with two little girls, maybe two years old and three and a half.

My longtime assistant, Toni, was with us. It was her birthday. As soon as we ordered, one in our group, Ralph Motley, stood up and screamed for the attention of everyone scattered throughout the restaurant and proceeded to announce it was Toni's birthday and for everyone to sing "Happy Birthday" to Toni. They did. Toni blushed, and the two little girls at the nearest table noticed Ralph and stared, mouths wide open.

What they saw when they watched Ralph was a grandfather of 17 (with another on the way) who was accustomed to little children. They also saw his white beard and slightly rotund belly, and they were mesmerized. They thought they knew who he was and pointed and whispered to their parents, "Santa Claus." From then on, they couldn't take their eyes off Ralph. And when Ralph realized what was happening, he became Santa Claus.

To our surprise, the parents eventually helped their children to the floor and watched them walk, arms outstretched, toward Ralph, who had turned at the end of our booth and was facing them. Both tables of adults and others nearby watched as "Santa" engaged the awestruck little girls in conversation, as the younger one balanced on his knee and snuggled into his waist. Later, he said, the two-year-old mostly said "yes" or "no" to his questions, but her older sister had a list and made sure to get everything in.

People throughout the restaurant were quiet and watched the conversations. As far as the little girls were concerned, they and Santa were the only ones there, but their daddy hovered nearby. The sisters never took their eyes off Ralph. After about five minutes, their parents picked them up and left. No matter how they held their daughters, the little girls managed to twist around to keep their eyes glued to Ralph, and they opened and shut their little hands slightly to wave goodbye as they exited to the street. We have a terrific photo of the admiration, but without knowing the children's names and checking with their parents, we won't use it.

Having thousands of people join me on the back porch every Saturday until this COVID is over? Wonderful. I'm so appreciative, and y'all are certainly invited to join us.

Having Neal Steele and some of his gang drive seven hours to NC and back in one day to be on my show? Unbelievable!

To be reminded of the awe of children during this busy season? Priceless.

To purchase Jeanne Robertson products, go to
www.JeanneRobertson.com/humor-store

Enjoy many of Jeanne's stories at
YouTube.com/JeanneRobertson